Tongues of Fire
and Other Sketches
EXPANDED EDITION

Algernon Blackwood

INTRODUCTION BY MIKE ASHLEY

Stark House Press • Eureka California

TONGUES OF FIRE AND OTHER SKETCHES

Published by Stark House Press
1315 H Street
Eureka, CA 95501, USA
griffinskye3@sbcglobal.net
www.starkhousepress.com

ISBN: 978-1-944520-98-4

Book design by Mark Shepard, shepgraphics.com
Proofreading by Bill Kelly
Cover illustration by C. B. Williams

First Stark House Press Edition: April 2020

Table of Contents

TONGUES OF FIRE

"Harold," she said in a very low voice, and as though it cost her enormous effort, "it's the same with both of us. And we've brought it on ourselves." Placing a hand on his smooth thick hair, though he shrank from her touch, she continued in a whisper: "And do you realise—it's something not of this world—quite?" She paused, drew back a step, and stared down at him…
"Flame that never dies."

Discover this strange tale of cosmic retribution, plus 20 more tales and sketches that illuminate the supernatural world of Algernon Blackwood. And for the first time in print since their original publication, three more stories are included to round out this rare collection.

ALSO BY ALGERNON BLACKWOOD

Novels:
Jimbo: A Fantasy (1909)
The Education of Uncle Paul
   (1909)
The Human Chord (1910)
The Centaur (1911)
A Prisoner in Fairyland (1913)
The Extra Day (1916)
Julius Le Vallon: An Episode
   (1916)
The Wave: An Egyptian
   Aftermath (1916)
The Promise of Air (1918)
The Garden of Survival (1918)
The Bright Messenger (1921)

Children's Books:
Sambo and Snitch (1927)
Mr. Cupboard (1928)
Dudley and Gilderoy: A
   Nonsense (1929)
By Underground (1930)
The Parrot and the - Cat (1931)
The Italian Conjuror (1932)
Maria (of England) in the Rain
   (1933)
Sergeant Poppett and Policeman
   James (1934)
The Fruit Stoners (1934)
How the Circus Came to Tea
   (1936)
The Adventures of Dudley and
   Gilderoy (1941)

Autobiography:
Episodes Before Thirty (1923)

**Original Short Story
Collections:**
The Empty House and Other
   Ghost Stories (1906)
The Listener and Other Stories
   (1907)
John Silence —
   Physician Extraordinary
   (1908)
The Lost Valley and Other
   Stories (1910)
Pan's Garden: A Volume
   of Nature Stories (1912)
Incredible Adventures (1914)
Ten Minute Stories (1914)
Day and Night Stories (1917)
The Wolves of God and Other
   Fey Stories, w / Wildred
   Wilson (1921)
Tongues of Fire and Other
   Sketches (1924)
Full Circle (1929) [single story]
Shocks (1935)
The Doll and One Other (1946)
The Mysterious House (1987)
   [single story]
The Magic Mirror: Lost
   Supernatural and Mystery
   Stories (1989)
The Face of the Earth &
   Other Imaginings (2015)

Plays:
Karma: A Reincarnation Play,
   w / Violet Pearn (1918)
Through the Crack w / Violet
   Pearn (1925)

Introduction

By Mike Ashley

In 1923 Algernon Blackwood believed he had completed his last book. "I have said all that was in me," he told his long-time Canadian friend, Professor George Wrong.

The book he had just finished was his autobiography, *Episodes Before Thirty*. It had required a difficult introspection of his younger self, although Blackwood only reported such that he wanted to. There were further "episodes" he did not record, many of which it is unlikely we shall now ever know.

Relieved of that pressure, Blackwood felt he could now support himself by journalism and occasional stories and articles. He was also writing for the theatre. He had already had several plays produced, most recently *Through the Crack*, with Violet Pearn, and other one-act plays written with Bertram Forsyth and Elaine Ainley. He was also looking forward to a fruitful collaboration with Kinsey Peile on stage drama. He had even acted on the stage in the role of Colonel Pemberton in John Drinkwater's *Oliver Cromwell*.

Perhaps the change of pace, the relaxation of his mental muscles and the sheer enjoyment he was gaining from life, helped his mind turn back towards fiction. But there was more. Blackwood had become fascinated with the teachings of the Russian mystic Georgei Gurdjieff and his rival on the earthly plane, P. D. Ouspensky. Blackwood attended their lectures and stayed at Gurdjieff's school at Fontainbleu near Paris. The activities he undertook there, some of which involved pushing his physical strength to the limit in order to release mental and spiritual energies, also brought his mind back to creative endeavours.

And there was more. Although J. W. Dunne did not hit the public imagination until the appearance of his book *An Experiment with Time* in 1927, Blackwood already knew of him through mutual friends, including Alice Perrin. I know he met with Dunne in 1925 but he may well have met him earlier, especially as the two stayed in nearby villages in Switzerland. Dunne had come up with this theory of a serial universe, meaning that all time co-existed at once, past, present and future. By recording his dreams Dunne believed that we had a greater awareness of our existence which we might perceive when asleep. Ouspensky preached something similar, and Blackwood had explored similar ideas in his readings and research since his teenage years, and his studies in the Order of the Golden Dawn. All of these activities inspired a relaxed and rejuvenated Blackwood. Stories again began to flow.

The ability to perceive through or across time had long intrigued Blackwood—he liked to refer to it as "Elsewhere and Otherwise". He had already used that concept in one of the John Silence Stories, "A Victim of Higher Space" which had been dropped from the original 1908 collection and was not published until 1914. Blackwood's mind focused again on the idea, now further bolstered by his studies of Gurdjieff, Ouspensky and Dunne.

One story, "Malahide and Forden", brought together all of his recent experiences, including his turn on the stage. It was inspired by the tour of the company through the English Midlands. Blackwood was with his friends Harcourt Williams (who becomes Forden) and Henry Ainley (who becomes Malahide). The narrator is Blackwood himself. On their travels they become dislocated in both time and space.

The ability to move through trans-dimensional space is central to two other stories. In "The Pikestaffe Case" a mirror serves as a conduit whilst in "The Man Who Was Milligan", it's a painting.

As a counter to these adventures was the horror of not being able to move through time or space at all, but to be utterly lost. The very title of the story "Lost!", set in the Alps, says it all. That fear of being trapped also surfaces in "Petershin and Mr. Snide" and "The Open Window".

It is clear that at this time Blackwood was relishing his freedom and channelling his previous fears of being trapped by the world about him. There is an exhilaration in these stories alongside an expansion of consciousness, dream-like visions that almost certainly came to him whilst exhausting his body at Fontainbleu. Both "Playing Catch" and "A Continuous Performance" consider how life continues in its inevitable cycle regardless of human involvement. They share the mood of an earlier, previously uncollected story, "The World-Dream of McCallister". There is the intriguing "Alexander *Alexander*" which envisages the ghost of a man with a split personality.

So when Herbert Jenkins approached Blackwood to see if there might be a chance for a new collection of stories, he had plenty. There were a few other earlier stories he had not included in previous collections, such as the wartime propagandist "Laughter of Courage" and a mood piece of childhood memories, "Picking Fir-Cones". But there are two stories which show the extremes of Blackwood.

The title story "Tongues of Fire" shows Blackwood at his most vitriolic. Doubtless at one of the weekend house parties he attended regularly as a "professional guest" he had witnessed two women spreading gossip about another. Here he seeks his revenge. "The Little Beggar", written a few years earlier, sees Blackwood at his most melancholic, envisaging the son he never had.

Tongues of Fire does not rise to the heights of *Pan's Garden* or *Incredible Adventures* but it has a diversity and honesty which allows the reader to experience a wide range of Blackwood's thoughts, experiences and emotions.

For this printing it's possible to include other previously uncollected material. There's an earlier story, completely forgotten until recently rediscovered by Johnnie Mains, "The Lock of Grey Hair", dating from 1909. There are also two mischievous pieces which show Blackwood in playful mood, and his passion for cats and dogs, "The Philosopher" from 1914 and "The Perfect Poseur" from 1919. They provide extra proof of the diversity and abilities of Algernon Blackwood, which are all too easily forgotten.

—January 2020

Tongues of Fire
and Other Sketches

By Algernon Blackwood

Tongues of Fire

I

The friendly little dinner party was over and Cecilia Lance had thoroughly enjoyed it; the Lindleys were kindly simple people; the gramophone had been turned on and her dancing partner, Harold Sharpe, had been there. Cecilia and Harold knew one another's steps as intimately as they knew one another's minds.

"Odd that Cecilia doesn't marry," Lindley remarked, half to himself, half to his wife, as they sat over a cigarette when the last guest had driven away. "She's still pretty. Everybody likes her. And such a cheery soul." He puffed his cigarette reflectively. "She has charm, too—eh?" he enquired presently, as his wife offered no comment. He glanced up affectionately at her.

"Always full of life, yes," came the belated reply. "I think she enjoyed herself to-night. I think they all did. They liked the new records, too."

Her husband smiled and nodded. The new records had cost money. "I wish we could do it more often," he mentioned, sighing ruefully. The Lindleys were hospitably inclined, but they were poor, and even a dinner party had to be calculated. "Now, that fellow Sharpe"—he went back to his first line of thought—"I thought at one time—they seemed to understand each other pretty well."

His wife hesitated a moment, gazing into the gas fire. "They still do, I think," she said. "Their views of life are the same"—then, after a second's pause, as though the words slipped out against her kindlier judgment—"and of people."

Her husband, however, discerned neither the hesitation nor the effort at restraint that caused it. Both had their tongues well under control, he by a natural good nature, she by education. They were an affectionate, devoted, faithful couple, to whom none but the most determined could impute deliberate evil. A little later, as they tidied away the records before going to bed, he remarked casually: "Sharp as a needle, though, isn't she? By Jove, yes." He laughed. "They both are, for that matter." And he chuckled again.

"They don't mean to be, I'm sure," was his wife's charitable comment.

Again, apparently, he did not notice anything. It was her usual way of talking, anyhow. The Lindleys invariably were kindly in their judgments of people. They did not criticise others—nastily.

"I'll put the lights out, Molly," he said presently. "You pop up to bed. It's late, and you must be tired." He kissed her, patting her on the shoulder. Fifteen minutes afterwards the room, so lately filled with music, whirling couples and merry voices, had darkness and the atmosphere of faded scent and stale cigarette smoke to itself.

Meanwhile, Cecilia Lance and Harold Sharpe were also talking in their taxi as he drove her to the widowed sister she lived with in Chester Street. They were in merry mood, satisfied with the evening just over. They discussed it in their usual way. Both voted it "ripping."

"Yet I never really care for a gramophone," Cecilia mentioned.

"It's better than nothing, though," her dancing partner agreed, while he qualified.

"Yes, I suppose so," she submitted, "only the records were so rotten, weren't they?"

"Putrid," said Sharpe.

"Why don't they get a few good ones, I wonder." She mentioned a few names. "If people use a gramophone for dancing, the least they can do is to have the latest tunes." To this her companion also gave assent. They both felt aggrieved. In a few minutes there was nothing bad enough left to say about the music, the floor, the cooking of the little dinner, and the heat of the room. They selected all the least favourable points and emphasised them, yet in their easy, natural way and without calculated motives.

Next they turned their attention to the other dancers, Cecilia leading the way, as before, with faint praise. "Not a bad lot," observed Harold patronisingly. "Quite nice," Cecilia qualified, "only I wonder where in the world they pick up such people." Her companion, while agreeing, mentioned that a certain girl "looked all right, I thought."

"What! That dowdy creature!" Whereupon he swore he had really only noticed one girl, whose name was Cecilia, and so remedied his mistake. The criticism of the dresses which followed was largely a monologue, since Harold Sharpe merely approved her verdict with "awful, perfectly awful" ; but when the taxi arrived after a drive of six minutes, the entire evening, including dinner, dance and dancers, had been so damned that no Recording Angel would have thought it worth even entering in his Book. The names of the destroyers, however, he possibly might have entered.

"Oh, come in for a minute and have a drink, my sister's sure to be up," invited Cecilia. Over his whisky and soda and her cigarette an opportunity was provided for chatting pleasantly about their late host and hostess, and without a chorus, since the sister had already gone to bed. "A good fellow, Jack Lindley," was Harold Sharpe's off-hand opinion, "though what he sees in *her*, I can't imagine." But Cecilia, feeling robbed of her accustomed right to start the line of criticism, assured him that he was quite mistaken, for Molly was the possessor of "such a good heart." "It's what

Molly sees in *him* that puzzles me! Still, she amuses herself with Sir Malcolm, the good-looking nerve specialist whom she's always going to see without the slightest reason."

"What ! That quiet old frump Molly has a lover!"

"Why shouldn't she?" Cecilia championed her doubtfully.

Before her cigarette was half-finished, Molly Lindley's character was demolished, and her husband, who was "gay enough when you got him alone," was insecurely balancing on one leg, which was certainly not fit to stand on. Husband and wife, a faithful, somewhat old-fashioned, devoted couple, who had just put themselves to trouble and expense to give the speakers a happy evening, had not a rag to their backs between them. Naked to the winds, vicious, false and stupid, they were heading full speed for that hell in which the speakers, their detractors, did not, of course, believe. There was not a nastier couple than the Lindleys apparently in all Chelsea. And this result had been accomplished by faint praise, offered with a pleasant smile; by careless suggestion, presented with a shrug of the shoulders; and by a series of innocent questions sprinkled with adjectives and adverbs that carried dark hints of hidden wickedness and double lives—but without a single scrap of truth to support the entire case. The Recording Angel, if he entered anything, entered it, indeed, as evidence the destroyers unwittingly gave against themselves—a confession that what they had in their own hearts and minds they saw most easily in others.

The case, moreover, presented with the skill due to long practice, was completed in ten minutes at the most. Without motive, without malice, without conscious intention to do harm or wish to injure, but merely obeying a habit to say something startling perhaps, Mr. and Mrs. Lindley were left naked to the cruel winds and without a leg to stand on.

Incidentally, just before Harold took his leave—in the space of two minutes or so—Cecilia's sister, asleep upstairs, lay also without covering.

"One of the best," Cecilia replied, as he dropped a polite word of casual enquiry, "but oh, so queer and moody sometimes."

"She's jolly good to you, Ceci," Harold considered, knowing of the generous allowance.

"Oh, she's a perfect brick. It's only her moods that I find trying sometimes."

"Ah!" His ears were hungry at once. He glanced at her enquiringly.

Cecilia lowered her voice. "It's drugs probably," she mentioned.

Harold laughed, nodding understandingly. "They all do it," he said with a shrug, swallowing a gulp of the lady's excellent whisky, while the kindly soul they discussed lay dreaming peacefully on the floor above, a homeopath ignorant of anything stronger than fairy doses of aconite for a cold or colocynth for indigestion. In future, however, whenever her name was mentioned in his presence, Harold Sharpe, with a look of knowing sympathy would say darkly, "Drugs, you know. Yes, I'm afraid it's drugs. Oh, her sister knows it ..."

"Well, good night, Cecilia. I must be getting on. See you again soon."

"At the Lindleys' probably. Molly said they'd give another gramophone hop before long. Good night."

An hour later, both of them lay sound asleep, at peace with all the world and entirely pleased and satisfied with themselves, their hearts harbouring no malice, envy or uncharitableness. Their tongues lay still. Their day, their evening, their conversation, had been an average sample of what occurred on the other three hundred and sixty-four days of their year. Fallen Reputations marked their course like birds before a skilful gun. These were not deliberately brought down, but when they aimed with deliberation they landed much bigger game, for they were both deadly shots.

Now, one of the latter, wounded but not killed, it so happened, traced the shot that hit him to its source. He was not only big game, he was dangerous big game, a man of personality, a man of power, a man of strange knowledge, too. And he did not bring the action for slander that he was justified in bringing, yet neither did he ignore the wicked snipers who used poisoned shafts in the darkness. He merely cursed them. He *cursed* them both. His curse, however, since he used a ritual known to few Westerners, was perhaps no ordinary curse....

II

On a lovely morning some weeks later Cecilia sat alone in a taxi, examining her face uneasily in the narrow mirror, as she drove to Grosvenor Street. The sun shone brightly and old grimy London laughed with happiness. Flowers shone in every corner, in every buttonhole. Birds were singing gaily. The air was sweet and fresh, for it was summer-time, and half-past ten was really half-past nine; but the pretty young face reflected in the taxi looking-glass betrayed no summer-time. It was neither sweet nor fresh. A haunting anxiety lay in the otherwise bright eyes. The corners of the little mouth turned down. From time to time she crushed a small lace handkerchief against her lips with violence. Occasionally, removing it quickly, she drew in a deep draught of the sweet air from the open window, inhaling and exhaling with fixed concentration in her face, then swiftly placing the handkerchief on her lips again. One might have thought she suffered toothache, neuralgia; some nerve attack perhaps that affected the mouth or lips or gums. Her behaviour indicated extreme uneasiness, if not actual pain.

At the door of No. 100A she dismissed the taxi, and was admitted with scarcely a minute's delay. The butler with the sphinx-like face bowed her smoothly into the waiting-room, closing the door behind her silently. Evidently, since he did not ask her name, he knew it already. Finding herself alone, she ran to the big mirror quickly, but had only time to catch a glance of a white frightened face before the door reopened and her name was softly spoken. Biting her lips, her hands clenched tightly at her side, she followed the sphinx into the consulting-room of Sir Malcolm, the famous nerve specialist. With an instinctive movement, as she crossed the threshold and saw the tall, dark-faced figure rising to greet her, she crushed the small lace handkerchief tightly against her lips....

The interview was a long one. When she came out again, the waiting-room was half-filled with fidgeting ladies who had been kept, they considered, unduly waiting. Her mind was too preoccupied to observe carefully, but she noticed, she fancied, one man among the women. Picking up her bag and parasol hastily, she looked into no single face. Her hands trembled, her breath came unevenly, her features were hard and aged, she kept the handkerchief pressed against her mouth. She hurried out; the sphinx called a taxi, she drove to her sister's house, ran quickly up to her room and locked herself in. The first thing she did on being alone was to collect several hand-mirrors and arrange them in such a way before the dressing-table that she could study her face from every possible angle. She studied herself thus for the best part of half an hour, her eyes too strained with intense anxiety for tears; her heart too over-loaded with a strange biting dread for her breath to behave naturally; her mind gone too far beyond control for her to remain still a single instant.

Cecilia Lance was terrified. But she had force, she had courage, her personality was not negligible; she could face anything, provided she first had time to decide upon her attitude and line of conduct. By the lunch hour, when she came down to meet her sister's guests, she had found herself again. If the face was somewhat drawn, it was not noticeably so. Her breath was normal, her manner quiet yet not depressed, her voice betrayed no trembling. She had faced the situation and taken her line of conduct.

"Ah, there you are! You were out early, Thompson told me. I missed you." And her sister came forward with her usual affectionate embrace.

Cecilia drew back sharply. "You mustn't kiss me, Gerty, I've—got a cold. Oh, it's nothing. But I don't want to give it to you."

The luncheon party passed off pleasantly. No one could have said that Cecilia was not her gay and normal self, nor could anyone have guessed from her lighthearted manner the amount of nervous power she exerted to appear so. It was with difficulty, none the less, that she ate her food or swallowed her wine. She did not smoke. There was a sinking dread, a constant terror in her that required all her skill and courage to conceal successfully. That inner gnawing never ceased. The wolf of horror tore steadily at her very vitals. The handkerchief went from time to time to her mouth, but in such a way that the maneuver seemed quite natural. In her mind still echoed the words the specialist had used a few hours ago. Her visit that morning to Sir Malcolm was not the first. It was the tenth. And after she had left him he made his next patient wait a little longer for her dreaded yet coveted ten minutes with him. In fact, he did a thing he rarely allowed himself to do —he saw another patient in her place, a man—and when the man had gone, he delayed the fuming lady still another ten minutes, while he made notes, consulted books, and looked generally more puzzled and interested, perhaps dismayed as well, than in the course of his strange practice he had ever looked before. With his subsequent visitors he was even a little absent-minded, though he was certainly too skilful for this cardinal mistake to be discovered....

"It seems more than curious—it's simply incredible," he thought to himself, as he glanced over his notes that night before going to bed. It was a thing he had never done before—to think of a case when the day's work was done. He particularly examined a sheet of tissue paper which had a circular hole in it with rough uneven edges, tinged slightly yellow, red and black. He wore an expression of bewilderment as he laid it down. He was evidently baffled. "I've never come across such a thing before. The books have no record of anything approaching it." He passed into a mood of deep reflection. "I'm damned!" he said aloud finally. "It's positively medieval. It's—it's uncanny." Sir Malcolm was baffled and admitted it—to himself only. "And two of them, by God!"

III

It was just as the last guests were leaving that Cecilia was called to the telephone by Harold Sharpe. He asked if he might look in for tea and whether she would be alone. His voice had an odd note of seriousness in it. But Cecilia excused herself on the plea that she was resting before the Lindleys' dance that night.

"Aren't you well?" he asked sharply.

"Oh—I'm all right, yes," with a moment's hesitation before she said it. Then Harold insisted. He was very urgent, very determined. "I simply *must* see you," he declared, "and alone, Ciss." A quiver ran down her, making her voice tremble a little. "Oh, all right," she yielded. "Gerty's going out. Only you mustn't stay long. I'm dead tired." Her body swayed slightly. She dropped into a chair, and hid her face in her hands. Ten minutes afterwards Harold was in the room with her alone.

"I haven't seen you for ages," he began. "What's up?" His manner was odd, it was strained and nervous. He spoke rapidly and his eyes had a hunted look. His skin was pale. Fingers and lips twitched badly. "What's been the matter, Ceci?" It was the form of her name he used when he was in earnest, which was not often. "You never turned up at Claridge's last night either." He coughed. The girl started, and asked quickly if he would smoke, but he declined with a gesture of impatience. He coughed a second time. His handkerchief came out. The girl started again, more violently than before.

"Harold—" she said abruptly, then stopped dead, and looked away. She had meant to say something else. "What does that cough mean?" she asked instead, keeping her face still turned from him. "I believe you're not—quite well. That wasn't a real cough."

His handkerchief was against his lips, and he did not answer.

"Harold?" she repeated, with a singular loudness, as though the word were produced by a shock. Slowly her head turned round towards him and their eyes met. "*Are* you," she insisted in a tense whisper that had an ominous tremor in it, "*quite*—well?"

Instead of answering, he asked a point-blank question, staring fixedly at her: "What were you doing in Grosvenor Street this morning, Ceci?" And as he said it her memory worked vividly. She remembered. He, of course, had been the one man in the waiting-room. This flashed across her. Her hand went to her handkerchief, but she did not use it. His eye, however, she saw, detected the movement—and understood it. They knew one another's minds so intimately.

"So it *was* you, Harold?" She could only whisper now. Control of her voice was gone.

Harold's face, already pale when he came in, turned a little paler. It went a shade more grey now. They stared hard into one another's eyes.

"I—" he began, then faltered. "What were *you* doing there?" he asked suddenly, and as he said it his gaze wandered down her face slowly, pausing at her lips. His eyes were fixed in a dreadful stare. Unutterable questions, she knew, lay in them. Her handkerchief again flew upwards. "Don't! Don't!" she cried vehemently, her voice muffled behind the pressing lace. "For God's sake, don't!"

He caught at her hand and wrenched it, so that the momentary pain gave her the energy to deflect her thoughts the least little bit. He was attempting—oh, she realised it quite clearly—attempting to look at her handkerchief, and the knowledge gave her the power to try and hide it, to prevent him seeing it, to smother it away. Only he was too strong for her.

He forced her palm open.

"You were there," he said in a voice that was calm but oddly stupid, "for the same reason I was." He dropped her hand, while she thrust the crumpled scrap of lace with violence into her tiny bag, yet knowing it was a useless thing to do, because he had already seen the strange, discoloured patch.

"How d-dare you?" she cried, stammering in her fear and pain. "You forg-get yourself, Harold Sharpe!" But he made no attempt at either apology or explanation, merely sinking back with a faint sigh into his chair and leaving his own crumpled handkerchief open for her to see in the palm of his effortless hand.

It, too, bore the same dread signature—a discoloured patch.

For several minutes of silence the pair of them sat thus, each staring— as though bereft of any power to move or speak—at that ghastly and significant patch. It had the appearance of having been burnt or scorched— by fire.

It was the girl who first recovered her self-control, though only in a measure. She rose from her chair and stood over him.

"Harold," she said in a very low voice, and as though it cost her enormous effort, "it's the same with both of us. And we've brought it on ourselves." Placing a hand on his smooth thick hair, though he shrank from her touch, she continued in a whisper: "And do you realise—it's something not of this world—quite?" She paused, drew back a step, and stared down at him. "It's from the d-devil."

He made no sign, no answer, but his whole body shivered.

"Do you understand what it m-means?" she went on. He sprang suddenly to his feet then, making strange gestures of futile violence with his hands.

"Ceci," he cried, "you're crazy. You're talking the damnedest nonsense in all the world. Pull yourself together—" And then his breath failed him and he collapsed in a stupid heap on his chair.

The girl shook him as though she could have struck his face for preference. There was great violence in her heart and mind. There was perhaps murder—or suicide, its equivalent.

"He told *you*—what he told *me?*" she asked in a voice that seemed without any emotion because its owner was beyond any feeling.

Harold nodded.

"He tried the tissue paper?"

He bowed his head.

"He told you what—what we have to expect?"

The only answer, the only sign that her words were heard, was a convulsive twitching movement of the body that somehow communicated horror more than any words could possibly have done. It was without intelligence.

"In-c-c-curable," she said in dead tones that conveyed even better than his convulsive gesture her blank, ultimate despair. The stammer added a touch of unintelligence similar to his own. It was dreadful.

He looked up then with an idiotic smile, while she responded, the mind in her obviously already clouded: "Flame that never d-dies."

"T-tongues of f-f-fire," he said with a feeble giggle. "We have tongues of f-fire—you and I—" He got up with a gesture as though to kiss her. In his hand fluttered his handkerchief, its awful patch apparent.

She did not move. "And afterwards, too," she whispered, the last gleam of reason fading from her eyes, "for ever and ever...."

The Little Beggar

He was on his way from his bachelor flat to the club, a man of middle age with a slight stoop, and an expression of face firm yet gentle, the blue eyes with light and courage in them, and a faint hint of melancholy—or was it resignation?—about the strong mouth. It was early in April, a slight drizzle of warm rain falling through the coming dusk; but spring was in the air, a bird sang rapturously on a pavement tree. And the man's heart wakened at the sound, for it was the lift of the year, and low in the western sky above the London roofs there was a band of tender colour.

His way led him past one of the great terminal stations that open the gates of London seawards; the bird, the coloured clouds, and the thought of a sunny coast-line worked simultaneously in his heart. These messages of spring woke music in him. The music, however, found no expression beyond a quiet sigh, so quiet that not even a child, had he carried one in his big arms, need have noticed it. His pace quickened, his figure straightened up, he lifted his eyes and there was a new light in them. Upon the wet pavement, where the street lamps already laid their network of faint gold, he saw, perhaps a dozen yards in front of him, the figure of a little boy.

The boy, for some reason, caught his attention and his interest vividly. He was dressed in Etons, the broad white collar badly rumpled, the pointed coat hitched grotesquely sideways, while, from beneath the rather grimy straw hat, his thick light hair escaped at various angles. This general air of effort and distress was due to the fact that the little fellow was struggling with a bag, packed evidently to bursting point, too big and heavy for him to manage for more than ten yards at a time. He changed it from one hand to the other, resting it in the intervals upon the ground, each effort making it rub against his leg so that the trousers were hoisted considerably above the boot. He was a pathetic figure.

"I must help him," said the man. "He'll never get there at this rate. He'll miss his train to the sea." For his destination was obvious, since a pair of wooden spades was tied clumsily and insecurely to the straps of the bursting bag.

Occasionally, too, the lad, who seemed about ten years old, looked about him to right and left, questionably, anxiously, as though he expected someone—someone to help, or perhaps to meet him. His behaviour even gave the impression that he was not quite sure of his way. The man hurried to overtake him.

"I really must give the little beggar a hand," he repeated to himself, as he went. He smiled. The fatherly, protective side of him, naturally strong, was touched—touched a little more, perhaps, than the occasion seemed to warrant. The smile broadened into a jolly laugh, as he came up against the great stuffed bag, now resting on the pavement, its owner panting beside it, still looking to right and left alternately. At which instant, exactly, the boy, hearing his step, turned round, and for the first time looked him full in the face with a pair of big blue eyes that held unabashed and happy welcome in them.

"Oh, I say, sir, it's most awfully ripping of you," he said in a confiding voice, before the man had time to speak. "I hunted everywhere; but I never thought of looking *behind* me."

But the man, standing dumb and astonished for a few seconds beside the little fellow, missed the latter sentence altogether, for there was in the clear blue eyes an expression so trustful, so frankly affectionate almost, and in the voice music of so natural a kind, that all the tenderness in him rose like a sudden tide, and he yearned towards the boy as though he were his little son. Thought, born of some sudden revival of emotion, flashed back swiftly across a stretch of twelve blank years ... and for an instant the lines of the mouth grew deeper, though in the eyes the light turned softer, brighter....

"It's too big for you, my boy," he said, recovering himself with a jolly laugh; "or, rather, you're not big enough—yet—for it—eh? Where to, now? Ah! the station, I suppose?" And he stooped to grasp the handles of the bulging bag, first poking the spades more securely in beneath the straps; but in doing so became aware that something the boy had said had given him pain. What was it? Why was it? This stray little stranger, met upon the London pavements! Yet so swift is thought that, even while he stooped and before his fingers actually touched the leather, he had found what hurt him—and smiled a little at himself. It was the mode of address the boy made use of, contradicting faintly the affectionate expression in the eyes. It was the word "sir" that made him feel like a schoolmaster or a tutor; it made him feel old. It was not the word he needed, and—yes—had longed for, somehow almost expected. And there was such strange trouble in his mind and heart that, as he grasped the bag, he did not catch the boy's rejoinder to his question. But, of course, it must be the railway station; he was going to the seaside for Easter; his people would be at the ticket-office waiting for him. Bracing himself a little for the effort, he seized the leather handles and lifted the bag from the ground.

"Oh, thanks awfully, sir!" repeated the boy. He watched him with a true schoolboy grin of gratitude, as though it were great fun, yet also with a true urchin's sense that the proper thing had happened, since such jobs, of course, were for grown-up men. And this time, though he used the objectionable word again, the voice betrayed recognition of the fact that he somehow had a right to look to this particular man for help, and that this particular man only did the right and natural thing in giving help.

But the man, swaying sideways, nearly lost his balance. He had calculated automatically the probable energy necessary to lift the weight; he had put this energy forth. He received a shock as though he had been struck, for the bag had no weight at all; it was as light as a feather. It might have been of tissue-paper, a phantom bag. And the shock was mental as well as physical. His mind swayed with his body.

"By Jove!" cried the boy, strutting merrily beside him, hands in his pockets. "Thanks most awfully. This *is* jolly!"

The objectionable word was omitted, but the man scarcely heard the words at all. For a mist swam before his eyes, the street lamps grew blurred and distant, the drizzle thickened in the air. He still heard the wild, sweet song of the bird, still knew the west had gold upon its lips. It was the rest of the world about him that grew dim. Strange thoughts rose in a cloud. Reality and dream played games, the games of childhood, through his heart. Memories, robed flamingly, trooped past his inner sight, radiant, swift and as of yesterday, closing his eyelids for a moment to the outer world. Rossetti came to him, singing too sweetly a hidden pain in perfect words across those twelve blank years: "The Hour that might have been, yet might not be, which man's and woman's heart conceived and bore, yet whereof time was barren...." In a second's flash the entire sonnet, "Stillborn Love," passed on this inner screen "with eyes where burning memory lights love home...."

Mingled with these—all in an instant of time—came practical thoughts as well. This boy! The ridiculous effort he made to carry this ridiculously light bag! The poignant tenderness, the awakened yearning! Was it a girl dressed up? The happy face, the innocent, confiding smile, the music in the voice, the dear soft blue eyes, and yet, at the same time, something that was not there—some indescribable, incalculable element that was lacking. He felt acutely this curious lack. What was it? Who was this merry youngster? He glanced down cautiously as they moved side by side. He felt shy, hopeful, marvellously tender. His heart yearned inexpressibly; the boy, looking elsewhere, did not notice the examination, did not notice, of course, that his companion caught his breath and walked uncertainly.

But the man was troubled. The face reminded him, as he gazed, of many children, of children he had loved and played with, both boys and girls, his Substitute Children, as he had always called them in his heart.... Then, suddenly, the boy came closer and took his arm. They were close upon the station now. The sweet human perfume of a small, deeply loved, helpless and dependent little life rose past his face.

He suddenly blurted out: "But, I say, this bag of yours—it weighs simply nothing!"

The boy laughed—a ring of true careless joy was in the sound. He looked up.

"Do you know what's in it? Shall I tell you?" He added in a whisper: "I will, if you like."

But the man was suddenly afraid and dared not ask. "Brown paper probably," he evaded laughingly, "or birds' eggs. You've been up to some wicked lark or other."

The little chap clasped both hands upon the supporting arm. He took a quick, dancing step or two, then stopped dead, and made the man stop with him. He stood on tiptoe to reach the distant ear. His face wore a lovely smile of truth and trust and delight.

"My future," he whispered. And the man turned into ice.

They entered the great station. The last of the daylight was shut out. They reached the ticket-office. The crowds of hurrying people surged about them. The man set down the bag. For a moment or two the boy looked quickly about him to right and left, searching, then turned his big blue eyes upon the other with his radiant smile:

"She's in the waiting-room as usual," he said. "I'll go and fetch her—though she *ought* to know you're here." He stood on tiptoe, his hands upon the other's shoulders, his face thrust close. "Kiss me, father. I shan't be a second."

"You little beggar!" said the man, in a voice he could not control; then, opening his big arms wide, saw only an empty space before him.

He turned and walked slowly back to his flat instead of to the club; and when he got home he read over for the thousandth time the letter—its ink a little faded during the twelve intervening years—in which she had accepted his love two short weeks before death took her.

Malahide and Forden

I

Our three-months' tour was drawing to its close—the Company playing in a midlands town at the moment—and Forden was chatting with me in the wings during the second act, when Malahide's great voice boomed in my ears as he hurried to his entrance. It startled me; the audience must surely hear it too. Forden gave me his quick smile, an understanding wink added to it.

"Hubert, old man!" cried the voice. "There's a place called Barton I want to see—Barton-in-Fabis. Let's go to-morrow. There's a train at 10.15. Forden, you come too!" His eyes blazed at us with an odd glare through the grease-paint, his great shoulders swept round the canvas, and he was gone on to the stage, where at once his voice became audible in the lines that ten weeks had made rather too familiar.

I experienced a twinge of surprise. Walking was little to Malahide's taste. He usually spent his spare time playing golf, and in the afternoon he invariably slept for a couple of hours, so as to be rested for the evening performance. That he should propose a whole day's walk, therefore, was unexpected.

My companion and I were left staring at each other.

"Does he mean it—d'you think?" I asked in a low voice. "It sounds such an odd name. You think it's real?" I laughed a little.

"A lovely name, though," came the whispered answer. "It's real enough. Yes—I've heard of it—"

"Oh, you've heard of it?" I interrupted, looking up at him.

He nodded. Always absent-minded rather, he was also always truthful. An expression on his face now puzzled me. He looked perturbed. I repeated my remark, anxious to press him for some reason.

"People make pilgrimages there—sometimes—I believe. There's an old church " Then his cue sounded, and he moved quickly away, but flinging over his shoulder, again with his quick smile, a final whisper: "Oh, it's real, yes, quite real. We'll go."

So it was the church and the odd name that had caught Malahide's romantic fancy. Yet such a flat and empty name, I thought, without the adjunct, which alone gave it atmosphere. "In fabis," I gathered from one of the local supers, meant "among the beans," and Barton was a village "with a lot of historic interest," he informed me proudly. The name and the historic interest, evidently, had taken Malahide's vagrant fancy. He was an incalculable fellow; but he was not a man to ply with questions. His temper was insecure as a wayward child's. I, therefore, asked no questions. Forden, too, was an elusive creature, where questions were concerned. There are people who instinctively detest having to give definite information in reply to definite questions. All the more, then, was I surprised to hear Forden ask one of Malahide—about the expedition. We passed the latter's dressing-room as we left the theatre to walk home together, and the door was open.

"Ten-fifteen, remember, Central Station," boomed Malahide, catching sight of us. "Single tickets to Stanton. We walk from Stanton." It again surprised me; he had actually thought out details.

It was then that Forden asked his question:

"I—I suppose," he ventured, faltering a trifle, "there's a train back all right?"

The evening performance, of course, involved an early meal, and the question seemed so natural that I thought nothing, but Malahide looked up from pulling on his big boots as though it startled him. He seemed taken by surprise. His eyes held the same blaze, the touch almost of glare, I had noticed before, but the startled air was added.

"We'll work round. What can it matter anyhow—provided we get there?" was all he vouchsafed, and in a tone that did not invite cross-examination.

So it was to be 10.15, with single tickets to Stanton, a walk thence to Barton among its Beans, with its old church and historic interest, and we were to "work round" to another station, and so home. Malahide had planned it all in advance. He wanted to go. Forden also wanted to go. It all seemed natural enough, ordinary, no exceptional feature anywhere about it beyond the trivial detail that Malahide did not care for walking as a rule. It is strange, therefore, that somewhere in my being lurked a firm conviction that the whole business was exceptional. For one thing, I felt sure that both Malahide and Forden did not really want to go. That they had to go, and meant to go, was the impression left upon my mind, not that either of them actually "wished" it.

During our supper of cold tongue, salad and beer, for instance, we made no further allusion to the expedition. Rather than actually avoided, it was just tacitly assumed. Forden, I partly gathered, realised that I still did not quite believe in the Barton walk, but was too delicately loyal to discuss our friend's delightful irresponsibilities. In his own mind, too, I fancied, lay the thought that Malahide would not turn up, and that he would lose his morning's sleep for nothing, but that he meant to keep the rendezvous none the less. My fancy may have been quite wrong, yet this, anyhow, was Forden all over. He was of finest material, something transparent and a trifle exquisite in him; and even when poorly cast—as in the present play—this quality shone beautifully through his acting.

We went soon to bed, but Malahide kept late hours, and Forden and myself were asleep long before he turned in. In the morning, however, he was waiting at the station when we got there. He had left the hotel before us. "I've been to look at the churches," was his unexpected explanation. "One of 'em was open, and I went in and sat a bit. A wonderful atmosphere of peace and stillness. By Jove, it makes one think," and he gabbled on about the charm and atmosphere of an empty, ancient church. It was surprising, of course, and it left us without comment. Yet I had known him before in this odd mood—when he was frightened about something, frightened usually, of death. Malahide, I understood, was frightened now, and his thoughts, for some reason, ran on death. In his eyes, moreover, I noticed, though veiled a little, a trifle deeper down, the same blaze I had seen the night before. And all the way to Stanton he gazed out of the window, humming to himself, the heap of morning papers beside him all untouched. The criticisms of his own performance, as, equally, mention of the Company, though of importance to the week's business, had, for once, no interest for him. His mind lay, evidently, upon other matters. He looked extraordinarily happy—happier, I thought, than I had ever seen him before; there was a careless indifference, a lightness, something, too, of a new refinement—to use a queer word his vehement personality did not ever suggest—I thought were new, yet all this lit, as from below, by the gleam of hidden fear I most certainly detected in him. And it was these contradictions, I think, these incompatibilities almost, that affected me so powerfully. Impressions began to pour and pour upon me. Emotions stirred. Things going on at a great speed in Malahide were things that I could not fathom.

To me, this short train journey to Stanton, *en route* for Barton among its Beans, already had the spice of something just a little unusual, of something a trifle forced. Unexpected touches played about it, as though a faint unknown light shone from the cloudless sky of that perfect April morning, but from *beyond* it. Forden, behind the transparent mask of his rather beautiful face, betrayed more than his customary absent-mindedness, sometimes to a point I could have thought bewilderment. Each time I spoke to him—to Malahide I did not once address a word—he started a little. In him there was no attempt at adjustment, no analysis, no effort to explain or query. He asked himself, I am sure, no single question. Whatever life brought him he accepted always. He was receptive merely; a recipient, but an extremely sensitive recipient, leaving all problems, all causes, to his God. Though without a formal creed, Forden was a deeply religious nature. And Forden now seemed to me—let me put it quite plainly as I felt it at the time—preparing, making himself ready, getting himself in hand, to meet something. Yes, to meet something—that is the phrase. And it was the search for this phrase, its discovery rather, that made me aware of an incomprehensible stress of subconscious excitement similarly in myself.

We were a queer enough trio, it may be, even in our normal moments. In myself, at any rate, being of different build to both Malahide and Forden, numerous little wheels were already whirring, gathering speed with every minute. This whirring one usually calls excitement. My own personal reactions to what followed are all, of course, that I can report. Though caught up, more or less, with the other two, I remained always the observer, thus sharing only a small portion probably of what my companions experienced. Another man, of different calibre, placed as I was, might have noticed nothing. I cannot say. My problem is to report faithfully what I observed; and whether another man would have observed the same thing, or nothing at all, is beside the mark.... Already, before the train stopped at Stanton, I felt—well, as if my feet did not quite touch the ground, and by the ground I mean the ordinary. It may, or may not, be an exaggeration to say that I felt both feet slightly off the earth. That my centre of gravity was shifting is, perhaps, the most truthful expression I can find.

By the time we reached Stanton, at any rate, the whirring wheels had generated considerable heat, and with this heat playing all through my system I had already begun to see and feel in a way that was not quite the ordinary way. I perceived differently: I experienced, as it were, with a heightened consciousness. Perception seemed intensified a trifle; but more than that, and chiefly, it seemed different.

Different is the right adjective, I think. Malahide and Forden were "different" to the Malahide and Forden I knew comfortably from long acquaintance. Very, very slightly different, however, not radically so. I saw them from another angle. There was nothing I could seize or label. The instant my mind fastened on any detail, it was gone. The "difference" escaped me, leaving behind it a wonder of enquiry, a glow of curiosity I could not possibly define.

One sentence, perhaps, can explain my meaning, both in reference to the men and to the inanimate things they moved among: I saw *more* of everything....

The fields, through the carriage windows, were of freshest green, yellow with a million buttercups, sparkling still from a shower that had followed sunrise, and the surface of the earth lay positively radiant in its spring loveliness. It laughed, it danced, it wept, it smiled. Yet it was not with this my mind was occupied during the half-hour's run to Stanton, but rather with the being of my two companions. I made no effort to direct my thoughts. They flowed of their own accord, with poignant, affectionate emotions I could not explain, towards Malahide and Forden...

II

Played about them, over them, these thoughts did, lovingly rather, and directed by a flair, so to say, of understanding that was new in me....

Neither would ever see forty again, yet to me they seemed young, their careers still in front of them; and each, though without much energy, groping a way honestly toward some ultimate meaning in life that neither, I fancied, was ever likely to discover. If not dilettantists, both shrank from the big sacrifices. They were married, and each, in this fundamental relationship, unsatisfied, though each, outwardly at least, had mastered that dissatisfaction. Accepting, that is, a responsibility undertaken, they played the game. There was fine stuff in them. And both sought elsewhere, though without much energy as I have said, an outlet marriage had accordingly failed to provide. Not immorality, of course; but a mental, maybe a spiritual, outlet. They sought it, I now abruptly judged, without success. Their stream of yearning, whatever its power, went lost among the stars and unremunerative dreams. The point, however, remains: this yearning did exist in each. Its power, I conceive, was cumulative.

Similarly, in their daily work as actors, and uncommonly good actors, one with a streak of fine inspiration, the other, Malahide, with a touch of fiery genius, both accepted an art that both held, mournfully, and secretly rather, was not creative. They were merely interpreters of other men's creations. And, here again, lay deep dissatisfaction. Here, indeed, lay the root and essence of a searching pain both shared—since, God knows, they were gifted, honest beings—that a creative outlet, namely, was denied to creative powers.

This fundamental problem—the second one—lay unsolved in both; hence both were open to attack and ready for adventure. But the lesser adventures, refuge of commonplace fellows, they resolutely declined. Were they, perhaps, worthy then of the greater adventure that circumstances, at length, with inexplicable suddenness, and out of the least likely material, offered to them ...?

Somewhat thus, at any rate, I saw my companions, as the train jolted us that sparkling April morning, many years ago, towards Stanton, Malahide humming his mood idly through the open window, Forden lying at full length, reading the papers with listless eye. But I saw another thing as well, saw it with a limpid clearness my description may not hold: something ahead—an event—lay in waiting for them, something they knew about, both not desiring, yet desiring it, something inevitable as sunrise.

We move towards and past events successively, calling this motion time. But the event itself does not move at all. It is always there. We three, now sitting in the jolting carriage, were approaching an event about which they knew, but about which I did not know. I received, that is, an imperfect impression of something they saw perfectly. And in some way the accumulated power of their combined yearnings, wasted as I had thought, made what happened possible.

It was an extraordinary idea to come to me with such conviction, and with this atmosphere of prophecy. I glanced at the two men, each like myself the victim, I remembered, of a strange, unhappy weakness. These weaknesses, too, I realised, contributed as well: un-balance, instability, were evidently necessary to the event. To steady, heroic types it never could have happened.

The train was stopping, and Malahide already had the door half-open. Forden, in his turn, sprang up.

"Stanton!" cried the former, as though he spoke a line of tense drama on the stage. "Here we are. Come on, you fellows!" And he was on the platform before the train drew to a standstill. His vehemence was absurd. He used it, I knew, to help him make the start, the fear I have mentioned prompting it. And Forden, like a flash, was on his heels. I followed, pausing a moment to collect the papers in case Malahide should ask for them, and then, thank heaven, as we stood on that ugly platform and asked the porter the way to Barton, my own strange feelings, heightened perception with them, dropped back with a jerk into the normal again. The uncomfortable insight was suddenly withdrawn. It had seemed an intrusion into their privacies; I was relieved to see them again as two friends merely, two actors, out for a country walk with me to a village called Barton-in-Fabis on a brilliant April morning.

One last flash only there was, as I followed them out, one final hint of what I have called "seeing more" of everything, seeing "differently," rather. The three of us left the carriage as described, in sequence; yet to me it flashed with definite though illogical assurance that only one got out. Not that one was gone and two were left, but that the three of us got out as one, simultaneously. One being left that carriage. The fingers of a hand, thus, may move and point in several directions at once, while the hand, of which they form parts, moves forward in one direction only, as a whole. The simile, occurred to me.... I perceive it, moreover, through what I can only call a veil of smoke.

III

"Oh, about three to four mile, maybe," the porter was telling Malahide, "an' you can pick up the Midland at Attenborough to get back.... Yes, it's a nice day for a walk, I dessay ..."

The name made us laugh, but the instructions as to paths, stiles, signposts, turnings, I, personally, did not listen to. I assumed, as most do, an air of intelligent comprehension. Forden, I saw, wore a similar expression, from which I knew that he, too, was not listening properly, but was leaving it to Malahide, wondering, like myself, how the latter could carry in his great slumbering mind so many intricate details whereas, actually, he was doing nothing of the sort. Malahide was merely acting, intent upon some other matter that was certainly not here and now.

We started off, therefore, with but a few details of our journey secure: "a mile and a half down the road, and bearin' to the right, you'll see a sign-post to Barton across the fields, and if you foller that a little way, bearin' to the left a bit now, you'll see a gate on the right just past some trees, but you don't go through that gate, you go straight on, bearin' to the right always, till you come to a farm, and then, through another gate...."

There was a definite relation between the length of description and a tip in the porter's mind, upon which Forden commented wittily, as we swung down the road, each relying upon the other two, and then exclaiming confidently, but with blurred minds, as we reached a signpost: "Ah! Here we are!" while we scrambled over a stile into enticing fields of gold.

We spoke little at first. "We must bear to the left, remember," mentioned Malahide once, to which Forden and I nodded agreement, adding however: "till we reach the gate," with Malahide's firm reminder: "which we do not go through," followed by my own contribution: "past some trees, yes, to another gate,"—and then Malahide's conclusive summing up: "always bearing to the right, of course ..."

We jogged on happily, while the larks sang overhead, the cuckoos called and the brilliant sunshine flooded a country-side growing more and more remote from signs of men and houses. Not even a thatched cottage or a farm-house broke the loneliness from humankind....

We spoke little, I have said; but my companions, presently, fell into a desultory conversation about their own profession, about present and future conditions on the stage, individual talent, rents of theatres, and so forth, to all of which, being an interloper merely, I listened with slight interest. It was the odd smell of burning, I think, that held my curious attention during this preliminary period, for I saw no cause for it, no smoke of rubbish being consumed, no heath-fire certainly. Malahide, I remember, coughed a little once or twice, and Forden sniffed like an animal that scents an untoward element in the atmosphere, though very faintly. They made no comment, I offered none. It was, obviously, of no importance. The beauty of the day in its fresh spring brilliance absorbed me wholly, so that my thoughts ran on of their own accord, floating on a stream of happy emotion, careless as the pleasant wind. The sentences I caught from time to time did little more than punctuate, as it were, this stream of loveliness that poured through me from the April morning. Yet at intervals I caught their words, a phrase or a sentence would arrest me for a second; and each time this happened, I noticed what I can only call a certain curious change, a change—in distance. Their talk, I mean, passed gradually beyond me.

There was incoherence, due partly of course, to the gaps I missed; and once or twice, it seemed to me, they were talking at cross-purposes, although tone and demeanour betrayed nothing of the sort. I remember that this puzzled me, that I registered the fact vaguely, at any rate; also, that an occasional comment of my own won no rejoinder from either Malahide or Forden—almost as though, momentarily, they had forgotten my existence and seemed unaware that I was with them.

Deeper and deeper into my own sensuous enjoyment of the day I sank accordingly, glad that I might take the beauty in my own little way. One thing only pierced my personal mood from time to time: the picture of Malahide's great head thrust forward a little when I glanced at him, the eyes turned upwards, carrying in them still that odd soft blaze, the glare, as I called it, now wholly gone; and that upon Forden's delicate face was a gentle expression, curiously rapt, yet with a faint brush as of bewilderment somewhere among the peering features. This impression, however, came back to me later, rather than held my attention much at the actual moment. We moved on deeper and deeper into the lonely countryside. With the exception of a man some fields ahead of us, I saw no living soul.

IV

Our path, meanwhile, crossed a lane, and a little later a road, though not a high-road since no telegraph poles marred it, and then Malahide remarked casually: "But, I say! It's about time, isn't it?" He stood still abruptly, staring around him. "It's about time—eh?"

"For what?" enquired Forden gently, not looking at him, a touch of resignation in his voice.

"That signpost, I mean. We should have come to it by now."

"Oh, that signpost," echoed the other, without interest.

Neither of them included me in this exchange, which had broken in upon a longish conversation, and I found myself resenting it. They had not so much as glanced in my direction.

"Signpost!" I exclaimed bluntly, looking straight at Malahide. "Why, we passed it long ago." And as I said it, my eye again took in the figure of the man three fields away, the only living being yet seen. Out of the corner of my eye I saw him merely, and a breath of sharper air, or something like it, passed quickly over my skin. "It said 'To Barton,'" I added, a flavour of challenge in my tone. I purposely kept my gaze hard on Malahide.

He turned slowly, with a look as though, casually, he picked me up again; our eyes met; that sharper air seemed in my mind now.

"We passed a signpost," he corrected me; "but it merely said 'Footpath.' And it pointed over there—behind us. The way we've come."

Forden, to my amazement, nodded in consent. "Over there, yes," he agreed, and pointed with his stick, but at right angles to the direction Malahide had meant. "And it said: '*From* Barton.'"

This confusion, produced purposely and in a spirit of play though of course it was, annoyed me. I disliked it, as though somewhere it reached a sad, uneasy region in my mind.

It was Malahide's turn to nod in consent. "Then we're all right," he affirmed with unnecessary vehemence in his deep voice. And that vehemence, again, I did not like. "Besides," he added sharply, pointing ahead, "there he is!"

A wave of vague emotion troubled me; for an instant I felt again that sharper air, and this time in the heart. "Who?" I asked quickly.

He replied carelessly: "The man."

"*What* man?"

Malahide turned his eyes full upon my own, so that their soft blaze came over me like sunshine, almost with a sense of warmth in them. On his great face lay a singular expression. I heard Forden, who stood just behind me, laughing gently. There seemed a drift of smoke faintly about them both. I knew a touch of goose-flesh.

"What man do you mean?" I asked with louder emphasis, and this time, I admit, with a note of exasperation that would not be denied, for the nonsense, I thought, had gone far enough, and there was a flavour in it that set my nerves on edge.

Malahide's reply came easily and naturally: "The man who plants them," he said without a smile. "He sticks them into the ground, that fellow. He's going about with an assortment of signposts 'To and From Barton,' and every now and again he plants one for us."

"We're standing under one now," Forden breathed behind me in his purring way, and looking up I saw that this was true. I read in black lettering upon a white background: "To Barton." It indicated the direction we were taking.

It occurred to me suddenly now that we had already walked at least four miles, yet had seen no farm, no trees, no garden. I had been sunk too deep in my own mood to notice things perhaps. This signpost I certainly had not noticed until Forden drew my attention to it. Malahide was tapping the wooden arm with the point of his stick, reading the lettering aloud as he did so:

"'Footpath *From* Barton,'" I heard him boom. And instantly my eyes fixed tightly on it with all the concentration that was in me. Yes, Malahide had read correctly. Only, the arm now swung the other way. It pointed behind us! And I burst out laughing. Sight and memory had, indeed, fumbled badly. I felt myself for a moment "all turned round," as the saying is. Malahide laughed too; we all laughed together. It was boisterous, not quite spontaneous laughter, but at any rate it relieved a sense of intolerable tension that in myself had reached a climax. This fooling had been overdone, I felt.

"So, you see, we *are* all right," Malahide exclaimed, and swung forward over the meadow, already plunged again in the conversation with Forden which he himself had interrupted. They had enjoyed their little game about the signposts, Malahide, in particular, his touch of fancy about "the man who planted them." It all belonged to the careless, happy mood of a holiday expedition, as it were—the nonsense of high spirits. This, at least, was the ready explanation my mind produced so glibly, knowing full well it would not pass the censor of another kind of understanding, a deeper kind, that sought hurriedly, even passionately, for the true explanation. It was *not* nonsense; nor was it acceptable. It alarmed me.

I repeat: this confusion about directions, the two men agreeing that opposite directions were one and the same, was not the nonsense that it sounds; and I affirm this in view of that heightened perception, already first experienced in the train, which now came back upon me in a sudden flood. It brought with it an atmosphere of prophecy, almost of prevision, and certainly of premonition, an atmosphere that accompanied me, more or less, with haunting persistence to the end.

And its first effect was singular: all that a man says, I now became aware, has three meanings, and not merely one. The revelation arrived as clearly as though it were whispered to me through the shining air. There is the literal meaning of the actual words; there is the meaning of the sentence itself; and there is the meaning, above and beyond both these, in which the whole of the utterer is concerned, a meaning, that is, which the unconscious secret part in him—the greater part—tries and hopes to say. This last, the most significant of all three, since it includes cause as well as result, makes of every common sentence a legend and a parable. Gesture, tone of voice betray its trend; what is omitted, or between the lines, betrays still more. Its full meaning, being in relation to unknown categories, is usually hidden both from utterer and hearers. It deals simultaneously with the past, the present and—the future. I now became aware of this Third Meaning in the most commonplace remarks of my companions.

It was an astounding order of perception to occur to me, and the difficulty of reporting it must be obvious from this confused description. Yet it seemed to me at the time so simple, so convincing, that I did not even question its accuracy and truth. Malahide and Forden, fooling together about the contradictory signposts, had betrayed this third meaning in all they said and did. Indeed, that it appeared impossible, absurd, was a proof, perhaps the only possible proof, of its reality. Momentarily, as it were, they had become free of unknown categories.

V

My own attitude contained at first both criticism and resistance; it was only gradually that I found myself caught in the full tide that, apparently, swept my companions along so easily. A first eddy of it had touched me in the train, when my feet felt a little "off the earth"; now I was already in the bigger current; before long I had become entirely submerged with them... Fields and lanes, meanwhile, slipped rapidly behind us, but no farm, no trees, no gate, as the porter described, had been seen. We were lost, it seemed, in the heart of the sparkling April day; dew, light and gentle airs our only guides. The day contained us.

I made efforts to disentangle myself.

"Barton's not getting any nearer," I expostulated once.

"Barton-in-Fabis," mentioned Malahide with complete assurance, that no longer held a trace of vehemence, "is there—where it always is," while Forden's breath of delicate laughter followed the flat statement, as though the larks overhead had sung close beside my ear.

"D'you think we're going right?" I ventured another time. "Our direction, I mean?"

Again, with that ghostly laughter, Forden met me: "It's the way we have to go," he replied half under his breath. "It's always a mistake to trouble *too much* about direction—actual direction, that is." And Malahide was singing to himself as though nothing mattered in the world, details as to direction least of all.... It was just after this, I remember, as our lane came to a stile and we leaned over it comfortably, all three, that the odour of burning touched my mind again, only with it, at the same time, a sight so moving, that I paused in thought, catching my breath a little. For the field before us sloped down into the distance, ancient furrows showing just beneath the surface like the flowing folds of a shaken carpet. They ran, it seemed, like streams. Their curve downhill lent this impression of movement. They were of gold. Every inch of the surface was smothered with the shimmering cream of a million yellow buttercups.

"Rivers of Gold!" I exclaimed involuntarily, and at the same moment Forden was over the stile in a single leap and running across the brilliant grass.

"Look out!" he cried, a bewitched expression on his face, "it's fire!"—and he was gone.

It was as though he swam to the neck in gleaming gold. He peered back at me a second through the shining flood—and it was in this instant, just as I caught his turning face, that Malahide was after him. He passed me like a wave, still singing; there was a rush of power in his speed. I followed at once, unable to resist. The three of us ran like one man over and through that flood of golden buttercups, passing, as we did so, every sign the railway porter had told us to look out for: the farm, the trees, the gate, the second gate—everything. Only, we passed them more than once. It was as though we swung in a rapid circle round and round the promised signs, always passing them, always coming up to them, always leaving them behind, then always seeing them in front of us again, yet the entire sequence right, natural and—possible.

Now, I noticed this. I was aware of this. Yet it caused me no surprise. That it should be so seemed quite ordinary—at the time....

We brought up presently, not even breathless, some half-way down that golden field.

"Nothing to what I expected," exclaimed Malahide, interrupting his singing for the first time.

"There was no pain," mentioned Forden, his voice soft and comforting, as though he spoke to a little child.

There was an instant of most poignant emotion in me as they said it; a certainty flashed through me that I could not seize; a sudden wave, as it were, of tears, of joy, of sorrow, of despair, swept past me and was gone again before I had the faintest chance to snatch at any explanation. Like the memory of some tremendous, rather awful dream, it vanished, and Malahide's quick remark, the next second, capped its complete oblivion:

"And there *he* goes again!" I heard. "He's stuck another one in!"

He was pointing to a hedge at the bottom of the field where, behind the veil of its creamy hawthorn, I just made out the figure of a man ambling slowly along, till the hedge, growing thicker, finally concealed him. But the signpost, when we reached it a few minutes later, showed an arm rotten with age, and only the faded legend on it, hardly legible: "Footpath," It pointed downwards—into the ground.

VI

We swung forward again, without a moment's delay, it seemed, my companions talking busily together as before, their meaning, also as before, far, far beyond me. They were talking, too, on several subjects at once. The odd language they had just used, the way we swung forward instantly, without comment or explanation, touched no sense of queerness in me— then. No comment or explanation were necessary; it was natural we should go straight on. Their talking on "several subjects simultaneously," however, did occur to me—yes, as marvellous.

Foolish, even impossible, as it must sound, it yet did happen; they talked on more than one subject at the same time. They carried on at least a couple of conversations at once without the slightest difficulty, without the smallest effort or confusion. My own admission into the secret was partial, I think; hence my trouble and perplexity. To them it was easy and natural. With me, even the strain of listening made the head swim. The effort to follow them was certainly a physical one, for I was aware of a definite physical reaction more than once, almost indeed of a kind of dizziness akin to nausea.

To report it is beyond my power. For one thing, I cannot remember, for another, the concentration necessary left me a little stupefied. I can give an instance only, and that a poor one. They used "third meanings," too.

Malahide, thus, while voluble enough in his normal state, was at the same time usually inarticulate. His verbosity, that is, conveyed little. The tiny vital meaning in him fumbled and stammered through countless wrappings, as it were. These wrappings smothered it. Now, on the contrary, he talked fluently and clearly. It was I who was puzzled—at first—to find the subject he discussed so glibly. And Forden, usually timid and hesitating in his speech, though never inarticulate, now also used a flow of fearless words in answer. Yet not precisely "in answer," for both men talked at once. They uttered simultaneously—on two subjects, if not on three:

"We all deserve, maybe," Malahide's deep voice thundered, "a divine attention few of us receive—God's pity. We are not, alas, whole-hearted. Few of us, similarly, deserve another compliment due to splendour—the Devil's admiration."

His voice, for once, was entirely natural, unselfconscious. There was the stress of real feeling and belief in what he said.

"I for one," he went on, "I take my hat off to the whole-hearted, whether in so-called good or evil. For of such stuff are eventual angels wrought ..."

Angels! The word caught me on the raw. Its "third meaning" caught me on the raw, that is, and with a sense of power and beauty so startling that I missed the rest. The word poured through me like a flame. Of what he spoke, to what context the strange statement was related, I had no inkling; yet, while he actually spoke the words, I heard Forden speaking to Malahide, who heard and understood and answered—but speaking, and simultaneously, on another matter altogether. And this other matter, it so chanced, I grasped. Remote enough from what Malahide was saying, and trivial by comparison, it referred to an Alpine sojourn with his wife a couple of summers before. Malahide, too, had been with them:

"Often, after the hotel dinner," Forden said contemptuously, "I heard them mouthing all sorts of lovely poetic phrases; yet not one of them would make the slight sacrifice of personal comfort necessary to experience that loveliness, that poetry, in themselves ..."

To which Malahide, though still developing "God's pity" and the "Devil's admiration" in phrases packed with real feeling, contrived somehow to answer, but always simultaneously, his friend's remark:

"They bring their own lower world," he boomed, "even into the beauty of the mountains, then wonder that the beauty of the mountains tells them nothing. They would find Balham on great Betelgeuse"—a tremendous laugh rang out—"and Clapham Junction on fiery Vega!"

"*Her* pity," came Forden's words, talking of another matter altogether, yet uttered simultaneously with his friend's laughing rhetoric, "is self-pity merely. She does these out-of-the-way things, you see, without sufficient apparent reason. It is not a desire for notoriety—that would shock her—but it is a desire to be conspicuous. Life, which means people, did not make a fuss about her in her youth. But the law of compensation works inevitably. Late in life, you see, she means to have that fuss ..."

It is the phraseology, perhaps, that enables me to remember this singular exchange. My head, of course, was spinning. For Malahide made a reply to this, while still discussing the poseurs in the Alpine hotel. And while they talked thus on two subjects simultaneously, Forden managed to chat easily too *with me*—upon a third.... It was as though a second dimension in Time had opened for them. Between myself and Forden, again, there was plainly some kind of telepathic communication. He had my thought, at any rate, before I uttered it aloud.

Of this I can give two instances, both trivial, yet showing that simultaneously with his Malahide-conversations he was paying attention to my own remarks, and—simultaneously again—was answering them. It was absolutely staggering.

Here are the instances memory retained:

Some scraps of white paper, remnants of an untidy picnic party, lay fluttering in the thick grass some distance in front of us, and at the first glance I thought they were not paper, but—chickens. Only on coming nearer was the mistake clear. Whether I meant to comment aloud on the little deception or not, I cannot remember; but, in any case, before I actually did so, Forden, glancing down at me with his gentle smile, observed: "I, too, thought at first they were chickens," He hit them idly with his stick as we passed.

The second instance, equally trivial, equally striking at the same time, was the gamekeeper's cottage on the fringe of a wood. It suggested to my mind, for some reason, a charcoal-burner's hut in a book of German fairy-tales, and I said so. This time I spoke my thought. "But, you know, I've just said that," came Forden's comment, his eyes twinkling brightly as before. And it was true; he had said it a fraction of a second before I did. During this brief exchange between us, moreover, he was still talking fluently with Malahide—on at least two subjects—and simultaneously....

Now, from the fact that I noticed this, that my mind made a note of it, that is, I draw the conclusion that my attention was definitely arrested, surprise accompanying it. The extraordinariness of the matter struck me, whereas to my companions it was ordinary and natural. I was, therefore, not wholly included in their marvellous experience. I was still the observer merely....

Immediately following the telepathic instances with Forden, then, came a flash of sudden understanding, as though I were abruptly carried a stage deeper into their own condition:

I discerned one of the subjects they discussed so earnestly together.

This came hard upon a momentary doubt—the doubt that they were playing, half-fooling me, as it were. Then came the swift flash that negatived the doubt. I can only compare it to the amazing review of a man's whole life that is said to flash out in a moment of extreme danger. This quality, as of juggling with Time, belonged to it.

Malahide and Forden, then, I realised, were talking together of Woman, of women, rather, but of individual women. Ah! the flash grew brighter: of their own wives. Yet that Malahide spoke of Forden's wife and that Forden discussed Mrs. Malahide. Each had the free *entrée* into the other's mind, and what each was too loyal to say about his own wife, the other easily said for him. This swiftest telepathic communication, as with myself and Forden, they enjoyed between themselves. With supreme ease it was accomplished.

It was an astounding performance. This discussion of their wives was actually, of course, a discussion of—well, not of Mary Forden and Jane Malahide individually, but, through them, of the deep unsolved problem of mate and sex which each man had faced in his own life—unsuccessfully. The fragments I caught seemed meaningless, because the full context was lacking for me. I got a glimmer of their Third Meanings, however, and realised one thing, at any rate, clearly: they were giving one another help. Forden's honeymoon, I remembered, had been spent in the Alps, whereas Malahide's wife had the lack of proportion which made her conspicuous by a pose of startling originality. This gave me a clue. Time, however, as a sequence of minutes, days and years, did not trouble either speaker. The *entire* matter, regardless of past and present, seemed spread out like a contour-map beneath the eyes of their inner understanding. There was no picking out one characteristic, dealing with it, then passing on to consider another. To *me* it came, seriatim, in that fashion, but *they* saw the matter whole and all at once; so rapidly, so comprehensively, too, that the sentences flew upon each other's heels as though uttered simultaneously by each speaker.

They were, it seemed, poised above the landscape of their daily lives, and in such a way that they were able to realise present, past and future simultaneously. It was no longer exactly "to-day," it was no longer necessarily "to-day." Temporarily they had escaped from the iron tyranny of being fastened to a particular hour on a particular day. They—and partially myself with them—were no longer chained by the cramping discipline of a precise moment in time, any more than a prisoner, his chains filed off, is fixed to a precise spot in his dungeon. *Where* we were in time, God knows. It might have been yesterday, it might have been to-morrow—any yesterday, any to-morrow—which we now realised simultaneously with the so-called present. It happened to be—so I felt—a particular to-morrow we realised, and it was something in the three of us (due, I mean, to the combination of our three personalities), that determined which particular to-morrow it was. The prisoner in space, his chains filed off, moves instinctively to the window of escape; and they, prisoners in time, moved now similarly to a window—of escape....

A flash of this escape from ordinary categories, of this "different" experience, had come to me as we left the railway carriage. It now grew brighter, more steady, more continuous. I seemed travelling in time, as one travels ordinarily in space. To the wingless creature crawling over fields the hedge behind it is past, the hedge beyond it future. It cannot conceive both hedges existing simultaneously. Then some miracle gives it wings. Hanging in the air, it sees both past and future existing simultaneously. Losing its wings once more, it crawls across the fields again. That air-experience now seems absurd, impossible, contradicting all established law. The same signpost points now as it always pointed—in one direction.

This analogy, though imperfect, occurred to me, while we brought up, but not even breathlessly, half-way down the field as already mentioned, and all I have attempted to describe took place in that brief interval of running.

Before entering that field with its rivers of gold, we had been leaning on a stile; we were leaning on that stile still. Or, it may be put otherwise: we were leaning on that stile again.

Similarly, the whole business of running, of passing the signs mentioned by the porter, the conversations, the emotions, everything in fact, were just about to happen all over again. More truly expressed, they were all happening still. Like Barton, in Malahide's previous phrase, it was all *there*. The hedge behind, the hedge in front, were both beneath us, existing simultaneously.... At a particular spot in the hedge—a particular "to-morrow"—we paused....

VII

... At my side, touching my shoulders, Malahide and Forden were quietly discussing the way to Barton-in-Fabis, and, as I listened, there came over me again that touch of nausea. For, while flatly contradicting one another, they were yet in complete agreement.

It was at this instant the shock fell upon me with its glory and its terror.

My companions stood back to back. I was a yard or so to one side. They both now turned suddenly—but how phrase the incredible thing?—they both came at me, while at the same time they went away from me. A hand, endowed with consciousness, a hand being turned inside out like a glove, might feel what I felt.

I saw their two faces. A little more, a little less, and there must have been a bristling horror in the experience. As it was, I felt only that a sheet of wonder caught us up all three. The odour of burning that came with it did not terrify; that drift of yellow smoke now deepening, did not wound. I accepted, I understood, there was even something in me had rejoiced.

In the twinkling of an eye, both men were marvellously changed: they stood before me, splendid and divine. I was aware of the complete being in each, the full, whole Self, I mean, instead of the minute fraction I had known hitherto. All that lay in them, either of strength or weakness, was magnificently fused.... The word "glory" flashed, followed immediately by a better word, and one that Malahide had already used. Its inadequacy was painful. Its third meaning, however, in that instant blazed. "Angels" in spite of everything, remains.

And, I, too, moved—moved with them both, but in a way, and in a direction, I had never known before. The glove, the hand, being turned inside out, is what my pen writes down, but accurate description is not possible. I moved, at any rate, on—*on* with my two companions towards Barton.

"It's all one to me," I said, perfectly aware that I suddenly used the third meaning of the phrase, and that Malahide and Forden understood.

"I've just said that myself," the latter mentioned—and this again was true. The smile, the happiness, on his face carried the very spirit of that radiant April morning, the essence of spring, with its birds, its flowers, its dew, it careless wisdom.

"Such things," cried Malahide, "are painless after all. It comes on me like sleep upon a child. Ha, ha!" he laughed, in his wild, vehement way. "It's all one to me now too. Escape, by God!"

The stab of fierce emotion his language caused me passed and vanished; afflicting memory of the burning odour was forgotten too. Everything, indeed, *was* one. Both men, I realised, gazed at me, smiling, wonderful, superb, and in their eyes a light, whose reflection apparently lay also in my own: an immense and awful pity that our everyday, unhappy, partial selves should ever have dared to masquerade as though they were complete and real....

"God's pity," sang Malahide like a trumpet. "We shall have deserved it …!"

"And the Devil's admiration," followed Forden's sweeter tones, as of a *vox humana*, both distant, yet like a lark against my ears. He was laughing with sheer music. "There was no terror. I knew it must be so…. Oh, the delicious liberty … at last!"

Both uttered simultaneously. In the same breath, anguish and happiness working together, my own voice cried aloud:

"We are, for once, whole-hearted!"

VIII

At the moment of actual experience a new category would not seem foolish or impossible. These qualities would declare themselves only when it passed away. This was what happened—gradually—to me now, and, alas, to my companions too. A searing pain accompanied the transition, but no shock of violence.

At the pinnacle there was a state of consciousness too strange, too "different," to be set down. The content of life, its liberty, its splendour, its characteristics of grandeur, even of divinity, were more than ordinary memory could retain. My own cry: "We are wholehearted" must betray how pitiful description is…. Thus, the lovely moment, for instance, when I first saw rivers of gold, kept repeating itself—because it gave me happiness, because it moved me. That field of golden buttercups was always—there. I lingered with it, came back to it, enjoyed it over and over again, yet with no sense of repetition. It was new and fresh each time. Now, Malahide and Forden, selecting other moments, chose these instead, and these, again, were moments easy to be remembered. Their finer instances baffle memory, although I knew and shared them at the time. Forden, for some choice peculiar to himself, was in the mountains which he loved; his honeymoon presumably. Malahide, on the other hand, preferred his stars, though details of this have left me beyond recovery…. Yet, while we lingered, respectively, among rivers of gold and stars and snowy peaks, we were solidly side by side in the actual present, crossing the country fields towards Barton-in-Fabis on this April morning.

The gradual passing of this state remains fairly clear in me.

There came signs, I remember, of distress and effort in our relationships. This, at least, was the first touch of sorrow that I noticed. I was coming back to the surface, as it were. The change was more in myself than in the others. There was argument about footpath, signposts, and the way to Barton generally.

"The fellow has planted his last post," I heard Malahide complaining. "Now he'll begin pulling them all up again. He both wants us to get to Barton, yet doesn't want it." He paused. His usual laugh did not follow. "You know," he went on, his whisper choking a little oddly in his throat, "he rather—puts the wind up me." A spasm ran over his big body. Then suddenly, he added, half to himself, with an effort painfully like a gasp, "I can't get my breath—quite."

Forden spoke very quickly in his delicate way, resignation rather sweetly mingled in it: "Well, at any rate, we're all right so far, for I see the porter's farm and gate at last." He stared and pointed. "Over there, you see." Only, instead of pointing across the fields, he—to my sharp dismay—looked and pointed straight into the sky above him.

It was the fear in Malahide that chiefly afflicted me. And the pain of this, I remember, caused me to make an effort—which was an unwise thing to do. I drew attention to the ordinary things about us:

"Look, there's a hill," I cried.

"God!" exclaimed Forden, with quiet admiration, "what amazing things you say!" While Malahide began to sing again with happiness.

His reaction to my sentence forced me to realise the increasing change in myself. As I uttered the words I knew their third meaning; in the plain sentences was something that equalled in value: "See! the Heavens are open. There is God!" My companions still heard this third meaning, for I saw the look of majesty in Malahide's great eyes, the love and beauty upon Forden's shining face. But, for myself, having spoken, there remained— suddenly—nothing more than a commonplace low hill upon the near horizon. The gate and farm I saw as well. A feeling of tears rose in me, for the straining effort for recovery was without result, anguished and bitter beyond words.

I stole a glance at my companions. And that strange word Malahide had used came back to me, but with a deep, an awful sense of intolerable regret, as though its third meaning were gone beyond recall, and only two rather empty and foolish syllables remained....

It was passing, yes, for all three of us now; the gates of ivory were closing; there was confusion, and a rather crude foolishness. Oddly enough, it was Forden—seeing that he was altogether a slighter fellow than Malahide—it was Forden who rose most slowly to the surface. Very gradually indeed he left the deeps we had all known together. To all that he now said and did Malahide responded with an aggravating giggle. He said such foolish things, confused, uncomfortable to listen to. His nerves showed signs of being frayed. The ordinary, inarticulate Malahide, with the unhappy weakness, was returning, had already returned in fact. He became a trifle sullen, a little frightened as well, and in his gait and gesture lay a disconcerting hurry and uncertainty, as though, hesitating to make a decision of some vital sort, he was flurried, almost in a frenzy sometimes, trying vainly to escape. This stupid confusion in him afflicted me, but the effort to escape seemed to paralyse something in my mind. It was petrifying.... And thus the sequence of what followed, proved extraordinarily difficult to remember afterwards. An atmosphere of sadness, of foreboding, of premonition came over me; there was desolation in my heart; there were stabs of horrible presentiment. All these, moreover, were ever vaguely related to one thing—that inexplicable faint odour of burning....

What memory recalls can be told very briefly. It lies in my mind thus, condensed and swift:

The storm was natural enough, but, here again, the smell of burning alarmed and wrung me. It was faint, it was fugitive. Our mistake about the river had no importance, for the depression in the landscape might easily after all have held flowing water. The roofs, too, were not the roofs of Barton, but of a hamlet nestling among orchards, Clifden by name, and it was here, Forden informed us, he had first met his wife and had proposed to her: this also of no importance, except that he went on talking about it, and that it surprised him. He suddenly recognised the place, I mean. It increased his bewilderment, and is mentioned for that reason.

The storm, then, came abruptly. We had not seen it coming. Following a low line of hills, it overtook us from behind, bringing its own wind with it. The rustling of the leaves was the first thing I noticed. The trees about us began to shake and bend. The sparkling brilliance, I saw, had left the day; the sun shone dully; the fields were no longer radiant; the flowers, too, were gone, for we were crossing a ploughed field at the moment.

The discussion between us may be omitted; its confusion is really beyond me to describe. The storm, however, is easily described, for everyone has seen that curious thickening of the air on a day in high summer, when the clouds are not really clouds, but come as a shapeless, murky gloom, threatening a portentous downpour while yet no single raindrop falls. In childhood we called it "blight," believing it to be composed of myriads of tiny insects. Lurid effects of lighting accompanied it, trees and roofs, against its dark background, looking as if stage flares illumined them. The whole picture, indeed, was theatrical in the extreme, artificial almost; but the aspect that I, personally, found so unwelcome, was that it laid over the sky an appearance of volumes of dense, heavy smoke. The idea of burning may, or may not, have been in my own mind only, for my companions made no comment on it. I cannot say. That it made my heart sink I remember clearly.

It was a sham storm, it had no meaning, nothing happened. Having accomplished its spectacular effect, it passed along the hills and dissipated, and the sun shone out with all its former brilliance. Yet, before it passed, certain things occurred; they came and went, it seemed to me afterwards, with the simultaneity of dream happenings. Forden, noticing the wall of gloom advancing, catching the noise of the trees as well, stopped dead in his tracks, and stared. He sniffed the air, but made no comment. An expression of utter bewilderment draped his face. He seemed once more bewitched. It was here the smell of burning came to me most strongly.

"Look out!" he cried, and started to run. He ran in front of us, we did not attempt to follow. But he ran in a circle, like a terrified animal. His figure went shifting quickly, silhouetted, like the trees and roofs, against the murky background of the low-hanging storm. A moment later he was beside us again, his face white, his eyes shining, his breath half-gone.

"Come on, old Fordy," said Malahide affectionately, taking him by the arm. He, for some reason, was not affected. "It's not going to rain, you know, and anyhow there's no good running. Let's sit down and eat our lunch." And he led the way across a few furrows to the hedge....

We ate our sandwiches and cake and apples. The sun shone hotly again. None of us smoked, I remember. For myself, the smell of burning had left something so miserable in me that I dared not smell even a lighted match. But no word was said by anybody in this, or in any other, sense. I kept my own counsel.... And it was while we lay resting idly, hardly speaking at all, that a sound reached me from the other side of the hedge: a footstep in the flowered grass. My companions exchanged quick glances, I noticed, but I did not even turn my head. I did not dare.

"He's putting it in," whispered Malahide, a touch of the old vehemence in his eyes. "The last one!" Forden smiled, nodded his head, and was about to add some comment of his own, when the other interrupted brusquely:

"Is that the way to Barton?" he enquired suddenly in a louder voice, something challenging, almost truculent, in the tone. He jerked his head towards the gate we had recently come through. "Through that gate and past that farm, I mean?"

The answering voice startled me. It was the owner of the footsteps, of course, behind the hedge.

"No. That's a dead end," came in gruff but not unpleasant country tones.

There was no more than that. It was all natural enough. Yet a lump came up in my throat as I heard. I still dared not look round over my shoulder. I looked instead into Forden's face, so close beside me. "We're all right," he was saying, as he glanced up a little. "Don't struggle so. It's the way we've got to go .." and was about to say more, when a fit of coughing caught him, as though for a moment he were about to suffocate. I hid my eyes quickly; a feeling of horror and despair swept through me; for there was terror in the sound he made; but the next second, when I looked again, the coughing had passed, and I saw in his face an expression of radiant happiness; the eyes shone wonderfully, there was a delicate, almost unearthly, beauty on his features. I found myself trembling, utterly unnerved.

"We'd better be getting on," mentioned Malahide, in his abrupt, inconsequent fashion. "We mustn't miss that train back." And it was this unexpected change of key that enabled me at last to turn my head. I looked hurriedly behind the hedge. I was just in time to see a man, a farmer apparently, in the act of planting a post into the ground. He was pressing it down, at any rate, and much in the fashion of Malahide's former play about a "fellow who planted signposts." But he was planting—two. Side by side they already stood in the earth. One arm pointed right, the other left. They formed, thus, a cross.

The very same second, with a quiver in the air, as when two cinema pictures flash on each other's heels with extreme rapidity, I experienced an optical delusion. I must call it such, at any rate. The focus of my sight changed instantaneously. The man was already in the distance, diminished in outline, moving away across the bright fields of golden buttercups. I saw him as I had seen him once or twice before, earlier in the day, a moving figure in the grass; and when my eyes shifted back to examine the posts, there was but a single post—a signpost whose one arm bore in faded lettering the words: "*From* Barton." It pointed in the direction whence we had come....

I followed my companions in a dream that is better left untouched by words. Led by Malahide, we passed through Clifden, we came to the Trent and were ferried across; and a little later we reached, as the porter had described, a Midland station called Attenborough. A train soon took us back to the town where we were playing. Malahide, without a word, vanished from our side the moment we left the carriage. I did not see him again until, dressed in his lordly costume, he stood in the wings that night, waiting impatiently for his entrance. I had walked home with Forden, flung myself on the bed and dropped off into a deep two-hours' sleep.

IX

A performance behind the scenes that night was more dramatic—to me, at least—than anything the enthusiastic audience witnessed from the front. The three of us met in the wings for the first time since Malahide had given us the slip at the station. High tea at six I had alone, Forden for some reason going to a shop for his meal. Malahide, for another reason, ate nothing. We met, anyhow, at our respective posts in the wings. Neither Forden nor I were on till late in the second act, and as we came down the rickety stairs from separate dressing-rooms, at the same moment it so chanced, I realised at once that he was as little inclined to talk as I was. My own mind was still too packed with the whirling wonder of the whole affair for utterance. We nodded, then dropped back towards the door through which he would presently make his entrance.

It was just then, while someone was whispering, "He's giving a marvellous performance to-night," that Malahide swept by me from his exit and ran to his dressing-room for a hurried change.

"Hullo, Hubert!" he cried in his tempestuous way. "I say …" as though it surprised him to see me there. "By the by," he rattled on, stopping dead for a breathless second in the rush to his room. "There's a place called Barton I want to see—Barton-in-Fabis. Let's go to-morrow. There's a train at 10.15. Forden, you come too!" And he was gone. Gone too, I realized with a dreadful sinking of the heart, a trembling of the nerves as well—utterly gone as though it had never happened, was all memory of the day's adventure. The mind in Malahide was blank as a clean-washed slate.

And Forden—standing close behind him within easy earshot—my eye fell upon Forden, who had heard every single word, I saw him stare and bite his lips. He passed a hand aimlessly across his forehead. His eyelids flickered. There was a quiver of the lips. In his old man's wig and make-up, he looked neither himself nor the part he was just about to play. Waiting there for his cue, now imminent, he stared fixedly at Malahide's vanishing figure, then at me, then blankly into space. He was like a man about to fall. He looked bewitched again. A moment's intense strain shot across the delicate features. He made in that instant, I am convinced, a tremendous, a violent, effort to recapture something that evaded him, an effort that failed completely. The next second, too swift to be measurable, that amazing expression, the angel's, shone out amazingly. It flashed and vanished…. His cue sounded. He, too, was gone.

How I made my own entrance, I hardly know. Five minutes later we met on the stage. He was normal. He was acting beautifully. His mind, like Malahide's, was a clean-washed slate.

X

My one object was to avoid speech with either Malahide or Forden. The former was on the stage until the end of the play, but the latter made no appearance in the last act. I slipped out the moment I was free to go. Malahide's door was ajar, but he did not see me. Foregoing supper, I was safely in bed when I heard Forden come upstairs soon after midnight. I fell into an uneasy sleep that must have been deeper, however, than it seemed, for I did not hear Malahide come in, but I was wide awake on the instant, dread clutching me with gripping force, when I heard Forden's voice outside my door.

"It's half-past nine!" he warned me. "We mustn't miss the train, remember!"

After gulping down some coffee, I went with him to the station, and he was normal and collected as you please. We chatted in our usual fashion. Clearly, his mind held no new, strange thing of any sort. Malahide was there before us….

The day, for me, was a nightmare of appalling order. A kind of mystical horror held me in a vice. Half-memories of bewildering and incredible things haunted me. The odour of burning, faint but unmistakable, was never absent….

We took single tickets to Stanton, Malahide reading a pile of papers and commenting volubly on the criticisms of the play. A porter at the station gave us confused directions. We followed faulty signposts, ancient and illegible, losing ourselves rather stupidly … and I noticed a man—a farmer with a spud—wandering about the fields and making thrusts from time to time at thistles. A sham storm followed a low line of hills, but no rain fell, and the brilliance of the April day was otherwise unspoilt. Barton itself we never reached, but we crossed the Trent on our way to a station called Attenborough, first passing a hamlet, Clifden, where, Forden informed us, he had met the girl he later made his wife.

It was a dull and uninspired expedition, Malahide voluble without being articulate, Forden rather silent on the whole … and at the home station Malahide gave us the slip without a word … but during the entire outing neither one nor other betrayed the slightest hint of familiarity with anything they had known before. In myself the memory lay mercilessly sharp and clear. I noted each startling contrast between the one and other. At the end I was worn out, bone-tired, every nerve seemed naked … and, again, I left the theatre alone, ran home, and went supperless to bed.

My determination was to keep awake at all costs, but sleep caught me too easily, as I believed it was meant to catch me. No such little thing as a warning was allowed to override what had to be, what had already been…. In the early hours of the morning, about two o'clock, to be exact, I woke from a nightmare of overwhelming vividness. Wide awake I was, the instant I opened my eyes. The nightmare was one of suffocation, I was being suffocated, and I carried over into waking consciousness the smell of burning and the atmosphere of smoke. The room, I saw at once, was full of smoke, the burning was not a dream. I *was* being suffocated. But in my case the suffocation was not complete, whereas Malahide and Forden died, according to the doctors, in their sleep. They did not even wake. They knew no pain….

Playing Catch

Mr. Anthony, a widower, was deeply interested in the big questions of life and death, and in philosophy generally. He liked to wonder where his wife was, what she was doing if she had survived the destruction of her pretty body, and how her spirit was engaged. Was she, for instance, in any way aware of him? ... Mabel, he remembered, had not been imaginative. Though sympathetic, she had contributed nothing to his mental life. When he referred any of his big questions to her, she would fix her patient eyes upon his own, and say: "I wonder! What do you think, dear?" Her disposition was gentle, but uninspiring.

Mabel apart, however, he pondered over many other things, being distinctly speculative: Why there was anything at all, and what—since there was a beginning—had existed before that beginning? What there might be on the other side of the moon, and whether the other planets were inhabited? The vast number of the heavenly bodies in particular perplexed him—a thousand million suns in the Milky Way alone!—It all seemed so unnecessarily enormous. He often wondered, again, about angels. Were there such beings, and, if so, what was their habit and nature? All races, all religions, all cosmogonies mentioned angels. Were they an invention of primitive imagining, or were they actual?

Dreams, too, interested him immensely. He declared all such enquiries stimulated him.

His speculations, it is seen, were sometimes grandiose, sometimes trivial. He read much, he brooded, he dwelt in an atmosphere of unanswerable questions. It argued, perhaps a strain of futility in the blood, but his love of the marvellous was ineradicable. That Mabel had not shared his divine curiosity had always been a secret grievance, rather shaking his belief in feminine intuition. She had never answered—anything. Could she answer anything now? By force of habit he still referred all his big questions to her mentally: Did Mabel know?

It was the advent of Mr. Einstein that dragged his anchor and set him sailing upon unchartered seas. Space, Time, Relativity, absorbed his entire thought. The mass of all his reading, knowledge, thinking, converged on this bewildering subject. No sympathy for a discredited Euclid troubled him. Time, as a fourth dimension, delighted him. He mastered the matter as well as any layman could. Though out of his depth, he was not afraid....

Meanwhile, he had no settled home, feeling himself a wanderer physically as well as mentally. He occupied lodgings in Dymchurch at the moment. Large foreign sea-shells stood, echoless and dismal, on the plush mantelpiece, and a yellow-faced clock, with hands always pointing to 4.20, reposed under a domed glass cover. There was brilliant gas, a horsehair sofa, and a painted fan before the grate. Long green bell-ropes hung against the walls, with two oil-paintings of violent Swiss scenery beside them. A framed photograph of a fat-faced man, wearing Masonic regalia, was perched above the door. The broad window-sills were littered with his books, volumes straggled over the sofa, and an atmosphere of relativity, of astronomy, of the marvellous generally, pervaded the false brightness of the sordid seaside lodgings out of the season.

One warm February evening, when the days were pleasantly lengthening, Mr. Anthony was coming home along the sea-front just after sunset, when a thing happened that enthralled him because it proved, as he had long suspected, that there were Beings in the Universe compared to whom the greatest human was the merest microbe. Were they, perhaps, angels? he asked himself. He was uncommonly intrigued.

The afternoon had been strangely warm. He had sat down under a breakwater to rest. The something that happened was as follows:

The moon, clean, bright and tender, and just off the full, stood well above the sea, when, from the western horizon, there rose without the slightest warning a gigantic arm, whose huge hand seized her, as a man might seize a tennis ball, and flung her away into space with a stupendous but quite effortless throw. The vast hand then dropped, as a man's hand drops after throwing, and the colossal arm, one instant level with the horizon, sank swiftly out of sight below the rim of the sea. The arm, Mr. Anthony noticed, was visible from the elbow only. The figure it belonged to, therefore, was standing in space at least one thousand miles below the spinning earth.

The grandeur of the gesture, magnificent, even godlike, left him breathless, but exhilarated. Yet it caused him no alarm, nor was he conscious of surprise. Such immense proportions, he reflected, must be angelic, surely. Why no head and shoulders were visible puzzled him—for his mind began to work at once—until he realised that, being of the same colour as the golden sunset, they merged into its background, so that the sky revealed no outline. Moreover, the arm, he observed, was slightly richer in red and gold than the tint of the air, and thus showed up nicely. The hand, of a splendid crimson, was fiery rather, and the colossal fingers that gripped the moon in their great curving clutch, stood out, dark-ridged like mountains, against the silver. It was an impressive and inspiring sight.

Mr. Anthony stood spell-bound, watching the moon as she flew plunging away into space. Such headlong speed enthralled him. It was thrilling, too, to remember that this outer space, being of ether only, was completely black. Had he been out there himself, he would have appeared as a solitary bright figure amid Egyptian darkness. This reflection, certainly, occurred to him. He would be a shining figure. Mabel, too, occurred to him. Did Mabel, he asked himself, witness what he witnessed? Was his strange privilege shared? …

He watched the flying moon. Already she was half her usual size. In fifteen seconds, she was no larger than a tangerine orange; in thirty, she resembled a sparkling marble; in forty, a shining pea; in sixty, a glittering bead; in seventy-five, a pin-head; and in ninety, a mere starry point that was barely visible at all against the sunset afterglow. The speed, the distance, the power behind the throw, the possible immediate effect upon the tide, the terror of any human beings who were looking on—all these details filled him with a high sense of happiness that was elation. He felt, to use his own favourite word, stimulated.

Then other points of view began to occur to him, modifying his first emotion of pure enjoyment. The human stand-point struck him. He noticed that the sky looked bare, undressed, naked somewhere, even—he used poetic license—a little lonely. He felt sorry that the moon had gone. He found that he missed her. He experienced regret. He was glad, therefore, to see that the point of light she had now become held stationary, and that no further dwindling occurred. The moon, then, had not completely vanished. Had she done so he would have felt bereft. Only a few days before he had told his landlady's child that he knew of no reason why the earth should have a moon at all, since not all planets had these pretty, faithful satellites, and the child had asked at once:

"But what would happen at night, then?"

It was this simple human point of view that now modified his first emotion somewhat. He felt precisely as the child felt: "What would happen at night without a moon?"

It was with sincere relief and pleasure, therefore, after the minute and a half had passed, that he noted she was now growing bigger again. She was returning. She was on her way back. He watched her rapidly grow larger, as she approached at appalling speed. The point, bead, pea, marble and orange sizes were reached and passed successively, and ninety seconds later she had almost resumed her normal size and appearance again. Mr. Anthony's fear that she would grow larger still and come crashing down upon the earth, obliterating perhaps Dymchurch, was hardly born before it was allayed. He watched with beating heart and straining eyes. He saw the gigantic arm and hand again shoot forth. The enormous fingers caught her, clutched her, then placed her with easy accuracy exactly where she would have moved to in these three minutes had her course not been interrupted. The same side as before shone placidly down. She was not a fraction turned. The stupendous arm and hand at once withdrew and sank below the sea. The sky was as it had been. Mr. Anthony, tears of joy in his eyes and wonder in his heart, but outwardly quite calm, resumed his walk home along the sea-front towards his lodgings....

The awful occurrence, for most, must have been dislocating, yet Mr. Anthony faced it with equilibrium. His joy was not hysterical. Accustomed to speculations concerning the unknown and unexpected, he maintained his poise quite admirably. He did not, so to speak, fall flat upon his face, prostrate in worship, although both awe and reverence were touched. The experience, he argued, was not merely a vision which could be analysed away next morning, for his mind retained its logical, observant processes, his reason worked as usual. Memory, judgment, imagination, the three great faculties, functioned properly. It was, therefore, no hallucination, in which these faculties are notoriously in abeyance. It was an honest, a genuine phenomenon.

He considered what he had seen, he made justifiable inferences, he drew sound conclusions. It pleased him particularly to find that these held water, as he called it. Thus he was delighted to establish—since the moon had been thrown away and then thrown back again—that two great figures were tossing her to and fro together across outer space, and that a spirit of amusement, even of sheer happy fun, evidently inspired the majestic spectacle. It was, perhaps, a game, a match possibly, a trial of skill at any rate, since one hand only was employed. The two gorgeous players were enjoying themselves. They were playing catch.

It made him happy to think that he had witnessed at least one mighty stroke in their magnificent game, and still more happy—comforted as well—to realise that, at long last, the intolerable quantity of the heavenly bodies, together with their overwhelming speeds and distances, were thus reasonably explained. He weighed his inferences cautiously, he examined his deductions; his logic and premises were sound, he could find no flaw in his reasoning. It was obvious to him that all the heavenly bodies, whose numbers had long dismayed him, as their *raison d'être* had thwarted him, that all of these—stars, suns, planets, comets—were being similarly thrown from hand to hand, most of them, with century-long, some with age-long tosses, and that the purpose of the colossal Universe was at last made clear.

He wondered if Mabel also knew; he hoped she did. To his boldest speculations her contribution had been invariably "But why bother, dear? What can it matter to *us?*" Did she now share the relief and wonder of his superb discovery that all the heavenly bodies were used by angels for the purposes of—happy play?

His mind, it is seen, worked admirably, his faculties retained their normal sharpness, the clarity of his thought was unimpaired. How, why, by what happy chance, he had witnessed only one stroke in the game, this, too, was quite clear to him at the moment, though he had difficulty in setting it down later in his written account of the occurrence. Relativity, of course, helped in the first easy stages of the explanation. Four measurements, he remembered, one of which is Time, are necessary to locate a point in space; and until that point is thus located and in position, it has not become an event—it has not "happened." Clearly, then, he had witnessed an occurrence in four-dimensional space. It was an event, it had happened, though not necessarily *now*.

This fourth measurement of Time troubled him for a moment, but for a moment only. He looked at his watch, he began to make elaborate calculations at the back of his head, and then confusion overtook him.... What remained, however, was the positive assurance that this playing catch with the moon filled him with the joy of a comfortable understanding. One of his big questions, at least, was satisfactorily answered.

He resumed his walk along the sea-front, therefore, at a steady gait, stimulated, though not unduly so, and by no means shaken. That his mental balance held true is proved by the fact that, as he turned homewards, his mind dealt with commonplace things quite naturally. He thought of his lodgings, remembering that he liked them because baths were included in the terms, that early morning tea was only three pence, and that he could turn the light out from his bed. Also, he once more remembered Mabel. And again he asked himself: was she aware of him in this magnificent moment? For Mabel, he suddenly realised with a qualm of peculiar distress, was involved somewhere in the entire business. This realisation, coming abruptly, caused an odd uneasiness, and the uneasiness spread, till it was established in his whole being. Mabel, it flashed through him, though involved, was not involved—quite openly. There was an unpleasant touch of subterfuge, a hint of plan, of purpose, almost of plot: his original idea of Mabel, his fond, admiring, yet rather stupid wife, had undergone a disagreeable change. It was as though she now stood mysteriously behind the scenes, unpleasantly concealed—secreted.

The confused conviction that Mabel played this hidden role began to trouble him....

Meanwhile, the splendour he had witnessed brought a touch of soberness in its train. The after-effect of splendour is invariably of a sedative description, and this reaction now set in, accompanied by a feeling of disappointment that just stopped short of distress and yet held the seed of faint alarm. The breath of uneasiness blew through him. It was slight, impossible to seize. He noticed it, no more than that, yet its presence lurked, if not definite enough yet to cause acute disturbance. It remained a vague sinking of the heart, due to something that was not fully explained. Mabel, however, he felt sure, would explain it—if she *could*. Here, at last, was something Mabel really knew. Here was a contribution she could make—if she *would*.

Confusion grew upon him. He had after all been privileged, perhaps, beyond what a man can bear with equanimity—this occurred to him as a solution of his distress. Being wise, therefore, he turned his thoughts deliberately upon more familiar things. He felt hungry. He hoped there might be a fried Dover sole for supper. Mabel, too, he remembered, was fond of that dish. He felt happier again. The wind had grown chilly, and he drew his light-blue dressing-gown more closely about him. The dark blue bathing-suit underneath looked a trifle tight, he thought, but there was no need to bother about that at the moment. The thought did not detain him. He must get home quickly now and change. He hurried....

In this frame of mind, therefore, Mr. Anthony made his way along the deserted front, and in so doing had to pass the row of bathing-sheds that stood high and dry upon the sandy ridge. The coarse grass bent ruffled and whistling in the wind. It was too early in the year for bathers, and the sheds were unoccupied. Rather dreary and melancholy it appeared, but this was all exactly as it should be, and his mind observed the fact, offering no comment on it. At the same time something about those white-washed bathing-sheds began to *draw* his attention. His mind was first arrested, then startled. There was a difference somewhere. Why, for instance, did it take so long to pass them? Why did they stretch into such an interminable distance? Why did the endless row of familiar ugliness now seem queer and ominous? ... He found himself counting them automatically. And his interest, on a sudden, became intense. He had discovered where the difference lay; there was an increase in their number. Multiplied by thousands, the row of sheds stretched horribly, hundreds upon hundreds, into a dim infinity....

His alarm deepened at once. There was something here he ought by rights to have known, but did not know; yet something, it occurred to him painfully, that Mabel knew already and had always known; something, again, that she was concealing from him deliberately.

He paused to consider the matter. It was, he realised, of immense importance, not so much the horrible increase in the sheds, as her reason for the deliberate concealment. A singular new dread invaded, clutched him. *What* precisely was it that Mabel knew, yet kept so mysteriously hidden from him? A dreadful curiosity attached itself to the interminable row of bathing-sheds. Their number, certainly, was sinister. But her reason for concealment was far worse. Terror touched him with an icy finger. He faced, with shrinking, a portentous and appalling thing.

In this predicament his native habit of philosophical enquiry amid unanswerable questions proved of some assistance. His mind switched automatically elsewhere. Turning his attention in another direction altogether, he glanced up at the sky, perceived the moon safely in her accustomed place, and noted, not without a faint annoyance, that he had mistaken her light a few moments before for sunshine. The bathing-suit he wore was out of place now. He had evidently lingered somewhere; he must hasten home and change. He therefore hurried. He passed the row of sheds without the slightest difficulty, intent only upon finding Mabel so that she might explain properly to him what she had so long been hiding. He reached and entered his lodgings, forgetting entirely that he had ever felt uneasy, and quite happy that everything was now all right again. Passing through the hall he saw his landlady *very* quickly close the kitchen door. She spoke to him, but he did not catch the words. Very quickly she closed that door. He caught but a glimpse of her vanishing face.

Things, however, were only fairly "all right," it seemed. For instance, he at once missed Mabel. There was no sign of her anywhere. A feeling came to him—it was in the very air—that she had never been in this particular house at all. For a second he felt sure it was the wrong house altogether. A wild bewilderment came on him. Mabel was lost, hopelessly, irrecoverably lost; and it was due to some stupid carelessness of his own that she was thus irretrievably mislaid. Somehow he had blundered; he had neglected some obvious precaution, had been somewhere he ought not to have been, had missed or overlooked a pre-arranged instruction of very simple kind—with the result that his wife was now finally and completely lost.

A realisation of his deep guilt overwhelmed him. A sense of hideous, imminent danger at once hung in the air. He had stolen upon the threshold of a mystery none but Mabel could possibly unravel—and she was lost. He felt it with capital letters: LOST. A sense of frantic hurry rushed upon him. It was tremendous, over-mastering. He knew himself hideously caught by the thing that all men dread—the panic sense.

He hurried, he rushed, he tore headlong....

In the confused and frenzied search that followed, Mr. Anthony experienced such acute anguish, such poignant, heart-felt sadness, such aching misery and distress of mind, that he realised it was altogether impossible to continue looking. It was a hopeless, an intolerable search; the strain was unbearable; the pain was more than he could support without a collapse that involved the awful disaster of some terrible extinction. He, therefore, gave up the search, and turned his thoughts to other things.... The power of detachment pertaining to a mind that dealt with unanswerable questions asserted itself once again. At the back of his head, moreover, was a feeling that really he knew all the time exactly where Mabel was, what she was concealing from him, and why she was concealing it; yet, further, that *when* she did reveal her secret it would prove to be something he had known all along quite well. What puzzled him a little, indeed, was *why* he hid this knowledge from himself? Why did he shrink from facing it? Why did he deliberately avoid it? Whence came this elaborate and artificial pretence? He raged, he shrank, he trembled....

Then, suddenly, the reason for his attitude flashed clearly. He understood the monstrous thing: if he faced it, his terror would be too appalling to contemplate and live. He must go mad, or die.

That Mabel grasped this and, out of love for him, still consented to remain Lost, brought a measure of comfort to his anguished soul, though it was in vain he tried to grasp its full significance. The full meaning of the whole episode continued to evade him. That her remaining lost bore some subtle relation to the throwing of the moon, he perceived vaguely, but what that relation precisely was he could not, for the life of him, determine. The effort to understand at length exhausted him. He dripped with perspiration....

With sharp, dreadful clarity, his intelligence then strangely opened, and—he knew.

Transfixed with terror, he could scarcely breathe. His voice failed him. He called out wildly, but no sound was audible. He screamed and shrieked for help, but no whisper left his lips. He was alone, entirely alone, lost in an infinity of emptiness. And—he was shining: a figure of light amid the Egyptian blackness of outer space.

He himself had been thrown away. He was falling, falling … and Mabel was aware of it....

In those awful seconds before he crashed upon some point in ultimate space, the full significance of the moon's return became at last quite clear. The revelation came with a final certainty there was no resisting. It was appalling beyond words. The Other Player, he realised, had held the catch—this time. But one day that catch would not be held. It would be *missed*. Another heavenly body would then be seized and flung, a constellation, perhaps the Pleiades, perhaps—the Earth herself!

"One day soon, we, too, shall be flung away!" he roared aloud, incoherent with the horror of his dizzy falling. But no sound left his lips. He heard instead—where, oh where, had she said this dreadful thing?—the voice of his landlady:

"The Pleiades would scatter in a handful of golden dust!"

His terrified thought could not grapple with such fearful words. Meanwhile, he rushed and tore and fell....

"Mabel!" he screamed, finding a strangled voice that hurt his throat in the effort to get out. "Mabel! Look out, dear! Look out! He's going to— *miss!*"

The odd thing—the first detail in the whole experience that occurred to him as really strange—the odd thing was that Mabel seemed quite unfrightened. She was not even interested, much less disturbed. She paid no attention to his frenzied warning, as she passed, prettily smiling, through the room. The sunlight fell on her smooth, comely body in its becoming bathing-suit that was dripping wet and clung tightly to her. She went very quickly towards the inner room to dry herself and put her clothes on. She came, evidently, straight from her dip in the sea, and it annoyed him that she had gone to bathe alone, without even letting him know that she was going.

This annoyance, however, lay far below his terror, barely recognisable at all. His terror usurped all, other feeling. Even the frightful descent through empty space was quite forgotten. It was the smile on her placid, patient face that petrified him. The ghastly horror of it, its indifference, its gentle sweetness, its fatuous imperturbability, froze his blood.

He understood at last—everything.

The tossed moon, the stupendous arm and hand that clutched her, the horrible increase of the bathing-sheds, his own fierce fling through blackness towards some final crash of extinction—all, all had a reason, an explanation, which had been concealed from him with cunning and diabolical success by—Mabel, by his own stupid, loving, faithful, yet *knowing* wife.

Mabel knew. She knew everything. Also—she had always known.

Yet his understanding, even now, was not complete. God! Would he never understand anything *completely?*

He slowly turned his head. Mabel, in the act of passing out of the room, was looking back at him over her wet, shapely shoulder. The line of her delicious body enticed him. Her lips were moving. She was mentioning something—by the way, as it were:

"He *has* missed, dear! But, why bother ...?"

Mr. Anthony, shivering with cold, opened his eyes, rose from his indifferent shelter below the breakwater, and walked home rapidly to his cheerless lodgings....

The Pikestaffe Case

I

The vitality of old governesses deserves an explanatory memorandum by a good physiologist. It is remarkable. They tend to survive the grown-up married men and women they once taught as children. They hang on for ever, as a man might put it crudely, a man, that is, who, taught by one of them in his earliest schoolroom days, would answer enquiries fifty years later without enthusiasm: "Oh we keep her going, yes. She doesn't want for anything!"

Miss Helena Speke had taught the children of a distinguished family, and these distinguished children, with expensive progeny of their own now, still kept her going. They had clubbed together, seeing that Miss Speke retained her wonderful health, and had established her in a nice little house where she could take respectable lodgers—men for preference—giving them the three B's, bed, bath, breakfast. Being a capable woman, Miss Speke more than made both ends meet. She wanted for nothing. She kept going.

Applicants for her rooms, especially for the first-floor suite, had to be recommended. She had a stern face for those who rang the bell without a letter in their pockets. She never advertised. Indeed, there was no need to do so. The two upper floors had been occupied by the same tenants for many years—a chief clerk in a branch bank and a retired clergyman respectively. It was only the best suite that sometimes "happened to be vacant at the moment." From two guineas inclusive before the war, her price for this had been raised naturally, to four, the tenant paying his gas-stove, light, and bath extra. Breakfast—she prided herself legitimately on her good breakfasts—was included.

For a long time now this first-floor suite had been unoccupied. The cost of living worried Miss Speke, as it worried most other people. Her servant was cheap but incompetent, and once she could let the suite she meant to engage a better one. The distinguished children were scattered out of reach about the world; the eldest had been killed in the war; a married one, a woman, lived in India; another married one was in the throes of divorce—an expensive business; and the fourth, the most generous and last, found himself in the Bankruptcy Court, and so was unable to help.

It was in these conditions that Miss Speke, her vitality impaired, decided to advertise. Although she inserted the words "references essential," she meant in her heart to use her own judgment, and if a likely gentleman presented himself and agreed to pay her price, she might accept him. The clergyman and the bank official upstairs were a protection, she felt. She invariably mentioned them to applicants: "I have a clergyman of the Church of England on the top floor. He's been with me for eleven years. And a banker has the floor below. Mine is a very quiet house, you see." These words formed part of the ritual she recited in the hall facing her proposed tenants on the linoleum by the hat-rack; and it was these words she addressed to the tall, thin, pale-faced man with scanty hair and spotless linen, who informed her that he was a tutor, a teacher of higher mathematics to the sons of various families—he mentioned some first-class names where references could be obtained—a student besides and something of an author in his leisure hours. His pupils he taught, of course, in their respective houses, one being in Belgrave Square, another in The Albany; it was only after tea, or in the evenings, that he did his own work. All this he explained briefly, but with great courtesy of manner.

Mr. Thorley was well spoken, with a gentle voice, kind, far-seeing eyes, and an air of being lonely and uncared for that touched some forgotten, dried-up spring in Miss Speke's otherwise rather cautious heart. He looked every inch a scholar—"and a gentleman," as she explained after-wards to everybody who was interested in him, these being numerous, of unexpected kinds, and all very close, not to say unpleasantly close, ques-tioners indeed. But what chiefly influenced her in his favour was the fact, elicited in conversation, that years ago he had been a caller at the house in Portman Square where she was governess to the distinguished family. She did not exactly remember him, but he had certainly known Lady Araminta, the mother of her charges.

Thus it was that Mr. Thorley—John Laking Thorley, M.A., of Jesus Col-lege, Cambridge—was accepted by Miss Speke as tenant of her best suite on the first floor at the price mentioned, breakfast included, winning her confidence so fully that she never went to the trouble even of taking up the references he gave her. She liked him, she felt safe with him, she pitied him. He had not bargained, nor tried to beat her down. He just re-flected a moment, then agreed. He proved, indeed, an exemplary lodger, early to bed and not too early to rise, of regular habits, thoughtful of the expensive new servant, careful with towels, electric light, and ink-stains, prompt in his payments, and never once troubling her with complaints or requests, as other lodgers did, not excepting the banker and the clergy-man. Moreover, he was a tidy man, who never lost anything, because he invariably put everything in its proper place and thus knew exactly where to look for it. She noticed this tidiness at once.

Miss Speke, especially in the first days of his tenancy, studied him, as she studied all her lodgers. She studied his room when he was out "of a morning." At her leisure she did this, knowing he would never break in and disturb her unexpectedly. She was neither prying nor inquisitive, she assured herself, but she *was* curious. "I have a right to know something about the gentlemen who sleep under my roof with me," was the way she put it in her own mind. His clothes, she found, were ample, including evening dress, white gloves, and an opera hat. He had plenty of boots and shoes. His linen was good. His wardrobe, indeed, though a trifle uncared for, especially his socks, was a gentleman's wardrobe. Only one thing puzzled her. The full-length mirror, standing on mahogany legs—a present from the generous "child," now in the Bankruptcy Court, and, a handsome thing, a special attraction in the best suite—this fine mirror Mr. Thorley evidently did not like. The second or third morning he was with her she went to his bedroom before the servant had done it up, and saw, to her surprise, that this full-length glass stood with its back to the room. It had been placed close against the wall in a corner, its unattractive back turned outward.

"It gave me quite a shock to see it," as she said afterwards. "And such a handsome piece, too!"

Her first thought, indeed, sent a cold chill down her energetic spine. "He's cracked it!" But it was not cracked. She paused in some amazement, wondering why her new lodger had done this thing; then she turned the mirror again into its proper position, and left the room. The next morning she found it again with its face close against the wall. The following day it was the same—she turned it round, only to find it the next morning again with its back to the room.

She asked the servant, but the servant knew nothing about it.

"He likes it that way, I suppose, mum," was all Sarah said. "I never laid a 'and on it once."

Miss Speke, after much puzzled consideration, decided it must be something to do with the light. Mr. Thorley, she remembered, wore horn-rimmed spectacles for reading. She scented a mystery. It caused her a slight—oh, a very slight—feeling of discomfort. Well, if he did not like the handsome mirror, she could perhaps use it in her own room. To see it neglected hurt her a little. Not many furnished rooms could boast a full-length glass, she reflected. A few days later, meeting Mr. Thorley on the linoleum before the hat-rack, she enquired if he was quite comfortable, and if the breakfast was to his liking. He was polite and even cordial. Everything was perfect, he assured her. He had never been so well looked after. And the house was so quiet.

"And the bed, Mr. Thorley? You sleep well, I hope." She drew nearer to the subject of the mirror, but with caution. For some reason she found a difficulty in actually broaching it. It suddenly dawned upon her that there was something queer about his treatment of that full-length glass. She was by no means fanciful, Miss Speke, retired governess; only the faintest suspicion of something odd brushed her mind and vanished. But she did feel something. She found it impossible to mention the handsome thing outright.

"There's nothing you would like changed in the room, or altered?" she enquired with a smile, "or—in any way put different—perhaps?"

Mr. Thorley hesitated for a moment. A curious expression, half sad, half yearning, she thought, lit on his thoughtful face for one second and was gone. The idea of moving anything seemed distasteful to him.

"Nothing, Miss Speke, I thank you," he replied courteously, but without delay, "Everything is really *just* as I like it." Then, with a little bow, he asked: "I trust my typewriter disturbs nobody. Please let me know if it does."

Miss Speke assured him that nobody minded the typewriter in the least, nor even heard it, and, with another charming little bow and a smile, Mr. Thorley went out to give his lessons in the higher mathematics.

"There!" she reflected, "and I never even asked him!" It had been impossible.

From the window she watched him going down the street, his head bent, evidently in deep thought, his books beneath his arm, looking, she thought, every inch the gentleman and the scholar that he undoubtedly was. His personality left a very strong impression on her mind. She found herself rather wondering about him. As he turned the corner Miss Speke owned to two things that rose simultaneously in her mind: first, the relief that the lodger was out for the day and could be counted upon not to return unexpectedly; secondly, that it would interest her to slip up and see what kind of books he read. A minute later she was in his sitting-room. It was already swept and dusted, the breakfast cleared away, and the books, she saw, lay partly on the table where he had just left them and partly on the broad mantelpiece he used as a shelf. She was alone, the servant was downstairs in the kitchen. She examined Mr. Thorley's books.

The examination left her bewildered and uninspired. "I couldn't make them out at all," she put it. But they were evidently what she called costly volumes, and that she liked. "Something to do with his work, I suppose—mathematics, and all that," she decided, after turning over pages covered with some kind of hieroglyphics, symbols being a word she did not know in that connection. There was no printing, there were no sentences, there was nothing she could lay hold of, and the diagrams she thought perhaps were Euclid, or possibly astronomical. Most of the names were odd and quite unknown to her. Gauss! Minowski! Lobatchewski! And it affronted her that some of these were German. A writer named Einstein was popular with her lodger, and that, she felt, was a pity, as well as a mistake in taste. It all alarmed her a little; or, rather she felt that touch of respect, almost of awe, pertaining to some world entirely beyond her ken. She was rather glad when the search—it was a duty—ended.

"There's nothing there," she reflected, meaning there was nothing that explained his dislike of the full-length mirror. And, disappointed, yet with a faint relief, she turned to his private papers. These, since he was a tidy man, were in a drawer. Mr. Thorley never left anything lying about. Now, a letter Miss Speke would not have thought of reading, but papers, especially learned papers, were another matter. Conscience, nevertheless, did prick her faintly, as she cautiously turned over sheaf after sheaf of large white foolscap, covered with designs, and curves, and diagrams in ink, the ink he never spilt, and assuredly in his recent handwriting. And it was among these foolscap sheets that she suddenly came upon one sheet in particular that caught her attention and even startled her. In the centre, surrounded by scriggly hieroglyphics, numbers, curves and lines meaningless to her, she saw a drawing of the full-length mirror. Some of the curves ran into it and through it, emerging on the other side. She knew it was *the* mirror because its exact measurements were indicated in red ink.

This, as mentioned, startled her. What could it mean? she asked herself, staring intently at the curious sheet, as though it must somehow yield its secret to prolonged even if unintelligent enquiry. "It looks like an experiment or something," was the furthest her mind could probe into the mystery, though this, she admitted, was not very far. Holding the paper at various angles, even upside down, she examined it with puzzled curiosity, then slowly laid it down again in the exact place whence she had taken it. That faint breath of alarm had again suddenly brushed her soul, as though she approached a mystery she had better leave unsolved.

"It's very strange—" she began, carefully closing the drawer, but unable to complete the sentence even in her mind. "I don't think I like it—quite," and she turned to go out. It was just then that something touched her face, tickling one cheek, something fine as a cobweb, something in the air. She picked it away. It was a thread of silk, extremely fine, so fine, indeed, that it might almost have been a spider's web of gossamer such as one sees floating over the garden lawn on a sunny morning. Miss Speke brushed it away, giving it no further thought, and went about her usual daily duties.

II

But in her mind was established now a vague uneasiness, though so vague that at first she did not recognise it. Her thought would suddenly pause. "Now, what is it?" she would ask herself. "Something's on my mind. What is it I've forgotten?" The picture of her first-floor lodger appeared, and she knew at once. "Oh, yes, it's that mirror and the diagrams, of course." Some taut wire of alarm was quivering at the back of her mind. It was akin to those childhood alarms that pertain to the big unexplained mysteries no parent can elucidate because no parent knows. "Only God can tell that," says the parent, evading the insoluble problem. "I'd better not think about it," was the analogous conclusion reached by Miss Speke. Meanwhile the impression the new lodger's personality made upon her mind perceptibly deepened. He seemed to her full of power, above little things, a man of intense and mysterious mental life. He was constantly and somewhat possessingly in her thoughts. The mere thought of him, she found, stimulated her.

It was just before luncheon, as she returned from her morning marketing, that the servant drew her attention to certain marks upon the carpet of Mr. Thorley's sitting-room. She had discovered them as she handled the vacuum cleaner—faint, short lines drawn by dark chalk or crayons, in shape like the top or bottom right-angle of a square bracket, and sometimes with a tiny arrow shown as well. There were occasional other marks, too, that Miss Speke recognised as the hieroglyphics, she called squiggles. Mistress and servant examined them together in a stooping position. They found others on the bedroom carpet, too, only these were not straight; they were small curved lines; and about the feet of the full-length mirror they clustered in a quantity, segments of circles, some large, some small. They looked as if someone had snipped off curly hair, or pared his finger-nails with sharp scissors, only considerably larger, and they were so faint that they were only visible when the sunlight fell upon them.

"I knew they was drawn on," said Sarah, puzzled, yet proud that she had found them, "because they didn't come up with the dust and fluff."

"I'll—speak to Mr. Thorley," was the only comment Miss Speke made. "I'll tell him." Her voice was not quite steady, but the girl apparently noticed nothing.

"There's all this too, please, mum." She pointed to a number of fine silk threads she had collected upon a bit of newspaper, preparatory to the dustbin. "They was stuck on the cupboard door and the walls, stretched all across the room, but rather 'igh up. I only saw them by chance. One caught on my face."

Miss Speke stared, touched, examined for some seconds without speaking. She remembered the thread that had tickled her own cheek. She looked enquiringly round the room, and the servant followed her suggestion, indicated where the threads had been attached to walls and furniture. No marks, however, were left; there was no damage done.

"I'll mention it to Mr. Thorley," said her mistress briefly; unwilling to discuss the matter with the new servant, much less to admit that she was uncomfortably at sea. "Mr. Thorley," she added, as though there was nothing unusual, "is a high mathematician. He makes—measurements and—calculations of that sort." She had not sufficient control of her voice to be more explicit, and she went from the room aware that, unaccountably, she was trembling. She had first gathered up the threads, meaning to show them to her lodger when she demanded an explanation. But the explanation was delayed, for—to state it bluntly—she was afraid to ask him for it. She put it off till the following morning, then till the day after, and, finally, she decided to say nothing about the matter at all. "I'd better leave it, perhaps, after all," she persuaded herself. "There's no damage done, anyhow. I'd better not enquire." All the same she did not like it. By the end of the week, however, she was able to pride herself upon her restraint and tact; the marks on the carpet, rubbed out by the girl, were not renewed, and the fine threads of silk were never again found stretching through the air from wall to furniture. Mr. Thorley had evidently noticed their removal and had discontinued what he had observed was an undesirable performance. He was a scholar and a gentleman. But he was more. He was frank and straight-dealing. One morning he asked to see his landlady and told her all about it himself.

"Oh," he said in his pleasantest, easiest manner when she came into the room, "I wanted to tell you, Miss Speke—indeed, I meant to do so long before this—about the marks I made on your carpets"—he smiled apologetically—"and the silk threads I stretched. I use them for measurements—for problems I set my pupils, and one morning I left them there by mistake. The marks easily rub out. But I will use scraps of paper instead another time. I can pin these on—if you will kindly tell your excellent servant not to touch them—er—they're rather important to me." He smiled again charmingly, and his face wore the wistful, rather yearning expression that had already appealed to her. The eyes, it struck her, were very brilliant. "Any damage," he added—"though, I assure you, none is possible really—I would, of course, make good to you, Miss Speke."

"Thank you, Mr. Thorley," was all Miss Speke could find to say, so confused was her mind by troubling thoughts and questions she dared not express. "Of course—this is my best suite, you see."

It was all most amicable and pleasant between them.

"I wonder—have my books come?" he asked, as he went out. "Ah, there they are, I do believe!" he exclaimed, for through the open front door a van was seen discharging a very large packing-case.

"Your books, Mr. Thorley?" Miss Speke murmured, noting the size of the package with dismay. "But I'm afraid—you'll hardly find space to put them in," she stammered. "The rooms—er"—she did not wish to disparage them—"are so small, aren't they?"

Mr. Thorley smiled delightfully. "Oh, please do not trouble on that account," he said. "I shall find space all right, I assure you. It's merely a question of knowing where and how to put them," and he proceeded to give the men instructions.

A few days later a second case arrived.

"I'm expecting some instruments, too," he mentioned casually, "mathematical instruments," and he again assured her with his confident smile that she need have no anxiety on the score of space. Nor would he dent the walls or scrape the furniture the least little bit. There was always room, he reminded her gently again, provided one knew how to stow things away. Both books and instruments were necessary to his work. Miss Speke need feel no anxiety at all.

But Miss Speke felt more than anxiety, she felt uneasiness, she felt a singular growing dread. There lay in her a seed of distress that began to sprout rapidly. Everything arrived as Mr. Thorley had announced, case upon case was unpacked in his room by his own hands. The straw and wood she used for firing purposes, there was no mess, no litter, no untidiness, nor were walls and furniture injured in any way. What caused her dread to deepen into something bordering upon actual alarm was the fact that, on searching Mr. Thorley's rooms when he was out, she could discover no trace of any of the things that had arrived. There was no sign of either books or instruments. Where had he stored them? Where could they lie concealed? She asked herself innumerable questions, but found no answer to them. These stores, enough to choke and block the room, had been brought in through the sitting-room door. They could not possibly have been taken out again. They had *not* been taken out. Yet no trace of them was anywhere to be seen. It was very strange, she thought; indeed, it was more than strange. She felt excited. She felt a touch of hysterical alarm.

Meanwhile, thin strips of white paper, straight, angled, curved, were pinned upon the carpet; threads of finest silk again stretched overhead connecting the top of the door lintel with the window, the high cupboard with the curtain rods—yet too high to be brushed away merely by the head of anyone moving in the room. And the full-length mirror still stood with its face close against the wall.

The mystery of these aerial entanglements increased Miss Speke's alarm considerably. What could their purpose be? "Thank God," she thought, "this isn't war time!" She knew enough to realise their meaning was not "wireless." That they bore some relation to the lines on the carpet and to the diagrams and curves upon the paper, she grasped vaguely. But what it all meant baffled her and made her feel quite stupid. Where all the books and instruments had disappeared added to her bewilderment. She felt more and more perturbed. A vague, uncertain fear was worse than something definite she could face and deal with. Her fear increased. Then, suddenly, yet with a reasonable enough excuse, Sarah gave notice.

For some reason Miss Speke did not argue with the girl. She preferred to let the real meaning of her leaving remain unexpressed. She just let her go. But the fact disturbed her extraordinarily. Sarah had given every satisfaction, there had been no sign of a grievance, no complaint, the work was not hard, the pay was good. It was simply that the girl preferred to leave. Miss Speke attributed it to Mr. Thorley. She became more and more disturbed in mind. Also she found herself, more and more, avoiding her lodger, whose regular habits made such avoidance an easy matter. Knowing his hours of exit and entrance, she took care to be out of the way. At the mere sound of his step she flew to cover. The new servant, a stupid, yet not inefficient country girl, betrayed no reaction of any sort, no unfavourable reaction at any rate. Having received her instructions, Lizzie did her work without complaint from either side. She did not remove the paper and the thread nor did she mention them. She seemed just the country clod she was. Miss Speke, however, began to have restless nights. She contracted an unpleasant habit: she lay awake—listening.

III

As a result of one of these sleepless nights she came to the abrupt conclusion that she would be happier without Mr. Thorley in the house—only she had not the courage to ask him to leave. The truth was she had not the courage to speak to him at all, much less to give him notice, however nicely.

After much cogitation she hit upon a plan that promised well: she sent him a carefully worded letter explaining that, owing to increased cost of living, she found herself compelled to raise his terms. The "raise" was more than considerable, it was unreasonable, but he paid what she demanded, sending down a cheque for three months in advance with his best compliments. The letter somehow made her tremble. It was at this stage she first became aware of the existence in her of other feelings than discomfort, uneasiness, and alarm. These other feelings, being in contradiction of her dread, were difficult to describe, but their result was plain—she did not really wish Mr. Thorley to go after all. His friendly "compliments," his refusal of her hint, caused her a secret pleasure. It was not the cheque at the increased rate that pleased her—it was simply the fact that her lodger meant to stay.

It might be supposed that some delayed sense of romance had been stirred in her, but this really was not the case at all. Her pleasure was due to another source, but to a source uncommonly obscure and very strange. She feared him, feared his presence, above all, feared going into his room, while yet there was something about the mere idea of Mr. Thorley that entranced her. Another thing may as well be told at once—she herself faced it boldly—she would enter his dreaded room, when he was out, and would deliberately linger there. There was an odd feeling in the room that gave her pleasure, and more than pleasure—happiness. Surrounded by the enigmas of his personality, by the lines and curves of white paper pinned upon her carpet, by the tangle of silken threads above her head, by the mysterious books, the more than mysterious diagrams in his drawer—yet all these, even the dark perplexity of the rejected mirror and the vanished objects, were forgotten in the curious sense of happiness she derived from merely sitting in his room. Her fear contained this other remarkable ingredient—an uncommon sense of joy, of liberty, of freedom. She felt *exaltée*.

She could not explain it, she did not attempt to do so. She would go shaking and trembling into his room, and a few minutes later this sense of uncommon happiness—of release, almost of escape, she felt it—would steal over her as though in her dried-up frozen soul spring had burst upon midwinter, as though something that crawled had suddenly most gloriously found wings. An indescribable exhilaration caught her.

Under this influence the dingy street turned somehow radiant, and the front door of her poor lodging-house opened upon blue seas, yellow sands, and mountains carpeted with flowers. Her whole life, painfully repressed and crushed down in the dull service of conventional nonentities, flashed into colour, movement, and adventure. Nothing confined her. She was no longer limited. She knew advance in all possible directions. She knew the stars. She knew escape!

An attempt has been made to describe for her what she never could have described herself.

The reaction, upon coming out again, was painful. Her life in the past as a governess, little better than a servant; her life in the present as lodging-house keeper; her struggle with servants, with taxes, with daily expenses; her knowledge that no future but a mere "living" lay in front of her until the grave was reached—these overwhelmed her with an intense depression that the contrast rendered almost insupportable. Whereas in his room she had perfume, freedom, liberty, and wonder—the wonder of some entirely new existence.

Thus, briefly, while Miss Speke longed for Mr. Thorley to leave her house, she became obsessed with the fear that one day he really *would* go. Her mind, it is seen, became uncommonly disturbed; her lodger's presence being undoubtedly the cause. Her nights were now more than restless, they were sleepless. Whence came, she asked herself repeatedly in the dark watches, her fear? Whence came, too, her strange enchantment?

It was at this juncture, then, that a further item of perplexity was added to her mind. Miss Speke, as has been seen, was honourably disposed; she respected the rights of others, their property as well. Yet, included in the odd mood of elation the room and its atmosphere caused her, was also a vagrant, elusive feeling that the intimate, the personal—above all, the per-sonal—had lost their original rigidity. Small individual privacies, se-crecy, no longer held their familiar meaning quite. The idea that most things in life were to be shared slipped into her. A "secret," to this expan-sive mood, was a childish attitude.

At any rate, it was while lingering in her lodger's attractive room one day—a habit now—that she did something that caused her surprise, yet did not shock her. She saw an open letter lying on his table—and she read it.

Rather than an actual letter, however, it seemed a note, a memorandum. It began "to J. L. T."

In a boyish writing, the meaning of the language escaped her entirely. She understood the strange words as little as she understood the phases of the moon, while yet she derived from their perusal a feeling of myste-rious beauty, similar to the emotions the changes of that lovely satellite stirred in her:

"To J. L. T.

"I followed your instructions, though with intense effort and dif-ficulty. I woke at 4 o'clock. About ten minutes later, as you said might happen, I woke a *second time*. The change into the second state was as great as the change from sleeping to waking, in the or-dinary meaning of these words. But I could not remain 'awake.' I fell asleep again in about a minute—back into the usual waking state, I mean. Description in words is impossible, as you know. What I felt was too terrific to feel for long. The new energy must presently have *burned me up*. It frightened me—as you warned me it would. And this fear, no doubt, was the cause of my 'falling asleep' again so quickly.

"Cannot we arrange a Call for Help for similar occasions in fu-ture?

"G. P."

Against this note Mr. Thorley had written various strangest "squiggles"; higher mathematics, Miss Speke supposed. In the opposite margin, also in her lodger's writing, were these words:

"We must agree on a word to use when frightened. *Help*, or *Help me*, seems the best. To be uttered with the whole being."

Mr. Thorley had added a few other notes. She read them without the faintest prick of conscience. Though she understood no single sentence, a thrill of deep delight ran through her:

"It amounts, of course, to a new direction; a direction at right angles to all we know, a new direction in oneself, a new direction—in living. But it can, perhaps, be translated into mathematical terms by the intellect. This, however, only a simile at best. Cannot be experienced that way. Actual experience possible only to *changed consciousness*. But good to become mathematically accustomed to it. The mathematical experiments are worth it. They induce the mind, at any rate, to dwell upon the new direction. This helps ..."

Miss Speke laid down the letter exactly where she had found it. No shame was in her. "G. P.," she knew, meant Gerald Pikestaffe; he was one of her lodger's best pupils, the one in Belgrave Square. Her feeling of mysterious elation, as already mentioned, seemed above all such matters as small secrecies or petty personal privacies. She had read a "private" letter without remorse. One feeling only caused in her a certain commonplace emotion: the feeling that, while she read the letter, her lodger was present, watching her. He seemed close behind her, looking over her shoulder almost, observing her acts, her mood, her very thoughts—yet not objecting. He was aware, at any rate, of what she did....

It was under these circumstances that she bethought herself of her old tenant, the retired clergyman on the top floor, and sought his aid. The consolation of talking to another would be something, yet when the interview began all she could manage to say was that her mind was troubled and her heart not quite as it should be, and that she "didn't know what to do about it all." For the life of her she could not find more definite words. To mention Mr. Thorley she found suddenly utterly impossible.

"Prayer," the old man interrupted her half-way, "prayer, my dear lady. Prayer, I find," he repeated smoothly, "is always the best course in all one's troubles and perplexities. Leave it to God. He knows. And in His good time He will answer." He advised her to read the Bible and Longfellow. She added Florence Barclay to the list and followed his advice. The books, however, comforted her very little.

After some hesitation, she then tried her other tenant. But the "banker" stopped her even sooner than the clergyman had done. MacPherson was very prompt:

"I can give you another ten shillings or maybe half a guinea," he said briskly. "Times are difficult, I know. But I can't do more. If that's sufficient I shall be delighted to stay on—" and, with a nod and a quick smile that settled the matter then and there, he was through the door and down the steps on the way to his office.

It was evident that Miss Speke must face her troubles alone, a fact, for the rest, life had already taught her. The loyal, courageous spirit in her accepted the situation. The alternate moods of happiness and depression, meanwhile, began to wear her out. "If only Mr. Thorley would go! If only Mr. Thorley will not go!" For some weeks now she had successfully avoided him. He made no requests nor complaints. His habits were as regular as sunrise, his payments likewise. Not even the servant mentioned him. He became a shadow in the house.

Then, with the advent of summer-time, he came home, as it were, an hour earlier than usual. He invariably worked from 5.30 to 7.30, when he went out for his dinner. Tea he always had at a pupil's house. It was a light evening, caused by the advance of the clock, and Miss Speke, mending her underwear at the window, suddenly perceived his figure coming down the street.

She watched, fascinated. Of two instincts—to hide herself, or to wait there and catch his eye—she obeyed the latter. She had not seen him for several weeks, and a deep thrill of happiness ran through her. His walk was peculiar, she noticed at once; he did not walk in a straight line. His tall, thin outline flowed down the pavement in long, sweeping curves, yet quite steadily. He was not drunk. He came nearer; he was not twenty feet away; at ten feet she saw his face clearly, and received a shock. It was worn, and thin, and wasted, but a light of happiness, of something more than happiness indeed, shone in it. He reached the area railings. He looked up. His face seemed ablaze. Their eyes met, his with no start of recognition, hers with a steady stare of wonder. She ran into the passage, and before Mr. Thorley had time to use his latch-key she had opened the door for him herself. Little she knew, as she stood there trembling, that she stood also upon the threshold of an amazing adventure.

Face to face with him her presence of mind deserted her. She could only look up into that worn and wasted face, into those happy, severe, and brilliant eyes, where yet burned a strange expression of wistful yearning, of uncommon wonder, of something that seemed not of this world quite. Such an expression she had never seen before upon any human countenance. Its light dazzled her. There was uncommon fire in the eyes. It enthralled her. The same instant, as she stood there gazing at him without a single word, either of welcome or enquiry, it flashed across her mind that he needed something from her. He needed help, her help. It was a far-fetched notion, she was well aware, but it came to her irresistibly. The conviction was close to her, closer than her skin.

It was this knowledge, doubtless, that enabled her to hear without resentment the strange words he at once made use of:

"Ah, I thank you, Miss Speke, I thank you," the thin lips parting in a smile, the shining eyes lit with an emotion of more than ordinary welcome. "You cannot know what a relief it is to me to see you. You are so sound, so wholesome, so ordinary, so—forgive me, I beg—so commonplace."

He was gone past her and upstairs into his sitting-room. She heard the key turn softly. She was aware that she had not shut the front door. She did so, then went back, trembling, happy, frightened, into her own room. She had a curious, rushing feeling, both frightful and bewildering, that the room did not contain her.... She was still sitting there two hours later, when she heard Mr. Thorley's step come down the stairs and leave the house. She was still sitting there when she heard him return, open the door with his key, and go up to his sitting-room. The interval might have been two minutes or two weeks, instead of two hours merely. And all this time she had the wondrous sensation that the room did not contain her. The walls and ceilings did not shut her in. She was out of the room. Escape had come very close to her. She was out of the house ... out of herself as well....

IV

She went early to bed, taking this time the Bible with her. Her strange sensations had passed, they had left her gradually. She had made herself a cup of tea and had eaten a soft-boiled egg and some bread-and-butter. She felt more normal again, but her nerves were unusually sensitive. It was a comfort to know there were two men in the house with her, two worthy men, a clergyman and a banker. The Bible, the banker, the clergyman, with Mrs. Barclay and Longfellow not far from her bed, were certainly a source of comfort to her.

The traffic died away, the rumbling of the distant motor-buses ceased, and, with the passing of the hours, the night became intensely still.

It was April. Her window was opened at the top and she could smell the cool, damp air of coming spring. Soothed by the books she began to feel drowsy. She glanced at the clock—it was just on two—then blew out the candle and prepared to sleep. Her thoughts turned automatically to Mr. Thorley, lying asleep on the floor above, his threads and paper strips and mysterious diagrams all about him—when, suddenly, a voice broke through the silence with a cry for help. It was a man's voice, and it sounded a long way off. But she recognised it instantly, and she sprang out of bed without a trace of fear. It was Mr. Thorley calling, and in the voice was anguish.

"He's in trouble! In danger! He needs help! I knew it!" ran rapidly through her mind, as she lit the candle with fingers that did not tremble. The clock showed three. She had slept a full hour. She opened the door and peered into the passage, but saw no one there; the stairs, too, were empty. The call was not repeated.

"Mr. Thorley!" she cried aloud. "Mr. Thorley! Do you want anything?" And by the sound of her voice she realised how distant and muffled his own had been. "I'm coming!"

She stood there waiting, but no answer came. There was no sound. She realised the uncommon stillness of the night.

"Did you call me?" she tried again, but with less confidence. "Can I do anything for you?"

Again there was no answer; nothing stirred; the house was silent as the grave. The linoleum felt cold against her bare feet, and she stole back to get her slippers and a dressing-gown, while a hundred possibilities flashed through her mind at once. Oddly enough, she never once thought of burglars, nor of fire, nor, indeed, of any ordinary situation that required ordinary help. Why this was so she could not say. No ordinary fear, at any rate, assailed her in that moment, nor did she feel the smallest touch of nervousness about her own safety.

"Was it—I wonder—a dream?" she asked herself as she pulled the dressing-gown about her. "Did I dream that voice—" when the thrilling cry broke forth again, startling her so that she nearly dropped the candle:

"Help! Help! Help me!"

Very distinct, yet muffled as by distance, it was beyond all question the voice of Mr. Thorley. What she had taken for anguish in it she now recognized was terror. It sounded on the floor above, it was the closed door doubtless that caused the muffled effect of distance.

Miss Speke ran along the passage instantly, and with extraordinary speed for an elderly woman; she was halfway up the stairs in a moment, when, just as she reached the first little landing by the bathroom and turned to begin the second flight, the voice came again: "Help! Help!" but this time with a difference that, truth to tell, did set her nerves unpleasantly aquiver. For there were two voices instead of one, and they were not upstairs at all. Both were below her in the passage she had just that moment left. Close they were behind her. One, moreover, was not the voice of Mr. Thorley. It was a boy's clear soprano. Both called for help together, and both held a note of terror that made her heart shake.

Under these conditions it may be forgiven to Miss Speke that she lost her balance and reeled against the wall, clutching the banisters for a moment's support. Yet her courage did not fail her. She turned instantly and quickly went downstairs again—to find the passage empty of any living figure. There was no one visible. There was only silence, a motionless hatrack, the door of her own room slightly ajar, and shadows.

"Mr. Thorley!" she called. "Mr. Thorley!" her voice not quite so loud and confident as before. It had a whisper in it. No answer came. She repeated the words, her tone with still less volume. Only faint echoes that seemed to linger unduly came in response. Peering into her own room she found it exactly as she had left it. The dining-room, facing it, was likewise empty. Yet a moment before she had plainly heard two voices calling for help within a few yards of where she stood. Two voices! What could it mean? She noticed now for the first time a peculiar freshness in the air, a sharpness, almost a perfume, as though all the windows were wide open and the air of coming spring was in the house.

Terror, though close, had not yet actually gripped her. That she had gone crazy occurred to her, but only to be dismissed. She was quite sane and self-possessed. The changing direction of the sounds lay beyond all explanation, but an explanation, she was positive, there must be. The odd freshness in the air was heartening, and seemed to brace her. No, terror had not yet really gripped her. Ideas of summoning the servant, the clergyman, the banker, these she equally dismissed. It was no ordinary help that was needed, not theirs at any rate. She went boldly upstairs again and knocked at Mr. Thorley's bedroom door. She knocked again and again, loud enough to waken him, if he had perchance called out in sleep, but not loud enough to disturb her other tenants. No answer came. There was no sound within. No light shone through the cracks. With his sitting-room the same conditions held.

It was the strangeness of the second voice that now stole over her with a deadly fear. She found herself cold and shivering. As she, at length, went slowly downstairs again the cries were suddenly audible once more. She heard both voices: "Help! Help! Help me!" Then silence. They were fainter this time. Far away, they sounded, withdrawn curiously into some remote distance, yet ever with the same anguish, the same terror in them as before. The direction, however, this time she could not tell at all. In a sense they seemed both close and far, both above her and below; they seemed— it was the only way she could describe the astounding thing—in any direction, or in all directions.

Miss Speke was really terrified at last. The strange, full horror of it gripped her, turning her heart suddenly to ice. The two voices, the terror in them, the extraordinary impression that they had withdrawn further into some astounding distance—this overcame her. She became appalled. Staggering into her room, she reached the bed and fell upon it in a senseless heap. She had fainted.

V

She slept late, owing probably to exhausted nerves. Though usually up and about by 7.30, it was after nine when the servant woke her. She sprawled half in the bed, half out; the candle, which luckily had extinguished itself in falling, lay upon the carpet. The events of the night came slowly back to her as she watched the servant's face. The girl was white and shaking.

"Are you ill, mum?" Lizzie asked anxiously in a whisper; then, without waiting for an answer, blurted out what she had really come in to say: "Mr. Thorley, mum! I can't get into his room. There's no answer." The girl was very frightened.

Mr. Thorley invariably had breakfast at 8 o'clock, and was out of the house punctually at 8.45.

"Was he ill in the night—perhaps—do you think?" Miss Speke said. It was the nearest she could get to asking if the girl had heard the voices. She had admirable control of herself by this time. She got up, still in her dressing-gown and slippers.

"Not that I know of, mum," was the reply.

"Come," said her mistress firmly. "We'll go in." And they went upstairs together.

The bedroom door, as the girl had said, was closed, but the sitting-room was open. Miss Speke led the way. The freshness of the night before lay still in the air, she noticed, though the windows were all closed tightly. There was an exhilarating sharpness, a delightful tang as of open space. She particularly mentions this. On the carpet, as usual, lay the strips of white paper, fastened with small pins, and the silk threads, also as usual, stretched across from lintel to cupboard, from window to bracket. Miss Speke brushed several of them from her face.

The door into the bedroom she opened, and went boldly in, followed more cautiously by the girl. "There's nothing to be afraid of," said her mistress firmly. The bed, she saw, had not been slept in. Everything was neat and tidy. The long mirror stood close against the wall, showing its ugly back as usual, while about its four feet clustered the curved strips of paper Miss Speke had grown accustomed to.

"Pulls the blinds up, Lizzie," she said in a quiet voice.

The light now enabled her to see everything quite clearly. There were silken threads, she noticed distinctly, stretching from bed to window, and though both windows were closed there was this strange sweetness in the air as of a flowering spring garden. She sniffed it with a curious feeling of pleasure, of freedom, of release, though Lizzie, apparently, noticed nothing of all this.

"There's his 'at and mackintosh," the girl whispered in a frightened voice, pointing to the hooks on the door. "And the umbrella in the corner. But I don't see 'is boots, mum. They weren't put out to be cleaned."

Miss Speke turned and looked at her, voice and manner under full command. "What do you mean?" she asked.

"Mr. Thorley ain't gone out, mum," was the reply in a tremulous tone.

At that very moment a faint, distant cry was audible in a man's voice: "Help! Help!" Immediately after it a soprano, fainter still, called from what seemed even greater distance: "Help me!" The direction was not ascertainable. It seemed both in the room, yet far away outside in space above the roofs. A glance at the girl convinced Miss Speke that she had heard nothing.

"Mr. Thorley is not *here*," whispered Miss Speke, one hand upon the brass bed-rail for support.

The room was undeniable empty.

"Leave everything exactly as it is," ordered her mistress as they went out. Tears stood in her eyes, she lingered a moment on the threshold, but the sounds were not repeated. "Exactly as it is," she repeated, closing the bedroom and then the sitting-room door behind her. She locked the latter, putting the key in her pocket. Two days later, as Mr. Thorley had not returned, she informed the police. But Mr. Thorley never returned. He had disappeared completely. He left no trace. He was never heard of again, though—once—he was seen.

Yet, this is not entirely accurate perhaps, for he was seen twice, in the sense that he was seen by two persons, and though he was not "heard of," he was certainly heard. Miss Speke heard his voice from time to time. She heard it in the daytime and at night; calling for help and always with the same words she had first heard: "Help! Help! Help me!" It sounded very far away, withdrawn into immense distance, the distance ever increasing. Occasionally she heard the boy's voice with it; they called together sometimes; she never heard the soprano voice alone. But the anguish and terror she had first noticed were no longer present. Alarm had gone out of them. It was more like an echo that she heard. Through all the hubbub, confusion and distressing annoyance of the police search and enquiry, the voice and voices came to her, though she never mentioned them to a single living soul, not even to her old tenants, the clergyman and the banker. They kept their rooms on—which was about all she could have asked of them. The best suite was never let again. It was kept locked and empty. The dust accumulated. The mirror remained untouched, its face against the wall.

The voices, meanwhile, grew more and more faint; the distance seemed to increase; soon the voice of the boy was no longer heard at all, only the cry of Mr. Thorley, her mysterious but perfect lodger, sang distantly from time to time, both in the sunshine and in the still darkness of the night hours. The direction whence it came, too, remained, as before, undeterminable. It came from anywhere and everywhere—from above, below, on all sides. It had become, too, a pleasant, even a happy sound; no dread belonged to it any more. The intervals grew longer then; days first, then weeks passed without a sound; and invariably, after these increasing intervals, the voice had become fainter, weaker, withdrawn into ever greater and greater distance. With the coming of the warm spring days it grew almost inaudible. Finally, with the great summer heats, it died away completely.

VI

The disappearance of Mr. Thorley, however, had caused no public disturbance on its own account, nor until it was bracketed with another disappearance, that of one of his pupils, Sir Mark Pikestaffe's son. The Pikestaffe Case then became a daily mystery that filled the papers. Mr. Thorley was of no consequence, whereas Sir Mark was a figure in the public eye.

Mr. Thorley's life, as enquiry proved, held no mystery. He had left everything in order. He did not owe a penny. He owned, indeed, considerable property, both in land and securities, and teaching mathematics, especially to promising pupils, seemed to have been a hobby merely. A half-brother called eventually to take away his few possessions, but the books and instruments he had brought into the lodging-house were never traced. He was a scholar and a gentleman to the last, a man, too, it appeared, of immense attainments and uncommon ability, one of the greatest mathematical brains, if the modest obituaries were to be believed, the world has ever known. His name now passed into oblivion. He left no record of his researches or achievements. Out of some mysterious sense of loyalty and protection Miss Speke never mentioned his peculiar personal habits. The strips of paper, as the silken threads, she had carefully removed and destroyed long before the police came to make their search of his rooms....

But the disappearance of young Gerald Pikestaffe raised a tremendous hubbub. It was some days before the two disappearances were connected, both having occurred on the same night, it was then proved. The boy, a lad of great talent, promising a brilliant future, and the favourite pupil of the older man, his tutor, had not even left the house. His room was empty—and that was all. He left no clue, no trace. Terrible hints and suggestions were, of course, spread far and wide, but there was not a scrap of evidence forthcoming to support them. Gerald Pikestaffe and Mr. Thorley, at the same moment of the same night, vanished from the face of the earth and were no more seen. The matter ended there. The one link between them appeared to have been an amazing, an exceptional gift for higher mathematics. The Pikestaffe Case merely added one more to the insoluble mysteries with which commonplace daily life is sprinkled.

It was some six weeks to a month after the event that Miss Speke received a letter from one of her former charges, the most generous one, now satisfactorily finished with the Bankruptcy Court. He had honourably discharged his obligations; he was doing well; he wrote and asked Miss Speke to put him up for a week or two. "And do *please* give me Mr. Thorley's room," he asked. "The case thrilled me, and I should like to sleep in that room. I always loved mysteries, you remember ... There's something *very* mysterious about this thing. Besides, I knew the P. boy a little—an astounding genius, if ever there was one."

Though it cost her much effort and still more hesitation, she consented finally. She prepared the rooms herself. There was a new servant, Lizzie having given notice the day after the disappearance, and the older woman who now waited upon the clergyman and the banker was not quite to be trusted with the delicate job. Miss Speke, entering the empty rooms on tiptoe, a strange trepidation in her heart, but that same heart firm with courage, drew up the blinds, swept the floors, dusted the furniture, and made the bed. All she did with her own hands. Only the full-length mirror she did not touch. What terror still was in her clung to that handsome piece. It was haunted by memories. For her it was still both wonderful and somehow awful. The ghost of her strange experience hid invisibly in its polished, if now unseen, depths. She dared not handle it, far less move it from the resting place where it rested in peace. *His* hands had placed it there. To her it was sacred.

It had been given to her by Colonel Lyle, who would now occupy the room, stand on the wondrous carpet, move through the air where once the mysterious silks had floated, sleep in the very bed itself. All this he could do, but the mirror he must not touch.

"I'll explain to him a little. I'll beg him not to move it. He's very understanding," she said to herself, as she went out to buy some flowers for the sitting-room. Colonel Lyle was expected that very afternoon. Lilac, she remembered, was what he always liked. It took her longer than she expected to find really fresh bunches, of the colour that he preferred, and when she got back it was time to be thinking about his tea. The sun's rays fell slanting down the dingy street, touching it with happy gold. This, with thoughts of the tea-kettle and what vase would suit the flowers best, filled her mind as she passed along the linoleum in the narrow hall—then noticed suddenly a new hat and coat hanging on the usually empty pegs. Colonel Lyle had arrived before his time.

"He's already come," she said to herself with a little gasp. A heavy dread settled instantly on her spirit. She stood a moment motionless in the passage, the lilac blossoms in her hand. She was listening.

"The gentleman's come, mum," she heard the servant say, and at the same moment saw her at the top of the kitchen stairs in the hall. "He went up to his room, mum."

Miss Speke held out the flowers. With an effort to make her voice sound ordinary she gave an order about them. "Put them in water, Mary, please. The double vase will do." She watched the woman take them slowly, oh, so slowly, from her. But her mind was elsewhere. It was still listening. And after the woman had gone down to the kitchen again slowly, oh, so slowly, she stood motionless for some minutes, listening, still intently listening. But no sound broke the quiet of the afternoon. She heard only the blundering noises made by the woman in the kitchen below. On the floor above was—silence. Miss Speke then turned and went upstairs.

Now, Miss Speke admits frankly that she was "in a state," meaning thereby, doubtless, that her nerves were tightly strung. Her heart was thumping, her ears and eyes strained to their utmost capacity; her hands, she remembers, felt a little cold, and her legs moved uncertainly. She denied, however, that her "state," though it may be described as nervous, could have betrayed her into either invention or delusion. What she saw she saw, and nothing can shake her conviction. Colonel Lyle, besides, is there to support her in the main outline, and Colonel Lyle, when first he had entered the room, was certainly not "in a state," whatever excuses he may have offered later to comfort her. Moreover, to counteract her trepidation, she says that, as she pushed the door wide open—it was already ajar—the original mood of elation met her in the face with its lift of wonder and release. This modified her dread. She declares that joy rushed upon her, and that her "nerves," were on the instant entirely forgotten.

"What I saw I saw," remains her emphatic and unshakable verdict. "I saw—everything."

The first thing she saw admitted certainly of no doubt. Colonel Lyle lay huddled up against the further wall, half upon the carpet and half-leaning on the wainscoting. He was unconscious. One arm was stretched towards the mirror, the hand still clutching one of its mahogany feet. And the mirror had been moved. It turned now slightly more towards the room.

The picture, indeed, told its own story, a story Colonel Lyle himself repeated afterwards when he had recovered. He was surprised to find the mirror—his mirror—with its face to the wall; he went forward to put it in its proper position; in doing this he looked into it; he saw something, and—the next thing he knew—Miss Speke was bringing him round.

She explains, further, that her overmastering curiosity to look into the mirror, as Colonel Lyle had evidently looked himself, prevented her from immediately rendering first-aid to that gentleman, as she unquestionably should have done. Instead, she crossed the room, stepped over his huddled form, turned the mirror a little further round towards her, and looked straight into it.

The eye, apparently, takes in a great deal more than the mind is consciously aware of having "seen" at the moment. Miss Speke saw everything, she claims. But details certainly came back to her later, details she had not been aware of at the time. At the moment, however, her impressions, though extremely vivid, were limited to certain outstanding items. These items were—that her own reflection was not visible, no picture of herself being there; that Mr. Thorley and a boy—she recognised the Pikestaffe lad from the newspaper photographs she had seen—were plainly there, and that books and instruments in great quantity filled all the near space, blocking up the fore ground. Beyond, behind, stretching in all directions, she affirms, was empty space that produced upon her the effect of the infinite heavens as seen in a clear night sky. This space was prodigious, yet in some way not alarming. It did not terrify; rather it comforted, and, in a sense, uplifted. A diffused soft light pervaded the huge panorama. There were no shadows, there were no high lights.

Curiously enough, however, the absence of any reproduction of herself did not at first strike her as at all out of the way; she noticed the fact, no more than that; it was, perhaps, naturally, the deep shock of seeing Mr. Thorley and the boy that held her absolutely spellbound, arresting her faculties as though they had been frozen.

Mr. Thorley was moving to and fro, his body bent, his hand thrown forward. He looked as natural as in life. He moved steadily, as with a purpose, now nearer, now further, but his fingers always bent as though he were intent upon something in his hands. The boy moved, too, but with a more gentle, less vigorous, motion that suggested floating. He followed the larger figure, keeping close, his face raised from time to time as though his companion spoke to him. The expression that he wore was quiet, peaceful, happy, and intent. He was absorbed in what he was doing at the moment. Then, suddenly, Mr. Thorley straightened himself up. He turned. Miss Speke saw his face for the first time. He looked into her eyes. The face blazed with light. The gaze was straight, and full, and clear. It betrayed recognition. Mr. Thorley smiled at her.

In a very few seconds she was aware of all this, of its main outlines, at any rate. She saw the moving, living figures in the midst of this stupendous and amazing space. The overwhelming surprise it caused her prevented, apparently, the lesser emotion of personal alarm; fear she certainly did not feel at first. It was when Mr. Thorley looked at her with his brilliant eyes and blazing smile that her heart gave its violent jump, missed a beat or two, then began hammering against her ribs like released machinery that has gone beyond control. She was aware of the happy glory in the face, a face that was thin to emaciation, almost transparent, yet wearing an expression that was no longer earthly. Then, as he smiled, he came towards her; he beckoned; he stretched both hands out, while the boy looked up and watched.

Mr. Thorley's advance, however, had two distracting peculiarities—that as he drew nearer he moved not in a straight line, but in a curve. As a skater performing "edges," though on both feet instead of on one, he swept gracefully and with incredible speed in her direction. The other peculiarity was that with each step nearer his figure grew smaller. It lessened in height. He seemed, indeed, to be moving in two directions at once. He became diminutive.

The sight ought by rights to have paralysed her, yet it produced again, instead of terror, an effect of exhilaration she could not possibly account for. There came once again that fine elation to her mind. Not only did all desire to resist die away almost before it was born, but more, she felt its opposite—an overpowering wish to join him. The tiny hands were still stretched out to greet her, to draw her in, to welcome her; the smile upon the diminutive face, as it came nearer and nearer, was enchanting. She heard his voice then:

"Come, come to us! Here reality is nearer, and there is liberty....!"

The voice was very close and loud as in life, but it was not in front. It was behind her. Against her very ear it sounded in the air behind her back. She moved one foot forward; she raised her arms. She felt herself being sucked in—into that glorious space. There was an indescribable change in her whole being.

The cumulative effect of so many amazing happenings, all of them contrary to nature, should have been destructive to her reason. Their combined shock should have dislocated her system somewhere and have laid her low. But with every individual, it seems, the breaking-point is different. Her system, indeed, was dislocated, and a moment later and she was certainly laid low, yet it was not the effect of the figure, the voice, the gliding approach of Mr. Thorley that produced this. It was the flaw of little human egoism that brought her down. For it was in this instant that she first *realised* the absence of her own reflection in the mirror. The fact, though noticed before, had not entered her consciousness as such. It now definitely did so. The arms she lifted in greeting had no reflected counterpart. Her figure, she realised with a shock of terror, was not there. She dropped, then, like a stricken animal, one outstretched hand clutching the frame of the mirror as she did so.

"Gracious God!" she heard herself scream as she collapsed. She heard, too, the crash of the falling mirror which she overturned and brought down with her.

Whether the noise brought Colonel Lyle round, or whether it was the combined weight of Miss Speke and the handsome piece upon his legs that roused him, is of no consequence. He stirred, opened his eyes, disentangled himself and proceeded, not without astonishment, to render first-aid to the unconscious lady.

The explanations that followed are, equally, of little consequence. His own attack, he considered, was chiefly due to fatigue, to violent indigestion, and to the aftereffects of his protracted bankruptcy proceedings. Thus, at any rate, he assured Miss Speke. He added, however, that he had received rather a shock from the handsome piece, for, surprised at finding it turned to the wall, he had replaced it and looked into it, but had not seen himself reflected. This had amazed him a good deal, yet what amazed him still more was that he had seen something moving in the depths of the glass. "I saw a face," he said, "and it was a face I knew. It was Gerald Pikestaffe. Behind him was another figure, the figure of a man, whose face I could not see." A mist rose before his eyes, his head swam a bit, and he evidently swayed for some unaccountable reason. It was a blow received in falling that stunned him momentarily.

He stood over her, while he fanned her face; her swoon was of brief duration; she recovered quickly; she listened to his story with a quiet mind. The after-effect of too great wonder leaves no room for pettier emotions, and traces of the exhilaration she had experienced were still about her heart and soul.

"Is it smashed?" was the first thing she asked, to which Colonel Lyle made no answer at first, merely pointing to the carpet where the frame of the long mirror lay in broken fragments.

"There was no glass, you see," he said presently. He, too, was quiet, his manner very earnest; his voice, though subdued as by a hint of awe, betrayed the glow of some intense inner excitement that lit fire in his eyes as well. "He had cut it out long ago, of course. He used the empty framework merely."

"Eh?" said Miss Speke, looking down incredulously, but finding no sign of splinters on the floor.

Her companion smiled. "We shall find it about somewhere if we look," he said calmly, which, indeed, proved later true—lying flat beneath the carpet under the bed. "His measurements and calculations led—probably by chance—towards the mirror"—he seemed speaking to himself more than to his bewildered listener—"perhaps by chance, perhaps by knowledge," he continued, "up to the mirror—and then *through* it." He looked down at Miss Speke and laughed a little. "So, like Alice, he went through it, too, taking his books and instruments, the boy as well, all with him. The boy, that is, had the knowledge too."

"I only know one thing," said Miss Speke, unable to follow him or find meaning in his words, "I shall never let these rooms again. I shall lock them up."

Her companion collected the broken pieces and made a little heap of them.

"And I shall pray for him," added Miss Speke, as he led her presently downstairs to her own quarters. "I shall never cease to pray for him as long as I live."

"He hardly needs that," murmured Colonel Lyle, but to himself. "The first terror has long since left him. He's found the new direction and moved along it."

Alexander *Alexander*

His Christian name and surname were the same, and the fact that he insisted upon their proper use, respectively, made things often most unpleasant. His sombre dignity forbade familiarity. If, greatly daring, I said "Hullo, Alexander!" using his Christian name, he would assume a stern and frightening air:

"*Alexander!* if you please," he would say icily. "Use my right name."

Herein lay, perhaps, the heart of that dark secret which deceived me for so many years, as also the essence of that horror his double masquerade concealed: Whereas, between Alexander and *Alexander* none knew which was which, he—alone of all the world—*he* knew!

To me, as a little girl, there was something portentous about him always. More than a common man, he was a Personage, a Figure. With the passage of the years my conception of him grew, for his bulk and stature grew at the same time, until, more than man, or personage, or figure, he became almost that emanation of legendary life—a Being. Although the original sharp outline remained, he spread himself out somehow over an immense, dim background, against which that first outline yet held itself fixed in vivid silhouette. I conceive him as both remote and very close, as shadow and substance, an unreality yet dreadfully composed of solid flesh and blood.

This confusion in my own mind added enormously to the mystery of his strange existence; but it was the mistake in the use of his name that remained chiefly serious, a crime of untold import, since it was I myself who first—christened him. To call him by a wrong name, therefore, was an insult to his actuality, a careless and unpardonable sacrilege that trifled with the essential nature of his personality.

I lived with an uncle, who was also my guardian, and this mystifying double role contributed, no doubt, an element to the birth of Alexander *Alexander*. Some childhood's divination dramatised itself perhaps. If so, this earliest creative drama had a prophetic, even a clairvoyant, quality that enabled him to endure until he had fully justified his dark existence. Both Alexander and *Alexander* persisted through my girlhood. Only at the threshold of womanhood, when I came of age at 21, did the dreadful pair pass hand in hand to their final distressing dissolution.

He—*Alexander*—often came to see my uncle, who, I divined, was a good deal afraid of him—a fact that impressed me painfully. He was tall, dark, angular, and so thin that he always looked cold, even in the sunshine; as though, having left off his flesh, as others leave off their thick underwear, he was for ever shivering in his bones. Of those mummied Pharaohs he reminded me. He had the great square jaw, deep eyes, heavy cheek bones, and copious hair those gloomy figures of prodigious personality bear tirelessly with them down the ages. He walked on his toes a little, adding thus to the appearance of his height. He took, too, an immense and swinging stride, with an easy gliding motion that seemed to flow. His extraordinary swiftness of movement made me think of running water.

Oh, Alexander—or do I mean *Alexander?*—how you impressed me when I was about six years old! Which "Alexander"? I don't quite know, to tell the truth. Years passed before I got even an inkling.

The names still flow, like parallel rivers, down and through my consciousness, to lose themselves in the depths of some mysterious dream-ocean where, at length and at last, they become merged, I believe, in one. There were certainly two of them—once. There was Alexander, and there was *Alexander*. I can swear to it.

It was his—*Alexander's* copious hair that impressed me vividly at the age of six. It was smoothed down with shiny grease whose faint, but not unpleasant, aroma came into a room before its wearer, and hung about in the air long after he had left. Hair, perfume, grease, all fascinated me.

"That's *pomade*," explained my nurse, answering a question and using a strange new word. Then, fearful of some wrong use I might make of the information, she added: "and no business of yours, remember, either." The queer word seized me; it remained hanging about my mind ... pomade, pomade. How vividly, with what lasting depth and sharpness these early impressions score the mind of a child, so tenderly receptive. No wonder the psychologists dive after them to explain the irregularities of nerve and memory that emerge in later life. The name Alexander, to begin with, carried me away. It bore me along with it. There was movement in it. Jones, Green, Brown, one syllable names, are stationary and fixed; but "Alexander" had a glide. It was a watery movement; I always connected it with water. It flowed round and through and under me. It bore me easily away with it. I saw a rapid stream, whose undulating surface had no actual waves, owing to its speed, but swept along in rhythmic rise and fall, liked a brimmed rivulet across a sloping meadow. My feet gave under me, and I was off. "Alexander, *Alexander*, oh, why cannot you meander?" I used to murmur to myself, using another strange new word I had discovered, a suitable word since it was the name of a river that also flowed. I saw copious hair, pomade, a lean dark, careering figure on its toes, swinging rapidly down my mind with a pulse of hurrying water.

He was a solicitor, I imagined, and the name only half understood, somehow to me suggested prison; and my uncle, who was also my legal guardian, I fancied had done something wrong. It was rather confusing having an uncle who was guardian too. It puzzled me. My Uncle was reserved, secretive—that is, as "guardian," he was reserved, secretive; for as "uncle" he was affectionate, playful, kind, and very dear to me. I had this mingled fear and love.

The name had a strange power. I was, perhaps, nine years old when the goose frightened me in the yard behind the stables, and some undigested fairy-tale made me think its cackling beak was going to bite me into pieces. Pulling down my little skirts frantically to protect my bare legs, I found the bad rhyme instantly, though I may have shaped it actually a little later:

> Alexander, *Alexander,*
> Oh, come down into the yard!
> For I'm frightened at the gander—
> Oh, come quick with your pomade!

And he came. That was what lived with me for years, increasing enormously his influence. He came at once. The glass door of the conservatory opened, and out he poured with amazing swiftness, on his toes, turning his thin, dark face and head towards me. His great stride brought him up to me in a moment. He was, I believe, really looking for my uncle, who was in the stables just then, examining the horses. But it was in answer to my cry that he was beside me in a second. I caught the whiff of the pomade.

"Oh, Alexander   !" I cried, relieved, but also alarmed.

"*Alexander*," he corrected me sternly, his deep eyes staring, while the gander retreated and left me safe at once. Yet, when I turned round again from watching the retreating bird, he—Alexander—had disappeared, and my uncle—or was it my guardian?—was coming towards me from the stables with a smile. The incident, at any rate, left a deep impression on me. The use—the correct use—of the great name evidently carried away with its own movement.

I saw him only occasionally as I grew older: during holidays, when home from school, and later, from a year in Paris to improve my French and acquire manners and deportment. He was aged in the eyes, and skin, and gait. The stream of his name no longer brimmed its banks as formerly. But the spell remained. And the pomaded hair kept young as ever. My uncle, I now realised somehow, welcomed his visits, while yet dreading them. I thought of the two at the time, I remember, as driver and driven in some mysterious enterprise of financial kind. They were. But Alexander was the driven, and *Alexander* held the whip. And once, lying half asleep in bed, a horrible suspicion came to me that my uncle—or was it my guardian?—knew. Knew what? Why "horrible"? I could not say, I felt it, that's all.

A week after my return from Paris—I was to be of age next clay—I was standing in the passage when he called. Thomas was leading the way. It was just outside the study door.

"Mr. Alexander to see you, sir," I heard him announced.

The visitor glowered with vexation. "Mr. *Alexander*," he rebuked the servant in a low tone, as he swung through the door on his toes into the study, where my uncle or my guardian, evidently awaited him. And as I heard the name, in the way *he* uttered it, a sudden wave of cold anxiety, more of acute distress, broke over me. As that lean, dark, pomaded head flowed round the open door with its extraordinary swiftness, and vanished, I felt afraid. The footman went past me with an expressionless face, but it seemed to me that his face was ghastly white. He disappeared in the empty hall beyond; I heard the green baize door into the nether regions swing to behind him with its customary gulp. But the draught of its closing came to me across all that distance; so that I felt it on my cheeks. And its touch was icy. I stood there shivering, unable at first to move or think. A vague dread and wonder held me. What were Alexander and *Alexander* saying to my uncle and my guardian?

What steps to take I knew not. For I was aware that I ought to take steps at once. My hesitation was caused by an inexplicable fear. It was the fear *of* my guardian, but *for* my uncle. Is that clear? While dreading my guardian, I felt, I knew, that I must help my uncle. Two courses seemed open to me: to enter the room, or to follow the footman and ask him an awful question.

I chose the latter. In a moment I was through the green baize door that led into the servant's quarters; but, as I ran, a new suspicion fastened on me. It fastened on my spine where the shivering was. I was amazed and horror-stricken. For the suspicion was so complete that it must actually have lain in me a long, long time already.

"Thomas," I said, breathlessly; "the gentleman you showed in just now— who was it?"

"I beg pardon, Miss," he said, staring blankly, I asked the question a second time, "Showed in, Miss," he repeated stupidly.

"The tall, dark gentleman," I insisted, in a failing voice, "you just showed in to—" I could not, for the life of me, say "my uncle's"—"into Mr. Burton's study, Mr.—Mr.—" I stammered and stuck fast.

The man paused a moment, with a puzzled air, He stared at me. "I showed no gentlemen in, Miss," he said, a trifle offended, his voice firm and decided. "Mr. Burton rang for—" it was his turn to hesitate—"for something to drink, Miss. And I just took it in to him."

I knew then. I knew it all at once, complete. I tore back. But my thought raced faster than my legs. An elaborate fabric built most carefully, and standing firm for years, collapsed into ghastly ruins. The footman's face, I remembered, was always white. My nurse, now dead, had always fallen in with my fancies. My uncle was tall and thin and dark, and had always worn pomaded hair. But it was only when I reached the study door that the final film cleared off, letting in the appalling light. For I suddenly remembered another thing as well: he acknowledged to a buried name. Hidden away among several others, he owned a name he never used. His full name, of course, was Frank Henry *Alexander* Burton.

I stood transfixed outside the door.

But precious minutes were passing. "Oh, Alexander, *Alexander,*" rushed down my mind. The childhood's rhyme was about to follow, yard, gander, pomade and all, when a sound inside the room sent the ice again down my spine. It made my will tighten at the same time. I might be too late even now. Without knocking, I rushed into the room. The desk was strewn with documents and papers. A decanter of spirits stood beside them, with a half-emptied glass. The French windows were open on the lawn. The summer air came in. There was a faint aroma of pomade. But I was too late. The room was empty. "Oh, Alexander!" I gasped, petrified by the emptiness, and was about to add *"Alexander"* when a horrid weakness came over me and a blackness rose before my face. My legs collapsed. I fell into a dead faint on the floor....

It was "by water" of course, and the verdict was death by drowning while of unsound mind. I saw the body next day. It was my uncle's, not my guardian's body. The hair, for the first time, I saw tangled.

Oh, *Alexander* Alexander! Merged at last in one! You, *Alexander*, left me a pauper. But for you, Alexander, I have still kind memories of a weak, affectionate, and sorely tempted uncle....

Lost!

There was something unusual in the village street that morning as I made my way to the chalet post-office to send a telegram, but the mind was only vaguely aware of it. A familiar detail seemed lacking; a difference had crept in. One noticed it—no more than that. Sunshine flooded the valley, the forests hung in purple shadow to the west, far overhead the snow shone dazzling against the turquoise blue, and the air was filled with the roar of falling water. Girls in yellow jumpers were going down to the tennis courts, tourists starting on their expeditions, mules clattering on the cobbles, and the priest went by, his face, as always, grave. All seemed as usual: the difference did not disclose itself. My mind, perhaps, was too preoccupied composing a complicated telegram in the fewest possible words to think about it. It was on my way back that I suddenly realised what was wrong: the familiar groups of guides, waiting for employment, were omitted from the picture. Something had happened.

A high Alpine climbing village is a sensitive organism, whose collective life responds swiftly to the least change—a new arrival, a departure, a summit conquered, but, above all, an accident. The news runs through it like a wind. On the way back to my friend's chalet the priest passed me again. "Yes, a man is lost," he said, his face graver than before. "He's been out all night, the search-parties have left."

He gave a few details, then hurried on, but in the twinkling of an eye the note of that brilliant, even gorgeous, morning had changed completely. The shadow of disaster dimmed the sunshine, the pleasant roar of falling water become ominous, the great peaks wore a forbidding air. Somewhere among their awful loneliness a man was lost. The thing all dread had happened. It was strange, at this early hour, how the undercurrent of news flashed so swiftly along the sunny street, touching some and missing others. To those who merely played tennis, danced, and went for walks, it meant less; to those who climbed and knew the wild places where the victim might be lying, it was poignant. One resented these careless, happy tourists, picking flowers, chasing butterflies, playing tennis in light-hearted safety. Through the mind flashed vivid pictures of the cold, dreadful heights, of icy slopes, of dizzy ledges, of perilous corners above an abyss of emptiness. One turned, rather, to the peasants who stood about in groups, some with telescopes, all with grave faces and sympathetic questions. A man was lost. He had been out alone all night. There had been a cold wind but a clear sky. He was still clinging, perhaps, to some ledge, unable to get up or down, shouting to the emptiness ... perhaps lying injured on some desolate pitch of rock … perhaps motionless.

My host, an old resident of the village, experienced climber as well, had all the available facts at his fingertips when I got back. He was ready to start too. We chose a route the other parties had not taken, and on the way up he gave me details of what was known. We took with us Zeiss glasses, food, brandy, extra ropes. It was a gloomy, mournful expedition. We went fast, much too fast for climbers; the feeling of hurry made it impossible to take it easy.

An odd thing was that, although the man had broken all the rules, no one had used a word of blame. He was not a climber, but one of those vigorous Englishmen of middle age who enjoy "a scramble." He wore nailed boots and carried an iron-shod alpenstock. He was married, his wife and children at Como, where he was to join them in a few days. He was a botanist. He took with him a knapsack with food and a thermos of tea. He had left his hotel at 2 o'clock on the previous afternoon, but he had *not* told anyone exactly where he was going. His direction was only vaguely known. He had not returned for dinner. He had been out twenty hours. Search parties had started at midnight; others had left at dawn. Three shots—echo carries the sound for miles—was to be the signal that he had been found.

We used the "botany" as our guide—taking a precipitous trail to a region of desolate rocks where rare saxifrages grew. Every inch of the ground was known to both of us. We climbed in silence, the pace leaving no breath for words, but the glasses were used constantly, and occasionally there was a pause to discuss direction. Such a man, it was certain, would not choose obviously dangerous places, although his enthusiasm for some rare plant, must remain an incalculable factor always. The probability seemed that his search had led him to some point whence descent became suddenly impossible. A common occurrence this, for to get up is frequently easier than to get down again. He had clung on through the darkness, beneath the stars, till his strength failed and exhaustion loosened his grip. Or, perhaps, on some steep pitch where ordinary care meant safety, he had slipped. There were ugly drops to the south in plenty. Anyhow, it was not the obviously dangerous places we need examine. The few peasants we met—all knew of the possible disaster—gave little help; some had seen a solitary figure, others had not; descriptions varied; there was nothing reliable to guide us. We hurried as the day wore on. Up by the torrent, through deep forest, past waterfalls, across bright green upper pastures, where a million flowers shone, scanning every *couloir*, examining every ledge where a man might venture, and especially the slope of shale at its foot. It was a familiar trail to both of us. The music of the cowbells filled the air. The gentians blazed. The snowfields sparkled far overhead, and the gay tourist village, except as the place where *he* had started 24 hours ago now, was quite forgotten. It was towards afternoon that I first noticed we began to speak of *it* instead of *he*. We were well up above the world by now, in the heart of the great heights, not far from the snow, the huge mountains coming more and more into their own. What we called the "saxifrage rocks" lay an hour below us. The sky wore a darker blue; the wind, creeping down from the glacier, had a nip in it; the flowers changed; and the immense desolation was emptied of any moving figures but our own. An occasional marmot whistled before diving into its hole, a bird flitted to another boulder, a white butterfly danced past, a stray fly buzzed and vanished. But that was all. Already the Oberland giants were peering at us from behind the ridges we had topped. The silence of the big mountains, their grandeur, their loneliness, their awe stole over us. The change one had noticed in the sunny village street below became increasingly manifest.

It was this change, though we did not speak of it at the time, that impressed us both, proving how the mood, the attitude of mind, determine selection. The familiar beauty retreated, letting terror in. The scenes we knew so well, had so often enjoyed with happy wonder, now wore another guise. The majesty turned awful, the splendour cruel, the indifference to human life stood out. This new significance in "scenery" we had admired countless times, at dawn, in the moonlight, in the fierce midday sunshine, became ever more apparent. The whole meaning of the high mountains altered, light and shade falling in unaccustomed places. Imaginatively, one became aware of the conspiracy that exists among these great inanimate peaks and precipices, first to entice, then to enforce the penalty for the least mistake. Every detail of crag and summit, every shoulder, *col*, and dangerous slope became invested with a dim sense of personality that clothed another type of life. And this life, as the shadows lengthened and darkness grew upon the eastern side, became for us, not merely indifferent, but definitely hostile. A hint of the monstrous crept into the lonely grandeur. These stupendous Powers, having claimed their victim, now tried to hide him. Other Consciousnesses now watched our puny efforts at discovery, peering down into our minds that still hoped to save. The sense of being watched was present. The weight of wonder, of admiration, of sympathetic tenderness certainly, was shifted from the mountains to the man. Awe was too strong for beauty any more. The eye searched, not for the marvel of form and colour upon these terrible heights, not for the mystery of their inaccessible and dreadful loneliness, but strained ever for a small, significant outline, lying broken among huge, misshapen boulders, the outline of a man, possibly of little importance beyond an immediate family circle, playing no big role in life that mattered, but—a human being, a member of the Race, a soul who, adventuring carelessly against too heavy odds, had lost.

Never again, for us, could these peaks and precipices, these flowers, snowfields, streams, seem quite the same. Into their collective being we called "scenery" a new ingredient had entered permanently so that their wonder must ever hereafter hold too much of respect for our former loving admiration. We should pass the slope of shale in silence, glance upwards at the treacherous ledge with a sigh, a shudder. Even on the brightest day, spring flowers carpeting our approach, this must be so. Nor would this emotion bear much relation to the wooden cross the peasants erect with reverence. The spot would be haunted by the shadow of an adventure against awful odds, but an adventure whose precise details none knew, because those lips were silent which alone could tell.

Half on the shale, half on a patch of turf where gentians actually brushed one cheek, we found him—motionless. Just before the darkness came the glasses picked out the significant outline. The unnatural shape betrayed it among the grim boulders. My friend merely pointed in silence, his face a little paler beneath the sunburn, as he held out the binoculars. The drop was perhaps one hundred feet, but death must have been instantaneous, for the neck was broken. The stick lay fifty yards away. In one hand a little saxifrage was still clutched tightly.

The Olive

He laughed involuntarily as the olive rolled towards his chair across the shiny parquet floor of the hotel dining-room.

His table in the cavernous *salle-à-manger* was apart: he sat alone, a solitary guest; the table from which the olive fell and rolled towards him was some distance away. The angle, however, made him an unlikely objective. Yet the lob-sided, juicy thing, after hesitating once or twice *en route* as it plopped along, came to rest finally against his feet.

It settled with an inviting, almost an aggressive, air. And he stooped and picked it up, putting it rather self-consciously, because of the girl from whose table it had come, on the white tablecloth beside his plate.

Then, looking up, he caught her eye, and saw that she, too, was laughing, though not a bit self-consciously. As she helped herself to the *hors d'oeuvres* a false move had sent it flying. She watched him pick the olive up and set it beside his plate. Her eyes then suddenly looked away again—at her mother—questioningly.

The incident was closed. But the little oblong, succulent olive lay beside his plate, so that his fingers played with it. He fingered it automatically from time to time until his lonely meal was finished.

When no one was looking he slipped it into his pocket, as though, having taken the trouble to pick it up, this was the very least he could do with it. Heaven alone knows why, but he then took it upstairs with him, setting it on the marble mantelpiece among his field glasses, tobacco tins, ink-bottles, pipes, and candlestick. At any rate, he kept it—the moist, shiny, lob-sided, juicy little oblong olive. The hotel lounge wearied him; he came to his room after dinner to smoke at his ease, his coat off and his feet on a chair; to read another chapter of Freud, to write a letter or two he didn't in the least want to write, and then to go to bed at ten o'clock. But this evening the olive kept rolling between him and the thing he read; it rolled between the paragraphs, between the lines; the olive was more vital than the interest of these eternal "complexes" and "suppressed desires."

The truth was that he kept seeing the eyes of the laughing girl beyond the bouncing olive. She had smiled at him in such a natural, spontaneous, friendly way before her mother's glance had checked her—a smile, he felt, that might lead to acquaintance on the morrow.

He wondered! A thrill of possible adventure ran through him.

She was a merry-looking sort of girl, with a happy, half-roguish face that seemed on the lookout for somebody to play with. Her mother, like most of the people in the big hotel, was an invalid; the girl, a dutiful and patient daughter. They had arrived that very day apparently.

A laugh is a revealing thing, he thought as he fell asleep, to dream of a lob-sided olive rolling consciously towards him, and of a girl's eyes that watched its awkward movements, then looked up into his own and laughed. In his dream the olive had been deliberately and cleverly dispatched upon its uncertain journey. It was a message.

He did not know, of course, that the mother, chiding her daughter's awkwardness, had muttered:

"There you are again, child! True to your name, you never see an olive without doing something queer and odd with it!"

A youngish man, whose knowledge of chemistry, including invisible inks and such-like mysteries, had proved so valuable to the Censor's Department that for five years he had overworked without a holiday, the Italian Riviera had attracted him, and he had come out for a two months' rest. It was his first visit. Sun, mimosa, blue seas and brilliant skies had tempted him; exchange made a pound worth forty, fifty, sixty, and seventy shillings. He found the place lovely, but somewhat untenanted.

He stayed on, however, caught by the sunshine and the good exchange, also without the physical energy to discover a better, livelier place. He went for walks among the olive groves, he sat beside the sea and palms, he visited shops and bought things he did not want because the exchange made them seem cheap; he paid immense "extras" in his weekly bill, then chuckled as he reduced them to shillings and found that a few pence covered them; he lay with a book for hours among the olive groves.

The olive groves! His daily life could not escape the olive groves; to olive groves, sooner or later, his walks, his expeditions, his meanderings by the sea, his shopping—all led him to these ubiquitous olive groves.

If he bought a picture post card to send home, there was sure to be an olive grove in one corner of it. The whole place was smothered with olive groves, the people owed their incomes and existence to these irrepressible trees. The villages among the hills swam roof-deep in them. They swarmed even in the hotel gardens.

The guide-books praised them as persistently as the residents brought them, sooner or later, into every conversation. They grew lyrical over them:

"And how do you like our olive trees? Ah, you think them pretty. At first, most people are disappointed. They grow on one."

"They do," he agreed.

"I'm glad you appreciate them. I find them the embodiment of grace. And when the wind lifts the under-leaves across a whole mountain slope—why, it's wonderful, isn't it? One realises the meaning of 'olive-green.'" "One does." He sighed. "But, all the same, I should like to get one to eat—an olive, I mean."

"Ah, to eat, yes. That's not so easy. You see, the crop is ..."

"Exactly," he interrupted impatiently, weary of the habitual and evasive explanations. "But I should like to taste the *fruit*. I should like to enjoy one."

For, after a stay of six weeks, he had never once seen an olive on the table, in the shops, nor even on the street barrows at the market-place. He had never tasted one. No one sold olives, though olive trees were a drug in the place; no one bought them, no one asked for them; it seemed that no one wanted them. The trees, when he looked closely, were thick with a dark little berry that seemed more like a sour sloe than the succulent, delicious spicy fruit associated with its name.

Men climbed the trunks, everywhere shaking the laden branches and hitting them with long bamboo poles to knock the fruit off, while women and children, squatting on their haunches, spent laborious hours filling baskets underneath, then loading mules and donkeys with their daily "catch." But an olive to eat was unobtainable. He had never cared for olives, but now he craved with all his soul to feel his teeth in one.

"Ach! But it is the Spanish olive that you *eat*," explained the head waiter, a German "from Basel." "These are for oil only." After which he disliked the olive more than ever—until that night when he saw the first eatable specimen rolling across the shiny parquet floor, propelled towards him by the careless hand of a pretty girl, who then looked up into his eyes and smiled.

He was convinced that Eve, similarly, had rolled the apple towards Adam across the emerald sward of the first garden in the world. The dull, accumulated resentment he had come to feel, subconsciously perhaps, against an elusive fruit, was changed in the twinkling of an eye, into a source of joy, a symbol of romance.

He slept usually like the dead. It must have been something very real that made him open his eyes and sit up in bed alertly. There was a noise against his door. He listened. The room was still quite dark. It was early morning. The noise was not repeated.

"Who's there?" he asked in a sleepy whisper. "What is it?"

The noise came again. Someone was scratching on the door. No, it was somebody tapping.

"What d'you want?" he demanded in a louder voice. "Come in," he added, wondering sleepily whether he was presentable. Either the hotel was on fire or the porter was waking the wrong person for some sunrise expedition.

Nothing happened. Wide awake now, he turned the switch on, but no light flooded the room. The electricians, he remembered with a curse, were out on strike. He fumbled for the matches, and as he did so a voice in the corridor became distinctly audible. It was just outside his door.

"Aren't you ready?" he heard. "You sleep for ever."

And the voice, although, never having heard it before, he could not have recognised it, belonged, he knew suddenly, to the girl who had let the olive fall. In an instant he was out of bed. He lit a candle.

"I'm coming," he called softly, as he slipped rapidly into some clothes. "I'm sorry I've kept you. I shan't be a minute."

"Be quick then!" he heard, while the candle flame slowly grew, and he found his garments. Less than three minutes later he opened the door and, candle in hand, peered into the dark passage.

"Blow it out!" came a peremptory whisper. He obeyed, but not quick enough. A pair of red lips emerged from the shadows. There was a puff, and the candle was extinguished. "I've got my reputation to consider. We mustn't be seen, of course!"

The face vanished in the darkness, but he had recognised it—the shining skin, the bright glancing eyes. The sweet breath touched his cheek. The candlestick was taken from him by a swift, deft movement. He heard it knock the wainscoting as it was set down. He went out into a pitch-black corridor, where a soft hand seized his own and led him—by a back door, it seemed—out into the open air of the hillside immediately behind the hotel.

He saw the stars. The morning was cool and fragrant, the sharp air waked him, and the last vestiges of sleep went flying. He had been drowsy and confused, had obeyed the summons without thinking. He now realised suddenly that he was engaged in an act of madness.

The girl, dressed in some flimsy material thrown loosely about her head and body, stood a few feet away, looking, he thought, like some figure called out of dreams and slumber of a forgotten world, out of legend almost. He saw her evening shoes peep out; he divined an evening dress beneath the gauzy covering. The light wind blew it close against her figure. He thought of a nymph.

"I say—but haven't you been to bed?" he asked stupidly.

He had meant to expostulate, to apologise for his foolish rashness, to scold and say they must go back at once. Instead, this sentence came. He guessed she had been sitting up all night. He stood still a second, staring in mute admiration, his eyes full of bewildered question.

"Watching the stars," she met his thought with a happy laugh. "Orion has touched the horizon. I came for you at once. We've got just four hours!" The voice, the smile, the eyes, the reference to Orion, swept him off his feet. Something in him broke loose and flew wildly, recklessly to the stars.

"Let us be off!" he cried, "before the Bear tilts down. Already Alcyone begins to fade. I'm ready. Come!"

She laughed. The wind blew the gauze aside to show two ivory-white limbs. She caught his hand again, and they scampered together up the steep hillside towards the woods. Soon the big hotel, the villas, the white houses of the little town where natives and visitors still lay soundly sleeping, were out of sight. The farther sky came down to meet them. The stars were paling, but no sign of actual dawn was yet visible. The freshness stung their cheeks.

Slowly, the heavens grew lighter, the east turned rose, the outline of the trees defined themselves, there was a stirring of the silvery-green leaves. They were among olive groves—but the spirits of the trees were dancing. Far below them, a pool of deep colour, they saw the ancient sea. They saw the tiny specks of distant fishing-boats. The sailors were singing to the dawn, and birds among the mimosa of the hanging gardens answered them.

Pausing a moment at length beneath a gaunt old tree, whose struggle to leave the clinging earth had tortured its great writhing arms and trunk, they took their breath, gazing at one another with eyes full of happy dreams.

"You understood so quickly," said the girl, "my little message. I knew by your eyes and ears you would." And she first tweaked his ears with two slender fingers mischievously, then laid her soft palm with a momentary light pressure on both eyes.

"You're half-and-half, at any rate," she went on, looking him up and down for a swift instant of appraisement, "if you're not altogether." The laughter showed her white, even little teeth.

"You know how to play, and that's something," she added. Then, as if to herself, "You'll be altogether before I've done with you."

"Shall I?" he stammered, afraid to look at her. Puzzled, some spirit of compromise still lingering in him, he knew not what she meant; he knew only that the current of life flowed increasingly through his veins, but that her eyes confused him.

"I'm longing for it," he added. "How wonderfully you did it! They roll so awkwardly—"

"Oh, that!" She peered at him through a wisp of hair. "You've kept it, I hope."

"Rather. It's on my mantelpiece—"

"You're sure you haven't eaten it?" and she made a delicious mimicry with her red lips, so that he saw the tip of a small pointed tongue.

"I shall keep it," he swore, "as long as these arms have life in them," and he seized her just as she was crouching to escape, and covered her with kisses.

"I knew you longed to play," she panted, when he released her. "Still, it was sweet of you to pick it up before another got it."

"Another!" he exclaimed.

"The gods decide. It's a lob-sided thing, remember. It can't roll straight." She looked oddly mischievous, elusive.

He stared at her.

"If it had rolled elsewhere—and another had picked it up—?" he began.

"I should be with that other now!" And this time she was off and away before he could prevent her, and the sound of her silvery laughter mocked him among the olive trees beyond. He was up and after her in a second, following her slim whiteness in and out of the old-world grove, as she flitted lightly, her hair flying in the wind, her figure flashing like a ray of sunlight or the race of foaming water—till at last he caught her and drew her down upon his knees, and kissed her wildly, forgetting who and where and what he was.

"Hark!" she whispered breathlessly, one arm close about his neck. "I hear their footsteps. Listen! It is the pipe!"

"The pipe—!" he repeated, conscious of a tiny but delicious shudder.

For a sudden chill ran through him as she said it. He gazed at her. Her hair fell loose about her cheeks, flushed and rosy with his hot kisses. Her eyes were bright and wild for all their softness. Her face, turned sideways to him as she listened, wore an extraordinary look that for an instant made his blood run cold. He saw the parted lips, the small white teeth, the slim neck of ivory, the young bosom panting from his tempestuous embrace. Of an unearthly loveliness and brightness she seemed to him, yet with this strange, remote expression that touched his soul with sudden terror.

Her face turned slowly.

"Who *are* you?" he whispered. He sprang to his feet without waiting for her answer.

He was young and agile; strong, too, with that quick response of muscle they have who keep their bodies well; but he was no match for her. Her speed and agility outclassed his own with ease. She leaped. Before he had moved one leg forward towards escape, she was clinging with soft, supple arms and limbs about him, so that he could not free himself, and as her weight bore him downwards to the ground, her lips found his own and kissed them into silence. She lay buried again in his embrace, her hair across his eyes, her heart against his heart, and he forgot his question, forgot his little fear, forgot the very world he knew....

"They come, they come," she cried gaily. "The Dawn is here. Are you ready?"

"I've been ready for five thousand years," he answered, leaping to his feet beside her.

"Altogether!" came upon a sparkling laugh that was like wind among the olive leaves.

Shaking her last gauzy covering from her, she snatched his hand, and they ran forward together to join the dancing throng now crowding up the slope beneath the trees. Their happy singing filled the sky. Decked with vine and ivy, and trailing silvery green branches, they poured in a flood of radiant life along the mountain side. Slowly they melted away into the blue distance of the breaking dawn, and, as the last figure disappeared, the sun came up slowly out of a purple sea....

They came to the place he knew—the deserted earthquake village—and a faint memory stirred in him. He did not actually recall that he had visited it already, had eaten his sandwiches with "hotel friends" beneath its crumbling walls; but there was a dim troubling sense of familiarity—nothing more. The houses still stood, but pigeons lived in them, and weasels, stoats, and snakes had their uncertain homes in ancient bedrooms. Not twenty years ago the peasants thronged its narrow streets, through which the dawn now peered and cool wind breathed among dew-laden brambles.

"I know the house," she cried, "the house where we would live!" and raced, a flying form of air and sunlight, into a tumbled cottage that had no roof, no floor or windows. Wild bees had hung a nest against the broken wall.

He followed her. There was sunlight in the room, and there were flowers. Upon a rude, simple table lay a bowl of cream, with eggs, and honey and butter close against a home-made loaf. They sank into each other's arms upon a couch of fragrant grass and boughs against the window where wild roses bloomed ... and the bees flew in and out.

It was Bussana, the so-called earthquake village, because a sudden earthquake had fallen on it one summer morning when all the inhabitants were at church. The crashing roof killed sixty, the tumbling walls another hundred, and the rest had left it where it stood.

"The Church," he said, vaguely remembering the story. "They were at prayer—"

The girl laughed carelessly in his ear, setting his blood in a rush and quiver of delicious joy. He felt himself untamed, wild as the wind and animals. "The true God claimed his own," she whispered. "He came back. Ah, they were not ready—the old priests had seen to that. But He came. They heard His music. Then His tread shook the olive groves, the old ground danced, the hills leapt for joy—"

"They called it earthquake! And the houses crumbled," he laughed as he pressed her closer to his heart.

"And now we've come back!" she cried merrily. "We've come back to worship and be glad!" She nestled into him, while the sun rose higher.

"I hear them—hark!" she cried, and again leapt, dancing, from his side. Again he followed her like wind. Through the broken window they saw the naked fauns and nymphs and satyrs rolling, dancing, shaking their soft hoofs amid the ferns and brambles. Towards the ruptured church they sped with feet of light and air. A roar of happy song and laughter rose.

"Come!" he cried. "We must go too."

Hand in hand they raced to join the tumbling, dancing throng. She was in his arms and on his back and flung across his shoulders, as he ran. They reached the broken building, its whole roof gone sliding years ago, its walls a-tremble still, its shattered shrines alive with nestling birds.

"Hush!" she whispered, in a tone of awe, yet pleasure. "*He* is there!" She pointed, her bare arm outstretched, above the bending heads.

There, in the empty space, where once stood sacred Host and Cup, He sat, filling the niche sublimely and with awful power. His shaggy form, benign yet terrible, rose through the broken stone. The great eyes shone and smiled. The feet were lost in brambles....

"God!" cried a wild, frightened voice, yet with deep worship in it—and the old familiar panic came with portentous swiftness. The great Figure rose.

The birds flew screaming, the animals sought holes, the worshippers, laughing and glad a moment ago, rushed tumbling over one another for the doors,

"He goes again! Who called? Who called like that? His feet shake the ground!"

"It is the earthquake!" screamed a woman's shrill accents in ghastly terror.

"Kiss me—one kiss before we forget again ...!" sighed a laughing, passionate voice against his ear. "Once more your arms, your heart beating on my lips ...! You recognised his power. You are now *altogether!* We shall remember!"

But he woke, with the heavy bed-clothes stuffed against his mouth and the wind of early morning sighing mournfully about the hotel walls.

"Have they left again—those ladies?" he enquired casually of the head waiter, pointing to the table. "They were here last night at dinner."

"Who do you mean?" replied the man stupidly, gazing at the spot indicated with a face quite blank. "Last night—at dinner?" He tried to think.

"An English lady, elderly, with—her daughter"—at which moment precisely the girl came in alone. Lunch was over, the room empty.

There was a second's difficult pause. It seemed ridiculous not to speak. Their eyes met. The girl blushed furiously.

He was very quick for an Englishman. "I was allowing myself to ask after your mother," he began. "I was afraid"—he glanced at the table laid for one—"she was not well, perhaps?"

"Oh, but that's very kind of you, I'm sure." She smiled. He saw the small white even teeth....

And before three days had passed, he was so deeply in love that he simply couldn't help himself.

"I believe," he said lamely, "this is yours. You dropped it, you know. Er— may I keep it? It's only an olive."

They were, of course, in an olive grove when he asked it, and the sun was setting.

She looked at him, looked him up and down, looked at his ears, his eyes. He felt that in another second her little fingers would slip up and tweak the first or close the second with a soft pressure

"Tell me," he begged: "did you dream anything that first night I saw you?"

She took a quick step backwards. "No," she said, as he followed her more quickly still, "I don't think I did. But," she went on breathlessly as he caught her up, "I knew—from the way you picked it up—"

"Knew what?" he demanded, holding her tightly so that she could not get away again.

"That you were already half and half, but would soon be altogether."

And, as he kissed her, he felt her soft fingers tweak his ears.

A Continuous Performance

While the Great Man was reading from his own Works to the ladies in the Duchess's blue drawing-room, O'Malley slipped out unnoticed and made his way into the garden. The Great Man's vanity, the collective pose of the adoring ladies, the elaborate parade and artifice of the human attitude generally, invited the sweetness of unadvertised open air. O'Malley, old poet whom lack of craft left inarticulate, so that he had never written a line, slipped past the roses towards the trees that fringed the ducal lawn. With him went an echo of the rotund period his exit had interrupted; a picture, too, of the human animal preening itself upon its hind legs in black coat and stiff white collar.

"That rubbidge!" came a gruff voice, as he passed a tool-shed. "Why, I cleaned it up long ago—lars' noight, if you want to know exact!" The undergardener spat on his hands, as he poured out some aggrieved explanation to the Head…. The voices died away. O'Malley entered the stillness of the pinewood, where only the murmur of the summer wind was audible. "It's rude of me," he reflected; "possibly it's affected. But, anyhow, my disappearance for half an hour won't be noticed …" He flung himself down in a sunny patch where a meadow, swinging its flowers gaily in the breeze, ran round the little copse. An old thatched summerhouse, neglected, to judge by its state of decay, stood on his right. "I can slip in again before the end," he finished his reflection, "and stand behind the chairs at the back …"

He lay and watched the world of sun and shade about him, the un-self-conscious, lovely wealth of colour, outline, graceful movement, mystery, and wonder. Not "wasting its sweetness on the desert air," he chuckled, "because I'm here to see it all!"

A momentary memory rose to jar the enjoyment of watching a bee, both clumsy and adept, bear down a head of golden blossom into a lovely curve the wind at once made lovelier—a memory of the Great Man's answer to a question recently: "They are tiresome, yes, I admit, these Readings; but a man must keep himself before the public, you know. One must adapt oneself to the Age one lives in. Money? Oh, no, of course not; yet—well, it *does* help one's sales a bit. When I was lecturing in America last spring, my publisher told me …"

The bee, happily loaded, had issued from the golden bell, and O'Malley watched it bear the pollen unconsciously to another honeyed blossom, then, presently, rise into the air, take several circles in a spiral flight before, finally, it darted off swiftly in a line due south. For some minutes he watched other bees behave similarly, and excitement grew in him. It was with difficulty, then, that he caught some half-dozen, one after another, in his coloured handkerchief, released them, watched their spiral flight of observation, and, noting the line all took due south, resisted the desire to be up and after them himself—in a bee-line to the nest in some old tree or broken wall. Many a wild-bees' nest had he tracked in this way as a boy. The old, first wonder, the enthusiasm, with a touch of worship added now, came back upon him. The gathering of honey, the carrying of pollen, the infallible sense of direction to a nest perhaps a mile or two away ... the Great Man's words were all forgotten. In their place he heard the siren voice of Shelley:

> "O follow, follow
> Through the caverns hollow,
> As the song floats thou pursue,
> Where the wild-bee never flew ..."

while, behind him, the pine-wood murmured with its delicate music "like the farewell of ghosts," as he turned to listen and to watch.

Nothing stirred, it seemed at first, so peaceful was the summer afternoon, but he remembered that Panthea, too, had heard this faint music in the Indian Caucasus—"kindling aeolian modulations in the waved air"—and had whispered her secret into Shelley's ear. Leaning on one elbow motionless, merged in the scene by the imaginative sympathy of his poet's heart, he watched and listened…. The ground, he saw, was alive with gentle, silent, unobtrusive movement, where half a million ants were busy upon their mysterious, communal purposes, while yet there was none to bid them labour, in ceaseless constructive activity that, beginning with sunrise, ends only with the dusk. He watched them lifting, pushing, piling up their burdens as though their lives depended on it, tiny, mighty engines of energy, each of which could drag 500 times its own weight, while a man, panting with effort, could barely move five of his own kind. The wonder of the insect world swept over him, and a fugitive memory flashed Blake's picture, The Spirit of the Flea, across his mind, a flea that can leap a thousand times its own height ... with the artist's explanation that God made it tiny lest its power and blood-thirsty nature might destroy the planet….

Plop! Something dropped upon the carpet of needles, and O'Malley, looking up, discerned two brilliant peeping eyes upon a branch, a bushy tail that twitched, and heard a squeaking voice that seemed to mock him. The squirrel was already making plans for its winter apartment, its winter store of food, its small head busily calculating months ahead. The human watcher moved cautiously to obtain a better view. Whisht! It was gone! An audacious leap through mid-air to another tree, perfect distribution of weight, consummate balance, precise relation between impetus and distance—powers no trained acrobat could ever hope to master....

A few scraps of bark fell slowly downwards through the air, but the squirrel was safely perched on a tree some twenty yards away. One scrap of bark, it seemed, caught on a floating spider's thread—a spider that unconsciously constructs a geometrical design a scholar can only make with the help of many instruments, and whose thread is the finest filament known, so that astronomers use it to map the heavens across the mouths of their huge telescopes.... No, it was neither bark nor spider's web after all, but a fly, apparently stationary, yet actually moving its wings with such rapidity that no eye could distinguish the separate strokes. How many times per second O'Malley could not remember. He could flap his own arms three or four times per second—*that* he knew....!

The minutes, meanwhile, were slipping away, while he watched a hundred marvels, unadvertised, performed daily, hourly, without Agents, without sales, without applause, mostly, indeed, without recognition. There, over a distant field, fell the tumbling plover under the very eye of a soaring hawk that made no attempt against them, knowing that their skill must ever elude its best endeavour. There, by chance, was the solitary wasp that stings exactly where paralysis, but not death, shall follow, so that its young shall feed on living food. There was the little trap-door spider, peeping, darting, cleverest of ingenious tiny carpenters. There was the beetle feigning death, as its enemy approached. There, again....

A new movement suddenly caught his eye, as he lay motionless, rapt with the wonder of it all. What was it? In the summer-house, along the darkened floor, a rat—yes, a rat—was advancing slowly and with utmost caution. O'Malley watched keenly, as closely as he dared. The bright-eyed creature was dragging a wisp of straw along the decaying boards. Another rat, tentatively rather, as though with uncertain movements, seemed following it, its nose ever against the tip of the drawn straw. The first rat, evidently, was leading the way, showing its companion where to go. But why? Was it a game? Improving his position for observation with extreme caution, O'Malley discovered the meaning of the strange pantomime: The second rat was blind; its companion was leading it to food....

O'Malley sprang up. The rats, the squirrel, the bees, ants, fly, wasp, spider, doubtless the plover and the distant hawk as well, all, saw him move. The various processes of mysterious Nature, for the fraction of a second, paused. The perfect performers desired no audience, certainly no applause; recognition, praise, admiration, meant nothing to them. They were not even aware that they were wonderful. O'Malley left them. The Continuous Performance went on. He left Nature and returned to Human Nature. The gardeners, as he passed the tool-shed, were still arguing together.

In the Duchess's blue drawing-room, when he stole back cautiously behind the chairs, the Great Man was still reading from His Own Works, to the assembled ladies, and some of the ladies were still listening, while all would presently tell him how wonderful he was.

Outside, in fragrant wood and meadow, the other performances, unadmired and unadvertised, went on as usual, and the Earth, nourishing all alike, turned calmly, faithfully, on her axis, continuing her journey at eighteen miles a second round a gigantic incandescent fire, some 93,000,000 miles away, that was too commonplace to call for remark as a rule, yet without which the entire Show would be snuffed out in a fraction of a second.

He got back just in time to be deafened by the applause, and to see the Great Man smile and bow.

The World-Dream of McCallister

Certain people, it would appear, are favoured with occasional dreams of so vivid a character that they leave on the mind an impression that lasts for hours, often, it may be, for the whole of the following day, while the dream itself is forgotten almost entirely upon waking. "Almost entirely"; for, possibly, some remnant is retained or half-retained, caught by the tail, as it were, in the act of plunging out of sight to rejoin the major portion—a fragment of glowing scenery, a voice, perhaps a sentence, halts long enough to be seen or heard (at any rate, to be remembered) before it is withdrawn swiftly from the consciousness.

Such remnants, moreover, though faint as moonlight—they vanish with extreme and urgent hurry, as though they had unduly lingered and were not intended to be more fully known—yet share this in common; that they pertain to some experience that has seemed infinitely desirable, since a peculiar yearning is awakened for their continuance or for their completion. Vague though the details have been, the emotion left is powerful and strangely haunting; and this emotion invariably seems due to a sense of having been in some familiar and enchanting place, and that a rarely privileged companionship has been interrupted by the act of waking. Life would be sweeter, bigger, indubitably more worth living—this is somewhat the feeling left behind—could the experience be entirely recaptured. The dream, at any rate, has been broken off before its end.

The emotion is so strong, so exquisite, indeed, that the mind makes a quick and vigorous effort at recovery—only to find that it is vain, and that such experiences are not recoverable at all. The dream is gone, and the more vigorous the effort, the more complete the disappearance. The remnant, moreover, soon vanishes as well: memory focuses it each time with less success; it grows blurred, confused, then artificial; a counterpart, half-invented, is erected in its place; and each attempt at recovery conceals the original more and more, while giving body to the substitute that mocks it. In the end the mind retains chiefly the emotion that filled it upon waking, and with that memory it must remain content.

This emotion, however, remains, according to circumstances, for a longer or a shorter time. It crops up unexpectedly at odd moments later; sometimes it haunts at intervals during the entire day, curiously persistent, eagerly, almost passionately desired, although each time a little weaker, a little fainter, than before. Rarely may it survive the twelve daylight hours of which the first announced its welcome birth and presence. The following night's sleep sets a term to its existence. Its loss is final. The sense that it *has* been alone remains. It has become the memory of an exquisite Memory.

And, since so little of the actual dream is caught, it would seem to be this accompanying emotion that lights the heart so strangely with the sense of elusive and enchanting glamour. For the emotion is, indeed, of an unusual kind: deep and tender, evasive yet profoundly real, a vague but persistent certainty that it refers to an experience more packed with life, more intense, more piercing, above all more joyous, than anything known in waking hours. It stands to the dreamer as full sunlight compared to palest moonlight—the most vivid emotions of his daylight life seem thin and temporary besides its permanent, though lost, reality. Almost it has suggested another order of existence, a richer state of consciousness, and hence the yearning in his heart for full recovery. He wonders, and he—sighs. He has touched a state that, to say the least of it, was satisfactory. Could he recall that state, the perplexities of his daily life would surely be explained; for, in some fashion beyond him to elucidate, that lost, happy dream pertained to a completer consciousness of which ordinary existence is but a broken, troubled shadow. He was then lit up and shining; he moves now in darkness....

Dreams of this kind, though rare, are known to many; the physiologists have, doubtless, a careful explanation of their origin, as of the effects which they produce. Upon their occurrence is possibly based that kind and ancient fantasy that persuades a few the spirit travels while the body sleeps, that things are then shown to it which the brain might scarce discover for itself; of which things, moreover, the intense or awful sweetness— as the case may be—were more than physical memory could retain without disaster to commonplace days and duties afterwards. To remember a state so perfect, yet so impossible of achievement, would involve a disappointment with the routine of normal difficulties that must border upon despair.... To deal satisfactorily with such delicate splendours, one should be, presumably, either fanatic or poet, the latter's hint, perhaps, remaining the sweetest hint we have: "Some say that dreams of a remoter world visit the soul in sleep ..."—and McCallister, at any rate, felt rather pleased that Shelley's line recurred to him during the day that followed his own particular experience.

For McCallister had such a dream one night, and in the morning behaved strictly according to precedent regarding it: That is, he registered the intensity and sweetness of the accompanying emotion, strove vigorously for full recovery, then went about his duties of the day with occasional moments when the emotion was hauntingly revived, and at the same time with a flickering consciousness—almost a memory—that he had been with someone in an enchanting place, and that this someone had told or shown him things of an authentic and privileged kind. Life had been full and rich and deeply splendid; but, more than that—it had been explained, because he understood it whole, instead of seeing it in broken fragments....

In his case the remnant caught by the tail was very slight indeed; many would have deemed it trivial, some ridiculous: perhaps it was both trivial and ridiculous. Only it shared the joyous and enchanting glamour of the whole, which yet remained obstinately hidden; and in this sense, while it teased him with unsatisfied yearning, it also blessed and comforted him with the feeling that Life was all right, could he but see it whole. For the fragment had in some fashion revealed an Entirety, to which his waking consciousness was stranger, yet to which desire and belief, half-buried, had, in moments of uplifting, bravest hope, distinctly pointed. Accordingly, he felt blessed and comforted; and, since these results assist a yet more valuable state of mind, he felt also—strengthened.

The remnant of the dream he retained was, indeed, but a fading sentence, consisting of seven commonplace words in daily use, uttered, moreover, by a voice of no particular calibre, yet of such happy and immense authority that he was instantly persuaded of its ultimate truth:

"So you see, it IS all right ...!"

Such was the detail memory retained, no more, no less. And, on waking, he yearned for its continuance, for its completion, struggling for a long time to recover the place, the person and the conditions which might reconstruct the entire dream and so explain it. For he had the delightful feeling—especially strong during the first ten minutes after waking—that, were it recoverable, he would be master of a point of view that must solve the perplexities of his life and make the puzzle of his somewhat muddled existence satisfactory. "If I could only get it *all* back," as he put it to himself, "I should get things straight—face everything happily—because I understood the lot!"

The remembered sentence, however, contained the essence of the vanished dream—"So you see—it IS all right!"—but the dream itself had disappeared....

He went, therefore, as already mentioned, about his duties of the day; and, doing so, he experienced—also according to precedent—those brief, flickering moments when the Emotion revived in haunting flashes, and was gone again as soon as recognised—unfulfilled, unrealised—yet each time leaving behind it a hint of that comfort and that blessing pertaining to its origin. With each flash, as it were, and with each haunting repetition, he recovered for that fleeting instant a singular consciousness of the splendid Whole to which the fragment still belonged.... He was lit up and shining.

As the day advanced, these moments of return became less vivid, though never less convincing. The first authority remained; it was the memory that faded.

These moments were as follows:

It was upon the one day in the seven that his work in the Censor's Office left him the afternoon free, and he went to tea with Her in the Enchanted Square. He was neither invited nor expected; he just dropped in. Later the husband dropped in, too, and all three talked together easily and naturally. The guest was obviously made welcome, there were no signs of restraint or awkwardness, far less of friction. Perhaps the husband guessed, perhaps he did not; possibly She knew—indeed probably—though assuredly not from anything McCallister had ever said, or done, or betrayed.... Neither he nor she troubled themselves about an after-existence: to McCallister, therefore, the one chance of possessing her was lost for ever. Although brains, as well as worldly success, had both been denied him, he had the great gifts of strength and loyalty and truth. He was known as a worthy, if perhaps an uninteresting man. Occasionally he went to call, like any other casual member of her circle—that and no more than that. His secret was a genuine secret, entirely his own and safely, honestly kept. He owned—and deserved—the friendship of the husband, too. And the position, while never beyond his strength, was the more difficult in that he was aware *she* felt for her husband affection, but not love.

And so he sat there in the enchanted house, silent and rather dull as usual, but blessed by her presence and therefore very happy. The only signs by which he persuaded himself she kept him in her thoughts during the longish intervals between his visits were that she divined his exact requirements when he came. She never asked. It was always sweet to him, and wonderful—such little yet enormous things: One lump of sugar in his tea; cream, but no milk; the hard chair with the stiff, upright back; the glaring lights turned out, leaving a single globe at the far end of the room to help the fire-light; and—the fragments of Russian music that he loved....

"I just want to try over this bit of Scriabin, if you don't mind," she would suggest, going across to the instrument without waiting for his answer. Or—"the piano's just been tuned; I really must play a chord or two"—and then, without further words, the pieces that he so particularly loved ... while he sat listening by the fire, watching, absorbed, strangely at peace and happy. There was no formality; he felt blissfully at home; the warmth of the fire, the shaded lights, the delicate sense of her perfume, her presence, her very thoughts, as he believed, brushing against his secret, and her music entering his inmost soul to phrase his dumb desire—all this filled him with strength and beauty that would help him in the long, long interval of loneliness to follow.

And then the door would open, and the husband enter with a clatter, bringing the atmosphere of the street and latest news of rumour thick about him.

"Jack, old boy! It's only you! Good. I was afraid it was a caller!"

But the husband did not care for music; he preferred the room well lit; and he was always ready for a hearty tea. He saw first to these three requirements, therefore, then kissed his wife while she put away the scores, and all three sat talking over the fire, the husband gulping his tea with audible satisfaction and munching his buttered toast as though he had earned it every bit—talking loudly with McCallister, whom he liked, and obliquely with his wife with whom he was so supremely satisfied that she could be neglected somewhat. His ownership of her, at any rate, was very manifest, and McCallister found these moments rather trying, especially when the music was interrupted earlier than necessary, perhaps in the middle of a piece....

They chatted happily for twenty minutes or so, and then, a natural pause presenting itself, McCallister rose to go. He said good-bye. For him it was a real goodbye—God-be-with-you, dear; for he could not know what might happen in the interval to follow, and, as with all real good-byes, the sense of separation was keen with possibilities that *would* leap into the mind and burden it. This moment of good-bye was always full of pain for him. But this time it was different. There was a smile in his eyes that many husbands must have noticed. For, suddenly, into that pause had flooded the motion of the vanished dream. It was, perhaps, but the memory of an unrecoverable Memory, yet with it an intense delight, a joy, a peace, swept over him. He was lit up and shining. He was not lonely. It seemed he knew more—far more—than he could quite remember. The very words came back:

"So, you see, it IS all right...."

The haunting emotion flashed and flickered like a swallow's wing, then vanished, yet left behind an instant of superb realisation that took his heart and blessed it. A high, sweet privilege he knew of, yet had somehow forgotten among smaller, troubling emotions of imperfect kind, was there to gladden life for ever—*now*. The instant's joy enthralled him, then was gone again. It was as if some absolute, some spiritual, possession of Her had been granted to him. He had amazingly overlooked it. Or, rather, having stupidly misunderstood this blazing fact, he now recovered it, complete and glorious—for the flashing instant. Their love was pure and flawless; they belonged to one another in the actual present: they were one. The emotion, evanescent though it was, involved the bliss of certain joy.

"So, you see, it IS all right," rose an inner voice behind the casual words he spoke aloud as he left the room....

And this joy that was real yet inexplicable, accompanied him down the steps after the maid had closed the big front door discreetly. He went out with a radiant happiness, as of a remembered ownership and dear possession in his soul. It hovered and lingered about him for some little time, as he walked down the murky street towards the Tube Station half a mile away. And then it faded. Trying to recover the dream itself, he lost hold of the emotion. It became confused. Its authenticity grew less and less. It grew unreal. Yet the certainty of his deep tie was strengthened unaccountably. She did belong to him in some odd sense that was not now, and yet was *now*…. The details of a Rumour in high quarters, uttered in the husband's decided voice, then replaced it with ringing insistence in his ears. The Memory grew very faint and died away. It was, in a few moments, quite unrecoverable. He remembered only that it had been there….

The other occasion when the dream haunted him had been earlier in the day; but, though first in sequence of time, it was, for some reason, less vivid than the instance just recorded. Perhaps the incident it lighted up, being of minor importance in his life, caused a less striking reaction. Yet the same conviction was present, the same hint of a richer, completer state of consciousness which must make life beautiful and solve its tribe of little puzzles, were he but master of it always. He groped among disconnected fragments; in the dream he had known the clue that slipped these angled fragments into the mosaic of a perfect pattern.

On the way to the Office he saw—in the distance but coming toward him—the Man he Loathed. The loathing was mutual, the deep antipathy of ancient standing. They were, however, on speaking terms, for they lived in the same small circle of friends and duties; there had been no open quarrel; but the nod, the meeting of the eyes, above all the uttered word—these were avoided whenever possible. In the language of the street, they could not "stand" one another. But now, with a stretch of empty pavement between them, growing every moment less as they approached, avoidance or decent escape was out of the question, and McCallister instinctively braced himself for the inevitable exchange of reluctant and half-hostile greeting. The conventional hypocrisy galled him. Far rather would he have dealt the man an honest blow, with a word to the effect that he was a cad and heartily deserved it.

They stopped, as such men will, talking a moment, with a bravish appearance of good-fellowship—less than a moment, indeed, for it was the merest half turn of the heel in passing, just enough to show the semi-smile of good manners, so that each might produce the impression—"*You* are the cad, not I; the fault is yours!" McCallister met the hated and the hating eyes, and looked deep into them. The same instant—the two hostile personalities facing one another upon that patch of deserted pavement at 8.45 a.m.—there flashed marvellously into his mind the emotion of the vanished dream. Born of nothing, apparently, it came and went. For a fleeting second memory recovered this Memory of a completer knowledge, and life was strangely beautiful. He was lit up and happy:

"So you see, it IS all right!" went down the morning wind like some fragrance of forgotten childhood flowers.

The gleam was there—then gone again like lightning. A hint of divinity came with the accompanying emotion; it did not wholly go. For in that evanescent flash, McCallister knew suddenly a large and driving, yet somehow perfectly natural impulse—that the mutual enmity was based upon an error, that in reality there was no enmity at all. This angled fragment fitted in somewhere, and fitted beautifully, could he but remember where.... Some such dazzling point of happiness, even of glory, pierced his being; peace, love and absolute comprehension bathed him, body, mind and soul. The flickering emotion blessed and comforted, even while it flashed beyond his reach. He and his enemy were one.

Another moment and he would have spoken frankly, made it up, explained, forgiven, and been forgiven. He felt positive of this, the power was in his grasp. He saw the enmity, the hatred, the latent loathing as nothing but a misunderstanding that must have suddenly dissolved in a smile of relief, born of happiness and springing out of love. The emotion of the forgotten dream was a salved fragment from some richer state of consciousness wherein the puzzles of daily life, seen from a bird's-eye point of view, explained themselves. The word that occurred to him was Unity.

But the emotion, fugitive as moonlight upon some wind-blown puddle, had disappeared again. The larger mood, the generous impulse, went with the gleam. He remembered that it had been, but he could no longer understand it. The brief greeting was over; the men passed on their way in opposite directions.... Before the next lamp-post was reached McCallister loathed the man as he had never loathed him before. Only the big impulse puzzled him still a little, for equally with the present hatred, it had been deep and genuine. He felt ashamed, first of the impulse, then of having disobeyed it.

"That's why some people are accused of falseness and insincerity," occurred to him. "They get a flash like that, and act upon it without reflecting first. Or else the other person doesn't get it at all, and so …!"

There remained, at any rate, in his heart, buried but alert, some haunting yearning for a lost, enchanting happiness which he had missed. He was aware of sadness, of regret. He could not understand it.... He reached the Office, saw his table piled up with letters in three foreign languages, realised that the writers, all of them, knew difficult, perplexing lives just now—and then, cutting open the first envelope with his special knife, forgot his dream, his enemy, and everything else in the world except his immediate and uncongenial duty.

The third and last incident—late in the evening—proved that the memory of the Memory was lost almost entirely. The emotion was present, indeed, but of exceeding faintness. It had faded so much that it seemed remote, unreal, not worth recovering. He had no longer any particular desire to recover it; the yearning had wholly left him. As for the words—*"So, you see, it IS all right"*—he recalled them, but found them ill-placed and without meaning or conviction. Their authority was gone. They came, moreover, in an artificial form, a substitute from some forgotten book or other—or was it from some advertisement upon the hoardings? His mind, clogged with the details of his work, with suspicion of certain letters and interest in others, with pity, boredom, exasperation, respectively, for the various writers, had no room for thoughts of unordinary kind. At any rate, this time he noticed the foolish words, the dying emotion, and no more: out of the corner of his tired eye, so to speak, he noticed them. But both were already centuries away.

The incident occurred in the darkened streets as he walked homewards carefully after ten o'clock, having spent the evening at his Club. He witnessed a distressing accident. The memories of the day lay somewhat jumbled in his mind, no one in particular dominating the rest. The meeting with his enemy twelve hours before had passed entirely, his work was deliberately set aside and forgotten, the Club had produced nothing to occupy his thoughts. With the latest evening paper in his pocket, still unread, he groped his way homewards, conscious perhaps, more than anything else, that the day had been of the red-letter kind because he had been to tea in the Enchanted Square. This memory wove itself softly, sweetly, in and out among his tired thoughts, when, at a certain crossing, the distressing accident occurred beneath his very eyes. A child was knocked down and killed by a passing taxi-cab.

Upon the sudden shock of horror that he felt, followed an abrupt paralysis of all his faculties. Every instinct in him leaped to render help—to prevent was already out of the question, alas—and the impotent desire to save, succeeded instantly by pity, sympathy, and pain, combined to arrest both his muscles and his breath. The affair was over with such hideous swiftness. Figures at once congregated about the dreadful spot, as though they had been lurking in the blackness, waiting for the thing to happen. Willing hands lifted the little body on to the pavement. The shadows swallowed everything.

McCallister, recovering the use of his muscles and his breath, moved on. A heavy sigh escaped him. But in moving away from the painful and unhappy scene, he moved away also—so it seemed—from a pause in life. Time, which had stopped a moment, flowed on with him again. Yet there had been this pause, this moment out of Time. He had forgotten himself; he now remembered himself again. And into that instant of pause, into that timeless, but also selfless moment, had poured the ghostly emotion of the vanished dream.

The emotion on this occasion, though still haunting as before, was almost too faint to be recognised; and though the familiar sentence rose scurrying to the surface of his mind, it took now another form—a substitute. This substitute, moreover, belonged to his waking, not to his dreaming, life. "God's in his Heaven; all's right with the world"—or some such words, taken if he remembered rightly, from the calendar on his walls in the Office. He had not the smallest idea whose words they were. They seemed to him rather foolish at the moment, an empty statement of some optimistic maker of phrases at the best. At the same time, the fading emotion left a vague suggestion of comfort in him somewhere: only he felt unable to accept it now; indeed, he resented and resisted it. He thought only of the mangled little body, of its being brought to the house, of the parents, and so forth. The cheap and facile sentence from the calendar excited his scorn, and his mind responded to it in kind with a touch of anger: "Why couldn't God in his Heaven have prevented it …?" He felt very near to that child—almost as if the accident had happened to himself.

For an hour before going to bed, he read the evening paper. Friends, he saw, had been wounded, taken prisoner, killed, and one was "missing." He entered the blackness, as many times before, experiencing once again the pity, anguish, despair the War had made familiar to most people. The Collective Sense took hold of him…. For a moment, now and again, he had a curious feeling of oneness with those interrupted lives…. He was aware, too, of the strength to make any personal sacrifice in order to help, the stolid determination (as though he were himself a Field Marshal or War Minister) to hold out until the diabolical immorality let loose upon the earth had been annihilated…. Yet, just as sleep took him, he felt another thing as well—an immense, incomprehensible hope that he somehow or other knew was justified. For, though unable to seize it for definition in his drowsy state, it came to him as being more than hope: a certainty, although a hidden one. But his mind was silent. He just felt it—felt sure of it—no more. "So, you see, it *is* all right," was as good a way of phrasing it as any other. Then thought grew hazy, curtains rose and fell. He had dreamed something very wonderful the last time he lay in bed…. Would the same dream recur, perhaps? He had not dreamed it alone either; surely the whole world had dreamed it with him. The haunting emotion touched him very faintly. A mist of forgetfulness rose over him. He was unable to think, much less to argue with himself about it. He fell asleep.

Next morning, his original dream, with the emotion that had accompanied it, were sponged completely from his consciousness. His egg for breakfast was not quite fresh, there was no butter, no marmalade, his fire was a column of thick, dirty smoke without flame or heat, his morning letters were unsatisfactory. He had a headache, he dreaded his day's work; nobody could have persuaded him that anything in the world was "all right." The war news, too, was depressing. In the newspaper he read an unflattering paragraph about his enemy, the Man he Loathed. He was delighted.

The very next second—almost the same second it was indeed, and for the first time in his life—he inconsequently felt sorry for him—rather. The loathing, he was aware, had unaccountably weakened somewhat. He noted the curious fact, for a moment, and then dismissed it. There seemed this change of attitude in him, very slight indeed, yet distinctly noticeable. This generalisation he dismissed as well.

Yet during the day it recurred; it refused to be dismissed. The change in his attitude, though slight, was very deep perhaps; it manifested from time to time, at any rate. He summed it up in this way: that there seemed less room in him, less time too, for personal emotions. He knew, among his little daily troubles, a bigger, braver, happier feeling. It was a great relief. He could not understand it; something in him had escaped, as it were. Hidden in the depths of his commonplace being was a new sympathy which is the seed of understanding, and so of forgiveness, and so, finally, of joy. This new attitude, as the day wore on, confirmed itself; it certainly was real. Not that he actively or deliberately thought about it, but as though the process went forward in him automatically, of its own accord, springing from some hidden and forgotten source of inspiration, leading him to certain very definite conclusions; conclusions, however, that wholly evaded him when he tried to put them into words.

He found himself, that is, with a new feeling, a new point of view, rather than with a new philosophy; with an approach to these, at any rate. The love he must, in one sense, renounce; the enemy he must forgive; the broken life of the little child; the killed, the maimed, the tortured, the bereaved; his own small personal difficulties and pains—towards all of these he felt as towards angled fragments of some mighty pattern which, could he but see it whole, must justify what seemed cruel and terrible merely. Occasionally, he felt them all as happening in himself. This seed of divine sympathy had singularly come to birth in him. The dream was forgotten, but this seed remained. He did not, perhaps, look happier, yet a possibility of joy had been experienced by him—the memory of a Memory. He was aware of a faint and childlike hope that something new was stealing down into the world.... It was all right.

The Other Woman

Not that it was so particularly lovely, but that it was so astonishingly real, perplexed him. This reality, the conviction that he knew it intimately, were the reasons why its appearance troubled him, though trouble is perhaps too strong a word, since it woke a yearning sweetness too. The root of the strange emotion doubtless lay in this: that the face, while curiously familiar, was not known to him. He did not recognise it.

It would rise before his inmost vision as in a cloud of silvery mist; memory would leap to claim it, pause, hesitate, and finally draw back in failure. "I know you intimately," he would whisper, deep inside himself. "I have always known you. But, for the life of me, I can't remember who you are!" Comforted, blessed, contented, he would give up the puzzle with a sigh.

Where had he seen this face before? When had he met the original? Under what conditions of time and space had he known in the flesh this woman whose eyes gazed with such sweet, haunting invitation into his own? It was not a memory he could trace, try as he would; it was not a dream—in his dreams he never saw her; she belonged to everyday working life and sunlight. Moreover, she was ever young. She matured, but did not age. In every true artist-soul lies something which is unageing. She kept pace in him with that.

She first appeared quite early in his life, in boyhood almost, but certainly when the boy slipped into the man; and he soon established the fact that it was invariably a girl or woman who evoked her. It was sufficient for a girl or woman to engage, or threaten to engage, his heart, for this other woman to rise inwardly and take possession of him, with the result that the attraction of the moment faded, then wholly died away. The exquisite invasion brimmed his entire being, leaving nothing over or unsatisfied. Her seductive power was so great that against her mere silent appearance, before the gaze of those inviting, gentle eyes, no other charm, no passing fancy, at any rate, could stand a moment. His soul soared upwards towards her. She seemed to offer a perfection which became for him a test and standard for all lesser beauty.... Did she, then, resent intrusion of such lesser beauty? Certainly she nipped in the bud each of his early love affairs, prevented serious attachment too. Absurd as it must sound, absurd as it was indeed, the Face forbade his marrying. His soul loved and yearned towards her alone. She became his faultless guide.

Having humour in his composition, he called her the Other Woman, and tried, but without success, to paint her. His skill, already famous, failed with each attempt. On the canvas she became too commonplace to finish, much less to frame. She eluded him completely. Thus he was unable to convince his friends, who flocked to the studio, that she possessed the qualities, above all the reality, he saw and felt in her. Moreover, she prevented other pictures too, landscapes even, or imaginative renderings of his inmost being that were not absolutely true—born of his highest inspiration. She resented, in a word, he came to realise, any aspect of Beauty not of the purest, sweetest, that threatened possession of him to her own exclusion. She insisted upon a standard he could not always reach. He made his name among the few. He made no money.

The relationship, thus established and accepted, ruled his life. He loved, he worshipped, he obeyed this Other Woman who so elusively filled the imagined roles of comrade, wife, and guide. Yet she troubled, even alarmed, him sometimes. It was not the conviction of precious intimacy, but the puzzling failure to recognise, that alarmed him, suggesting some grave dislocation of memory. Somewhere he *must* have seen her original, perhaps in a picture, perhaps fugitive in the street, or at another's house.

"You see, I *know* her," he told his friend, "know her as well as I know my own mother. Yet I cannot recall her name, or who she is, or where we met, or anything about her. And that's amazing—like forgetting all about the wife you love except that you know her, love her, and belong to her. Now—I ask you!"

"But you're a painter," the friend explained. "This is some ideal or other you visualise pictorially. It's probably some childhood memory suppressed years ago. Find the original and it will cease to haunt you."

"But *she* knows me, too, I tell you," insisted the artist, already regretting the confidence given. "That's the uncanny part of it." The other stared a moment with embarrassment. "It is," he repeated, as with a mental shrug of the shoulders. "It is a bit uncanny, as you say." He changed the subject, and presently made an excuse to go.

The painter passed through many love affairs; they had no result; they interfered with his work; they dimmed his sweetest vision as they passed; but each time, with the appearance of the haunting eyes that gazed so yearningly into his own, power was restored to him. Each frustration added to his power; he was enriched. He wanted wife and children ... their lovely ghosts walked through his canvases. The artist soul is notoriously passionate and fickle, exacting too; the Other Woman led him victoriously, clean, unsoiled, through all adventure. To be false to her was to be faithless to the highest, deepest, truest, in his life. He suffered, hut he did not fail her. He saw then in her dear eyes a new expression—majesty. His genius knew fulfilment.

"You say you have already tried to paint her?" asked a wise woman who loved him for himself, but loved his genius more. "Her expression would interest me enormously—"

"Tried till I'm tired," he interrupted. "She fades instantly. Elusive beyond capture. That's just it, you see." There was a note of reverence in his voice.

"And pain—?" she asked softly, the sympathy of real understanding dangerously in her eyes.

He signified assent. "I yearn towards her," he confessed, gazing at his companion as though he begged forgiveness, then gazing suddenly past her. "I'm beginning to think—" He paused; the sentence remained unfinished. Ineffable yearning filled his heart as the Other Woman rose in that instant before his inmost sight, exquisite, majestic, with her final, unquestionable power. The love offered him seemed tawdry by comparison. The full confidence was not given.

From his earthly eyes she remained concealed until the very end. It was at the very end only that he knew and recognised her. At the moment of death she gave herself into his full keeping, because she had already been in his full keeping always, and because he had proved faithful to her through all his minor faithlessness.

"Forgive me," he murmured, in the confused rambling they mistook for incoherence; "forgive my times of doubt and question.... O my Great Loveliness....!"

Beside the bed they listened to his whisperings:

"It is worn thin with words.... I heard them discuss it often ... the artist.... I see now it's true.... Alone of men the artist has within himself the perfect mate. He needs no other. The feminine lies divinely in his being, his own perfect soul-mate...."

He held out his hands, raising his head a moment from the pillow.

"It was you, and only you, I really loved. I have been true.... O my Great Loveliness!" And, with a smile of joy upon his face, he went to meet her.

Picking Fir-Cones

I

Among my earliest recollections of any vividness is a voice saying "yes" across the darkness of my winter bedroom. My exact age at the time is difficult to fix, but since I have no memories of anything before I was six, it may be set, perhaps, safely at seven years old. The voice seemed outside myself; it issued apparently from the shadows as a whole, rather than from a particular corner of the fireless room.

I had been lying awake, wondering "frightfully hard" about everything, why so much was forbidden, and how disappointing it was to be blocked by rules and parents and nurses, and so on, when there stole out of the hush this whispered "yes," as if in answer to my puzzles. It gave me the feeling that life was intended to be lived. All sorts of things were going to happen at once: I would do, accept them all. An exultant happiness burst up in me. I was alive!

"I'm at it all again," came to me.

Questions as to goal or origin there were none, but the feeling of "again" was vivid. This idea of resumption was certainly present. I resumed a journey; the train had stopped, but now went on again…. It was to be a long, long, business, yet stuffed with interest and excitement, to which I looked forward with zest, with positive joy. I had been "at it" for ages already, the journey by no means just begun. I was hungry to live, but to live again, and this hunger was familiar to me. My questions, my wonder, seemed like efforts to remember things just out of reach, yet not impossibly, finally, out of reach. They were recoverable. Meanwhile, I wished "fearfully" to live and experience again, avoiding nothing. "Getting on," I called it, though growth, *quâ* development, was certainly not present in my mind at that tender age.

I woke next morning with the excitement to do things in my blood, and to do them as soon as possible. I did them. I turned on all the taps in the bath-room, tried to set fire to a hay-rick to see the blaze, and let the pigs out of their pens into the stable-yard and thence into the garden. I remember lifting a broken hop pole to hit the coachman's daughter with. I did everything I could, taking the consequences, painful though these were, and puzzling too. For no one really explained to me, but merely said No, and then hurt me physically. It made no difference apparently. I meant to live, to miss no opportunity of doing things and enjoying the experience, pleasant or unpleasant. To avoid and shirk merely because it hurt was to lose an opportunity I was alive to know; whereas to suppress a desire, find no outlet for it, filled me with a choking violence that poisoned my whole being—what my elders meant by wickedness, I suppose.

Keen regret invariably followed such repression: I had missed an opportunity that might never come again, The hunger to live had been denied. To suppress without regret was a stage, of course, I reached much later; to divert this energy into other channels, transmuting it, came later still. If intensity was my native gift, at any rate, I think my energy was merely wasted rather than used for evil. This analysis, moreover, belongs to maturity, when reason loves laborious explanations; at the time I accepted and believed: I only felt and acted.

Evil! It was just this word, so often on father's lips, that, with its opposite, good, made me feel sure there was some state superior to either, and that this state I had experienced already. I had known it before, but had now forgotten. It was recoverable, however, only I must be jolly quick about recovering it, for once I was grown up it would be too late. It involved an experience of strange, enormous, universal conditions difficult to describe. I wanted to get into everything, to do everything and to do it all at once, to be everywhere, and to be everywhere simultaneously. The fir-cone incident was the only practical proof I had that it was possible. It will be described presently.

Here, then, was a definite, though wholly undetailed, memory. Belief, so called, played no part in my attitude towards it. I *knew*. I was haunted at this very early age by a dim recollection of some state superior to good and evil, and it betrayed itself, briefly, in an intense longing for things to be otherwise than they were—entirely otherwise.

This sounds so ordinary, it was actually so significant. No intellectually devised Utopia was involved: an *absolute* change was what I so ardently desired. Hints of it came to me—came back; in fairy-tales, in poetry, in music, yet most frequently and with a closer sense of validity, from the beauty of Nature, especially in wild and lonely places; though as I grew older I grew, it seemed at the same time, smaller, and the chances of recovery rapidly decreased. I was settling in among conditions that excluded full recollection. Soon I should forget altogether.

The memory, as I have said, was undetailed, but two conditions stood out in the recovery so ardently desired: I wanted goodness to be more good, wickedness more wicked. This was the first step. People of both types were so tame, insipid, colourless, so oppressively alike. The good were only just good by the skin of their teeth, as it were, their goodness managed by an effort that left no energy over; they laboured for goodness, and for happiness, at some future time. Good to me meant positively shining. Yet the good folk had no particular joy. I wanted people who were shining and radiant *now*. Children had more of the quality I meant than older people, but no one had it properly at all.

With what my parents called "evil" it was similar. Depravity there was in plenty, but that was negative: an open wickedness, strong and unafraid, I did not find. What passed for wickedness was a hole-and-corner, afraid-of-being-caught, a shamefaced business; what passed for goodness an equally negative state that denied living and kept certain rules grudgingly and with sighs for the sake of safety and some reward in the future. Energy, raised to the intensity where it involved worship—though I did not phrase it so at the time—did not, exist at all. It was such a trumpery affair, the way folk lived. I wanted an intenser and quite different life that was somewhere within reach, within recovery. Memory played faintly round it like a flame, but a flame that was slowly and surely dying as I grew older. I longed to lift a curtain, to stretch the scale, to open life to some gigantic flood that was brimming just outside, ready to pour through and sweep me into joy and power. This immense tide hung waiting only just beyond the way we lived, but some small personal fear of its depth and extent alarmed us all. The key-note, at any rate, of this superior state I refer to was certainly joy. Joy was the quality that no one had—that joy, as I knew later, which is the essential quality of wisdom. The surprise, the unearthly touch, of wisdom, are mothered always by this towering sense of joy. It was the denial of joy everywhere that chafed and bruised me at a very early stage of my development, since it was, of course, a denial of life itself. That "yes" in the darkness of my bedroom was an affirmation of its accessibility. And memory was an ingredient.

The accessibility of this superior state I dreamed about remained my firm knowledge for a long time. It lay within reach still, here and now; it was really everywhere. Any moment I might pop back into it—at the end of the wet brambly lane, round the bend of a passage in the old house, behind the huge cedars, across the pond, a little further down the river. It was not in the future, but now; it was not away, but here. When least expecting it, I should come upon the exit through which I had slipped down into "this"—this life with parents, brothers, sisters, servants, governesses, gardeners, coachmen and policemen, all saying No from morning till night. And, once I came upon the exit, I could slip in again. But the way of slipping in or out I also had forgotten, and I made no special effort to recover it because it seemed so amazingly easy—a mere question of mood almost—that no effort was really necessary. It would come of its own accord. If people would only stop saying No so loudly, it would surely be upon me any moment.

Yet the actual way and method became more and more uncertain. Some kind of distance shrouded it in haze. It was then that I *tried* to get it back, but found that no mental effort was of any use, thinking and longing least of all. The conviction of genuine belief alone could manage the desired recovery, and it was this belief precisely that had begun to waver and grow dim in me as I got older. I must keep very still, intensely still, but with an interior stillness that was now escaping me, because no one knew of it, practised it least of all: this stillness within me I must find if I was to recover what I longed for before it was too late.

Then one day, quite suddenly, it came to me of its own accord. I did not discover it, but just knew. I did it. We called it—do you, my brother, as you read these notes, remember?—by a word of our own invention: *dipping*.

II

On the back lawn you and Val and I (Val just back from his first term at Charterhouse) were picking fir-cones that crackled sharply to the touch and had earwigs crawling between the dark little gaping crevices. A penny a hundred was the rate of payment father made, half in play and half in sermon-earnest, and the cones were burned eventually in the drawing-room fire, with the remark (if we happened to be present): "See how useful your labour was, my boys! No work is lost, nothing in life is wasted!" The sentence always made me feel rude; I wanted to deny it angrily, but never dared to. The actual picking, however, was rather fun. The crinkly cones with their ugly brown inhabitants were mysterious; the pincers of the insects fascinated me. As a rule, too, this collecting seemed important; it made a difference to the world; yet ever with this half-concealed provision, that it was actually a sham, and that one day some person or other would catch us at it and laugh. The humbug of it would be shown up.... One thing that held my interest, perhaps, was the quantity, and the way the cones deceived me. At first they appeared so few upon the lawn, so thinly scattered; yet half an hour's labour apparently made no difference to the numbers left. The quantity, indeed, increased; the lawn seemed blacker. I could not make it out. And a hundred cones took up so small a space in the gardener's wooden basket that smelt of leaves and mould.

On this particular occasion we were picking hard, with remarks at intervals about the number, the prospective pennies, and speculations as to which of us had collected the greater quantity, when, quite suddenly, there was a change.

I was kneeling up at the moment, watching Val—Val, who was so clever, who explained things and "knew it all";—my head swam a little with the rush of blood from stooping; Val had filled his straw hat, but, forgetting the blue cord fastened to his button-hole, reached out an arm with a careless jerk that upset his entire store. He uttered an exclamation of disgust with a wry grimace, glancing round at me as though he hoped I had not seen the accident. I thought for a moment he was going to cry with disappointment. It was just then that a new mood—the change—came on me as with a burst of dazzling light.

The tiny comedy was set upon the big green lawn, the towering cedars behind, the vast summer sky of blue above. Such was the background to the trivial accident—an insignificant human miscalculation of time and distance, framed by the steady, unalterable immensities. The contrast made me catch my breath. I did not laugh, I felt no triumph or pity; I felt, indeed, no interest of any kind, but knew suddenly that I was unutterably bored. The occupation *was* a sham, it was absurd and trumpery. Some-one—father perhaps—was laughing at us. This was not living, it was merely making the time go by without being counted. There were better things to do, real things, immense opportunities sliding past unclaimed. Indeed, we were humbugging as well as being humbugged. I, at any rate, could manage things differently, otherwise, quite otherwise. The sense of the superior state I had forgotten and was in danger of losing altogether came breathlessly close to me. I shivered.

I stopped. A huge simple joy stole over my whole being. I had a sense of awe that made me hold my breath and at the same time intensely happy. The thing I so yearningly desired was near to me as air, not in the future, not away, but here and now, I only had to claim it. There was rapture. I trembled, as though interiorly I was a sheaf of fine, taut wires drawn thin as silk, and a wind passed over them.

I waited, kneeling upright on the grass and staring. Nothing happened at first. All my activities, not merely the gathering of the fir-cones, came to rest. My inner being had become intensely still. Of Val I was no longer aware, I hardly saw him; but I saw you, my brother; I stared, watching you in your alpaca suit of overalls, as you stooped and picked and stretched out your arms and legs in the sunshine. You moved slowly; and I marvelled why you continued grubbing so contentedly on one spot of ground. You crawled laboriously over the lawn, a few inches at a time, panting with effort, like some monster-insect badly made, clumsily jointed: even the ear-wigs moved with more skill and cleverer energy.

It was ludicrous; yet I realised you were doing this on purpose and had not really "forgotten" any more than I had. It was a phantom you I watched; the real you looked on, looked down, from this superior state. You yourself watched the phantom "you" with detachment that was not quite indifference. Sharply then I realised another thing: you picked fir-cones with all your energy, because you knew it was the purpose for which you were here. I was vividly aware in that instant of those two different points of view respectively: neither of us had "forgotten"; but, whereas I revolted and wished to be otherwise, you accepted the present and were content. I felt ashamed of myself while this flashed through me. With its passing, however, my own point of view shot uppermost again. I thought you ob-stinate, stupid, but knew that I loved you dearly.

"You are my darling brother," I thought to myself, "only it's stupid-silly— (you remember our childhood superlative?)—of you to be satisfied with this. Why in the world don't you ...?"

But the actual word escaped me; there was a gap where the right word should have been. The swift, fluttering effort to find it bore fruit afterwards only with the invention of "dip" and "dipping."

"Let's go!" I cried instead. "Let's go on!" It was the nearest I could come to the meaning of what I felt, but could not say. There was an abrupt and passionate vehemence in my voice; in my heart there was absolute conviction. Quietly, without looking up, you replied, "There are more over here," and continued to fill your basket. The rattle of the cones, as you tossed them in, came to me already from a distance.

"Yes, yes," I exclaimed excitedly, for I had the horror that you were missing an amazing opportunity, "but why stick in one place like this? It's awful. We can be anywhere—everywhere at once—doing everything!" I remember the frantic impossibility of finding words to express what I felt so sure of—"Come on, Dick! Come with me!"

Caught by something in my voice, perhaps, you stopped picking and looked up; there was a steady expression in your big blue eyes. You said nothing. I felt that you knew more than I did after all. You wished to restrain me, though at the same time you would have liked to "go."

I sprang up quickly, lest forgetfulness of the way should catch me.

"Anyhow," I cried, "I'm going—!"

And then I heard your solemn whisper: "Look out!" you said softly, "it's not allowed, you know. You mayn't be able to get back. They'll cry about you. Mother'll be in a state. Besides, you'll only miss all *this*—"

There was a catch in your voice and breath as you said it; you were eager and ready; you knew the way; but, for some wiser reason than I guessed, you thought it a mistake to go. I confused, I think, the real you and the other that picked fir-cones and objected. I hesitated for a fraction of a second, the merest fraction. At the same moment I saw Val watching us—watching me in particular—and the startled expression on *his* face decided me. For he was afraid. I realised his vanity, his self-importance, his ignorance; either he had never known, or had entirely forgotten; remembering nothing of this "other" state, he was a sham, unreal, supremely satisfied with himself and with his condition. "Oh, dear," I thought, "almost everybody's like that!" And I cried at the top of my voice, bursting with joy and confidence, "I'm off!"

Val gave a gasp, and shouted "Where?" And I wanted to reply, but had no time to get the words out; besides, the right words would not come.

"Look, Dickie! Look!" I cried happily. You smiled into my eyes, but said no word. And I went.

The effort, if effort there was at all, was of some interior and delicious kind that was familiar. It was not muscular, though it was accompanied by a certain tautening of the muscles about the heart and abdomen—a sensation of heat in the pit of the body—followed instantly by a complete and comforting relaxation. It seemed a species of inner determination; perfect assurance, absolute conviction made it possible and even easy. I had no doubt that I could "go." I knew. And there was joy in me beyond anything my words can possibly explain.

I went. It was a change of condition really, but the terms of physical motion describe it best. I went out gliding, as in those flying-dreams so many know, and the slight effort was due to the fact that I had forgotten how to exercise the power properly. As in the flying-dream, I now recovered this half-forgotten power. "I can do this again when I wake," thinks the dreamer. "I've remembered at last," I thought; "how jolly!" Had I then known Bergson's suggestion that the flying-dream is due to the feet being deprived of their customary support, I could have given him the lie. The flying-dream is a racial, but also an individual, memory of the means of transition to this other "state." It is supremely easy; only it must be recovered young, before Reason and excess of physical sensation obliterate instinctive knowledge of the method.

I went out gliding, gliding over the summer lawn. I looked down—down upon the fir-cones and the baskets, the cedar tops, the crescent flower-beds, the bushy horse-chestnut and its bulging shadow, the gravel drive, the squat, fore-shortened Manor House. All lay beneath me, curiously flat. You I saw clearly, I saw Val in a haze; and while you increased for me somehow, there was about Val that flat and meaningless quality, as of an empty shell almost, which touched the other objects also with unreality.

And the expression in *his* face I cannot forget: the staring eyes, the mouth wide open, the perspiration on the puckered forehead, the coat pulled out where the hat-cord tugged at it, and then the look of sheer amazement passing into terror, as he stretched his bare arms out, turned jerkily, as though the power of co-ordinating his movements were impaired, and ran headlong towards the house. He had no breath to scream, or possibly the sound did not reach me; for his attitude was a scream materialised. He disappeared. Yet not by going into the building; it was more a fading out, a dying away, as a reflection fades from a pool when the sun is hidden or a puff of wind obliterates it. He vanished into a depth. He was withdrawn from my consciousness. The phantom Val was all I knew. He was unreal.

With you, however, precisely the opposite took place; you became instantly more real. It seemed I knew you for the first time fully, and understood the reason for the deep tie between us. We both shared another, bigger, but quite different state. The little figure in alpaca overalls picking fir-cones was not really you at all. It was a phantom you. We now came together for the first time properly, or, as I felt it then, "we were together again—at last." There was union and the full, rapturous joy of union. The idea of being everywhere at once, of sharing everything, seemed amazingly justified.

I cannot say that you joined in my actual physical motion, that you definitely came with me on my gliding, sliding change. It was rather that when I arrived I found you already there; and "there" was a state we had both left temporarily, come down from, as it were, in order to pick fir-cones and do other little necessary things—little things, trivial and unimportant in themselves, yet the doing of which increased our value, our reality. Everybody in the world had similarly "come down," but the majority became so absorbed in the "little, trivial things" that they forgot. Father, for instance, though he went to church as regularly as to the Treasury where he worked, had not the least idea—he denied that there could be a way back at all. And this was why everyone said No so often and so loudly. The important thing was to continue picking fir-cones as long as possible and as many as possible. Whatever enfeebled or endangered the picking faculties must be prevented. Picking to fill one's basket, and to fill it first before anybody else, was the sole criterion of reality and a useful life. Church and the Treasury were both, to father, a form of picking fir-cones, and any suggestion that reality lay in a different state was merely stupid-silly. This flashed into me as clearly as the meaning of cake and jam at tea-time....

We were properly together, anyhow, you and I, and the joy was wonderful; but not only was I properly with you, for I was in everything everywhere, not stuck in one spot any more, but able to do anything everywhere at once. I had this power, this rapture.... At the same time, *you* understood, apparently, that picking cones on a single spot, and so forth, was worth doing, and worth doing well. It was not to be shirked by any means. We picked experience while we did so, experience that was carried over and stored up in our "other" state, making us more real, and our eventual happiness even more complete. This, too, was very clear to me, simple, easy, and overwhelmingly convincing.

"We mustn't stay too long," you said at once. "They'll be frightened, you see. Besides"—and you laughed happily, as though you referred to a brief, almost an instantaneous interlude—"we want to finish, don't we? Let's get it done. Then we can be together ..."

There was more I cannot remember, but what I do remember with vividness is the feeling of deep, lasting joy that accompanied your phrase, "then we can *be* together." For it involved everything that those who love, yet fear separation, most ardently desire—complete and permanent union. I was too young, of course, in those days to have realised death, yet I saw clearly as in brilliant sunshine that death, where love is, meant only the transition into this other "state" where separation was not even a possibility. It was, I suppose, my first experience of a spiritual value. The meaning of *Now* was shown to me.

But another thing was also clear: Val had looked on death, or on what he thought was death. For him the only reality was picking fir-cones, and the Val that picked them was the only Val he knew. He had "forgotten" everything. Thinking I was dead, he experienced the nameless terror that is the bogey of his kind—of those who have forgotten.

▌▌▌

I found myself in bed. There was a darkened room full of soft rustling and whispering. Busy figures moved to and fro on tiptoe like ghosts amid a general sense of hush. Mother and nurse were bending over me. There was a cold sponge and a feeling of anxiety and awe. I felt this anxiety, this awe, this fear, but I wanted to laugh; I could not understand this peculiar atmosphere of dread. It was unnecessary humbug. I could have screamed. A yearning sadness next came over me. Then I laughed. And the laughter brought relief, although it frightened the others. Afterwards—long afterwards—it was reported that I hung between life and death. Isn't that delicious? A comic statement—the sort of thing a grub might say about a chrysalis: it hung between life and death before it emerged and flew as a butterfly! ... A hand stroked my forehead, I knew half-sensations.

Of these half-sensations I was uncomfortably aware. With an effort I had come back, I was shut in again, enclosed, confined in something that had the pain of limitation, yet of limitation that was somewhere valuable. The truth was I had forgotten again, or was beginning to forget, and hence the half-sensations.... They explained presently that I had fainted in the sun; "a touch of sun," they called it; and when I laughed at this the cold sponge descended on my neck and forehead and the whispers multiplied.

"Lie quite still, my darling, quite, quite still. Do not excite yourself. You're safe at home, and Mummie's looking after you!"

It never occurred to them that I might have looked after Mummie.

It was marvellously sweet and tender, but O, how futile and how ignorant! I knew so much; I could tell so little—nothing and less than nothing. I had come back, I was caught again. They could not know, because they had "forgotten." At last the cold sponge ceased descending on my neck and forehead; I fell asleep; and when I woke again the curtains were drawn back and the sun poured over the room. "That's real, at any rate," I remember thinking, as I felt the warmth upon my skin. The light made me happy, though I knew not exactly why.

I recovered very quickly. It had been something of a false alarm apparently. There were no ill results, although hourly warnings about the sun continued for a long time, and Val was afraid of me for the rest of the holidays. "I thought you were dead," was all he said. "I saw you tumble down flat, you know." He was white as he spoke of it. "Once I saw a chap fall on his head from the parallel bars and kill himself," he added. "By Jove, you know—it's awful," Having looked on death, he was afraid of life.

What *you* thought and felt you never said. You were a solemn little owl. Our love seemed more near and understanding than before. I date our realisation of it from that time, at any rate. But, also, from that moment I knew another thing that lay at the back of my brain; I knew it subconsciously perhaps without explanation or analysis. What one knows and believes subconsciously affects all one does in a natural, instinctive way, whereas what one reasons out is a matter of calculation—one is for ever persuading oneself that it is true. This thing I now knew was, perhaps, that daily life was but an interlude of no real duration in a bigger but a different matter, and that death simply closed the interlude—if a state without duration can be said to have an end. My intense desire for things to be "quite otherwise" was actually a memory therefore, true and deep, yet hidden with extraordinary care behind my brain. My true self was not involved with this fir-cone picking business except to watch it and be wise; it dwelt apart, detached from good and evil, so-called; it was everywhere and for ever. It was my "otherwise." To be identified with it meant to know peace and joy and those indescribable states which are of the spirit and of eternity, but to know them *Now*. To forget—as Val forgot it—meant to be unreal. As a dream of ten seconds may seem indefinitely prolonged, so it was with daily life. At the close of the dream the sleeper wakes and says: "Is that all?" The dream has been an interlude without duration.

Although I can give no further details of what I experienced after I went out gliding, I remembered it for a long time with happy wonder. The tang of its unforgettable ecstasy came back with me. I had known power, sweetness, joy; it was complete and satisfying; I had been everywhere, dipped and merged in everything; and you were with me. Young as I was, I realised this great completeness. "It was all right," as I said to you; and the phrase seems to me now significant: *all* and *right*…. My yearning to be "otherwise" had been justified. I *had* been otherwise. I had been dipped, then come up to the surface again. And I remember saying this to you, wondering at your owl-like silence, although you knew far more about it all than I did, and then your remark at the end: "Yes. It's all right, but I vote we stay down for a bit all the same. I think we've got to—don't you see?"

Then, gradually, as we grew older, the memory of the experience faded and grew dim. At school it became heavily obscured, at Sandhurst I forgot it. I did not forget the experience, that is, but I forgot the feelings that accompanied it. I could not reconstruct those feelings; I did not even wish to.... Only much later, with the thrill and the opening of the heart by beauty, did the *feelings* partially return to me....

I know now, of course, that it is possible to pick fir-cones on the surface, yet to dip and be otherwise, simultaneously; that this, in fact, is really living. Picking fir-cones helps to build empires, but builds the empire of oneself as well; it is human and necessary, whereas "dipping" is exceptional and divine. Everybody wants to be dipped, yet knows not how to achieve it. Being afraid of death, they are afraid of life—afraid to live. They think that picking fir-cones is the way. They have "forgotten." For, instead, it is the *way* they pick fir-cones that is the Way!

The Open Window

The bungalow stood in some twenty acres. Three hundred yards away, across the field, ran the dense belt of woods—oak, chestnut, larch—that closed the view to the south, but kept the house so delightfully shut in. This belt, a hundred yards deep, with undergrowth of thick holly, formed a wall none could look over, the bungalow nestling, so to speak, within its encircling arm of leaves. A track meandered through it lengthwise, but there was no straight way across to the path that ran along its outer edge, linking the village to the church. Beyond it lay the common, wild with gorse and scattered pines, rising to the deep Sussex sky....

The owners, imaginative folk, having lived there ten years without moving, were proud of The Wood: "It keeps us so private, you see. No one can look through at us. It's so protective." Wild horses could not have dragged them from this bit of rural England that was "so private … so protected by our belt of woods ..." whose effect, indeed, pervaded even one's outlook upon life—the great life outside, beyond. The mind dwelt securely under that "protection." One's very ideas were screened and sheltered from the big winds that blow.

From the bungalow verandah it rose with fine dignity against the sky; no gleam pierced its impenetrable tangle. The crowding holly saw to that. The dogs hunted in it, the children picked firewood, the little pigs and chickens sometimes got lost in its depths, but its only real inhabitants were grey squirrels, a pair of wood-peckers, and a dozen screaming jays. And on windy nights it roared like the surf against some lonely island shores.... "It's the making of the place, *we* think"—the guests who came and went invariably in agreement. "Rather!" they said. "You're so nice and cozy behind it, aren't you? You can't see through." Then one adventurous and tactless fellow changed the formula, offering a new, upsetting point of view: "But you can't see through it anywhere, can you?"

"No—rather not," the owners assured him.

"Not even a bit of light—of sky—a glimpse of the horizon beyond?"

There was a silence. "What d'you mean?" they asked. His suggestion seemed almost rude. Then, shading his eyes with one hand, the fellow added the words that seemed so unnecessary: "I mean—you can't see—*out!*" And the fat was in the fire.

He didn't stay long, this adventurous guest, being, it seemed, of a roving disposition, an uncomfortable man accustomed to open spaces. The wide seas and the mountains called him. And grey dawns saw his "camp-fires in the rain" sort of person, who mentioned before he left that

> Even the mighty winds that range the seas
> In water-spouts, typhoons, and hurricanes
> Begin by chasing leaves down window-panes.

An unsettling creature, on the whole, with his travel talk, and in his eyes that long-distance look which tells of great horizons, wild, free winds, and the mystery of stars in lonely places. Moreover, he was "uncomfortable" to his hosts, too, because, in their otherwise delightful bungalow, he had an air of being somehow caught, imprisoned, trapped, while it was not, they perceived, the walls and roof that did this, but the encircling wood they thought so protective and so nice. "You can't see *out!*" It was so unnecessary, but there it was. The seed was sown....

There stole upon them gradually, insidiously, from that moment a strange new restlessness. For they were imaginative folk. It was queer but undeniable. Curse the fellow! "A bit of light," indeed! "A glimpse of the horizon," forsooth! ... They hid it from one another; they scoffed openly, ignored, tried to hold firm against such disturbing, dangerous ideas. They fortified themselves by combined resistance. But—well, there it was! The seed grew horribly. Why did both lawn and garden seem darker now than formerly? Why did thought travel in odd moments far afield? Why did the husband sometimes surprise his wife with dreaming eyes, and she catch him once or twice with that new, that awful expression, which meant—only too plainly desire to escape? It was most upsetting. Those gaudy books, too, from the Library, illustrated, of course ... and a faint suggestion—it was quite absurd!—that there was less air about, almost a hint of suffocation on windless days, as though the view from the south windows were now small, suddenly, and limited. "Did *you* order this, Maud?" fingering the yellow volume. "No, but I thought you might like to glance at it, dear." The Marquesas, she remembered, were at a safe distance, but the gipsies camped upon the common, with their gleaming fires, their tents, their sweet blue smoke, and the yellow gorse hung ever shining to an open sky....

Imagination is a wicked phagocyte, whose poison works apace beneath dull skies. Leaden days suggest pictures of blue seas and golden sunsets to the heart. The trees turned red and yellow, the smoke of burning leaves hung over the lawn, the shortening days and slanting sunlight laid the melancholy of autumn over the quiet place. But some nights the winds were loose.... Once she heard him mumbling: "Even the mighty winds that range the seas ..." And then, one still November morning, very early, a sound on the paved garden below her window led to a full betrayal. For there he was, in pyjamas and dressing-gown, marking an arrow on the stones. She drew back, catching her breath a little. That arrow pointed south towards the wood. "Oh, I was just taking a line," he explained at breakfast. "If we cut a little vista—oh, the *tiniest* little slit, of course—our windows would look—er—further." She watched his face. "We should see a bit of sky, I mean."

"Something quite informal," she offered, "a mere track?"

"Oh, dear me, yes," he agreed; "the merest little tiny glade that would let the light through, you know."

They did it themselves; no workmen helped; they chopped the trees, uprooted the holly, made great bonfires that crackled and clothed the garden with a sweet blue gipsy smoke. Bit by bit light sprinkled and peeped in ... and at last the great day came, a wild February morning with glad lengthening hours, when the sky was visible, the horizon beyond shone through. That night from the verandah they saw the gipsy fires gleam, they saw the moonlight's silver on the stems, and down the little vista thought travelled magically to mysterious, far horizons beneath other stars. In the daytime the south wind blew softly through, bringing her messages of blue seas, of flowers, of enchanted islands far away...

It was dusk when they saw the figure come towards them down the little winding glade, his outline just discernible against the fading sunset. "You!" they exclaimed. "Why, where in the world did you drop from?" He explained that he was staying in the neighborhood. He looked about him. "But—how splendid," he remarked casually. "It's twice the place it was. You can see out now! You've opened a window."

They begged him to stay the night. "We're off to Egypt," they explained, "in a few days." But he declined the offer. "My tent," he mentioned, "lies just out there," pointing through the glade towards the common, "I'm on the wander too. I must be pushing off.... But, I say—what a lovely place to—come back to!"

They watched his figure melting out into the darkening sky as he went silently down the glade, finally disappearing from view as though merged in the horizon.

Petershin and Mr. Snide

Petershin, a retired Insurance Surveyor, had always nursed a private terror that one day the night express would catch him on a level crossing, that his foot would get jammed between the rails, and that he would not have the courage to saw it off with his penknife.

This secret dread had haunted his mind since childhood.

Owing to circumstances that need no particular mention at the moment, he let out his secret one evening to a valued acquaintance. He spoke of it, in some detail, to John Snide, a book-seller in a small way and a publisher of occasional pamphlets, a married man of education and authority.

"Really, Petershin," observed Mr. Snide. "Now, that's very odd. It's a co-incidence, I might say. For, d'you know, now that you mention it, I may say I've always had a similar dread myself." He took off his glasses and wiped them thoughtfully.

"No," exclaimed Petershin with lively interest. "Have you really?"

He was relieved to find that his terror was not so peculiar after all that no one else could share it. Raising his eyebrows he listened attentively.

"I have, indeed," Mr. Snide assured his friend. "Only in my case"—he put his glasses on his nose and looked over them at his companion—"in my case, Petershin, there's—a difference." He was addressing, of course, an inferior fellow.

Both voice and manner betrayed a slight suggestion of superiority, as though it would hardly do to feel precisely what the other felt. Apparently, a shade more value had to be inserted.

Petershin accepted the slight rebuke. "A difference, Mr. Snide!" he echoed, as one whom a fellow-sympathy made intelligently understand-ing. That he was accustomed to keep his place was conveyed in the fa-miliar yet respectful "Mr."

"In my own case," resumed the other, nodding with what he might have called, had he been pressed, a "soupçon" of advantage, "the difference is, that, while my foot will be jammed somewhat as you describe, I shall have," he went on carelessly, "no penknife on me."

"Really! Now, if that isn't peculiar!" declared Petershin, where an infe-rior mind must have phrased it "Well—I'm damned!" He hoped he had suitably conveyed the admiration of his friend's courage.

Mr. Snide nodded with comfortable assurance, and the talk, thus begun, continued volubly for an hour or so, Mrs. Snide not being in the particu-lar building at the time....

Petershin liked Mr. Snide. He rather looked up to him as being a cultured man, learned in books, even something of a scholar. The way he quoted from authors proved this. He saw little of him, however, because he was afraid of Mrs. Snide, whom he considered "too particular." Once or twice he had gone into the shop, just a little before lunch time, and had invited Mr. Snide to join him in a few minutes' stroll, and Mrs. Snide had distinctly mentioned that it was inconvenient—"Gentlemen didn't go for a stroll just before meal-time—when it was raining." She had noticed, too, his celluloid collar, with a remark he did not quite catch, but an unfavourable remark, he felt sure; because, later, when Petershin advised Mr. Snide to use one, the latter said: "Yes, Petershin, they *are* practical, I admit, and a saving too, no doubt, but—er—the wife thinks they're not quite the thing for me, being—as I might say—among books, you see."

"*Reely* they don't catch fire," explained Petershin eagerly, not understanding at first what was meant. "There's not the smallest danger of that sort—"

"A man—the wife holds—is what he wears," Mr. Snide interrupted him.

From which moment Petershin despised and feared Mrs. Snide, realising that she was "too particular." The phrase, moreover, was obviously a quotation from some book, and a quotation from a great author invariably overwhelmed Petershin with a painful sense of his own inferiority, reducing him to an uncomfortable and admiring silence.

Mrs. Snide, Petershin had ascertained, disapproved of him for another reason than that of his external appearance, for her husband had been detained one night, getting home at 3 a.m., to be exact—and his explanation had not quite satisfied "the wife."

"Oh, I was out with an insurance man," he said. "A surveyor, my dear," he added, when pressed, "with Mr. Petershin, in fact."

That was all Mr. Snide said; but, apparently, his wife had said a good deal more. Mr. Snide had mentioned the matter to him afterwards—briefly. Wherefore it was that Petershin did not see as much of his friend as he would have liked to see, and was, in addition, rather afraid of Mrs. Snide.

The tendency to coincidence already mentioned continued, nevertheless, to bring the two acquaintances together by chance, finding both, as if by chance again, affected by a similar, or as Mr. Snide might have said, an identical emotion. This emotion they shared accordingly, exchanging confidences, as two intelligent men will when actuated by the same desire simultaneously. Yielding to Mrs. Snide's disapproval, however, they were cautious in the matter of referring to these chance meetings afterwards— at least Mr. Snide was, being a tactful and experienced man. Nor again, respecting Mrs. Snide's wishes, did they meet before a meal. Petershin no longer called at the shop just before luncheon for a little stroll. It was usually after dinner that the spirit of confidence brought one across the other's path.

These occasions began invariably with Petershin's saying invitingly:

"Now, here we are! And what's it going to be, Mr. Snide? Eh?"

They ended invariably with an observation from Mr. Snide—much later:

"Well—I'll be getting on, Petershin. Time slips away on rapid wing. The wife'll be expecting me," a glance at his friend's collar conveying the hint that its wearer was not expected to accompany him, and the quotation, if it were such, having its invariable effect,

One of these occasions, however, though inaugurated by Petershin's usual greeting, did not end quite according to formula, the reason being that Mrs. Snide had gone to the country to see her mother who was very ill, and had telegraphed that her return that night was uncertain: "Mother very gravely ill indeed may not be back to-night. Ada."

"Dear me," offered Petershin, by way of sympathy. "Worse, is she?"

"Much worse, yes, apparently," replied Mr. Snide. "In fact, I might say, dying."

"Dear me, dear me!" repeated the other, his voice lower, his eyebrows higher. "Is she *reely?*"

"I'm afraid so," was Mr. Snide's considered opinion, given slowly and repeated for the sake of emphasis. "I'm afraid she is." He reflected a moment, idly fingering a glass that happened to be near his hand, then adding as a result of his reflection: "I might say I'm sure of it." And immediately thereafter, before his friend could offer anything further by way of condolence, he brushed the entire matter from his mind with a free gesture of the hand and elbow, and invited Petershin to join him in the discussion of the various interests they possessed in common.

"For why meet trouble half-way?" he added, as an afterthought. "A wise man should float above sorrow and keep his head well above water always."

"Say when," Petershin interrupted, happening to be pouring out some water at the moment.

"And that's courage, it seems to me?" the other finished his sentence, ignoring the interruption, though quickly holding up two fingers in an absent-minded yet peremptory manner.

"It is indeed," concurred Petershin sympathetically, and with a touch of respect due to his persuasion that he had listened to a quotation from some famous author. "That *is* courage, yes," he repeated, adding with a slight inconsequence, "Here's *to* you, sir!"

Whereupon the conversation led easily into exchanges of a personal, even of a confidential nature, the two friends being evidently in a chatty and exuberant mood that favoured such intimate exchanges.

Outside, the weather was cold and dreary, a bitter wind from the north threatening snow. Darkness had fallen, as with a clap of suddenness, before its time. It was inclement weather, as Mr. Snide might have said, or, as Petershin in other company would have described it—filthy. Unfavourable, anyhow, each felt in his own particular way, to Mrs. Snide's mother.

"No weather for an invalid, Mr. Snide, this—is it?" was what Petershin remarked, to which the other replied briefly but with energy, indeed, with gusto, as he might have said—"dangerous, I call it dangerous."

Both references, it is seen, were indirect; an allusion of sympathy to the illness, each felt, was proper and desirable, while yet it need not detain them. There were other matters to discuss.... The sense of leisure was pleasant, the warmth of the room was comfortable, each man found the other's conversation stimulating. Ideas certainly flowed. The hours slipped easily away....

It was Petershin who made the first move to leave: "You'll be getting anxious, Mr. Snide," he observed. "I mushtn't keep you up." He crossed cautiously to the window and, wiping the moisture off with the curtain, peered out into the night. "Shnowing, by gad!" he exclaimed. "Shnowing thickanfasht!" His manner held an unaccustomed dignity. It was a stiff, exaggerated dignity.

Behind his back Mr. Snide, first looking at his watch, replied easily, as one who is master of circumstances, "Not a bit, Petershin. Be an optimist, my lad. Those whom the gods love die young—"

"But, I tell you it *is*," interrupted Petershin brusquely, thinking his veracity was called in question. "Evershing's white already. The air's thick with it. Like a Chrismhascard." Then, returning to his seat, he caught his companion's powerful eye fixed on him. "Mr. Shnide," he added, with an effort, "beg pardon, but it izsch—reely."

He sat down, fumbling with his watch. He did not want a disagreement with his superior friend. He made no further comment.

"The nightsh still young," Mr. Snide mentioned presently. "Let it snow. Wha'dowe care, Pee'shin?"

And they chatted on for another timeless interval....

"Shtill snowing, I igspec'," Petershin offered in the middle of something Mr. Snide was saying with great deliberation. He had not gone to the window to look. It was merely that Mr. Snide had been talking for a very long time about a "sosh'listic pamphlet" he was publishing, and that he, Petershin, had the impression it was time for him to say something by way of comment. Only, not having listened attentively, he could find no "reely" intelligent comment.

Mr. Snide paused, glowering heavily at him.

"To hell withyer shnow," he said angrily. "You've not been lis'ning to what

I washayin." And before Petershin could find a tactful answer by way of soothing him, Mr. Snide looked at his watch, rose from his chair, stood for a moment hesitating, and then abruptly sat down again, a broad smile upon his face.

"Pe'ershin, my boy, the night is young," he said with the emphasis of one who knows. His momentary annoyance was quite forgotten. "Time wearsh along but the night, I shure you, ish still young. And Mrs. Shnide is far from—far from 'ome."

Petershin agreed with a nod. It was partly a quotation.

An hour later, when they rose to take their leave (as Mr. Snide might have said, but did not actually say), the driving snow was so thick in their faces and upon the ground that Mr. Snide, catching his companion by the arm with delightful friendliness, observed:

"We'll take zhe shor'cut. Thaswashwe'll do. An' you come to my placesh. Accept my hospital'ty for the night. I'll put you up, Pe'shin. She's probly dead. Sh'll right, old boy. The godsh love thoshwho die young."

"No thanksh," Petershin replied with dignity, "prefer to be excushed," but, perhaps yielding to the spell of the quotation about the gods, he accompanied Mr. Snide forthwith arm in arm, into the inclement snowstorm.

It was what Snide might have called "reely a heavy storm." Thick snow swirled about them, drove into their faces, plastered their clothes with big clinging flakes, so that in five minutes they were white from head to foot. They panted with effort. It was no time for speech. Petershin, blindly confident in his friend's leadership, ploughed forward heavily. No other pedestrians were out on such a night. They passed no single person, and the snow lay six inches deep upon the ground. It was the wind, of course, that made them sway.

To Mr. Snide first occurred the idea of calling a halt to recover breath; he accompanied the action with an observation of some violence which his companion did not quite catch.

"Pardon?" bawled Petershin, looking up a second into a red face whose eyebrows and moustache were hung with white dripping flakes.

"Thisis an orspishcashun," roared Mr. Snide, but again the words were whirled from his lips by the tremendous wind. He stood with his back to the gusts, Petershin facing him.

"Can't hear wotyoushay," yelled the latter, and then turned his back to the storm. He now stood sideways to his friend, and being sheltered a little he glanced up and repeated very loudly "What?"

Mr. Snide roared back at him: "I only said orspishcashun"—the wind again whipped the syllables into space, while at the same time it upset his balance a trifle, so that he reeled slightly towards his companion. They collided, in fact, though speedily separating themselves again and standing upright.

"Ver' sorry," screamed Petershin, still anxious to hear what the lost sentence was, but feeling the fault lay with himself. "Aw fly sorry, but I didn't qui' hear." He glanced up at the same time, and the red face he saw, plastered with wet snow, the hat crooked and the end of a necktie sticking up through the coat collar towards the mouth, made such a funny picture that he burst suddenly into a spasm of uncontrollable laughter.

"Woshthematter, you idjiut?" cried Mr. Snide, suddenly angry. "I only said that was an"—he articulated very clearly, roaring his syllables against the storm—"orspishush'cashun. What the devil—"

Petershin's laughter died away on the instant. "Oh," he yelled back. "Pardon me, Mr. Snide. Awspishush'casion, yes. So it is. Qui' right, of course." It cost him a prodigious effort, but the words, despite the wicked wind, rang true and clear.

"Tha's woshIsaid," came back the angry roar. "Why don' you liss'n?"

Petershin, crestfallen and ashamed, tried to pull himself together, and as the mental effort involved also the physical effort of standing erect, he was surprised to find that there was something the matter with his feet. With one foot, that is. The left foot refused to follow the right. Mr. Snide, he became aware, was standing on it. It was an awkward moment. He did not quite like to mention it, but neither did he quite like to push Mr. Snide away. He wriggled. Nothing happened. Again he wriggled—furiously. It was no good. Mr. Snide was firmly planted apparently on his left foot. Petershin, still wriggling, was in the act of losing his balance altogether, when suddenly his companion stepped aside with a curiously unnatural movement. A clear space of two feet now lay between the two men; Mr. Snide could not possibly still be standing on his companion's left foot and yet that left foot would not budge.

Petershin struggled. Mr. Snide, he perceived, was struggling too. Each man, apparently, was making violent efforts to extricate his foot from the clutch of deep snow that somehow held it. Each had one leg stretched out stiff and straight at an awkward angle that provided leverage. But Petershin was the first to realise what had happened. He was the first to put it into words at any rate:

"Me foo's cau'," he gasped.

At the same moment both men lost their balance and fell sideways into a deep white drift.

Petershin, again, was the first to pick himself up—into a sitting position. He brushed the snow violently from his person. Immediately opposite to him, about three feet away, he stared into a red face with glaring, bloodshot eyes, cheeks, moustache and eyebrows caked with white, necktie askew, and one arm gesticulating vehemently in the air. For a second the impulse to burst out laughing was very strong, for Mr. Snide's appearance was grotesque beyond description. The same instant, however, the laughter died away in his throat. His friend was bawling something at him. The words were thick—with snow and wind. They horrified him:

"Me foo's cau' too! We're on the ra'way track! God shave us!"

The dreadful situation produced one immediate effort—both men found their mother tongue and were able to use it without difficulty, and simultaneously. They recovered their lost distinctness of utterance. Mr. Snide in particular, having the louder voice of the two, dropped his pose of quoting from better minds than his own, and became at once natural and sincere:

"You damned idjiut," he roared. "What possessed you to ta' the shor' cu' on a night like this?" He stood upright again, after a tremendous struggle. He shook his fist, lost his balance in doing so, and collapsed again into the snow, still shouting as he floundered.

"*You* led me into this," Petershin was shouting simultaneously. "It was *your* damfool s'gesstion."

Then he collapsed beside him and, like two violent turkeys beating furious wings, or two veterans in a three-legged race with ankles fastened together, they made the snow fly in all directions, pulling vainly at each other in their attempts to rise, roaring imprecations while they did so. It was a grotesque and painful sight. Breathless at last, with right hands clasped for a final pull, arms taut and shoulders braced there came a pause.

"Now," cried Mr. Snide. "Are you ready? One, two, and—away!"

They rose together as though a spring released them. Facing each other in a standing position, as if they were shaking hands, Petershin then turned his head sideways a moment and listened. A sound came to him that was not the wind.

"Snide!" he screamed. "It's the ni' express!"

"And me foo'sstill cau'!" both roared in the same breath.

In the distance was a faint glimmer of reddish light just visible through the driving flakes. It was growing larger, brighter. There was a deep sound like thunder. It was growing every second louder. And, without a word at first, both figures stooped, bent double, fumbling at their feet with frozen fingers that were all thumbs.

"Lend me yo' penknife," both shouted frantically together.

"Lef' it at home," bawled two minds with but a single thought.

"Got a match?" yelled Snide. "Li' it at once. Li' a bit o' paper, can't you?" Petershin did not answer. Not even an oil-can could have burned in such a wind.

"Cut the laces!" It was Petershin's generous idea. He suddenly shoved an open penkife at his friend, as though he wished to stab him.

"Good man!" Snide seized it and made frantic slashes at his imprisoned boot.

"Hurry up, for God's sake! Haven't done me own yet!" from Petershin.

The red light had come much closer, the roar of the approaching train already shook the ground and made the metals tremble.

"Lemme do it for you," bawled Snide. "I'm free!" He leant over, he bent himself double, his arm was stretched towards his friend's boot, but in the attempt he lost his balance and fell   outwards, away from the

track. At the same instant, when the awful engine was not ten yards from where he had been standing, Petershin, making a desperate wrench of final, superhuman, almost acrobatic violence, extricated his own foot too. The wind from the engine flung him with violence against Mr. Snide's prostrate body. His foot had torn loose, leaving the boot tight in the rails beneath the thundering wheels. It was an effort that would have surprised an osteopath.

The night express, oblivious of two human hearts within an inch of its flying mass, roared past into the darkness and, light, thunder, rattle, bulk and all, was lost in the storm. The wind and the driving snowflakes resumed their unchallenged occupancy of the night.

"Get orf of me, you lout!" was the first sound audible, after the bang and clatter were gone. It was Mr. Snide's voice, muffled by something that impeded clear utterance. A big, white, shapeless substance rolled slowly to one side—and Petershin stood up.

"It passed right over us—I do believe," he gasped. "Are we alive?" He felt himself over. A second shapeless white mass rose gradually beside him. "*I* am," it shouted. "But no thanks to you!"

From the path of a slow-moving luggage train on the other track where they were now standing, they moved shakily aside. The great, endless thing went lumbering past them with convulsions, jolting and shuddering, the enormous tarpaulins over the piled-up freight looking like white mammoths galloping on short legs and with hidden heads, back to the shelter of their primeval forests.

The two men watched it slowly vanish. For a long time neither spoke a word. The appalling fate they had escaped left them half-stunned.

"Have you done with my penknife—Mr. Snide?" Petershin enquired presently, shouting as usual to make himself heard. Mr. Snide replied that he had and added "Thank you" while a search for the knife began, ending some minutes later by its being discovered still tightly clasped in the right hand of the man whose life it had undoubtedly saved.

"With many thanks," repeated Mr. Snide, more composedly now. He handed over the object with a mixture of carelessness and *empressement* in his manner.

"Don't mention it, please," said Petershin. Both men were very shaky still. Indeed, they were trembling. But recovery was on the way.

The search for two boots then followed. Of these, however, little remained beyond the soles and some scraps of frayed laces. Wearing these sandal-wise, and complainingly bitterly of the cold, the two friends eventually resumed their journey arm-in-arm. They spoke little.

"I—er—should like to say thank you," repeated Mr. Snide, as they presently reached the comparative shelter of the houses. "Your knife—the loan of it—was a great help to me. So small a thing can change the waysh of fate! Indeed, I might say—"

"Oh, please. It's nothing, Mr. Snide," interrupted Petershin. "Only too glad I had it with me—after all."

"I might say," continued the other, ignoring the interruption, "that it saved my life." He pressed his friend's hand, as they reached the door. A lump rose in Petershin's throat. He was not far from tears. The proximity of the forbidden door, however, exercised a sobering effect. Mrs. Snide, of course, might have returned, he reflected. He paused inside the iron garden gate, then made a move as though to go.

"One minute," enjoined Mr. Snide, observing his hesitation, but sympathetically. "Allow me," he added in the tone of a host, as he passed in front and inserted his latchkey with some difficulty. The proprietor pushed open his faded blue door and turned up the light in the little hall. His sandal had slipped off, but he did not notice it perhaps, as he moved on tiptoe to the table below the hat-rack where a telegram was visible.

Petershin, watching him from the snowy step with anxious eyes, was not even aware that his left foot was freezing in the icy slush. He picked up his friend's lost sandal and laid it cautiously inside the passage.

"One minute," enjoined Mr. Snide, glancing back over his shoulder as a man who hesitates between authority and subservience. He opened the telegram.

"Ah!" he ejaculated, tapping it like an actor, then reading it again a little closer to the light. "It's or' ri'," he added, a happy smile spreading across his red face.

"I beg your pardon?" offered Petershin, choosing the longer form to gain time. Usually he was content with "pardon." He wished to make quite sure.

"It's or' ri', I said," repeated Mr. Snide briefly. "Come in, Pe'shin, come in, lad." He hung his hat up with an air.

Petershin advanced slowly into the forbidden hall. "Your wife, I trust—?" He meant to ask after the wife's mother, but his mind was a trifle confused, it seemed. "Everything's s'asfactry, I hope?" he faltered.

His host turned round and gazed at him, an expression of false gravity unable to mask the smile of genial hospitality that overpowered it.

"Qui' or' ri,' thank you," he replied. "Hang yer hat up!" He moved past and closed the door with a bang that echoed through the house and made

Petershin jump. "It's an inclement night. I'll get some shlippers."

"Thank you, thank you," murmured Petershin, shaking the snow from his hat, but still hesitating before he hung it up as bidden. "And your mother-in-law," he hastened to correct his little mistake. "I trust—"?

"It's or' ri', I've told you once," was the reply, given with some impatience. "She's dead. And my wife returns in the morning. Now, please make yourself at home, Pe'shin, my lad."

Petershin attempted a hasty calculation in his mind, but failed to arrive at a conclusion. Times, trains and distances were too involved for him at the moment. All he knew was that it was now somewhere about 3 o'clock in the morning.

"Come in and have a spot," Mr. Snide was saying pleasantly. "The mills of the godsh grind surely, but they grind uncommon slow. Those whom the godsh love die sooner or later. It's all ri'. I'll put the kettle on and find the slippers…. We'll have it hot."

And Petershin followed his friend into the dining-room. It was at this moment that a new sound became audible behind him. It was a sound that froze his blood. His host, Mr. Snide, had evidently not heard it, for he was just then occupied in pouring out whisky with a generous air into two glasses, and he continued the operation steadily enough. He did not jump, at any rate. But neither did Petershin jump—for the simple reason that he could not jump. He could not move at all. He experienced a total paralysis of all his muscles. Tongue, legs, arms, head, all were held motionless in a vice of terror. Petershin was petrified, for the sound that thus turned him into stone was a voice—the voice of Mrs. Snide:

"Is that you, Richard Snide?" she asked, as she came slowly down the stairs towards the hall.

No answer was forthcoming; the question, with a slight change in the wording that rendered it doubly awful, was repeated:

"Then it *is* you, Richard Snide?"

Petershin, still unable to move a muscle, was aware that the speaker now stood close behind him. She could see his celluoid collar. He could not turn his head, even had he dared. An acute anguish twisted his very entrails. His position became suddenly more than he could bear, so that he made an effort of supreme violence, even though he felt it might burst his heart: he tried to run.

The result was suffocating. He could not breathe properly. A second later he could not breathe at all. God! He was going to die! An awful yell for help escaped him, though meant at the same time to warn his companion. Mr. Snide, to his intense relief, looked round.

The red face was tilted back a little, as its owner poured into his mouth the contents of his glass, and a moment or two later rose in an oddly laborious way and remarked solemnly:

"Pe'shin, me lad, you've had 'nough—more than 'nough, I might say. You've slept past closing time and your cell'ioid collar's choking you...."

"Pe'shin, me lad, you've had 'nough—more than 'nough, I might say. You've slept past closing time and your cell'ioid collar's choking you...."

The Man Who Was Milligan

Milligan looked round the dingy rooms with an appraising air, while the landlady stood behind him, wondering whether he would decide to take them. She stood with her arms crossed; her eye was observant. She, in her turn, was appraising Milligan, of course. He was a clerk in a tourist agency, and in his spare time he wrote stories for the cinema. What attracted him just now in the very ordinary lodgings was the big folding-doors. All he really needed was a bed-sitting-room, with breakfast, but he suddenly saw himself sitting in that front room writing his scenarios—successfully at last. It was rather tempting. He would be a literary man—with a study!

"Your price seems a trifle high, Mrs.—er—?" he opened the bargain.

"Bostock, sir, Mrs. Bostock," she informed him, then recited her tale of woe about the high cost of living. It was unnecessary recitation, for Milligan was not listening, having already decided in his mind to take the rooms.

While Mrs. Bostock droned monotonously on, his eye fell casually upon a picture that hung above the plush mantelpiece—a Chinese scene showing a man in a boat upon a little lake. He glanced at it, no more than that. It was better than glancing at Mrs. Bostock. The landlady, however, instantly caught that glance and noticed its direction.

"Me 'usband"—she switched off her main theme—"brought it 'ome from China. From Hong-Kong, I *should* say." And the way she aspirated the "H" in Hong made Milligan smile. He perceived that she was proud of the picture evidently.

"It's wonderful," he said. "Probably it's worth something, too. These Chinese drawings—some of 'em—are very rare, I believe."

The little picture was worth perhaps two shillings and he knew it; but he had found his way to Mrs. Bostock's heart, and, incidentally, had persuaded her to take a shilling off the rent. The picture, he felt sure, had been stolen by her late husband, a sea captain. To her it was a kind of nest-egg. If she ever found herself in difficulties, it would fetch money. Milligan, by chance, had stumbled upon what he called a "good line."

Being an honest creature, he had no wish to use his knowledge, but every week thereafter, almost every day, indeed, some remark concerning the Chinese drawing passed between them: with the natural result that, while it bored him a good deal, he cultivated the theme, and in so doing gazed much and often at the Chinaman. That Celestial, sitting in the boat with his back to the room, rowing, rowing eternally across the placid lake without advancing, he came to know in every detail.

Every time Mrs. Bostock chatted with him, his eye wandered from her grimy visage to the drawing. He used it to end the chat with.

"I like your picture so much," he observed. "It's nice to live with." He put it straight, he flicked dust from the frame with his handkerchief. "It's so much better than these modern things. It's worth a bit—I dare say—"

It chanced, at the time, that Lafcadio Hearn, the writer about Japan, was in his mind. He had once arranged a successful trip to Japan for a client of his firm, and the client had made him a present of one of Hearn's strange and wonderful books. It was hardly in the line of Milligan's reading, for it had no "film value," and he had sold the book—a collection of Chinese stories—to a second-hand bookseller for a shilling. But he had glanced at it first, and a story in it had remained sharply in his mind: a story about a picture of a man in a boat. An observer, watching the picture, had seen the man move. The man actually began to row. Finally, the man rowed right out of the picture and into the place—a temple—where the observer stood.

Milligan thought it foolish, yet his memory retained the details vividly. They stuck in his head. The graphic description was realistic. Milligan caught himself thinking of it every time he met a Chinaman in the street, every time he sold a ticket to China or Japan. It rose, it flitted by, it vanished. The memory persisted. And the moment his eye first saw Mrs. Bostock's treasure over the plush mantelpiece, this vivid memory of Hearn's story had again risen, flitted by, and vanished. It betrayed its vitality, at any rate. Wonderful chap, that Hearn, thought Milligan.

All this was natural enough, without mystery, without a hint of anything queer or out of the ordinary. What was a little queer—it struck Milligan so, at any rate—was an idea that began to grow in him from the very first week of his tenancy.

"That *might* be the very drawing the fellow wrote about," occurred to him one night as he laboured at a lurid scenario which was to make his fortune. "Not impossible at all. It's an old picture probably. Exactly what Hearn described, too, I wonder! Why not?"

Why not, indeed? A fellow—especially a literary fellow—should use his imagination. Milligan used his. Sometimes he used it in prolonged labour till the early hours. The gas-light flickered across his pages, across that lake in China, across the boat, across the back and arms and pigtail of that diminutive Chink who rowed eternally over a placid Chinese lake without advancing an inch. The scenario of the moment brought in China, aptly enough. A glance at the picture, he found, was not unhelpful in the way of stimulating a flagging imagination.

Milligan glanced often. The gas-light was always flickering. Shadows were for ever shifting to and fro across Mrs. Bostock's worthless nest-egg. It was easy to imagine that the boat, the water, even the figure moved.

Those dancing shadows! How they played about the arms, the back, the outline of the boat, the oars!

And when it was two in the morning, and the London streets lay hushed, and a great stillness blanketed the whole city, Milligan felt even a little thrilled. It was, he thought, "imaginative," to catch these slight, elusive movements in the drawing. He imagined the fellow rowing about, changing his position, landing. It helped his own mood, his incidents, his atmosphere. He had read Thomas Burke, of course. His scenarios always referred to Chinamen as "Chinks."

"That Chink's alive!" he whispered to himself. "By Jove! He moves in the picture. His place changes. It's an inspiration. I must use it somehow—!" And imagination, eerily stimulated in the deep silence of the sleeping city, was at work again.

This was the beginning of the strange adventure which befell the literary Milligan, whose imagination worked in the stillness of the small hours, but whose scenarios were never used.

"For why write scenarios," he said to me, "when you can *live* them?"

In Peking, ten or twelve years later, he said this to me, and I am probably the only person to whom this scenario he "lived" was ever confided.

In Peking his name was not Milligan at all. He was not working in a tourist agency. He was a rich man, aged thirty-eight, a "figure" in the English community there, a man of influence and position. But all that does not matter. What matters is the story of how he came to be in China at all—and this he does not know. He does not know how he came to be in China at all. There is no recollection of the journey even. Nor can he state precisely how he began the speculations and enterprises that made him prosperous, beyond that he suddenly found himself concerned in big, fortunate undertakings in the Chinese city.

There is this deep gap in the years.

"Loss of memory, I suppose they call it," he mentioned, after our chance acquaintanceship had grown into a friendship that gave me his confidence. What he *could* tell he told me frankly and without reserve, glad to talk of it, I think, to someone who did not mock, and making no condition of secrecy, moreover.

There was some link, apparently, between myself and the man who had been Milligan. Chance, that some call destiny, revealed it. And, as I listened to his amazing tale, I swore that on my return to London I would visit Mrs. Bostock and buy the picture. I wanted that Chinese drawing badly. I wanted to examine it myself. Her nest-egg at last should be worth something, as Milligan, ten years before, had told her.

What happened was, apparently, as follows: Milligan, first of all, discovered in himself, somewhat suddenly it seemed, a new interest in China and things Chinese. If the birth of this interest was abrupt, its growth was extremely rapid. China fairly leapt at him. He read books, talked with travellers, studied the map, the history, the civilisation of China. The psychology of the Celestial race absorbed him. The subject obsessed him. He longed to go to China. It became a yearning that left him no peace day or night. In practical terms of time, money and opportunity, the journey was, of course, impossible. He lived on in London, but actually he lived already in China, for where a man's thought is there shall his consciousness be also.

All this I could readily understand, for others, similarly, have felt the call and spell of countries like Egypt, Africa, the desert. There was nothing incomprehensible nor peculiar in the fascination China exercised upon the imaginative Milligan. It was his business, moreover, to sell exciting tickets to travellers, and China happened to have fired his particular temperament. Natural enough!

Natural enough, too, that, through this, the picture in his lodgings should have acquired more meaning for him, and that he should have studied it more closely and more frequently. It was the only Chinese object he had within constant reach, and he told me at wearisome length how he knew every tiniest detail of the drawing, and how it became for him a kind of symbol, almost a kind of sacred symbol, upon which he focused his intense desires—frustrated desires. Wearisome, yes, until he reached a point in his story that suddenly galvanised my interest, so that I began to listen with uncommon, if a rather creepy, curiosity.

The picture, he informed me, altered. There was movement among its details that he already knew by heart.

"Movement!" he half-whispered to me, his eyes shining, a faint shudder running through his big body.

The sincerity of deep conviction with which he described what happened left a lasting impression on my mind. His words, his manner, conveyed the truth of a genuine experience. Hitherto only the back of the Chink's head had been visible. Then, one night, Milligan saw his profile. The face was turned. It now looked a little over the shoulder, and towards the room.

From this moment, though he never detected actual movement when it occurred, the alteration in the drawing was marked and rapid. The face retained its new position; the angle of the profile did not widen, but the position of oars and boat, the attitude of arms and back, their size as well, these now changed from day to day.

There was a dreadful rapidity about these changes. The figure of the Chink grew bigger; the boat grew bigger too. They were coming nearer. "I had the awful conviction," whispered the man who had been Milligan, "that they were coming—to fetch me. I used to get all of a sweat each time I saw the size and nearness grow. It was appalling, but also it was delightful somehow—"

I permitted myself a question: "Did your landlady notice it too?" I enquired, concealing my scepticism.

"Mrs. Bostock was ill in bed the whole time. She never came into the room once."

"The servant?" I persisted. "Or any of your friends?"

He hesitated. "The girl who did the room," he said honestly, "observed nothing. She gave notice suddenly without a reason. So did the next girl. I never asked them anything. As for my friends"—he smiled faintly—"I was too scared—to bring them in."

"You were afraid they might *not* see what you saw?"

He shrugged his shoulders. "It scared me," he repeated, looking past me towards the shuttered windows of his study where we sat.

The account he gave of it all made my flesh creep even in that bright Peking sunshine. He certainly described what he saw, or believed he saw, as, day after day, night after night, that Chink rowed his boat slowly, slowly, surely, surely, very gradually, but with remorseless purpose, nearer, nearer—and nearer. The lodger watched. He also waited.

"The man," he whispered, "was rowing into the room. It was his purpose to row into the room. He was *coming to fetch me.*" And he mopped his forehead at the thought of what had happened ten years ago.

Suddenly he leant forward.

"In the end," his thin voice rattled almost against my face, "he—did fetch me. I'm in that picture with him now. I'm not in China, as *you* think I am. This"—he tapped his chest, the chest of a successful business man—"is not me. I'm not Milligan. Milligan is in that picture with the Chink. He's in that boat. Sitting beside that Chink. Motionless. Being stared at by a succession of lodgers. Sitting in that stiff little boat. Very tiny. Not dead, but captive. Sitting without breath. Without feeling. Painted, yet alive. Caught on the surface of that placid Chinese lake until time or death dissolve the drawing—"

I thought he was going to faint, but, oddly enough, I did *not* think him merely mad. His mood, his crawling horror, his intense sincerity took me bodily into his own deep nightmare. He recovered quickly. He was a man who had himself always well in hand. He told me the end at once.

He had been to a dance and he came home tired, sober, having well enjoyed himself, it seems, about four in the morning. The time was early spring, and dawn was just giving faint signs of breaking, but the hall and passage of the house were still dark.

He entered his room and lit the gas, going at once to the mirror to have a look at himself. This was the first thing he did, he assured me, and in the mirror he saw, behind himself, the boat and the Chinaman, both of them—gigantic.

Gigantic was the word he used, though he used it, of course, relatively.

The Chinaman was standing in the room. He was in the lake in front of the plush mantelpiece. The wall was gone—there was a sort of hazy space. Close at the Chinaman's heels lay the boat, both oars resting sideways on the water, their heads still in the rowlocks. Water was up to his feet, to Milligan's feet, for he not only felt his shoes soaked through, but he also heard the lapping sound of diminutive wavelets on the "shore."

He gave a great sigh. No cry, either of terror or surprise, he said, escaped him. His only sound was this great sigh—of acceptance, of resignation, of a mind benumbed and yet secretly delighted. The big Chink beckoned, smiled, nodded his yellow face, retreating very slowly as he did so. And Milligan obeyed. He followed. He stepped into the boat. The Chink took up the oars, and rowed him slowly, very slowly, across the placid lake, into the picture and out of his familiar, known surroundings, rowed him slowly, very slowly, into the land of his heart's deep desire.

All the way home to England in the steamer this strangest of strange narratives haunted me. I still saw the man who was Milligan sitting in the study of his big, expensive house as he told it to me. His shrewd business brain had built that house; the fortune he had made provided the good lunch and cigars we had enjoyed together. From the moment of entering the boat his memory had remained a blank. Continuity of personality, though still, it seemed to me, rather uncertain somewhere, had revived only when he was already a rich man who had spent years in China. This big gap in the years remains.

In my mind lay every detail of the story; in my pocketbook lay the address of Mrs. Bostock's rooms. I prayed heaven she might still be living, even if aged and crumpled by ten more English winters.

I had arranged to cable "Milligan" at once; we had selected the very words I was to use: "Two figures in boat," or "One figure in boat." He asked for the message in these words. Fortune favoured me: I found the rooms; Mrs. Bostock was alive; the rooms were unoccupied; I looked over them; I saw—the picture.

Before visiting Mrs. Bostock, however, I had visited the newspaper files in the British Museum, and the "Disappearance of James Milligan" was there for all to read. Millions had evidently read it. It had been *the* news of the day. Columns of space were devoted to it; dozens of false clues were started; crime was suggested, of course. His disappearance was complete. Milligan was a case of "sunk without trace," with a vengeance.

It was in the dingy front room that I experienced what was perhaps the most vivid thrill of wonder life has ever given me. I stood, appraising the room as a would-be lodger. Behind me, her arms crossed, appraising me in turn just as she had appraised her former lodger of ten years ago, stood Mrs. Bostock. Probably I looked more prosperous than he had looked; her attitude, at any rate, was attentive to a fault. Why I should have trembled a little is hard to say, but self-control was certainly not as full as it might have been, for my voice shook a trifle as, at length, I drew her attention with calculated purpose to the picture above the plush mantelpiece. I praised it.

"Me 'usband brought it back from Hong-Kong," I heard her say.

My breath caught a little, so that there was a slight pause before I said the next thing. My voice went slightly husky.

"I have a collection of Chinese drawings," I mentioned. "If you cared to sell, perhaps—"

"Oh, many 'as wanted to buy it," she lied easily, hoping to increase its value.

I mentioned five pounds. I mentioned another figure too—the figure in the boat.

"That single figure," I explained in as calm a tone as I could muster, "is so good, you see. The Chinese artists never overcrowded their paintings. Now, if—instead of that single figure—there were two"—I moved closer to the picture, hoping she would follow—"the value," I went on, "would, of course, be less."

Mrs. Bostock had followed me. I had tempted her greed; I had tested her truth as well. We stood side by side immediately beneath the drawing. We examined it together.

At the mention of five pounds the woman had given a little gasp, jerking her body at the same time. Now, at such close quarters with the thing she hoped to sell me, her voice was dumb at first. At first. For a moment later a strange sound escaped her lips, a sound that was meant to be a cry, but only succeeded in being a wheezy struggle to get her breath. Her mouth opened wide, her eyes popped almost from her face. She staggered, recovered her balance by putting a hand on my arm for support, then stepped still nearer to the mantelpiece and thrust her head and shoulders close against the drawing. Her blind eyes peered. Her skin was already white.

"Two of 'em!" she exclaimed in a terrified whisper. "Two of 'em, so 'elp me, Gawd! And the other's *him!*"

I was ready to support. I had expected her to collapse perhaps. I felt rather like collapsing myself. She swayed, turning her horror-stricken countenance to mine.

"Mr. Milligan!" she screamed aloud, then, her voice returning in full volume: "It's Mr. Milligan. All this time that's where 'e's been. And I never noticed it till now!"

She swooned away.

The second figure faced the room, for the boat was in the position of being pushed by the oars, not rowed. The features were unmistakable.... Half an hour later I sent a cable to Peking: "*Two figures in boat.*"

The real climax, I think, came three days later, when, with the picture safely in my rooms, I had arranged for "specialists" to call and examine it. A chemist, an experienced dealer, and a sort of expert psychic investigator were already upstairs when I reached my flat.

The picture was in my bedroom. I had examined it myself—examined Milligan's face and figure—hour after hour, my flesh crawling, my hair almost rising, as I did so. My guests were in the sitting-room, the servant informed me, handing me a telegram as I hurried up in the lift. My three friends were already known to each other, and, after apologising for the delay, I brought in the drawing and laid it before them on the small table. I intended to tell them the story after their examination; the psychic investigator I meant to keep when the other two had left. Setting the drawing in front of them, I looked over their shoulders at it.

There was only one figure—the Chink. He sat alone in the little boat. He was rowing, not pushing; his back was to the room.

The dealer said the drawing was worth a shilling; the chemist said nothing; I, too, said nothing; but the psychic investigator turned sharply and complained that I was hurting him. My hand, it seems, had clutched the shoulder nearest to me, and it happened to be his. I allowed him to leave when the other two left....

I was alone. I remembered the telegram. More to steady my mind than for any interest I felt in it, my fingers tore it open. It was a cablegram from—Peking, signed by a friend of Milligan and myself:

"Milligan died heart failure yesterday."

The Falling Glass

The preparations were so interesting and suggestive that they almost compensated for the temporary loss of our expedition. For three days the calm and cloudless sky pretended that bad weather had left the world for ever. This sunny peace, this heaven without a stain, surely must always be. Our peak ran sharp and still into the spotless blue, looking as though it never could be otherwise. Its serene majesty seemed unassailable by any troubling thing, by weather least of all. Then, just when our security was greatest and we had resolved to start next day at dawn, my companion came in to supper, with the ominous remark: "The glass has begun to fall a bit." This, for us, was the beginning of the change, the first *we* knew of it; in reality, of course, the actual beginning lay leagues away—many leagues and many hours—in Siberia or Norway, far out on the Atlantic or between the Sahara and the Mediterranean. The glass falling in our little mountain valley was in reply to changes *there*. And this first hint of trouble communicated itself instantly to ourselves; it might be nothing or it might be grave. There was menace in it, and our sense of security was shaken, for the hearts of climbing men lie close enough to Nature; we were aware of resistance, even of possible attack. That tremor of the sensitive mercury was a presage of something coming; at any rate, of something trying to come. In spite of the depression, however, the warning brought a thrill of pleasure with it; the instinct of self-protection stirred; it woke that adorable element in life—resistance against a hostile power that could not be trifled with, certainly not ignored. Somewhere, somehow, it was known that we had planned our great attack at dawn, and so a whisper travelled down from the enormous heights: "Beware! The enemy is on the move!" All this, and more, lay in the casual phrase: "The glass is falling."

Side by side with a natural annoyance there was this stimulus as well. For the beginnings of things are always very wonderful; alteration of what has been before, a new direction, purpose and independence, all these are involved in every true beginning. There is anticipation and surprise, promise of novelty, too; something is going to happen; it may be something quite unprecedented. Beginnings, being in the nature of creation, are beyond language marvellous: the beginning of a day or of a night; of anger, when a rising temperature and the hasting run of blood betray in us the lurking savage who kills naturally; of illness, with its sharp reminder that life one day *must* stop; of love, when the sound of a voice changes the universe; or of spring, when a new softness in the air, nameless by any sense, proclaims the arrival of gigantic, flooding life. But the beginning of a storm is so wonderful that it can easily eat up disappointment. For the preparations are so long and gradual, so sure, so steadily matured, so cumulative; at first so negligible, yet with a hint of genuine grandeur coming, that the blood is stirred, and the heart, first warned, then awed. He is a fortunate man who, in these sophisticated days, can find it in him to acknowledge this trace of the primitive spirit of worship. That faint, mysterious tremor that runs through Nature everywhere is divine in its first gentle yet calculated insignificance.

The animal and vegetable world at once respond to it; birds and fishes know, the insects know as well; trees note it and keep very still; all take instantly their best precautions; and only men, not aware of it until it is too late, disregard the delicate warning at their peril. Few humans can feel that the pressure of the air has altered. They watch an instrument and whisper: "Ah, the glass is falling!" The change is born, of course, so very far away. How *should* they know? Culture has dulled their primitive awareness.

And that night the stars were ominously clear and brilliant. In the morning there were other signs as well. At three o'clock just when the east was blushing, my companion called me, or rather came into my room. "Up already!" he exclaimed; "I just came in to see. What do you think of it? That barometer was a fraud." We went out upon the wooden balcony and saw the distant ridges mercilessly outlined in the growing light; the summits were near enough to throw a rope across.

"Too close," I said, with misgivings born of long experience.

"But look!" he objected, "there's not a single cloud." He loathed my caution, deeming it proud imagination only. "It's simply brilliant," he added, his young eagerness unspoilt by knowledge. I shook my older head. Some inborn instinct made me firm for once. Ten years before I should have been overridden, and have started on our perilous two-days' climb with ample hope.

"It's a whole day to the hut," I reminded him, "and then—suppose we wake to mist and wind and possibly driving snow? Let's wait till we're certain and the glass is rising slowly. For instance, look at *that!*" And I pointed to a narrow straw of vapour that trailed clingingly across the first huge precipice, five hours away, good going. It was tinged with a faint, transparent pink—unduly luminous.

"That's nothing," he exclaimed contemptuously, "mere bit of early morning mist. Why, I've known—"

"But it's too low down," I interrupted. "On the top it would not matter, it has no business *there.* It means changed or changing temperature."

He shivered in his thin pyjamas, yet did not realise that *dry* cold would not have made him shiver. In the night a new thing had crept in upon the valley—dampness.

"And listen," I added, as the tops of the pines below the balcony stirred with a rustling sound that as quickly died away again.

"The morning wind," he cried, "that's all."

"But the sound of falling water with it. The north or east—good winds—would not move a single branch down here. Observe the lie of the land." He did so grumpily enough.

"It's from the south," I observed, "and it's blowing *up* the valley."

"There's hardly any wind at all, anyhow," he said impatiently.

"But what there is is southerly. The wind has changed. You feel its dampness? That damp is evil. Why, man, you can smell it!" For a strong odour of earth and grass and growing things lay behind the exquisite morning freshness of the dawn, and the fragrance, though so pleasant, was suspicious. It was moisture that brought it out.

"Oh, you know best, I suppose," he growled, "though it looks all right, and I should call it perfect." He glanced at me with a trifle more respect, however—that change of wind *had* shaken his confidence!—then shrugged his shoulders and moved off reluctantly to bed. "You tell the guides, then," he added, with resignation, and was gone before he caught my answer: "if they're fools enough to come!"

But the guides, of course, put in no appearance. They ought, by rights, to have ascertained the "Herr's" decision, but took it for granted his opinion would be their own. I admit there was this childish pride and pleasure in the disappointment, and to be right even in prophesying disaster holds a faint satisfaction. It was the "Herr's" pleasure, however, to sit up and watch this marvellous beginning of a storm. The preparations for its splendid climax were so indecipherably faint, yet so carefully planned, that though the brilliance of last night's stars had announced their coming, six hours had passed and brought them apparently no nearer. The storm was being massed for attack below the edges of the visible world. One thought of it as a living monstrous thing that would presently come crowding and crashing down the heavens, alive for miles, and full of violent fury. It was too gigantic to move quickly; each separate detail must be trained and ready before the accumulated blow could fall; but hints of wind and moisture, like delicate antennae, were stretched out in advance to warn the sensitive nerves of those who had them.

I brewed some chocolate, and, with rugs and blankets on the narrow balcony, I watched the paling stars. This slow beginning of terrific weather thrilled me. It was unbelievably slow, unnecessarily cautious; its growth, unhasting but unhindered, brooked no interference, however, and there was a hint of diabolical thoroughness in the steady way beginning crept towards fulfilment. All Nature was pressed into the service; the entire firmament laboured to one given end. The imagination became conscious almost of personal direction in this consummate marshalling of such huge forces in sympathetic combination. Yet once or twice, for all my pride of certainty—particularly at half-past five, for instance, when the advance seemed stayed—I confess I had misgivings, and was tempted to wake my friend again and scold the guides for their inexcusable delay. For the weather held so still and brilliant. "Look at the sky!" I would have cried to the men. "How could *you* have been deceived by those false, transient signs of change?" Some deity of luck preserved me from their inevitable answer: "We thought the 'Herr' could have told what's surely coming!"

It was of marvellous, though sinister, beauty, well worth the loss of hours of beauty sleep, even worth the loss of the expedition as well, to see the wonder of the dawn across the awful heights, falling on cliff and ridge, and stealing along the high, faint snowfields in the break between the periods. The colours may be guessed, but not described, with the aspect of veiled terror that they wore, of menace in the strange diffusion of the light, and in the apparent innocence of sun and shadow that masked their changed expression. For nowhere was expression quite the same as on an innocent morning. The rising of the valley out of sleep, the creeping light, the guileless freshness of the air that brought the tumbling water loud and close, the general stillness, peace and calm—all these were different, but oh! so little different, to their normal aspect when the glass stood high. It was mere pretence, of course. The coming violence attempted to steal unnoticed and unawares upon the sky. Behind that treacherous calm it piled up forces that presently would shake the mountains and make the old woods howl. Yet at six o'clock the big peaks still looked friendly in the crystal atmosphere, and it was not till nearly nine that these first assurances of a perfect day began to fade. They passed, slipping away with an unnoticed skill that suggested cunning. No clouds were visible, and no wind to mention stirred, but there crawled into the air a certain dimness that lessened the first unearthly brilliance. Something waned, and the sting of the sharp, delicious heat was gone. Less than haze, it yet took the flash out of the sunshine, and while sound grew clearer, closer, the outlines of both trees and peaks stood blurred a little. Few would have noticed any definite change as yet, none, perhaps, but very keen observers with an interest at stake; but by half-past ten there lay an observable shadow over the entire heavens, cast by no cloud, but as though the tide of light rushed down, then halted and drew back. Before eleven it was a curious, faint veil, and an hour later it had dimmed the normal blaze of noon. There was a glare of unpleasant brilliance that hurt the eyes.

Then, from noon till perhaps after two o'clock, there came a pause when nothing happened, and only a great thick stillness settled over everything. And the pause was ominous, freighted with presentiment; the freshness of the upland world was gone entirely; it seemed a dull, exhausted, burnt-out day. The smell of grass and earth became more marked, and there were soft touches of moisture in the eyes and on the skin; the flies were "sticky," their tickling of the face and hands persistent, and that state of irritation known as "nerves on edge" required steady handling. But though outwardly all this time the signs had seemed minute, they had really been immense, and the entire heavens wrote the letters clear. For as the light had piled in waves upon the eastern sky, the west had given its too early answer, and the suspicious radiance that had brought so grand a dawn was of the same evil quality that had lit the stars too brilliantly the night before. By four o'clock, then, just as the shadows lengthened steeply in the nearer gorges, a delicate trail of fine-spun cloud came thinning down the sky from south to north at an incredible height above the tallest peaks. So tenuous as to be scarcely visible, it lined the atmosphere where no clouds were, and at five o'clock, when the afternoon was waning, there appeared as if by magic, in several spots at once, small patches of isolated mist that had darkness on their underside. Below the giddy ridge where our proposed night shelter perched—the hut—they gathered suddenly into a single line, and fifteen minutes later there was a barrier of dirty-looking cloud that was rising—rising in places at considerable speed. On the edges it leaped and coiled with a kind of hurrying impatience. Yet all this time—these twenty hours of interval— the entire heavens had conspired together to produce no more than this thickening cloud that was the first visible sign a townsman need have noticed with anxiety. The peaks, however, were close enough now to touch; a stifling, oven heat, airless as a concert hall, hung everywhere; there was a strange, deep stillness; and from the distant upper pastures the sound of cow-bells came queerly down the village street. The birds had ceased their singing long before.

The wreaths and lines of vapour meanwhile spread and thickened, gaining ground, some rising, others sinking, new centres forming everywhere with a rapidity that argued admirable preparation. A coiling mist wrapped hurriedly about one summit after another, yet leaving the actual top in shining light. A ring was round the sun, immensely distant from it, with a diameter of many miles of sky. The heat in the valley, pressed down and running over, made breathing increasingly oppressive; the sunlight filtered badly and unevenly. The peasants looked skywards and said no word, but barn doors were shut and the cattle came to water early in the nearer pastures. In spots the air grew colder, and suddenly, with dramatic abruptness, solitary puffs of heated wind came rushing up our valley from the south. Heralded by clouds of dust they passed and went their way, first having tossed the waiting trees, not twice, but once, rattled the windows, closed the open doors—went their way upwards to bear word that all was ready for the main attack.

Long, ominous silences followed, but with the lurid sunset the change, so long maturing, now dropped swiftly. At dusk there was heavy roaring in the mountains as the winds let loose against the darkening cliffs. It was audible even on our balcony. And, before the appointed time, there fell a sea of blackness on the world that blotted out in less than a dozen minutes the last vestiges of sunset or of gleaming, distant snow. By 7.30 the true wind began to rise, or, properly speaking, began to reach us in our sunken hollow. Up the valley like a crying voice it swept, in no puffs now, but in a steady torrent. It wailed and moaned. None perhaps but a climber knows that desolate sound, that strange, wild whistling among rocks and trees, that shrill and angry calling to the earth. It is a threatening sound. He hears a host of javelins and lances flying, for he knows the sting and pierce of that sharp, wetted wind. There is grim foreboding in it, and presentiment in the hot and empty pauses that lie between the heavy gusts. And the upper wind came down to meet it. Again the deep roaring became audible, though where no man could tell, for it was everywhere and filled the inky sky. It descended with its battle howl from the iron fastnesses of scree and precipice and from the bitter snowfields that had iced its fury. It was a wind that could blow a man from the securest foothold into space, mow down the older trees like matches, and even loosen rocks. It seemed the mountains stooped to heave their shoulders, driving it down with crushing power upon our village between the forests.

We had little sleep that night. The storm was, of course, the worst that had ever been known. It lasted with unabated fury and with torrential rain for forty hours. Its suddenness, the unenlightened said, was so extraordinary. It came, as it seemed, out of a clear and harmless sky. Only the few who watched as we had watched knew of its marvellous genesis and careful growth, its gradual and distant preparation, the birth of its small beginning hours and hours before it came.

The Spell of Egypt

The return of Tut-ankh-Amen into the sunshine after 3,000 years in stifling darkness has a drama both majestic and pathetic. There is a poignant contrast in it. After thirty centuries of peace and silence, he re-enters a world that, apparently, has little changed so far as human nature is concerned. The bickerings about precedence and pecuniary values, about the ownership of the treasures, the commercial exploitation generally, he would find, in principle, similar to the squabbles he was familiar with in his own day. That kingly figure, blind, deaf, unfeeling, is fortunately unaware of the violent contrast his resurrection emphasizes: the strident chorus of modern voices—his own *silence*.

It is an eloquent silence. He emerges from his ancient tomb with dignity, with grandeur, bringing with him into our practical twentieth century a sense of mystery, of star-like leisure, of wonder; something of awe, and a strange, forgotten beauty too. There is about him almost an unearthly touch, not dissimilar, perhaps, to the emotion wakened in Kinglake by the Sphinx, his fellow-splendour, so briefly and so adequately described in "Eothen": "Comely the creature is, but with a comeliness not of this earth"—a pregnant sentence that lays upon the mind again, with Tut-ankh-Amen, that singular Egyptian glamour, which is, indeed, a mysterious, almost an unearthly spell.

A considerable amount of nonsense has been written about it. Cheapened by exaggeration, vulgarized by familiarity, it has become for many a picture-post card spell, pinned before the mind like the posters at a railway terminus. The moment Alexandria is reached, this huge post card hangs across the heavens, composed of temples, pyramids, palm-trees by a shining Nile, and the inevitable Sphinx. And the monstrosity of it paralyzes the mind. Memory escapes with difficulty from the insistent, gross advertisement. It deafens imagination. Behind it, however, there hides a potent yet a nameless thing, not acknowledged by all, perhaps, because it is so curiously elusive, yet surely felt by all, because it is so true. An effect that does not pass away is wrought subtly upon the mind, an effect that not being properly comprehensible, is nameless. Having once "gone down into Egypt," one is never quite the same again; having drunk of the water of the Nile, there is a yearning to drink of it again. Moreover, it is the casual visitor, unburdened by antiquarian and archaeological knowledge, who may best estimate this power: the tourist who knows merely what he has gleaned, say, from Baedeker's general synopsis, is more freshly sensitive to it than the excavator or official who has lived long in the country. He becomes aware, too, that it is all the more enchanting because he is unable to define and analyze it.

All countries, of course, colour thought and memory, stirring imagination in any but the hopelessly inanimate—whence the educational value of travel-psychology—but, whereas from Greece, Japan, India, the traveller returns with reports he can evoke at will and label, he returns from Egypt with a marvellous blur that defies detailed description. Saturated, maybe, with overmuch, the mind recalls with definiteness nothing coherent. There comes to its summons a colossal medley that half stupefies: immense stretches of tawny sand drenched in a stinging sunlight; dim, solemn aisles of granite silence; stupendous monoliths that stare unblinking at the sun; a shining river licking its slow way across a murderous desert; an enormous night-sky drowned in brilliant stars. A score of temples merge into a single monster; great pyramids float across the sky, like clouds; palms rustle in mid-air; and from subterranean gloom there issue muffled voices that seem to utter the hieroglyphics of a long-forgotten tongue.

The mental horizon, oddly lifted, brims with this procession of gigantic things, then empties again without a word of explanation, leaving behind a mere litter of big adjectives—unchanging, formidable, amazing, and the like; while the coherent single memory that should link all these together hides too deep for articulate recovery. The Acropolis, the wonders of Japan, of India, the mind can grasp; but this composite enormity of Ramesseum, Serapeum, Karnak, Cheops, Sphinx, with a hundred temples and a thousand miles of sand, seem to have bludgeoned it into temporary silence. That dreadful post card, moreover, rises like a wall. Yet, behind the post card, behind the adjectives, and sure to emerge for full recognition in due course, the mind remains aware of some huge, alluring thing, alive with a pageantry of ages, strangely brilliant in blue and gold, magnificent, appealing almost to tears—something that drifts past like a ghostly full-rigged ship with crowded decks and painted sails, too vastly scaled for sight to take it in. The spell, that is, has become operative.

I remember asking myself what I had gained, and I remember the fruitless result. Nothing came but that abominable, shouting post card, endlessly extended. Its very endlessness, however, was a clue. Egypt *is* endless and inexhaustible; some hint of eternity lies there, an awareness of immortality almost. To-day, after a doze of four or five thousand years, subterranean Egypt peeps up again at the sun. The vast Memphian cemetery that stretches from Sakkhâra to the Mena House has begun to whisper in the daylight. The Theban worship of the sun is being reconstructed. There is a sense of deathlessness about the ancient Nile, about the grim Sphinx and Pyramids, on the very colonnades of Karnak, whose pylons now once more stand upright after a sleep of forty centuries on their backs; above all, in the strength of the floating, rustling sand—something that defies time and repudiates change in death. Out of that flat, undifferentiated landscape which is Egypt, still stand the unconquerable finger-posts of stone, pointing, like symbols of eternity, to the equally unchanging skies. The spell is laid upon you once you have looked into the battered visages of those Memnon terrors, which reveal, yet hide, far better than the Sphinx. They have neither eyes nor lips nor nose; their features, as their message, inscrutable. Yet they tell this nameless thing plainly *because* they have no words. Out of the green fields of millet they stand like portions of the Theban Mountains that have slid down into the plain, then stopped for a few more centuries to stare across the Nile and watch the sunrise. From them, as partly from the opened tombs of priest and Pharaoh, comes some ingredient of this singular Egyptian spell.

Unguessed at first, because sought for in some crude, tangible form it never assumes, it flames up unexpectedly—perhaps in a London street when fog shrouds the chimneys; perhaps at a concert; perhaps in a tea-room among perfumed, gossiping women; in church, at the club, even in bed when falling asleep just after a commonplace evening at a commonplace play. A sound recalls the street cries of the Arabs, with its haunting sing-song melody; a breath of air brings back the heated sand, the rustle of the curtain whispers as the palms and acacia whisper—and the truth is realised. Up steals the immense Egyptian glamour. It pours, it rushes up. It is over you in a moment. All this time it has lain coiled in deep recesses of the inner being—recesses, where there is silence because they are inaccessible amid the clamour of daily life. There is awe in it, a hint of cold eternity, a glimpse of something unchanging and terrific, yet, at the same time, soft and very tender too.... The pictures unroll and spread. You feel again the untold melancholy of the Nile. The grandeur of a hundred battered temples beats upon the heart. There is a sense of unutterable beauty. Something in you bows to the procession that includes great figures of non-human lineage. Up sweeps the electric desert air, the alive wind, the wild and delicate perfume of the sand; the luminous grey shadows brush you; you feel the enormous scale of naked desolation which yet brims with strange vitality. An Arab on his donkey flits in colour across the mind, melting off into tiny perspective. A string of camels stands against the sky, swaying forward the same moment as though it never ceased. A dozen pyramids cleave the air with monstrous wedges, pointing holes in space. In peace and silence, belonging to a loneliness of ages, rise heads and shoulders of towering gods of stone, little jackals silhouetted, perhaps, an instant against deific thighs half buried in sand. Great winds, great blazing spaces, great days and nights of shining wonder float past from the pavement or the theatre stall, and London, dim-lit England, the whole of modern life indeed, are reduced sharply to a miniature of trifling ugliness that seems the unreality. Egypt rolls through the heart for a second and is gone.... Conventions drive you ... there are letters to be answered, appointments to be kept, calls to be paid, and a new umbrella to be bought.... But out there the days swam past in a flood of golden light, and, caught in a procession of ancient splendours, changeless as the leisured Nile, majestic as the desert, and fresh still with the wonder that first created them, you moved with the tide as of some unconditioned world. Egypt steals out and whispers to you in your dreams. Once more you float in an atmosphere of passionate marriage....

Egypt with a power of seduction almost uncanny, has robbed the mind of a faculty best described perhaps as the faculty of measurement. Its scale has stupefied the ability to measure, appraise, estimate; and this balance, once destroyed, wonder and awe capture the heart, going what pace they please. Size works half the miracle, for it is size including a quality of terror—monstrous; and, but for the noble beauty that thunders through it, this sheer size might easily work a very different spell—dismay. The modern mind, no longer terrified by speed, to which it has grown contemptuously accustomed, yet shrinks a little before this display of titanic and bewildering size. Egypt makes it realize that it has no handy standard of measurement. It listens to words that are meaningless. The vast proportions uplift, then stupefy. The girth of the Pyramids, the height of the Colossi, the cubic content of the granite columns and the visage of the Sphinx expressed in yards—these convey as little truth as the numbered leagues of the frightening desert or the length of that weary and interminable Nile. You draw a deep breath of astonishment—then give up the vain attempt to grapple with a thing you cannot readily assimilate. A dizziness of star-distances steals over you; there is a breathlessness of astronomical scale in it that exhilarates while it stuns. What mind can gain by the information that our sun, with all its retinue of planets, sweeps daily 1,000,000 miles nearer to Hercules, yet that Hercules *looks* no closer than it did thousands of years ago, when Tut-ankh-Amen was laid to rest? Such distances lie beyond comprehension. Similarly, in Egypt, there is something that for ever evades capture in the monstrous details of sheer size, beautiful with majesty, that tower above the shrinking reason. The land exhales a steam of enchantment that lulls the senses. You move through this almost visible glamour. All about you is a high, transparent screen, built by the centuries, and left standing; modern life, cast like a cinema-picture upon this screen, becomes the unreality. Herein lies one letter at least, of the spell of Egypt—the mind is for ever aware of something that haunts from the further side of experience.

For some, a rather dominant impression is undoubtedly "the monstrous." A splendour of awful dream, yet never quite of nightmare, stalks everywhere, suggesting an atmosphere of Khubla Khan. There is nothing lyrical. Even the silvery river, the slender palms, the fields of clover and barley and the acres of flashing poppies convey no lyrical sweetness, as elsewhere they might. All moves to a statelier measure. Stern issues of life and death are in the air, and in the grandeur of the tombs and temples there is a solemnity of genuine awe that makes the blood run slow a little. Those Theban hills, where the kings and queens lay buried, are forbidding to the point of discomfort almost. The listening silence in the grim Valley of the Tombs of the Kings, the intolerable glare of sunshine on the stones, the naked absence of any sign of animal or vegetable life, the slow approach to the secret hiding-place where the mummy of a once powerful monarch lies ghastly now beneath the glitter of an electric light, the implacable desert, deadly with heat and distance on every side—this picture, once seen, rather colours one's memory of the rest of Egypt with its sombre and funereal character. And with the great deific monoliths the effect is similar. Proportions and sheer size strike blow after blow upon the mind. Stupendous figures, shrouded to the eyes, shoulder their way slowly though the shifting sands, deathless themselves and half-appalling. Their attitudes and gestures express the hieroglyphic drawings come to life. Their towering heads, coiffed with zodiacal signs, or grotesque with animal or bird, bend down to watch you everywhere. There is no hurry in them; they move with the leisure of the moon, with the stateliness of the sun, with the slow silence of the constellations. But they move. There is, between you and them, this effect of a screen, erected by the ages, yet that any moment may turn thin and let them through upon you. A hand of shadow, but with granite grip, may steal forth and draw you away into some region where they dwell among changeless symbols like themselves, a region vast, ancient and undifferentiated as the desert that has produced them. Their effect in the end is weird, difficult to describe, but real. Talk with a mind that has been steeped for years in their atmosphere and presence, and you will appreciate this odd reality. The spell of Egypt is an other-worldly spell. Its vagueness, its elusiveness, its undeniable reality are ingredients, at any rate, in a total result whose detailed analysis lies hidden in mystery and silence—inscrutable.

A Man of Earth

John Erdlieb used to tell this story—occasionally and with reluctance. It had to be dragged out of him. He seemed to feel it was telling something against himself, but that was because he didn't believe in "the kind of thing," and felt that he did himself a wrong and strained the credence of his listeners as well. Hence, probably, the strange impressiveness of the quaint recital; it had indubitably happened to him.

Though of German origin, he was English, stolid, steady, inarticulate English, and a rare good fellow, whose character emerged strongly in those difficult circumstances known as "tight places." He was a mining engineer by profession; he loved the earth and anything to do with the earth, from a garden he played with half tenderly, to a mountain he attacked half savagely for tunnelling or blasting purposes. He never left the earth if he could help it; both feet and mind were always planted firmly upon *terra firma*; figuratively or actually, he never flew. And his physical appearance expressed his wholesome, earthly type—the rumbling, subterranean bass voice, the tangled undergrowth of beard that hid his necktie, the slow, stately walk as of a small hill advancing. Moreover, you might dig in him and find pure gold—the mass of him covered the heart of a simple, tender child, honest and loving as the day. A child of earth, in the literal sense he was, if ever such existed.

"The first time," he said moving his words laboriously, as though they weighed, "was a June evening in Surrey, when I was going along a lane to catch a train to London. I was carrying a bag. It was a quarter-past ten, the train was 10.30, and I had a mile to go. I had come down in the afternoon to advise a friend about the laying of his tennis court—not professionally," he explained, with a booming laugh, "but because I knew he was going the wrong way about it—and he had persuaded me to stay to dinner. He had seen me to the gate and given me directions about short cuts. It was near the longest day, and there was light still hanging from the sky, but the lanes and paths ran along deep gullies in the sandstone, which the trees and bushes turned into tunnels of black. It was very warm and without a breath of air. Rain in the afternoon had left the atmosphere heavy, thick, and steamy. I perspired awfully, my wrist began to ache with carrying the bag, and half-way down one of the deep sandy lanes I stopped a moment to rest. I put the bag down, and struck a match to see my watch. There were seven minutes left to do a long half-mile." He paused a moment, and we concluded from that pause that he would miss his train.

"Now, I'm not the sort of man," he continued simply, "that a tramp would be likely to attack. I don't look opulent, and I'm big. Until I struck that match I hadn't passed a living soul. But my friend's wife had told me the tramps were thick about the roads this summer, and had been pretty bold as well. I'd quite forgotten all this; it wasn't in my mind. So when the glare of the match showed me a man standing close in front of me—so close I could have touched him—I got a start. He saw my watch, of course. But I saw his face. And he was looking straight into my eyes, just as though he had been staring at me in the dark before. The light, I mean, caught him in the act. There was no surprise in his face. Now I must tell you another thing as well: his face was smeared with earth." He laughed again as he said it. "The fellow looked as if he had been buried and just crawled out. It was a big bearded face, and the eyes were like an animal's—quite frank. But what struck me at the moment—I'm telling this badly, I'm afraid—was that, just as I stopped to strike that match, I noticed a strong smell of earth, of soil and mould I mean. If you've ever turned up real virgin soil you'd know exactly what it was like—same sort of smell you get when digging up a wet bit of field, only ten times stronger. A good smell; I love it.

"Well, the match went out, and the blackness after it was like a wall. I just thought I'd be getting on as quick as I could or I'd miss the train— no feeling at all that the fellow meant me any harm, you see—when I heard him say, 'I'll carry it for you. Come up this way. It's the best.' And before I could answer or object—do anything at all, in fact—the fellow had snatched my bag and made off with it, I suppose he had been waiting just at this darkest part of the lane on purpose. He went up hill, and I after him, striking angrily with my stick in the hope of tripping him up. But he had the start, and I was winded already, and uphill I'm not as quick as I used to be ten years ago. I heard his running tread along the sandy ground, light as a child; and, while I stumbled in the darkness among the loose stones and ruts, two other things flashed into my mind. I can't say what made me think of them. But it seemed to me that the fellow was very short and had been standing on tiptoe when he stared into my face; and the other thing was this: that in this sandy soil—it's mostly sand and heather and pine trees in that part—it was curious that the smell of *earth* should have been so strong. For it was rich, black earth I smelt."

John Erdlieb stopped again. He had reached a difficult place, we felt, a place where he wanted help. We gave what help we could, urging him to tell the rest, whether it seemed credible to him or not.

"He kept just ahead of me," he continued, in his growling tones that were like the deep string on a double bass, "and didn't seem a bit anxious to escape from me. He could easily—he ran so lightly—have nipped up the banks and disappeared, and I could never in this world have caught him.

But he kept ten yards in front. In the patches where the trees were thinner I saw his outline plainly; he'd run a bit, then pause, then start again just when I got too close. I shouted and cursed him, but he said no word. And at length—oh, we'd been running four or five minutes, I should think—he stopped dead, and waited. It was an open space, where the banks on both sides were clear of trees or bushes, and the light from the sky, as well as the sort of radiance that sand gives out—you know—showed him distinctly, crouching in the path, the bag beside him. I came up with a rush, my stick raised to clout him on the head, when—of course, you can't believe it—he simply wasn't there. I heard his voice, but—well, I can only tell you how it seemed to me—I heard it underground. It was muffled and smothered, as though it came through earth." Erdlieb said this very low; he almost growled it; he was ashamed to tell it. "You want to know what it was he said? I'll tell you in three words: 'Now you're safe.' That was what I heard, and I heard it as distinctly as I hear my own voice now. The fellow had disappeared, as if the thing had been a dream, and I'd just wakened up." He shut his mouth with a snap, as though there was no more to tell.

A lot of questions were discharged at him, of course, but chief among them, or first, at any rate, "And did you catch your train?" He had made such a point of catching that particular train.

"Luckily," he said, "I missed it by three minutes. Yes, I did say 'luckily.' In the tunnel that begins a mile beyond the station there was a bad cave-in—it had been an exceptionally wet summer, and the first three coaches, the only first-class coaches on the train, had every occupant killed. Yes, it's a fad of mine," he answered a final question. "I always go first-class."

He gave the second incident as well. He was very shy about it; but for the dusk on the verandah, where he told it, one could have seen him blush.

"It was last year, when I was in the Caucasus—the Lesser Caucasus, some 50 miles south-east of Batoum, where there are copper mines, first worked by the Phoenicians ages ago, but covered now by a forest of rhododendrons and azaleas. The ore is visible to the eye, and they get it out with pickaxes. It's a marvellous country, wild as ever it can be, and the men wilder still, a difficult crew to manage, Georgians, Persians, Tartars, all Mohammedans, and all free with knife and pistol. We were 5000 feet above sea-level. You could see Ararat in the distance, a pyramid of snow, and even Elbruz and Kasbek to the north, when the air was clear.

"One of my younger engineers was an American, capable as they make 'em, but with one curious drawback—he spouted Shakespeare and saw visions! A poetical sort of chap, but sober, reliable, and awfully good at his work. I think, you know, the power of the place got into him a bit—you can believe anything," he explained apologetically, "in the Caucasus—and just across the next ridge was a settlement of Ossetines. The Ossetines are said to be older than the Egyptians, and no one knows exactly where they come from; they worship the soil, pray to heaps of earth, with the idea that it expresses deity or something, offer salt and milk to open places in the ground, and all that kind of thing. They're a wild lot, too. But they didn't bother us much, although some of our workmen were afraid of them. The idea was, you see, that they resented our cutting holes in the body of their deity.

"Apart from stories, that grew big unless stopped instantly"—he said this significantly—"I had no trouble with the men at all, and the Ossetines I only saw—er—this once. My American engineer was the bother, with his imaginative talk of nature-spirits, his seeing things about the mountains, and all the rest. The Caucasus just there is not exactly the place to talk that kind of stuff. It's marvellous enough—without additions!

"Well, one afternoon this chap and I were out prospecting together—his geology was splendid, a sort of instinct in him—prospecting for new veins and outcrop and what not, and in the most gorgeously savage scenery you can possibly imagine. The mountain side was smothered with azalea bushes, all in bloom, every shade of colour, and the smell of them was almost more than I could stand. Azalea honey, you know, has a kind of intoxicating effect, like a drug, and the natives use it for that purpose, and, perhaps, the smell of these miles of blossom, taken in such enormous doses, affects the nerves a bit. I can't say about that, but anyhow, Edgar began talking his nonsense about it in his peculiar way—clear-headed enough at the same time to trace his strata with amazing accuracy and judgment—and saying that his eyes were opened, and he could see down into the ground, and talking about the Ossetines and the Powers of the Place, and all mixed up with quotations from his Shakespeare and the rest. Well, it was no business of mine to stop him. He did his work all right. I let him go on fifteen to the dozen until at last it got on my nerves, and I told him to quit it. He didn't mind a bit; just looked at me, and said, 'I've had my eyes opened by the place; I can't help it. Why, I can see your glassy essence. You're an earth-person. You ought to feel what I feel. I think you *do!*' That 'glassy essence,' you know, is in *Measure for Measure*, only I forget the whole quotation. And then he said excitedly, 'The worship of these Ossetines up here has done it. The place is all stirred up. I shouldn't be a bit surprised if we saw—'

"I interrupted him and told him to stow all that. The Ossetines, I told him—taking it that he referred to them and not to—er—other things—were over the next ridge, anyhow, five hours' climbing away—when just at that very minute he came at me like a football player on the charge. He caught my shoulders and stared at me with terror in his face. 'They're coming!' he cried out. 'Can't you hear them? They're coming!'

"And there was a curious, deep, roaring sound up in the mountains to the north, a tremendous sound. It was like thunder. Yet it was a sunny, windless day without a cloud; there was not even falling water near us. I couldn't believe my ears. And I turned and saw what at first I thought were sliding masses of earth and stones moving down towards us from the heights a mile away. There were boulders, rolling and dancing down ahead of the general mass, only they moved so slowly and with such an extraordinary kind of motion altogether that I stood and stared in complete amazement. It all bewildered me. The sound was appalling somehow. It was like an upheaval of the earth. Then Edgar shouted, 'Run, man, run for your life. They're out!' and started off downhill like a frightened deer.

"It takes a good deal to move me, however"—he smiled at us through the dusk so that his teeth were visible—"and I stood still a minute longer, watching the strangest thing I'd ever seen. For those stones and rolling boulders were not rock, but people. It was a crowd of people. Not Ossetines, though. I could see *that*. They were small and stunted. Even at that distance I could swear they were very small. They were like dwarfs. They *were* dwarfs. It took my breath away; but, I swear to you, they were just like that tramp who snatched my bag in the Surrey lane five years before, and they made the same strange impression upon me of being—er—out of the ordinary." He paused a moment, wondering most likely how much more he cared to tell. "I picked up our instruments and ran downhill after Edgar," he told us simply, "ran as hard as I could pelt. You can judge the pace when I tell you I caught him up in something under ten minutes, too." That didn't impress us much, perhaps, because we had never seen the other man, but it meant a lot to Erdlieb apparently. Edgar, of course, was a younger man. "And then we ran on together side by side, not looking back, but feeling exactly as if the mountain-side was at our heels. The roaring sound had stopped. Once within sight of the Works we stopped, too. Nothing unusual was anywhere to be seen. The heights stood out clear and sharp against the brilliant sky. Nothing moved. Not a living soul was visible in any direction upon the enormous slopes. Edgar, however, was white as a ghost, scared stiff, as he phrased it himself. He declared he had seen

> 'A shadow, like an angel with bright hair
> Dabbled in blood.'

"I was in no mood for quotations. I could have knocked him down on the spot.

"That night, an hour after sunset, when the stars were out, and all the mountains peaceful, no wind, no noise of any kind, no hint of warning either, the landslide came. You know about it because I've already described it to you at dinner. It's why I'm in England now instead of super-intending the copper mines out there in the Caucasus. The Works were smothered, the loss of life appalling. I told you how we escaped, Edgar and I, by the skin of our teeth and—er—luck. The spot among the azaleas where we first heard the noise in the afternoon—several hours before a single pound of earth had begun to shift—by eight o'clock lay under several hundred feet of fallen mountain, still slowly sliding. I doubt if the Works will ever be dug out. It would cost a fortune. I have advised against it."

The Laughter of Carthage

It was at a big cinema house. The lights were turned down and the general audience was a blur, faces at a few feet distance not clearly discernible. On the screen a comic story was being shown, some scenes very comic, and amusement was audible all over the crowded building. There was tittering, sniggering, gasps of surprise, and occasionally an exclamation. Everybody seemed sufficiently tickled to make a noise of one kind or another, when suddenly a new sound was heard, a sound that presently dominated the entire house. A man was—laughing.

At first, so concentrated was attention on the screen, that his laughter did not attract attention. It merged in the general murmur of the crowd. But gradually it differentiated itself from this general murmur, and rose above it. It became a sound apart. More than mere amusement, more than a pleasant sense of the ludicrous made audible, it drew attention to itself. It was a genuine, hearty laughter.

And people turned their heads. First one, then another, looked away from the screen to see who was so unadulteratedly happy, enjoying himself with such spontaneous hilarity. One must be a child to laugh like that, felt many, with a touch of envy, perhaps, at the thought. No grown-up could forget himself for so slight a cause. It certainly was unaffected laughter, the man was unselfconscious. He did not know he was making such a noise. And everybody looked at the rows behind them, peering eagerly to see his face; they made remarks to their neighbours; they waited, listening for the next outburst, then nudged each other again—and finally began laughing themselves.

They laughed with the man, not at him, for it was such infectious laughter that bubbled from him in a ceaseless stream. Actors on the stage must have been seriously disconcerted, but the pictures, of course, showed no signs of injured vanity; for the fact was that, while the comic story lasted, the entire audience laughed with the man instead of with the moving photographs. The screen was neglected shamefully; its changes merely supplied the question from one moment to another—"Listen! That will set him off again! You see if it doesn't!" And off he went—the stream of delicious, unselfconscious, heart-felt laughter that it did one good to hear.

There was no marked peculiarity about it, the voice was not unusual in any way, there was nothing about it that made one inclined to laugh at instead of with him. It was the genuine, happy joy in the sound that caught so many hearts along. The desire to see the man became, apparently, universal; what was he like, what sort of fellow to look at, what age, what size, what type of man—that he could laugh like this? People leaned forward, backwards, sideways, to discover him; but the semidarkness screened him from their view; they could not see the shaking sides, the merry eyes, the jolly mouth and cheeks. He was audible only, not visible. The few in the back rows who sat near him had him to themselves.

But all listened with keen delight. Every few seconds the spontaneous laughter broke forth with what seemed new freshness. It cheered, it made the day seem brighter, there was more happiness in the world than one knew, evidently; life itself took on a gayer, and more careless aspect with such a proof of brave enjoyment in one's ears. The screen amused, but this man's laughter heartened. It was very good to hear. He must, indeed, be a jolly, reckless, light-hearted fellow, without a care or worry in the world. If only that laughter could be bottled up and delivered by cartloads in the unhappy houses of the world! There was such hope and courage in it. The man must be an optimist with confident outlook.

And everyone who heard it shared one longing—for the story to end and the lights to be turned up that the laugher might be visible. For it seemed that no one cared any longer what happened on the screen; all wanted to see the jovial face of the jolly, happy man who had cheered them up without knowing that he did so. And at last the story ended, the lights began to rise. Hundreds of necks were craned.

I shall never forget him. He was still laughing, though not loudly now. He leaned over to a pal to talk about the pictures. He was utterly oblivious of the sensation that he caused—this happy, cheerful, jolly man who was a wounded soldier, holding two crutches lightly against his shoulder. I saw his grim, determined face; I saw his bright blue eyes, laughter still in them; and, when the performance ended, I also saw him carried out tenderly by his two pals. He was young, perhaps twenty-six at most, and his body ended at the knees. And a sigh went through the great silent audience as, without watching, they yet saw—a sigh of wonder and admiration, of gratitude, also, I think, of love. There was a feeling of reverence; there were certainly moistened eyes.

S.O.S.

It is a question how many witnesses shall be required to establish the veracity of an occurrence so singular, especially when one of such witnesses is a dog.

Three of us, two men and a girl, had skimmed the snow-covered Jura slopes on our *ski* since noon, arriving toward four o'clock at the deserted chalet where the fourth was to meet us. Upon the arrival of that fourth hung all the future happiness of the girl, and he was to come from a village far away on the other side. The Christmas rendezvous had been carefully arranged.

We had brought provisions for making a hot supper in the empty building, a lonely farm-house used only in summer, and our plan was to ski back all together by moonlight.

"Put on your extra sweaters before you begin to cool," said the older man, coming round the corner with an armful of logs from the frozen woodpile. "I'll get the fire going. Here, Dot,"—turning to his niece—"stack your ski, and get the food out. He'll be hungry as a bear."

The three of us bustled about over the crisp snow, and the older man had a wood fire blazing upon the great open hearth in less than ten minutes. The interior of the big room lit up, shadows flew overhead among the rafters, and shafts of cheery yellow light flashed even into the recesses of the vaulted barn that opened out into the cow-sheds in the rear. Outside, the dusk visibly deepened from one minute to the next.

The cold was bitter; but our heated bodies fairly steamed. The big St. Bernard ran, sniffing and prancing, after each of us in turn, and from time to time flew up the mounds of snow outside, where he stood, with head flung back and muzzle up, staring against the sunset. He knew perfectly well that someone else was expected and the direction from which he would come. The effect of the firelight streaming through door and cracks of muffled window into the last hour of daylight was peculiar; night and day met together on the threshold of the chalet, under the shadows of that enormous snow-laden roof. For the sun was now below the rim of the Suchet ridges, flaming with a wonderful sheet of red and yellow light over the huge white plateau, and the isolated trees threw vague shadows that easily ran into a length of half a kilometer. Rapidly they spread, assuming monstrous shapes, half animal, half human; then, deceiving the sight, merged into the strange uniform glow that lies upon a snow-field in the twilight. The forest turned purple; the crests of the pines cut into the sky like things of steel and silver. Everything shone, crackled, sparkled; the cold increased.

"Dorothy, where are you going?" sounded the older man's voice from the door, for the girl was out on her ski again. Her slim young figure, topped by the pointed, white snow-cap, was sprite-like.

"Just a little way over the slopes—to meet him," came her reply. She seemed to float above the snow, not on it.

With decision he called her in, and it was the warning in his tone that perhaps made her obey.

"Better rest," he said briefly, "we've got a long run home in the moonlight." On her ski she came "sishing" back down the gleaming slope to his side, neat and graceful, her shadow shooting ahead like black lightning, enormously elongated. "The Creux du Van precipices, besides, lie over that way," he continued. "They begin without warning—a sheer drop, and nothing to show the edge."

"I know them," she said, pouting a little.

"He knows them, too," her uncle answered, putting a hand on her shoulder. "He'll take the higher slopes. He'll get around all right." He had noticed the look in her soft, brown eyes that betrayed—it was the merest passing flash—an eagerness lying too close upon the verge of anxiety. "Harry knows these ridges even better than I do."

He helped her stack the ski, then turned to whistle in the dog, which had stayed behind on the summit of the slope she had just left, and it was at this instant, I think, that I first suddenly became aware of an unusual significance lying behind the little scene. Such moments are beyond explanation or analysis; one can only report them. They pertain, some hold, to a kind of vision. I can merely affirm that the flash came to me in this wise: I saw the big dog, his outline sharply silhouetted against the skyline and his head turned westward, refusing for the first time that day to obey instantly a whistle that for him was a summons always to be obeyed. His master, noticing nothing, had already gone inside; but the girl saw what I saw, caught a flash similar to my own, and recognised in the animal's insignificant disobedience a corroboration of something in herself that touched uneasiness. I cannot prove it—she has never spoken of it—only, as she stood there a moment, with the sunset in her face and her tumbled hair half over her eyes, I intercepted the swift glance that ran upward to the St. Bernard, travelled beyond him to the huge, distant snow-slopes, and then fell upon me. It was love, perhaps, that carried and interpreted thus the instantaneous wireless message—the love that lay undelivered in my heart, as in her own, and since she was forsworn already, lay unrecognised. In view of what followed, I cannot wholly say. My sight held clearer and steadier than her own, and it came to me that my strange perception, sharpened to bitter sweetness as if by sacrifice, approached possibly to some kind of inferior divination of the wounded soul.

The next minute the great dog came bounding down, and we entered the chalet together, busying ourselves with fire, benches, table, and supper. The portable little kettle of aluminum already steamed upon the hearth.

With us—with myself, at any rate—came into the cozy fire-lit interior a sensation that was new. I felt the terror and desolation of these vast, snow-covered mountains, immense, trackless, silent, lying away from the world of men below the coming stars. Winter, like a winter of the polar regions, held them fast. In the brilliant sunshine of the day they had been friendly, enticing, sympathetic. Now, with the icy dusk creeping over their bare, white faces, the freezing wind sifting with long sighs through the forests below, and the silent Terror of the Frost stalking from cliff to ridge with his head among the stars, they turned terrible. With the coming of the night they awoke to their true power. They showed their teeth. Our own insignificance became curiously emphasised. I thought of the Creux du Van precipices, sweeping, crater-like with their semicircle of dark grandeur, a gulf of snow-drifts about their dreadful lips, six hundred feet of shadows yawning within, and shuddered.

"You're cold," said Dot softly, pulling me to the fire, where she warmed her steaming boots. "I'm cold, too." We piled the wood on; the flames leaped and crackled; shadows flew among the rafters.

"Harry's due any minute," said her uncle. "We'll drop the eggs in as soon as we hear his whistle." He stooped down to pat the St. Bernard, which lay now with head stretched on his forepaws before the fire, staring, listening. "You'll hear him first," he laughed cheerily, giving the beast a resounding pat, "Long before we do."

The dog growled low, making no other response to a caress that usually brought him leaping to his master's breast. We heard the wind keening round the wooden walls, rushing with a long faint whistle over the roof, and we drew closer to the fire. For a long time no one spoke. The minutes passed and passed.

It was then, quite suddenly, that we heard a step in the snow; but not before the dog had heard it first and bounded to his feet with a growl that was more like a human roar than any animal sound I have ever heard. He fairly leaped toward the door, and the same second Dot and I were also upon our feet.

"What's the matter?" exclaimed her uncle, startled and surprised. "That's only wind, or snow falling from the roof."

Behind us the wooden walls gave out sharp cracking reports as the heated air made them expand; but in my heart something turned into ice with a cold that lay beyond all cold of winter. The terror I at first experienced, however, was not for myself, but for this soft, brown-eyed little maid who shot so swiftly by me and opened the heavy door. I was ready there to catch her, ready to protect and shield, yet knowing by some strange authority within me that she stood already safe, held by a power that lay beyond all little efforts of my own.

For into that great, fire-lit interior stepped at once the figure of a peasant, large, uncouth, lumbering, his face curiously concealed either by the play of the shadows or by the fall of his hair and beard—to this day I know not which—filling the threshold with his bulk, the freezing wind rushing in past his great, sheathed legs, and an eddy of dry snow veiling him like a flying cloak beyond. He stood there a second with an atmosphere of power about him that seemed to dwarf everything, and of such commanding stature that into my mind, bewildered and confused a little with the sudden entrance ran the thought of a bleak and towering peak of mountain. It came to me that the chalet must crumble, the huge beams split, and fall upon our heads. There was a rush of freezing wind, a touch of ice, and at the same time I was aware of some strange, intolerable beauty, as of wild nature, that made me hide my eyes. It was only long afterward that I remembered there was no snow upon his feet, that his eyes remained hidden, and also that he spoke not a word.

"The door's blown open!" cried the uncle. "For God's sake—"

All this, moreover, in the tenth of the first second, for immediately I saw that the St. Bernard was bounding round the figure with an unfeigned delight that knew no fear; and next, that he had stretched his arms out toward the girl with a gesture of tenderness and invitation possible only in this whole world to the arms of a woman. Terrible, yet inconceivably winning, was that gesture, as of a child. And the same moment, to my amazement, she had leaped forward and was gone. With her, barking and leaping, went the St. Bernard dog.

"Dot, you silly child, where in the world are you going? Do shut the door! It's not Harry yet. It was a false alarm." It was the matter-of-fact tone of her uncle's voice that let me into the secret—that only she, I, and the dog had witnessed anything at all.

"I'll go with her and see her safe," I shouted back, and it was only then, as I turned toward the door again after saying it, that I understood there was no one standing there, and that her leap had been really a springing run toward the corner where her ski lay. Already, I saw, they were on her feet. She was away. I saw the dog bounding over the frozen slope beside her. He was a little in front. He held her skirt in his teeth, guidingly. In that pale wintry light of the rising moon, I saw their two outlines against the snow. They were alone.

"Bring brandy and a blanket!" I had the sense to call back in to the room, and was after her in my turn. But the frozen fastenings of my ski had never seemed so obstinate. It was a whole minute before I was whizzing down the mile-long slope. The speed was tremendous, and the ski skidded on the crust. She left only faint indications of her trail. It was the barking of the dog that guided me best, and far away below me in the yellow moonlight, the little speeding spot of black that showed me where she flew, heading straight for the Creux du Van.

At any other time such a descent as we two then made would have been sheer lunacy, even in daylight. The tearing speed, the angle of the huge slope, the iciness of that gleaming crust, all were invitations to disaster; and with the gaping chasm of the Creux du Van lying waiting at the bottom, it was simply a splendid race into suicide. The water poured from my eyes, the frozen mounds whipped by like giant white waves, and no sooner was the black line of some isolated pine-tree sighted than it was past, like the telegraph poles to an express train. Only the yellow face of the big rising moon held steady.

She had soon outstripped the dog, and as I shot past him, wildly cantering, with his tongue out and steaming, open jaws, he caught vainly at my puttees. The next moment he was a hundred yards behind me.

But Dot, guided by some power that the mountains put into her little feet, knew her direction well, and went as straight as a die to the edge of the awful gulf; then stopped dead, buried to her neck in a drift that climbed wave-like upon the very lips of the chasm. It stopped her, as ten minutes before it had also stopped another, coming down from the slopes that lay to the westward. I saw the hole of the valley gaping at our very feet as a successful "telemark" flung me backward beside her just in the nick of time. "Quick!" I heard her cry. "He's still sliding!" It was then that I realised that the third body, lying there unconscious where the drift had likewise stopped it, was slowly moving with the weight of snow toward the edge. One ski already projected horribly over the actual brink. I heard a mass of snow detach itself and drop even as she said it.

It took less than a second to detach my belt and fasten it to his leg; but even then I firmly believe the strain of our slow pulling must have landed us all three into the gulf below had not the arrival of the St. Bernard put a different complexion upon the scene. It was the grandest thing I have ever witnessed. A second he stood there, the supreme instinct of his noble race judging the problem. He knew the softness of the drift that must engulf him if he advanced; he also saw it sliding. Very slowly, like a courageous human being, on all fours, calculating distance, angle, and tensions, as it were, by his superb animal divination, he crawled round to another side. He crept gingerly along the very edge. His teeth fastened upon the boot and ski-straps. We pulled together. God! I cannot understand to this day how it was that the four of us were not gone! He knew, that splendid dumb creature. We merely followed his magnificent lead.

A moment later we were safe on hard, solid snow. As we lay back exhausted, the snow immediately at our feet slid with a hiss, and disappeared into the valley hundreds of feet below. But the St. Bernard, still pulling carefully and gently by himself, was next busily licking the boy's white face and breathing his heat upon him, when help arrived with the brandy and the blankets. I believe it was the tireless and incessant attentions of that great dog that really saved the life, for he lay upon the form with his whole body, keeping him warm, and letting go only when he understood that the blankets and our arms, carrying him to the chalet, might replace his own self-sacrificing love.

"I heard a voice crying outside the door, in the wind," she told me afterward. "It was his voice, you see, and it called me by name. I don't know what guided me to the place, for I think I shut my eyes the whole way till I fell at his side."

Nephelé

I

The change of atmosphere at Carsholt began probably soon after Sir Mark's discovery of the Roman cinerary urn that very morning, but the discordant element in the castle household was not noticeable until Lady Shute betrayed her jealousy with the remark: "It's that interfering girl again! Why in the world should she go digging about the grounds like this?" Her eyes were questioning; her lips became very thin. "Above all, what possessed her to do it *now?*"

Her husband, the famous archaeologist, a sternfaced, elderly man, with an expression, evidently habitual, of great concentration yet aloofness, replied without looking up at first. The mouth was kindly, even tender, though it wore no smile at the moment. "Marjory is invaluable to me, you forget, dear; her memory, accuracy, insight—" he raised his eyes to his wife a moment. "Her knowledge of Roman things in particular is unusual. I often wish she had been with me in Crete and Egypt—"

He spoke soothingly, but the words were evidently the reverse of what his wife desired.

"Miss Trench," came the sharp interruption, "was an excellent governess before you stole her from the children for your archeology. I don't grudge you her invaluable services," with a tiny sneer of disbelief. "You know that. It's her taking up your time and attention at this particular moment that's so annoying. The house full of guests, the Christmas Theatricals coming on to-night, the children helpless without her—for rehearsals, dresses, everything—and then she must needs go and dig up a buried antiquity in the Park, and carry you off, and—"

"*I*—not she—dug it up, Emily," he corrected her, with a patient smile that secretly enraged her. He knew of her jealousy of his passionate work and, indirectly, of all concerned with it. "As a matter of fact, it was Tiger's burrowing that did it. A mass of earth, softened by the rain, buried the dog; I went to extricate him—and there—think of it, Emily!—there was the stone work, leading to a cavity"—his eyes shone with the smile of an enthusiastic boy—"a stone cist! I put my hand in. An urn, a lead casket, a Roman burial-place beyond question not far away—!"

"Mark, dear," interrupted Lady Shute, her voice harsh yet pleading, as of one bearing a grievance nobly, "they had lain there several hundred years. It wouldn't have hurt them to lie a few days longer, would it?"

The conversation was interrupted by a servant, and Sir Mark, outwardly apologetic, but inwardly glowing with his discovery, watched his wife disappear upon some urgent errand, then slowly made his way down a corridor to his study.

"We must be patient, Marjory, for another twenty-four hours or so," he mentioned, on finding her waiting for him to examine the treasures they had brought into the house only a few hours before. "Once the performance is over, and the people gone, we can get to work again." And he explained the situation in his blunt fashion, while the girl watched with eager, close attention his slightest word and gesture. The urn had not yet been thoroughly examined. Sir Mark now brought a movable electric lamp from another table. It was a moment of real life for the two delighted experts. The enthusiastic pair could contain themselves no longer.

"Still quite untouched," said the girl, in a tone a devotee might have used about some holy relic. "How lucky that you found it, instead of some clumsy workman with the point of a pick!" With her experienced, clever fingers she began to clear away the earth and stains of mould that still clung to the entrancing object. Her voice almost trembled with excitement as she added in a quick whisper: "Look, Sir Mark, look!" She pointed. "There's an inscription on it! I do believe—yes, there's an inscription! Look!"

He lowered his grey head beside her own, and thrust the light against the beautifully curved side of the precious urn.

"Nephelé," she whispered, making out the Greek letters before he did, "Nephelé—"

"The Dancer"—he deciphered the Latin words that followed. "Nephelé the Dancer," he repeated, easily deciphering the full inscription, now that she had shown the way. "Nephelé the Dancer," he repeated to himself.

He suddenly straightened up and stared hard at her, "Marjory!" he exclaimed, as though for the first time he realised her presence close beside him as a human being and not a secretary merely. "Marjory!"

She stared back at him, a light in her eyes that was not a reflection from the electric lamp he now held askew. "Nephelé the Dancer," she replied, looking straight into his face, and standing upright, while her breath came quickly. "That means no ordinary slave girl, but probably a celebrated dancer—someone exceptional—"

"They took Greek names, yes—the best of them. It was the fashion, wasn't it, in those days?" It seemed he asked her, as though he leant upon her special knowledge. The pair of them certainly were thrilled. Yet he was the great expert, she the assistant merely. He waited for her words, a curious look of expectancy in his eyes.

"A pure-bred Roman most likely!" she replied, after a moment's pause. "The villa that stood here, remember, was the residence of the District Governor. We are reasonably sure of that. And he"—the sudden curious inflexion in her voice he did not notice, nor the bolder expression that flamed an instant in her usually veiled eyes—"and he would certainly have the best—the very best obtainable—wouldn't he—"

"No ordinary slave girl, no mere dancer, as you say"—his words went fumbling rather—"would have been buried in this careful, honoured way—that's certain," he agreed, regarding her with the first touch of personal, admiring wonder he had ever shown. "Marjory!" he exclaimed again, "it's wonderful—very, very wonderful!"

There fell a momentary pause between them that was broken by Sir Mark suddenly rubbing his hands with pleasure and excitement, as he summoned his thoughts back to the consideration of the present. He turned to fetch some other objects to the light, objects that only an expert could have recognised at all, so broken and fragmentary were they, for the small metal box containing them beside the urn had not been properly fastened, the damp had entered, and the result was little more than a discoloured dust.

"A tibia, evidently," said Miss Trench, quietly; "this was once a little sweet-toned tibia, a flute of sorts you remember." She took up the crumbled atoms with loving care, as a mother might have lifted the tiny offspring of her own flesh and blood. "And this," she went on, half to herself, "quite possibly—I wonder?—might well have been a lyra that twanged the accompaniment to the dancing."

"My dear!" exclaimed Sir Mark with keen interest, and yet keener surprise. "You may be right. How clever of you—"

"The merest guesswork," replied the girl. "I may just as well be quite wrong, though somehow—I don't think I am." Her manner was intent, absorbed; he was as moved as she was. They handled and fingered the mysterious little things of dust and powdery wood, piecing them together again, as it were; making technical, expert comments; yet both stirred to their hearts by the human emotions that seemed still clinging about these pathetic symbols of ancient joy and gaiety.

"The casket! Now for the little casket!" exclaimed the archeologist, his eyes lighting up afresh. He glanced at his companion. "We will open it together, you and I—eh?" He went over quickly to another shelf, the girl so close on his heels that unconsciously she laid her hand upon his arm, and her shining face almost brushed his cheek as they bent down together, then carried back to the light a small, dull object that had lain for twenty centuries beside the urn—the leaden casket. "The chisel, Marjory! The cold chisel—quick—where is it?" But already her swift fingers had passed it to him, and she watched his deft movements as he gently prised up the lead all round the top.

"It overlapped, you see," she remarked. "It was hammered down to the sides so as to form an air-tight joint all round. You can see the scallop-shell moulding too."

"Admirable, admirable!" he murmured. "If only you had been with me years ago in Crete!"

"It's the Roman things I'm best at," replied the girl simply.

The opening of the casket was accomplished without damage, revealing inside a second box, whose lid threatened to crumble as they touched it. "Cedar wood," said Miss Trench, "fastened with a leather thong." The leather was in good preservation. They peered inside. Two flat, brownish objects lay at the bottom of the little cedar box that still exhaled a faint aroma of its original fragrance; and as Sir Mark, puzzled at first, lifted them out tenderly for examination, the emotion of the archaeologist rose in him to a degree he had never experienced before, not even in his former Egyptian days of wonderful excavation and discovery. For a second his sight dimmed and became curiously blurred. "Footwear of some kind," he muttered, "slippers probably, or—"

"Sandals," came the low, clear voice at his ear, even before his own sentence was completed. "Her dancing sandals. Nephelé's!"

Her employer turned and stared at her without a word for several seconds; then presently passed over to her, almost automatically, the precious remnants of the centuries. In spite of their great age, the sandals were still soft and pliable, the thongs that once bound them to the twinkling feet still serviceable.

"How neatly made and finished! How strong and flexible!" the girl said in a low voice, holding them to her eyes. "The leather—some imported hide, from Africa probably—gazelle, most likely. And what small feet she had—Nephelé. How marvellously light they are—feel them, Sir Mark— they seem almost alive. And her jewellery—some of her jewellery, too!"

The girl held in her hand a square piece of crystal attached to a fine gold chain. For a moment she hung it upon her dress, the gold chain touching the skin of her neck, the crystal swinging to and fro against her bosom. Very becoming to her was this ornament of the Roman dancing-girl of two thousand years ago. "It was in the bottom of the cedar box," she explained in a slow, quiet voice, looking down admiringly at it. "Nephelé wore it, of course, when she danced. I feel—somehow—she loved dancing to this Roman Governor. She gave of her very best. I'm sure she danced divinely, and perhaps"—her voice sank away, fading curiously in volume—"she loved him—"

Her companion, examining the crystal and gold chain in his fingers, was not listening, apparently, to her fanciful description. "Of no great value," he remarked, "of no particular value, but interesting all the same—extraordinarily interesting. One can see the whole thing," he continued, half to himself, half to her, "the scene itself, the girl dancing, the great Roman looking on. One can hear the flutes, the twanging of the harps. It's easily reconstructed, isn't it? I wonder what she wore, and what he wore; what she felt, and what he felt? She must have been beautiful, yes, a beautiful dancer, of course, and, as you say, she may—"

The hoot and drone of arriving motors broke in upon his words; the sound of a dressing-gong followed harshly; a servant knocked and entered, bearing an urgent message "from her ladyship" that the dinner guests were already within the castle gates and both archaeologist and his assistant were needed by the tyrant Present. Sir Mark broke off, listening with a vague impatience.

"Thus," he said, turning with a smile to Miss Trench, "do the centuries repeat themselves—eh? Somewhat in this way, perhaps, Nephelé herself was summoned to prepare for *her* performance!"

They exchanged an understanding glance which proved that one and the same sympathy taught both minds, and that both shared a similar vision of reconstruction. Behind the servant, meanwhile, came Hugo Trench, already dressed; as Judge of the rival factions which were to perform after dinner, he was alert and interested like themselves, though in a different way.

"The audience is pouring in," he announced laughingly, "and as I'm a famous dramatic critic as well as arbiter, I insist upon your being ready, Marjory. Every child in the castle's calling for you, and Lady Shute"—with a glance at his host—"declares you're wanted in every room at once." He turned to Sir Mark, as his sister hurried away. "You must let me into the secret too," he observed, "as soon as the great performance is over. I'm not an expert, like my sister, but I'm eager to see and learn."

And Sir Mark, drawing up his mind and manners to the surface of to-day again, explained briefly what the precious objects were. "Marjory," he mentioned, "your sister—her instinct is quite extraordinary where Roman things are concerned, really wonderful. I hope—she won't overtire herself to-night with all this acting, children business. She seemed to me a trifle—overwrought—just now. It's the twofold excitement, of course."

"Her own part is a small one," replied his guest, "and she knows it backwards, she tells me, though I've no idea what it is myself. But she's stage-manager, dresser, scene-shifter, and prompter in addition. How she loves and enjoys it all, though!"

"She's most competent, most gifted," added Sir Mark, hurrying off with an excuse to make himself ready, and leaving the critic in charge of the relics on the table.

Hugo Trench, left alone with the musty treasures on the table before him, examined them with the merely curious interest of a well-read, cultivated mind. The sandals in particular he looked at closely for some minutes, since dancing was his absorbing hobby, and it was his "Study of Classical Dancing in Relation to the Modern Ballet" that had won for him his present eminent position in the artistic world.

At the moment, however, a more human interest, and one nearer to his heart, divided his attention. He was thinking of his sister's passionate adoration for a man thirty years her senior; wondering whether Lady Shute had—and why her husband had not—divined it; hoping that no unhappiness need result from so strange a relationship, involving perhaps the loss of lucrative and pleasant work; asking himself chiefly, however, wherein lay the cause of the recent and sudden increase in the girl's emotion. It had become so intense that her face betrayed her. Its radiance lent her positively a new beauty. Holding the sandals in his hands, stroking, examining them, his real interest was not with Nephelé, their wearer, whose name even he did not know, but with his sister Marjory, who, it seemed to him, was becoming somewhat deeply entangled in an awkward set of circumstances.

II

The Hall had certainly come into its own to-night, with a quiet air of grandeur, a dignity, a spaciousness which had accumulated during the passing of the ages.

Two immense log-fires roared upon capacious hearths that once had roasted oxen whole; and near the roof, lost among shadows, the faded battle flags of inter-tribal battles long ago hung motionless and grim. The fitful light gleamed on the stands of armour round the walls, and the big candles that alone lit the table might have been torches of resinous wood flaring upon boar's head, mead in goblets, tankards of foaming ale, instead of upon champagne for the elders and lemonade for the children who formed a large proportion of "those present."

These annual festivities were a serious affair at Carsholt. Before the climax of the Christmas Tree, there would take place the time-honoured rivalry between the Shutes of the Upper and the Lower Valley, each side giving its performance respectively amid keenest competition. Children, of course, were the actors, only two grown-ups, one of either sex, being permitted to take part; and Lady Shute of Carsholt, zealous partisan of her own Lower Valley, was persuaded that Miss Trench, though her part was a small one, would this time lead her side to victory. The girl's ten minutes on the stage affected the entire cast, lifting the little play to almost a professional standard. The Upper Valley, she was convinced, could boast no such talent among its grown-up helpers. The prize, an enormous box of chocolates, she did not care about; it was the honour of the Lower Valley she had at heart. There were cousins, too, she longed to see crestfallen after defeat, and the fact that her own children were performing was, of course, an added incentive to her keen desires. Both sides, with a hundred performances behind them, were at present equal. This was a decisive occasion. She certainly counted upon Miss Trench.

The Judge, moreover, was Miss Trench's famous brother, whose unanimous appointment lent a further distinction to the occasion. Amid much excited laughter and applause he was duly installed after dinner in the stiff chair belonging to his exalted office, the few electric lights Sir Mark permitted were turned out, and in the soft glow of a hundred candles the troupe from the Upper Valley gave a finished performance of the piece they had been rehearsing for weeks, if not for months, beforehand.

Its success, judging by the spontaneous applause from both sides, was beyond question, and Hugo Trench, busily making the notes he was expected to make, watched by numerous anxious eyes, registered as well the mental comment that "if the Lower Valley is going to beat *that*," the Shute tribe would indeed be an uncommonly gifted set of people. For the excellence of the performance had genuinely surprised him; he had expected to be mildly bored, but instead had been an admiring and interested spectator. Sir Mark, beside him in the background of the crowded room, clapped long and loudly, while Lady Shute flashed acutely enquiring glances in his direction, though forced to conceal her anxiety, and to applaud as well. Only Marjory, in a chair just behind her host, gave no outward sign of approbation, an omission her brother ascribed to her preoccupation with her own part in the following rival piece. The Banqueting Hall echoed with enthusiastic curtain-calls, and in the general buzz of voices and bustle of excited movement, neither he nor Sir Mark noticed exactly when she left her seat. Being behind them both, indeed, and this end of the hall being but dimly lit by the big fires, her actions were easily concealed. Shadows draped all three of them, for that matter, and several empty rows intervened between them and the main body of the audience. What happened to Marjory Trench at the moment, in any case, no one apparently observed.

Suddenly there came an abrupt lowering of voices everywhere, and the appearance of a figure on the stage announced the approaching excitement of the rival troupe. In the hush that instantly descended upon the audience, the boy of fifteen, stage-manager and impresario, stood with shy self-consciousness before the row of candles and made his solemn announcement. After telling the "ladies and gentlemen" that what they were about to see was "of an unparalleled nature," and had "never been excelled on any stage," he added: "And I'm very sorry, ladies and gentlemen, we hope you won't mind much, but really we must turn all the lights out for it, please!"

The chorus of protest, half-shudderingly made, might have overwhelmed any less confident public man than this one who stuck manfully to his guns, and, availing himself of a pause the Judge obtained for him, carried his point at length successfully. "You see, ladies and gentlemen, the night has turned out fine, and there's a lot of moonlight now, so the place won't really be a bit too dark, and the bright light would spoil our piece. Thank you very much, ladies and gentlemen"—and he was gone again behind the curtain to the sound of clamorous applause. A moment later a footman appeared and extinguished the footlight candles, while another servant drew back the heavy curtains from the narrow, deep-set windows. The great body of the hall sank down into obscurity. At once a soft stream of moonlight stole upon the stage with a delightful and mysterious effect.

It was at this moment, perhaps, that the change of atmosphere, lurking hitherto unnoticed behind the general details of the day, stepped forward a little from the background and proclaimed itself a recognisable item in the programme. A soft, mysterious gloom pervaded the whole place, and a shudder of enjoyable creepiness ran among the children in an audible wave. The hall now doubled in size, the lofty ceiling reared away among deep shadows that blurred all outlines, and the sudden absence of glare from the stage candles made it difficult to welcome the swift change from brilliance to obscurity.

It is a fact, moreover, that into this pause when the voices ceased and talk died away, there fell abruptly an unexpected sound—the barking of dogs, muffled by distance, but answering one another with distinctness in the night outside. With the faint moonlight, now streaming across the stage from the uncurtained windows, entered also this curiously mournful sound. The Carsholt hounds were baying the wintry moon, no more, no less; yet over that packed audience, obeying automatically the spell of semi-darkness—as men and women must and ever will—stole the faint presage of the singular change. It almost seemed that the deep baying of the uneasy dogs, as by some preconcerted signal, had announced it.

"Admirable—quite admirable, really!" exclaimed the Judge beneath his breath, as though both baying and the moonlight were artificial tricks of the producer's—and at the same time wondering whence came the shiver that chilled his skin uncomfortably and made him look across his shoulder. "A wonderful *mise en scène*, isn't it—so dramatic?" he whispered to his host, who stood upright at his side, one arm resting on the stiff-backed chair. "We're going to see something exceptional, I do believe!"

Sir Mark, apparently, was too intent upon the empty stage to answer; his eyes stared fixedly, he showed no sign of having heard; and Trench turned next to take an impression of his sister, whose chair, placed behind and below his own, left her in shadow somewhat. But before sight picked her up, he forgot his first intention. The performance had begun. From that moment, in any case, Hugo Trench, as critic, as man, as Judge, forgot everything in the world except the thing he saw and heard upon the little improvised Carsholt stage.

"It's really capital, first class!" ran his murmured exclamations, as the strings stole deliciously across the dark spaces of the immense old hall. "How in the world do they manage it? It's too delightful!" For this sound of harp-strings plucked very far away seemed to enter the room from the Park beyond the narrow windows; the players, no doubt, were standing, muffled to the eyes, upon the moonlit lawns outside; and the effect, as the soft twanging sent its small vibrations through the vaulted hall, was most cleverly conceived and carried out. As the strings grew louder, the sense of anticipation became yet more keen, and when low flutes took up a delicate melody to the harps' accompaniment, the critic knew a moment of positive enchantment that he, for one, had never yet experienced upon any stage before.

"The youthful impresario was right," he whispered to his host. "Where— who are the players? How do they manage that sound so well?" He interrupted himself with a long-drawn "Sshhh" to the audience, who still kept up their whispering too loudly. "Very, very clever!" he went on, "but I wish they'd shut that door or window—ugh!" and he shivered a second time, then gave a little start. Sir Mark, in an effort to see and hear better, had leaned over and lurched rather heavily against his chair, but the same second almost was rigid again.

"Harps! Flutes! It's astonishing!" he was muttering, though to himself rather than to his guest. "A curtain has been drawn," his whisper continued, "and someone looks forth on us!"

"Perfect, perfect!" repeated the Judge, as the tune quickened and the strings now sounded close behind the curtain. "It's Marjory's idea, no doubt," he added proudly, too excited to notice the strangeness of the other's language, and then came once more his vehement hiss, half-angrily this time, since the audience obstinately refused to maintain a proper silence. It was in the obedient hush following this time the authority of the Judge's chair, that a figure all had been waiting for slipped round the edges of the immense plush curtains and began to dance.

Trench was aware of two things: that someone had omitted to close the open door through which the cold winter's air came in with the musicians—and that he was spellbound. He forgot even to chide the stupid, chattering audience into silence. He watched with an amazement that increasingly mastered him. "I didn't know—I simply never guessed she had it in her ...!" he exclaimed aloud once to his neighbour, then fell to silence, enchanted, strangely moved, caught out of himself by something he had never seen before on any stage.

In his day he had known much solo interpretative dancing, the best the capitals of Europe had to offer, and his criticism had picked out its almost invariable weakness—the inability to tell the story clearly. Hence, then, the miracle that now arrested the experienced soul in him, with a startled wonder and wholehearted admiration that took his breath away. The story that the figure interpreted in her dancing was clear as print. It was, moreover, a deep, a subtle story. How many, he wondered maliciously, among that country audience grasped it too?

For all that, his mind seemed confused—and curiously confused—between two sets of values. He watched, he felt, he analysed; he did not wholly understand; there was a missing item of immense importance somewhere that evaded him. That his sister possessed this touch of genius, that it explained her previous odd excitement, that her performance really *must* be seen in London, Paris, Milan—herein lay one set of values he could deal with easily enough. It was the other that puzzled him, even to laying a shadow upon his heart and mind.

In some way he could not define exactly, the exquisite performance he witnessed slipped just, though only just, beyond the edge of what was explicable and normal. This fact both puzzled and enthralled him, but it was the *type* of dancing that added the element of distress. Never before had he seen its like; its *genre* was unfamiliar; wholly new to him indeed. There were moments when Hugo Trench, who signed weekly articles in a newspaper of authority, doubted his own eyes. This lovely draped figure with the masses of dark, unfastened hair falling below her waist, a jewel gleaming on her breast, her bright feet flashing, twinkling; these gestures and movements that so superbly rendered the drama, now passionate, now pathetic, of a soul in the anguish of a great yet unuttered love—that this was his own sister Marjory, dancing upon the Carsholt stage for a Christmas gathering seemed incredible. For the face, hidden by falling hair and flowing drapery, was never clearly visible in the uncertain moonlight, while the sound of the little feet, well-nigh inaudible too in their fairy lightness, was drowned even by the faintly plucked strings and soft-blown flutes. He was aware of a deep lost meaning that went drifting, fluttering, hanging in the air before him, though of one he could not wholly seize....

Yet the story itself certainly unravelled itself clearly enough before his enchanted eyes, and to a setting of deep emotion only great art and even greater conviction could have hoped to waken: the story of a faithful love divinely felt, but of a love unspoken because unrecognized by the object of its worship; a love, therefore, heroically concealed. By what power, by what art, was conveyed, further, the spiritual grandeur belonging to a passion that was unearthly in the sense that it was deathless, able to survive all possible barriers of space and time? It was this touch of majesty that arrested the critic's soul with a wondering amazement, making him ask himself repeatedly: "How can she do this thing? Can this really be Marjory?"

So profound was the impression made upon him by the interest of the story, that he was less surprised than might otherwise have been the case when, to questions his brain asked occasionally, there rose from somewhere instantaneous and adequate replies. That an inner voice came to his assistance in this way, answering questions in his mind, satisfying moments of doubt he felt from time to time in the dance—he was as positive of this, as he was that these replies were absolutely true. Did he fail sometimes to follow the rapid, concentrated drama, did the meaning become momentarily obscure or wavering, then instantly rose this voice with a few true words that supplied the lost intention. Guided by these infallible, mysterious comments, he followed the brief story with a divination beyond his normal powers. For it was not the action merely that he sometimes failed to grasp, but rather the motives, desires, hopes and fears that lay deeply buried in the dancer's beating heart; it was these the mysteriously understanding voice made clear ...

Far from her native land, beneath skies alien yet not unfriendly, the girl danced this great love she could not, dared not, otherwise express. Her secret was her life; she told it, offered it, in ecstasy. And not entirely in vain; her lavish giving of all she had to give was not wasted utterly; for though unrecognised by him who called it forth, her passionate beauty enriched the curtained eyes, sweetened the heart, of him who thought he delighted merely in her perfect art. His days stole some strange added happiness, whose origin he did not trouble himself to ask....

"He never knew, he never recognised...." rose the inner voice in explanation. "He remained blind—almost to the end ..."

The figure bent lower, as the dance now drew towards its close; the jewel flashed in the moon upon her heaving breast; she kissed the alien soil *he* also trod; the masses of dark hair fell forward abruptly in a final gesture of sacrificial pain and happiness, covering her young face and outline as with the night of death.

" ... until she died at his very feet, falling with his name upon her lips, her secret told in the eyes' last look ... so that too late ... he *knew*—"

A shock of surprise and fear fell suddenly on the listener's heart. This voice was real. It was not an inner, an imagined voice, but one he knew and recognised. It was close beside him, against his very ear. It was his host's. Also he now recognised the jewel, the sandals too; the very music was not what he had the right to hear. This, beyond all question, was his sister Marjory, but in what borrowed, stolen guise, he asked himself? The blood for a moment left his heart, then rushed back with uncomfortable pressure, as he turned to the man at his elbow who had all along been supplying him with these uncanny, whispered explanations.

An instant of blinding confusion, of values that refused to right themselves, swept over him. Added to this, came the rising whispers of the impatient audience, but whether in praise of the performance just over—the figure had disappeared—or to welcome the young stage manager who now tried to stammer a few words, he could not say. This, too, remained a blurred picture in his troubled mind. Memory, indeed, hardly registered normally for some minutes, and it was partly the marble-white face of his host, and partly another thing as well, that undoubtedly caused his momentary loss of self-control. Sir Mark lurched heavily, a second time against his chair. A sound immediately behind them both had rendered his balance insecure. Trench turned in the grip of a supreme amazement. The voice was that of his sister. It issued from the lips of Marjory, as she collapsed yet deeper into the chair she had never, he now realised, for one moment left.

"Help me! We must get her out—away from this," cried Sir Mark, yet quietly, his tone perfectly steady and controlled. It was exactly as though he knew and understood something his guest just failed to grasp—the very item, indeed, that had eluded him during the entire evening. It was he, the brother, however, who divined the fuller truth, and divined it perhaps alone—that the girl had been unconscious during the whole of the little act. Her cry was not uttered in the moment of fainting, but uttered out of an unconscious state she had lain in for the past half-hour and more.

Trench, though he made a great effort to recover his mental balance, was too surprised, too shocked still, to succeed entirely, He moved as in a dream. He remembers inaccurately what happened. He had just lived a dream; that dream continued oddly. The interest of the audience in the second piece, now about to begin, enabled the two men to carry the girl out of the room unnoticed; the rows of empty seats, the darkness, and the proximity of a side door helped them further. Once in the lighted passage outside, he remembers hearing, with a vague dull anger in his heart, some words his host muttered about "the sandals, the very sandals … and the jewel. I saw them on her. I must—forgive me a moment—I'll see if they're still safe …" He broke off, almost letting drop the feet he carried, and was gone, deep in the preoccupation of his personal and passionate concern, shaking the little human interest from his obstinate mind, as though he shook off at the same time the recognition of something that he knew was true, yet dreaded.

Trench managed to carry his sister, unaided, to her room. Before he reached it, however, her eyes had opened and her normal state already begun to return. It was the rapidity of this return from unconsciousness, together with the first words she uttered, that confused her anxious brother even more, but at the same time convinced him finally that he had indeed witnessed something that had not been "seen on any stage before."

"Nephelé ..." she murmured, staring at him with moist eyes and quivering lips; "she told him... she gave her secret. But did he realise ... understand?"

"N-no, no," stammered her brother in reply. "He never understood. He never will!"

He was shaking. He spoke with curious conviction, wondering at himself. His words—her own as well—came evidently from the glamour of his dream, belonged still to the story that had so vehemently possessed him. He supported the girl's arm as he led her to the sofa. Who was she? Who was Nephelé? Who was Majory? Who, above all, was—this other? The questions rose flooding into his bewildered mind.

"He's gone to make sure his precious relics are safe," came lamely, stupidly from his lips, as he watched his sister now putting her hair tidy before the mirror. She had refused to lie down. She declared she felt all right again. "You—you wore them, you know—Marjory," he added, in spite of his desire not to say this thing.

She did not understand apparently, perhaps she did not catch his words. The normal expression rapidly reestablished itself on her face. She was calm.

"I fainted—didn't I?" she was asking quietly. She looked about her, her grey eyes clear and soft, her voice quite steady. "Where are we? Oh, my room, of course. How idiotic of me! I've never fainted in my life before."

For a moment there passed through her eyes a distant expression as of things remembered but not explained, then vanished again. "Where is—" she had an air of searching vaguely—"I mean—has the second piece begun?" She changed the sentence. "Quick, Hugo, I must hurry! Lady Shute will never forgive me if I'm late." With a few deft touches to her dress, she ran with anxiety, yet laughingly, to the door. "You too, Hugo," she exclaimed, as she opened it to the sound of excited voices coming up the passage. "You're Judge, remember!"

Following the excited voices, in came the young stage manager and the breathless Lady Shute herself.

"Oh, I say, Miss Trench, wherever have you been?" cried the aggrieved boy.

"We have *all* been waiting for you," put in the exasperated lady, a jealous anger gleaming behind the frigid manner. "You were nowhere to be found. It's really unforgivable—"

The Judge took the blame upon himself as they hurried downstairs; but the second piece, thus delayed, went poorly, for the players were upset, and Miss Trench, herself flustered and apologetic, gave an uninspired, even a mediocre performance of her own particular part. The Judge was forced to decide in favour of the Upper Valley, to the intense and venomous annoyance of his hostess. Sir Mark was not present. He arrived only just in time to make his customary little speech to the assembled rival tribes, and to hand the prize to the delighted winners.

"That stupid, selfish, irresponsible girl!" his wife relieved her mind at the first opportunity afterwards. "Her mind was elsewhere the whole time. And I'd counted on her so *absolutely*. Really she might—you, too, Mark—might have left your dead specimens in their grave just *one* day longer! I think," she added acidly, "it's time that Miss Trench's work was done by a man."

He made no adequate reply, his wife's grievance was admitted.

"The girl could hardly help fainting, I suppose," he mumbled. "She's been over-doing it lately a bit perhaps—"

"Men don't faint," his wife informed him. "You should have a man secretary. As for the girl—I've packed her off to bed, and I think it's time you engaged another assistant, dear."

Sir Mark sympathised, staring at his enraged wife somewhat blankly. There was justice and common sense in what she said. He was aware of this. Then, suddenly, he was aware of another thing—that an unalterable firmness lay in him with regard to something she had said, a fixed decision. He would never dismiss Miss Trench from his employment ...

It was long after midnight, the last guests gone, the children sound asleep, and the moon looking down softly upon Carsholt and the time-worn valley of the Shute.

In the mind of the archeologist, as he stood gazing down upon his treasures before going to bed, stirred a faint, inexplicable warmth of awakened imagination, whose trail, as he followed it, led him out into the wintry sky beyond the old stone walls. Upon one open palm lay the little pair of shining sandals, upon the other gleamed the bright crystal jewel. He gazed down at them in silence, forgetting that his guest sat smoking by the fire, watching him.

"They say," he murmured, "that history repeats itself. It certainly was passing strange and wonderful! Can I believe that—?"

"Genius," remarked the critic, not wishing to play unwilling eavesdropper, "is ever strange—particularly in its spasmodic appearances." Sir Mark's face was not visible, his back being to the glare of the electric light. "Never on any stage before," he went on, slowly, "have I witnessed anything—"

His host turned sharply with a look on his face that stopped his companion dead. Tenderly laying down the treasures, he came over to the fire where his guest sat watching, listening, wondering.

"Let me tell you this," he said thickly, "that what we witnessed to-night is something that our old world has not seen for close upon—two thousand years."

He laid a hand gently upon the other's shoulder. "I suggest, Trench," he added in a lowered voice trembling with emotion, "that it remain *our* secret, since you and I were the only witnesses. To-morrow I shall replace these relics in their ancient tomb. I shall bury them again."

He did, then, an amazing thing. Turning back to the table, he raised the sandals to his lips and kissed them with a reverent devotion. He kissed the shining jewel too.

"Let us, too, bury in our hearts," he said softly, "those treasures which we appreciate—but may not use."

Additional Sketches

By Algernon Blackwood

The Lock of Grey Hair

It hung so conspicuously there amid the surrounding mop of fine dark hair that it piqued the curiosity of Dr. Blane's friends more than any other detail of his very distinguished appearance. Grief, said a good number, had caused it; anxiety, declared others; but the majority, including servants and women, plumped of course for love. He was successful and he was unmarried: the evidence was unanswerable. I believe, however, that I am the only living person who holds the true secret.

"Most people who have really lived," he used to say, "possess some singular experience or other that they do not care about telling indiscriminately. And this is mine. I'm a little ashamed of it," he added, "for now-a-days we explain everything—or confess ourselves unscientific. Besides,"—he shrugged his shoulders—"my conduct, I always feel, was not strictly professional perhaps in the best sense. And, also,—it was the only time in my life when I was obliged to acknowledge a sense of unreasoning fear;—and yield to it!"

And the story, it must be confessed, certainly would have claimed belief more readily in those picturesque times when "Possession," diabolical or otherwise, was a prevalent superstition, and when the post-mortem activity of a disembodied spirit was held to be often exceedingly lively.

It happened before the days when Dr. Blane's skill had earned for him the honours of knighthood, together with the privilege of Inspectorship of Royal Diseases. This, somewhat, is as he told it to me shortly before his own death:

With an intimate friend, it appears, he was revisiting a little village in the Swiss Jura where had been to learn French as a boy, when the friend incontinently was laid low with diphtheria, and he stayed out perforce to nurse him. Both men had their meals in the cosy little Pension de La Poste, where twenty years before they had studied grammar and irregular verbs together; but Dr. Blane, who wanted quiet, had his work- and bed-room in Michaud's new house at the other end of the village where the vineyards begin.

Now, the epidemic, it so happened, was a severe one, and two other persons—but for whom this thing might not have come about—were also laid low: one, the villa aesculapius, Dr. Ducommun, the other, Mlle. Udriet, a wealthy but avaricious old woman whose personality was of dark and sinister odour throughout the whole countryside, and who on account of her intense miserliness, was known generally as *'la mauvaise riche.'* And she was well named, for village wit has a way hitting the nail on the head. She was an evil woman, with great force of individuality, dreaded by all; and her fear of spending money went to amazing lengths. It was even reported of her that she enticed her neighbours' cats into her big house, slew and cooked them with her own hands, and ate them to save a butcher's bill. Her long finger-nails, and certain other unappetising peculiarities, were evidence, the village held, for anything and everything.

And Dr. Blane, who was sent for to prescribe in the temporary absence of Dr. Ducommun, admits that the moment he crossed the threshold of the ill-smelling room and saw the old miser staring fixedly at him from her bed, he was inspired by an instant and singularly powerful aversion for her. The face he always described as truly venomous, and her thin fingers lying on the coverlet were "taloned and be-clawed," he used declare with a shuddering laugh, "like the feet of a great bird of prey." Here, for the first time in his life, was a patient, he hinted afterwards, whom he would rather have helped to die than to live.

Though ashamed of his revulsion, he could not quite conceal it. The fact that she would never pay his fees was nothing. It was the woman herself. "She was like some great loathsome insect in that dark room," he said; "some insect whose sting was death!"

The situation at first was merely unpleasant, but a little later it became more awkward and furnished Dr. Blane with the excuse for what he terms his unprofessional attitude. For the village doctor got better—well enough to crawl out and see his pet patients—and *la mauvaise riche* got steadily worse. Moreover, she insisted on sending for Dr. Blane because she preferred his greater skill, and Dr. Blane as often as possible shelved the unpleasant responsibility upon the shoulders of the local practitioner.

Plainly put, he avoided seeing her—even refused point blank to do so, and the old woman, when she found that he no longer came, suffered paroxysms of rage that were positively terrifying in their concentrated fury.

It was one night towards the end of March when the matter came to climax. Earlier in the evening Mlle. Udriet, apparently at her crisis, had sent him an imperious summons, and Dr. Blane, not without pricks of conscience, had passed on the summons by messenger to his colleague at the other end of the village. Dr. Ducommun, however, was delayed for several hours, with the unfortunate result that *la mauvaise riche* lay neglected to the end. The Englishman, of course, knew nothing of this. He was in the Pension sitting by the bedside of his friend, reading. It was ten o'clock. Shaded candles stood on the little table and the sick man was sleeping peacefully the sleep of recovery. For twenty-four hours there had been no return of the delirium. At the end of the darkened room, Mme. Favre who owned the Pension and had proved herself a devoted helper, was in the act of mixing a tumbler of Thé St. Germain—her invariable remedy for all complaints—when suddenly two things—two surprising things—happened simultaneously: the sick man sat bolt upright in bed with startling abruptness, stared fixedly into the dark room in front of him, and pointed; while Mme. Favre let fall her tumbler with a crash upon the floor and cried in a voice of genuine alarm, "Who is it? Somebody pushed past me! There's someone else in the room!"

The singular way these two persons acted on the same instant impressed Dr. Blane unpleasantly—curiously. He was conscious at once of a disagreeable thrill—of something that brought the water with a rush to his eyes and made the skin of his back crawl. Yet, of course, he never for once believed that anyone had really entered the room through the closed doors.

"A return of the delirium," he said quietly, as his friend continued to glare about him and to point. And then added more sternly. "There's no need for alarm, Mme. Favre, I assure you;" for the old lady was leaning, pale and terrified, against the cupboard, and staring towards the bed as though her eyes would drop out.

But the patient, of course, absorbed his immediate attention. To the doctor there could be nothing very unusual about a scene of delirium; yet about this particular scene of delirium, he became sharply and unpleasantly aware, there was something very unusual indeed. It was convincingly and horribly real. To begin with, though the sick man had forgotten his French almost to the simplest phrases, he was now gabbling the language with a speed and fluency that were positively uncanny; and at the same time with a vehemence, a passion, a fury that had characterised none of his former attacks: moreover—most disquieting of all—with a thin whispering voice that was beyond question, not his own.

But of the whole wild torrent, all he, or that matter all Mme. Favre, could catch before it subsided again into abrupt silence were the short phrases, uttered with eyes fixed upon the doctor and a hand pointing into his very face: "You passed me by. But now I am out—and I shall not pass you by!"

The singular thing however—and it was this that gave the good woman the *crise de nerfs* that ended in a fainting fit—the singular and horrible thing was that as the changed voice poured out of the sick man, his face altered visibly as well, altered too into the lineaments of another visage that they both knew. How the eyes and mouth of a man could slip into the expression of a woman—an evil, vindictive woman—is beyond the power of description, yet the calm, experienced Dr. Blane as well as the frightened old lady at the end of the room both recognised beyond possibility of discussion that voice, face and manner belonged to the evil personality of that perverted old woman, *la mauvaise riche*. In the eyes, perhaps, the resemblance lay chiefly. It was unmistakeable. It was weirdly impressive.

Then it all passed as quickly as it came. The sick man slept peacefully once more. Mme. Favre pulled herself together, assisted by the judicious aid of cold water, and half an hour later Dr. Blane, battling already with vivid sensations of alarm such as he had never known before in his life, left the Pension to go back his own rooms.

His shortest way lay down the village street, past the house of Mlle. Udriet and so home. Yet the doctor deliberately chose the longer route. He admits it frankly. He did not wish to pass the woman's house. "I was curiously nervous, almost frightened," he said; "though exactly of what I could not tell. I came out of La Poste into the night all trembling. It was the most unaccountable sensation I have ever known. Rather than pass the door of that woman's house I have walked a mile."

So he went home by a roundabout way of perhaps fifteen minutes. The village was utterly deserted, and the night air swept about him with the scents of early spring from the surrounding forests. In his mind however he still saw his friend's changed face and heard the whispered words so vindictively uttered, "You passed me by. Now I'm out. I shan't pass you by!" And do what he might he could not dismiss them. The words kept time with the echo of his feet on the hard road.

A little more than halfway his path joined the main street by the fountain and then turned to the right and ran between low stone walls to Michaud's house. Beyond the walls were vineyards with hundreds of bare sticks already planted in the earth. And it was here, as he passed the fountain, that he first heard a noise that sent the blood tingling up about his ears. The mountain water splashes there all the year round with a steady fall, but what he heard had nothing to do with that. It was the sound of small feet pattering along under the deep shadow of the houses.

Something was following him. "It's a dog," he said, yet at the same time he knew quite well that it was not a dog. It was on two feet, not on four. Fear dropped cold and wet over his face. The road slopes the whole way to where the Michaud house stands isolated from the rest of the village among the vineyards, and Dr. Blane quickened his pace almost to a run. He found the excuse that he was cold, though he was perfectly well aware that the cold he felt was not the common cold of night.

For a time he resisted the desire to look round, but before he was half way down the hill the moon emerged from the clouds, and at last, with a sudden movement as though he expected to be attacked from behind— he stopped short and turned.

The village street in the pale wintry moonlight was empty. Black shadows lined its sides; the church pierced the sky; far above gleamed the spectral snows on the heights of Mont Racine, and the great mountain of Boudry with its dark army of pines hung, immense and forbidding, in the air. Nothing moved. But from the spaces of open moon-lit road close behind him came the sound of light pattering. The sound still followed him.

The way this creeping fear had begun to master him was beyond all things strange. He pulled himself together with a great effort of will and continued his way, this time without undue haste; for to run, he realised, was to admit that terror was in his heart. Yet, along some dark by-way, it had undoubtedly established itself already in his blood beyond all reach of argument. He walked with firm and measured steps, and as result he at once noticed that the sounds were no longer audible. The moment he asserted his will, apparently, they ceased. The whole thing was, of course, imaginary, born of the night, of the deep wintry silence and of the unpleasant memory that vivid scene in the sick-room had marked on his brain: in a word, nerves!

Leaving the village behind him he entered the section of road where low walls separated it from the vineyards on either side. But before he had gone a dozen yards, he became aware that something was running stealthily among the serried ranks of vinesticks over the wall on his left. The soft pattering on the earth was distinctly audible. The thing was keeping pace with him still, yet always a little behind. It was holding him in view—watching, waiting. "This," he says, "I realised above all else—that I was being followed with some sinister purpose."

Keeping to the middle of the road, however, Dr. Blane refused now to quicken his steps. It was remarkable how dead, how deserted, the mountain village seemed. No one was about; lights were out in every house. Wind, the night, and the timid mood with her fugitive gleams held possession of the world. And those swift, pattering footsteps, making their way without a single false tread between thousands of upright stakes, was ever beside him on the other side of the wall.

At last the outline of the house loomed welcome before him, and he entered the iron gates, slowly, still master of himself, and fumbled in the lock with his key. A space of gravel path led up to the door, and as he stooped to insert the key he was positive that he heard something leap the wall and land with kind of hushed shuffle on the shingly path close behind him. He turned with an exclamation, half cry, half curse,—again with the instinctive idea of protecting himself from attack, when suddenly a light shone through the door and Michaud, his landlord, opened it from the inside.

The sounds ceased. Dr. Blane passed hurriedly in. Never was light or human presence more welcome.

"I'll close after you," said Michaud, a little man with a jolly, smiling, fat face. "I knew your step."

Before shutting the door he peered out into the night. "Tiens!" he said, looking about him, "I thought I heard someone!"

"It's a dog or something that followed me down the road," said the doctor. He was glad to be with another man—uncommonly glad.

Michaud closed the door and locked it, but as he did so Dr. Blane got the curious impression that something darted in past his legs like a quick shadow into the house. At the same moment the lantern standing on the steps behind fell with a crash, as though knocked over, and the light was extinguished. Michaud laughed as he struck a match to relight it. He looked rather closely at his lodger for a moment. Dr. Blane declares that to the end he could never be certain that he had not himself stumbled against the lantern and so kicked it over.

"They've been here several times to fetch you," the man said, the moment the door was fastened. "But I told them you were out."

"Who came?" asked the other with an odd catch in his voice.

"I couldn't see. I called down from the window but didn't recognise the voice—some woman, I think. It was too dark to see. I told them to get Dr. Ducommun. She's dead, you know," he added abruptly. "Gone to her account at last."

"Who—who is dead?"

Michaud's voice was curiously hushed as he replied. "*La mauvaise riche*." He shrugged his shoulders.

Presently they said good-night and Dr. Blane went up to his room to work or to sleep. They were alone in the house these two, for Mme. Michaud was away visiting her mother at La Chaux-de-Fonda, and there were no other occupants. He heard the little man thumping about for a space in his bed-room below. Then, presently, all sounds ceased.

Dr. Blane's room was on the top floor—an attic room really. There were double windows, a cupboard, a bed in one corner with a mountainous duvet, hot-air pipes, a wash-hand stand opposite, and in the centre his worktable with two lighted candles. By the bed and table two strips of carpet—the rest pine boards, not even stained. It was all very primitive.

At first he tried to work—in vain. Then, turning his thoughts inwards, he deliberately attacked the problem with a view to solving it and recovering his normal state of balance. He brought bear upon it all the force of his acute mind, together with his great medical knowledge and experience. But analysis only confirmed things: he was suffering from a singular invasion of utterly unreasoning fear. He was afraid in the depths of his soul; cold and perspiring in turns; horribly creepy about the skin; and his hair ready at the least sound to rise upon his head. Yet, in his search, he could find nothing that seemed an adequate cause. His neglect of a patient, not even properly his, he admitted was not wholly pardonable, but, after all—! His mind, in spite of all efforts, came back always to the thought of that horrible changed expression his friend's face—the expression of that evil woman's eyes, and to the whispered words that had seemed like a curse. "I'm out. You passed me by. I shall not pass you by!"

Finally, to steady his mind and possibly find a measure of relief in expression, he sat down to put an analysis of his mental state on paper. He worked hard. But presently he paused and looked about him. He heard the wind. It had changed and *la bise* was blowing up over the lake of Neuchâtel. Now and again it rose to a wild, whistling cry that made him shiver. The clocks of Colombier struck one in the morning.

At length, in a calmer state of mind, Dr. Blane, half wondering, half laughing, but still strangely nervous, put out the candles and got into bed. And the moment the room was dark the noise began again.

There was no interval of guesswork; he knew at once what it was. Something was scratching at the door—outside. And the curious part of it was that the instant he heard it he realised that the door was no sort of protection. That it was locked was all a useless pretence. The thing could, and would, get in to him. And the next minute, with a nauseous rush of terror, he knew that it was in. It had somehow squeezed itself underneath the door—and was pattering across the bare boards to the side of his bed. And as he heard it, that vile pattering seemed inside him—on the very substance of his heart.

The actual distance between door and bed was small enough, but in those few seconds of intense horror it stretched into a hundred yards, and he knew all the prolonged agony of the steady, merciless approach that a man fastened to the rails must know when in the distance he hears the first rumble of the coming train. For a kind of paralysis crept over him so that he could not move. His heart dropped like lead. The perspiration that drenched him froze instantly into ice.

Then the steps quickened for a running leap; there was a sound of rushing through the air; a gust of glacial wind; and something dropped heavily upon the bed by his feet—and then began to climb quickly upwards towards his face.

Dr. Blane says he tried furiously to shout but could get no sound out above a whisper. The sensation of the footsteps treading up the whole length of his paralysed body was the most horrible thing he had known. But his climax of terror brought with it at least a certain power of movement, and he was just able to bury his face beneath a pile of clothes and pillows when the thing settled down with a clinging grip like wire netting upon his head and there began the most dreadful struggle imaginable in the thick darkness.

But it was an unequal fight. His hands were so moist with the clamminess of fear that the sheets slipped through fingers, and inch by inch the strength of his adversary succeeded in uncovering his face. First he felt it against the skin of his neck where thin fingers that gripped like cold iron caught him behind in a suddenly exposed place. The rest went swiftly: for that touch of ice somehow seemed to paralyse all the nerve centres at a stroke and bereft him of any power he had left. In a moment the clothes were torn from off him and he lay there helpless and motionless on his back, his face at last wholly uncovered.

And then, so close to his ear that the breath touched him as though the *bise* had forced its way in through the open window, he heard a thin whisper of words: "You passed me by. Now I'm out. I shall not pass you by!" and immediately after it came a smothering sensation over eyes and mouth as though a weight of snow had fallen to suffocate him, while creeping through it a stinging pain moved slowly down the sides of his face towards the throat. It was like claws of iron entering his flesh.

The freezing air of night blowing upon his face revived him after what must have been a long period of unconsciousness, for the grey light of early morning was in the room when he opened his eyes again and there was a sound of movement in the house below. With the precision of a strong mind accustomed to quick reflection and decision Dr. Blane at once realised the situation. There was no groping of memory. It all came back vividly, and in that very final minute of returning consciousness he was aware clearly of two things: first that it had all been real and no dream; secondly, that the terror had passed completely from his soul.

Wholly master of himself, yet with a feeling that was bruised and battered, he got out of bed and examined the room. And to his amazement he noticed for the first time that the double-windows were wide open and the *bise* was blowing straight into the room.

Wondering greatly—for they had been closed and fastened when he went to bed—he shut them tight. Then he crossed the floor to turn on the supply of hot air in the radiator. It was on his way back that he caught the reflection of his face in the mirror that hung by the window. The morning light fell full upon it. Down both cheeks ran dull red lines that ended in marks round the neck like the marks of the rope that he had known years before as prison doctor on the neck of a hanged man. There was no blood—merely a dull contusion under the skin; and almost as he looked the lines faded away and were gone.

But above them, a signature of his great terror, was something else that did not fade, and that remained to the day of his death. A lock of hair over the right temple had turned grey in a single night.

The Philosopher

A very nice old lady stood with a very big dog on the edge of the pavement. It was in the outskirts of a country town; the sun was shining, the birds were singing, and May smothered the hedges like fresh-fallen snow. Dressed in shiny black, with objects in her bonnet that jerked and waggled, the old lady was a pleasant thing to see, for she expressed exactly what a typical old lady ought to look like. She was what is called "a perfect dear," and the dog, who seemed enormous beside her frailty, was what is called "a perfect beauty." She was vigorous, yet used a stick, a stick of gleaming ebony with a polished ivory handle. She was full of life, and obviously satisfied with life; had undoubtedly made her will—there was lots to leave as well!—and had no quarrel with existence on any score whatever. For life was kind to her, and illness had forgotten to interfere with her digestion. Peevishness was a stranger to her. She was happy. You could hear her in the drawing-room at home laughing with the best of them and teasing people far younger than herself in a deep and musical voice. You could hear her saying "People as young as I am, my dear," before half the sentences she uttered; and she was going now on foot into the little town with her black stick, her neat black reticule, and her big, protective dog, upon good works intent. You could hear her laughing on the front-door steps as she came down into the garden while her son, or possibly her grandson, chided her: "It's absurd of you to walk, Grannie, when there are four motors and fourteen horses dying to pull you; but you are so obstinate in your young days—"

"I *am* young, Charles. You forget that I'm not yet seventy-eight!"

"Caesar will look after you, then, if you really won't let me come—"

"Better than you could," she smiled; then added slyly in her deep, teasing voice, "you have someone else to look after—a little younger than I am!"

It was the joke she had made first with his father thirty years before, probably with his grandfather as well a quarter of a century before *that*. She would surely live for ever. Death and illness had both forgotten her. The male figure on the steps watched her go until the shrubberies hid her, then turned and disappeared inside the ivy-covered old house that one day would be his own. She was a dear and wonderful old lady.

The day was glorious and very peaceful, with the calm beauty of a spring morning upon the entire country side. The stillness seemed too deep for anything to break it, for anything to happen. Beside her fragile figure the dog looked more than large—he looked massive and gigantic, powerful as a pony, very steady, very sure of himself. The whip she carried with her reticule would hardly have disturbed a fly. But Caesar loved and followed her as though she were at least a lion-tamer.

He obeyed with a slavish smile in his great brown eyes her slightest order. He kept brushing up against her to inquire what her wishes were. He protected her. He could have held the traffic up if necessary while she passed very slowly with him into safety.

And there she stood on the edge of the pavement, waiting to cross the road. Her stick was a foot in front of her as she leaned a little forward. She left the curb and stood a moment in the cobbled gutter. She looked steadily up the road, then down the road, then straight in front of her to choose her footsteps well. No tram, no car, no tradesman's cart was visible; the air was without dust; there was no sound but the piping of the birds. She glanced inquiringly at Caesar, and Caesar agreed, wagging his bushy tail with authority and confidence.

Four of her little steps fitted into one leisurely stride of his great legs. His eyes said plainly: "Yes, you may cross with safety now, my dear. Keep close to me," as he sedately led the way. He never followed at such moments; he helped by guiding; and if he felt concern he did not show it. He invariably waited till the "old thing," as he called her to himself, was out of danger, and then he barked and bounded with tremendous energy just to inform the world at large the worst was over. But he *was* anxious all the same. He had known her to "bundle about" most stupidly sometimes when sudden danger confused her and surprised the muscles into acting without an order from the brain. For, of course—and this was what he never could understand or realise—she had not got his absolute alertness and instinctive action. Where he could act instantaneously she had to think before the proper movement followed. She could neither leap nor bound nor save herself five times in thirty seconds before the horses' very hoofs.

And so in the middle of the road, when the reckless car came tearing round the unexpected corner at its wicked pace, and she pirouetted apparently on the point of her ebony stick, unable to execute the sudden leap of six inches that could have saved her—he merely barked at her to hurry up, with a helpful push of his great shoulder in the right direction. He wagged his beautiful tail and pranced. It was true he pushed her with his shaggy head, but he did not realise that she could be so clumsy, so dreadfully maladroit, as to let the stick catch right between her little feet. "If she had bounded sideways or even backwards! If she had dropped on all fours and leaped six inches after me...!" But she hadn't.

He observed the subsequent proceedings solemnly, ignoring the little dogs that came to whisper things about the pleasant weather; and he followed the car to the building in the town where his dog licence came from, and so eventually back to the house where he had his meals and kennel, wondering why they went so slowly and why she lay so still and made no sign to him. And on the steps he gambolled. He pranced and barked, thinking it strange that no one noticed him. And when his master spoke sadly to him, saying something about "Grannie was in *your* charge," he cocked his great head sideways and wagged his tail and gave a backwards leap in splendid spirits, and barked again, utterly puzzled why the whip came down and cut his glossy back. "Keep quiet, you brute, can't you?" explained nothing at all to him.

That is, it explained Fate to him as little as the skidding, hooting car had explained Fate to her. The car, the whip, his master, he himself as well, were symbols of some bigger Power that had to hurt things somehow for their own good—for everything in the happy, careless, lovely world was good, of course. He accepted things as they were, unable to understand very well. It all lay just beyond his powers of comprehension. It was all right somewhere, and some day he would know it all.

The occupants of the car, meanwhile, were acquitted of reckless driving, because Caesar was the only witness against them, and they silenced him by saying "the great brute" pushed the deceased inadvertently right under the wheels. But Caesar was not told of this. Nor did he understand quite why his master did not take the trouble to find the "old thing" and bring her out of her hiding place, but went about the house exactly as though she were not there, and as though he did not care a plate of dog-biscuit whether she was there or not. He had inherited, of course. Caesar noticed certain changes in the household. Life was a puzzle indeed. Then he forgot about it all, and just went on wagging his huge tail, and bounding and barking as before.

The Perfect Poseur

They sat by the open window after dinner as the first stars appeared in the hot, cloudless sky. The view from this top-floor flat was big; the Crystal Palace was visible in daylight. The sky looked unusually enormous, full of possibilities. "Except rain," said someone. The man who owned large strawberry beds complained bitterly, and the man who wanted to play tennis opposed him. "But it's food," said Strawberries. "But it's exercise," countered Tennis, "and exercise means health, which is of the first importance. We can live without strawberries; they're poison to lots of people, anyhow." The other stated the amount of capital invested in the industry, the number of hands affected by a failure of the crop. "The greatest good of the greatest number," he brought in with an air of victory. Whereupon a woman demolished them both, and at the same time set the note of conversation that followed: "Oh, you two," she said, "stop posing!" And they did stop, with apologies and many excuses. "Don't pose" is a criticism that hits everybody very hard. "To pose or not to pose" called forth points of view from everyone in the group, and of astonishing variety. It was defended and attacked with heat. The dread of posing must lie in every heart perhaps.

"A pose," said the novelist, "is due to a sense of inferiority in the poseur. It's assumed to conceal a vacuum. The personality knows its nakedness, and is afraid to show it."

The pontifical utterance annoyed a girl, clever but poor, who kept a dressmaking shop "Yet in another sense," she protested, "posing is a kind of creation. A creative impulse prompts it. 'I don't care for myself as I am. I will create another and better person in my place.'"

"I like that idea, Iris," remarked the hostess, pleased to help the talk along, but unable to inspire it. A dull, honest woman, who could not have posed to save her life. People "simply loved her." She was so dependable.

"A disconcerting and dangerous gift," suggested the novelist. "Unless the creation is successful, the comedy gets very near to tragedy. Everybody sees through its failure, and smiles contemptuously. And the contempt is deserved."

"Agreed; that's true of all creation," the girl rejoined. "And women, I think, pose more successfully than men. That's why they like dressing up, and dress up so effectively—a scrap of ribbon, a bow, a wisp of feather, and lo, they are changed!"

"I simply love dressing up," interrupted the hostess, with happiness.

"It's very interesting, that dressing-up business," agreed a painter. "In an old country suit I'm one man; in my immaculate evening clothes I am another. I live up to the latter with an effort, but in the first I'm my natural, spontaneous animal self."

"Clothes *do* make a difference," the hostess murmured to herself.

"Priests know that," said a new voice, "and kings and queens."

"And above all, children," the girl put in, "they are the consummate little poseurs of the world. Life is a Fancy Dress Ball to them."

"Ah!" exclaimed the novelist, "but that's real. I'm talking of affectation." He returned to his muttons with a rush of breath rude folks call hot air. "Affected people are invariably empty. Their affectation is an instinctively assumed defence to conceal their poverty; an elaborate business involving constant effort they dare not relax for fear of ridicule. The nervous energy, measured in foot-pounds, must be enormous."

"Goodness!" put in the hostess, impressed by his emphasis of the word enormous. No argument dared become unpleasant or personal when she was present.

The novelist glanced appreciatively in her direction, yet not meeting her eye. "Enormous," he repeated. "All available energy is laid under contribution if the pose is to be maintained consistently and to be convincing. Nothing left over, you see"—another glance towards his hostess—"for honesty. Something not really possessed is assumed, the idea being to persuade the world it *is* possessed. Affectation is fundamentally dishonest."

"Dear me!" came a whisper, a tongue clicking three times running against the teeth.

"Useless as well," he resumed his exposition, thus encouraged. "It never succeeds for long. Yet the poseur, head in sand, believes it does succeed. Why, there are cases, you know, where the constant effort has ended by producing the reality affected—the poseur actually becomes his pose."

"Auto-suggestion," remarked the elderly psychologist, speaking, for the first time, and somewhat drily, "runs through life everywhere, of course, as you say. But pose and affectation are not synonymous, are they? The first is consciously insincere; the latter—"

The hostess, turning round deliberately to listen more attentively, emitted an audible sigh. "Ah!" she said, as one who recognises wisdom when she hears it.

"—may be, and often is, quite genuine. A pose, as with good dressing-up which involves real imagination, is very probably, I feel, another aspect of the personality struggling for breath. A part of the self that has never had its chance strives to manifest. Local conditions have suppressed it. It must out. It may be ill-conceived, it may act and dress up badly, but its will to live demands expression. In more or less appropriate clothes—physical as well as mental—out pops the new fresh self and enjoys itself. Only, it is real."

"True," observed Tennis. "And such a relief. One gets so tired of one's old self."

"Then, which *is* the real self?" asked the novelist. "Potentially, we're all Sally Beauchamps, I suppose?"

"Undoubtedly. You 'dress up' in your stories, the doctor in his patients, provided he is sympathetic enough to feel with them, the painter in his pictures—"

"The poser in his poses," added Strawberries, thinking it was time he made a remark.

"Our hostess in her guests," added Iris, with a laugh, "and I in my rare customers. A person who cannot pose is a shallow person. *Au fond* this dissatisfaction with self is a healthy sign: imperfection, incompleteness, inadequacy are realised."

"The pity being," suggested the psychologist, "that, when selecting a new self, one doesn't take the best. It's such a bargain sale. Most poseurs are such amateurs. 'I'm a King and Queen,' swears the child; and, by gad, he *is*."

"I'm afraid I'm a very shallow person," said the hostess. "At least—at any rate—I do love new clothes and dressing-up."

"No, no, dear," exclaimed Iris, laughing. "That means all your other selves are harmonised. You're at one with your Self."

"It's not very exciting—"

"But it's very dependable. It's why we all love you so."

During which desultory conversation this hot summer night, searching more or less painfully for Reality, all posing en route with more or less success, unaware that the process was nakedly observable—all this time there sat behind them before the empty grate a strange dark being, with cold green eyes, a being whose pose of indifference, superiority, aloofness, of wickedness, and of alien remoteness from the world of human interests, yet semi-divine, at the same time, sacred, unapproachable—a being whose pose and affectation were sublimely achieved with a minimum of effort, the one perfect poseur on the planet: Pharaoh, the big black cat.

THE END

Classic Fiction from

ALGERNON BLACKWOOD

**The Empty House & Other Ghost Stories /
The Listener & Other Stories**
978-1-933586-45-8 $19.95
Blackwood's first two story collections, which
include such classics as "The Haunted Island,"
"The Insanity of Jones," "The Dance of Death"
and his best-known tale, "The Willows."
New introduction by Storm Constantine.

**Ten Minute Stories /
Day and Night Stories**
978-1-933586-62-5 $19.95
Two more superlative story collections of ghost
stories, strange nature tales, weird events and
dark fantasy from one of the greatest writers of
supernatural fiction in the 20th century.
Includes a new introduction by Mike Ashley.

Jimbo / The Education of Uncle Paul
978-1-933586-13-7 $19.95
Two mystical adventures set in the world of
children. "I have rarely read a book that has
given me such unqualified delight."
—Sidney Dark, *Daily Express*.
New introduction by Mike Ashley.

Pan's Garden / Incredible Adventures
978-1-933586-15-1 $23.95
Classic stories that defy categorization—
introductions by Mike Ashley and Tim Lebbon.
"[Has] no rival at all for strength, sincerity, and
poetic vision." —*The Standard*.

The Lost Valley / The Wolves of God
978-1-933586-04-5 $23.95
Two classic short story collections in one
volume, including the "The Wendigo."
Introduction by Simon Clark.

Julius LeVallon / The Bright Messenger
978-0-9749438-7-9 $23.95
"The culmination of a lifetime's experience... you
will encounter nothing like them anywhere else
in the whole of fantastic literature."
—Mike Ashley, from his introduction.

The Face of the Earth
978-1-93358670-0 $19.95
Blackwood biographer Mike Ashley has created
a new collection of stories and essays, most of
which have never been in book format before.
Also included is a definitive bibliography of
Blackwood's writings as well as a new
introduction.

The Human Chord / The Centaur
978-1-944520-01-4 $19.95
"The masterpiece of the new romantic
movement... It is quite the best thing that Mr.
Blackwood has given us." —*The Bookman*.

**John Silence—Physician Extraordinary /
The Wave**
978-1-944520-25-0 $21.95
A classic collection of supernatural horror tales,
plus a masterful novel of reincarnation. Includes
a new introduction by Stefan Dziemianowicz.

The Promise of Air / The Garden of Survival
978-1-944520-50-2 $15.95
"...a buoyant emotional statement of the
restlessness of the race." —*Theosophical
Outlook*. New introduction by Mike Ashley.

Stark House Press
1315 H Street, Eureka, CA 95501, 707-498-3135, www.StarkHousePress.com
Retail customers: freight-free, payment accepted by check or paypal via website.
Wholesale: 40%, freight-free on 10 mixed copies or more, returns accepted.
All books available direct from Publisher, Ingram or Baker & Taylor Books.